I turn my back to him and summon my wings, stretch them over my head, flex. When I glance over at him again, he's standing, staring with a kind of yearning admiration at my feathers, which gleam white in the sun.

He wants to touch them.

"Clara—" he says breathlessly, and takes a step forward, and reaches out.

I leap off the rock.

BOUNDLESS

CYNTHIA HAND

An Imprint of HarperCollins*Publishers*

For Rod, my dad

Excerpts from Memorial Church pamphlet
© Office for Religious Life, Stanford University

HarperTeen is an imprint of HarperCollins Publishers.

Library of Congress Cataloging-in-Publication Data
Hand, Cynthia, 1978–
    Boundless : an Unearthly novel / Cynthia Hand. — First edition.
        pages   cm.
    Summary: "As the battle against the Black Wings and Their min-
ions looms on the horizon, part-angel Clara Gardner is finally ready to
fulfill her destiny, even though she knows she may have to make the ultimate sacrifice"— Provided by publisher.
    ISBN 978-0-06-199621-4 (pbk.)
    [1.   Angels—Fiction. 2.   Supernatural—Fiction. 3.   High
schools—Fiction. 4. Schools—Fiction. 5. Family life—Wyoming—
Fiction. 6. Jackson (Wyo.)—Fiction.] I. Title.
PZ7.H1917Bou   2013   2012045522
[Fic]—dc23   CIP
                                                              AC

Typography by Andrea Vandergrift
13   14   15   16   17   LP/RRDH   10 9 8 7 6 5 4 3 2 1
❖
First paperback edition, 2014

He who, from zone to zone,
Guides through the boundless sky thy certain flight,
In the long way that I must tread alone,
Will lead my steps aright.
—William Cullen Bryant

PROLOGUE

The first thing I'm aware of is the dark. Like somebody just shut off the lights. I squint into the inky nothingness, straining to see something, anything, but my eyes don't adjust. Tentatively I feel with my feet along the floor, which is oddly slanted, as if the room is being tilted downward. I take a step back, and my leg strikes something hard. I stop. Try to regain my balance. Listen.

There are voices, faint voices, from somewhere above.

I don't know what this vision is about yet, where I am or what I'm supposed to be doing or who I'm hiding from. But I do know this: I'm hiding.

And something terrible has happened.

It's possible that I'm crying. My nose is running, but I

don't try to wipe at it. I don't move. I'm scared. I could call the safety of glory, I think, but then they would find me. Instead I draw my hands into fists to stop the trembling. The darkness closes in, encasing me, and for a moment I fight the urge to call glory so hard that my fingernails break the surface of my palms.

Be still, I tell myself. *Be quiet.*

I let the darkness swallow me whole.

1

WELCOME TO THE FARM

"How you holding up, Clara?"

I jolt back to myself in the middle of my bedroom, a pile of old magazines strewn around my feet, which I must have dropped when the vision hit. My breath is still frozen in my lungs; my muscles tense, as if they are preparing me to run. The light streaming through the window hurts my eyes. I blink at Billy, who leans against the door frame of my bedroom and offers up an understanding smile.

"What's the matter, kid?" she asks when I don't answer. "Vision got you down?"

I gulp in a breath. "How did you know?"

"I get them, too. Plus I've been hanging around people

who have visions for most of my life. I recognize the post-vision face." She takes me by the shoulders and sits down with me at the edge of my bed. We wait until my breathing quiets. "Do you want to talk about it?" she asks.

"There's not a lot to it yet," I say. I've been having this vision all summer, since Italy with Angela. So far there hasn't been much to go on but darkness, terror, an oddly slanted floor. "Should I tell you anyway?"

Billy shakes her head. "You can if you want, if it would help you get things off your chest. But visions are personal, for you and you alone, in my opinion."

I'm relieved she's so laid-back about it. "How do you do it?" I ask after a minute. "How do you go on living like normal when you know that something bad's going to happen?"

There's pain in her smile. She puts her warm brown hand over mine. "You learn to find your happiness, kid," she says. "You figure out those things that give your life meaning, and you hold on to them. You try to stop worrying about the stuff you can't control."

"Easier said than done." I sigh.

"It takes practice." She claps a hand on my shoulder, squeezes. "You all right now? Ready to come up swinging?"

I conjure a weak smile. "Yes, ma'am."

"All right, then, get to work," she says playfully. I resume packing, which is what I was doing before the vision clobbered me, and Billy grabs a tape gun and starts sealing up the finished boxes. "You know, I helped your mom pack for

Stanford, back in the day. 1963. We were roomies, living in San Luis Obispo, a little house by the beach."

I'm going to miss Billy, I think as she goes on. Most of the time when I look at her, I can't help but see my mom, not because the two of them look anything alike, outside of being tall and gorgeous, but because, as my mom's best friend for like the last hundred years, Billy has a million memories like this one about Stanford, funny stories and sad ones, times when Mom got a bad haircut or when she lit the kitchen on fire trying to make bananas flambé or when they were nurses in World War I together and Mom saved a man's life with nothing but a bobby pin and a rubber band. It's the next best thing to being with Mom, hanging with Billy. It's like, for those few minutes, when she's telling the stories, Mom's alive again.

"Hey, you okay?" Billy asks.

"Almost done." I cough to cover the catch in my voice, then fold up the last sweater, lay it in a box, and glance around. Even though I haven't packed everything, even though I've left my posters on the walls and some of my stuff out, my room looks emptied, like I've already moved out of this place.

I can't believe that, after tomorrow, I won't live here anymore.

"You can come home anytime you like," Billy says. "Remember that. This is your house. Just call and tell me you're on your way and I'll run over and put fresh sheets on the bed."

She pats my hand and then heads downstairs to load boxes

into her truck. She'll be driving to California tomorrow, too, while Angela's mom, Anna, and I follow along behind in my car. I go out into the hall. The house is quiet, but it also seems to have some kind of energy, like it's full of ghosts. I stare at Jeffrey's closed door. He should be here. He should have already started his junior year at Jackson Hole High School. He should be well into football practice and his disgusting early-morning protein shakes and tons of mismatched stinky gym socks in the laundry basket. I should be able to go to his door right now and knock and hear him say, *Go away*, but I'd go in anyway, and then he'd look at me from his computer and maybe turn his throbbing music down a notch or two, smirk, and say, *Aren't you gone yet?* and maybe I'd think of something smart to fire back, but in the end we'd both know that he would miss me. And I would miss him.

I miss him.

The front door bangs shut downstairs. "You expecting company?" Billy calls up.

I become aware of the sound of a car pulling up in the driveway. "No," I holler back. "Who is it?"

"It's for you," she says.

I book it down the stairs.

"Oh, good," says Wendy when I open the door. "I was afraid I missed you."

Instinctively I look around for Tucker, my heart doing a stupid little dance.

"He's not here," Wendy says gently. "He, uh . . ."

Oh. He didn't want to see me.

I try to smile while something in my chest squeezes painfully. Right, I think. Why would he want to see me? We're broken up. He's moving on.

I make myself focus on Wendy. She's clutching a cardboard box to her chest like she's afraid it might float away from her. She shifts from one foot to the other. "What's up?" I ask.

"I had some of your stuff," she says. "I'm headed to school tomorrow, and I—I thought you might want it."

"Thanks. I'm leaving tomorrow, too," I tell her.

Once, when her brother and I first got together, Wendy told me that if I hurt Tucker, she'd bury me in horse manure. Ever since we broke up, some part of me has been expecting her to show up here with a shovel and bean me over the head with it. Some part of me thinks that maybe I'd deserve it. Yet here she is looking all fragile and hopeful, like she missed me this summer. Like she still wants to be my friend.

"Thanks," I say again. I smile, reach for the box. She smiles shyly back and hands it over. Inside there are a couple DVDs, magazines, my dog-eared copy of *Vampire Academy* and a few other books, a pair of dress shoes I loaned her for prom.

"How was Italy?" she asks as I set the box down next to the door. "I got your postcard."

"It was beautiful."

"I bet," she says with an envious sigh. "I've always wanted

to backpack around Europe. I want to see London, Paris, Vienna. . . ." She smiles. "Hey, how about you show me your pictures? I'd love to see them. If you have time."

"Um, sure." I run upstairs to get my laptop, then sit down with her on the living room sofa and cruise through my photos of this summer, her shoulder pressing into mine as we look at pictures of the Coliseum, the Roman arches, the catacombs, Tuscany with its vineyards and rolling hills, Florence, me making that dumb "I'm holding it up" pose at the Leaning Tower of Pisa.

And then up flashes a picture of Angela and Phen at the top of St. Peter's.

"Wait, go back," Wendy says as I click past it.

I reluctantly press the back button.

"Who's that?" she breathes.

I get it. Phen is hot. There's something magnetic about those brown eyes of his, the manly perfection of his face and all that, but sheesh. Not Wendy, too.

"Just a guy we met in Rome," I tell Wendy. That's about as close to the truth as I can come without going into the gory details of Angela and her secret, "swear you won't tell anybody, Clara" boyfriend. Who is, according to her, a summer thing only. She's been all "Phen who?" ever since we returned to Wyoming, like she never even met the guy.

"Did I mention that I want to go to Italy?" Wendy says, raising her eyebrows. "Wow."

6

"Yeah, there are a lot of hot guys there," I admit. "Of course, then they become beer-bellied middle-aged men in Armani suits with slicked-back hair who look at you like 'How you doing?'" I give her my best pervy Italian grin, tilt my chin up, blow an air kiss at her.

She laughs. "Ew."

I close my laptop, glad to get the subject off Phen. "So, that was Italy." I pat my stomach. "I gained like five pounds in pasta."

"Well, you were too skinny before, anyway," Wendy says.

"Gee, thanks."

"I hate to be the party pooper, but I should go," she says. "I've got loads to do at home before tomorrow."

We stand, and I turn to her, instantly choked up at the idea of saying good-bye. "You're going to do awesome at Washington State and have all kinds of fun and become the best vet ever, but I am so going to miss you," I say.

Her eyes are misty, too. "We'll see each other on breaks, right? You can always email me, you know. Don't be a stranger."

"I won't. Promise."

She hugs me. "Bye, Clara," she whispers. "Take care."

When she's gone, I gather up the box, take it to my room, and close the door. I dump the box out on my bed. There, among the things I loaned Wendy, I find some items from Tucker: a fishing lure that I bought him at a tackle shop in Jackson—his lucky Carrots lure, he called it—a pressed wildflower from one of the wreaths he used to make for my hair, a mixed CD I made him last year, full of songs about cowboys and songs about flying and songs about love, which he listened to a bunch of times even though he must have thought it was corny. He's giving it all back. I hate how much this hurts me, how much I'm clearly still hanging on to what we had, so I put the stuff all carefully back in the box, and I seal the box with tape and slide it into the shadows at the back of my closet. And say good-bye.

Clara.

I hear the voice in my head, calling my name, before I hear it out loud. I'm standing in the quad at Stanford University, in the midst of more than fifteen hundred teeming freshmen and their parents, but I hear him loud and clear. I push through the crowd, looking for his wavy dark hair, the flash of his green eyes. Then suddenly there's a break in the people around me and I see him, about twenty feet away, standing with his back to me. As usual. And as usual, it's like a bell chimes inside me in a kind of recognition.

I cup my hands around my mouth and call, "Christian!"

He turns. We weave toward each other through the crowd. In a flash I'm by his side, grinning up at him, almost laughing because it feels so good to be together again after so long.

"Hey," he says. He has to talk loudly to be heard over the people around us. "Fancy meeting you here."

"Yes, fancy that."

It doesn't occur to me until right this minute how much I've missed him. I was so busy missing other people—my mom, Jeffrey, Tucker, Dad—caught up in all that I was leaving behind. But now . . . it's like when part of you stops hurting and suddenly you're yourself again, healthy and whole, and only then do you understand that you've been in pain for a while. I missed his voice in my head, in my ears. I missed his face. His smile.

"I missed you, too," he says bemusedly, bending to say it next to my ear so I can hear him over the noise.

His warm breath against my neck makes me shiver. I step back awkwardly, suddenly self-conscious. "How was the boonies?" is all I can think to say.

His uncle always takes him into the mountains during the summers, spends the whole time hard-core training, away from the internet and television and any other distractions, and makes him practice calling glory and flying and all other angel-related skills. Christian calls it his "summer internship," acts like it's only a step up from army boot camp.

"Same old routine," he reports. "Walter was even more intense this year, if you can believe that. He had me up at the crack of dawn most days. Worked me like a dog."

"Why?" I start to ask, then think better of it. *What's he training you for?*

His eyes get serious. *I'll tell you later, okay?*

"How was Italy?" he asks me out loud, because it'll look

9

weird to people if we're standing here facing each other, not saying anything, while we carry out an entire conversation in our heads.

"Interesting," I say. Which has got to be the understatement of the year.

Angela picks this moment to appear at my side. "Hi, Chris," she says, lifting her chin in greeting. "How's it going?"

He gestures at the crowd of excited freshmen milling around us. "I think reality is finally starting to settle in that I'm going here."

"I know what you mean," she says. "I needed to pinch myself when we drove down Palm Drive. What dorm are you in?"

"Cedro."

"Clara and I are both in Roble. I think that's across campus from you."

"It is," he says. "I checked."

He's glad that he ended up with a dorm across campus from us, I understand as I look at him. Because he thinks I might not like it if he's always around, picking the random thoughts out of my brain. He wants to give me some space.

I send him the mental equivalent of a hug, which surprises him.

What was that for? he asks.

"We need bicycles," Angela's saying. "This campus is so big. Everybody has bikes."

Because I'm glad you're here, I say to Christian.

10

I'm glad to be here.

I'm glad you're glad to be here.

We smile.

"Hey, are you two doing the mind-meld thing?" Angela asks, and then, as loudly as she can, she thinks, *Because it is so annoying.*

Christian gives a surprised laugh. *Since when does she talk telepathically?*

Since I've been teaching her. It was something to do on an eleven-hour flight.

Do you really think that's a good idea? She's loud enough as it is. . . . He's joking, but I can tell he doesn't love the thought of Angela being part of our secret conversations. That's between us. It's ours.

So far she hasn't been able to receive, I say to ease his mind. *She can only transmit.*

So she can speak, but she can't listen. How appropriate.

Ann-oy-ing, Angela says, folding her arms across her chest and glaring at him.

We both laugh.

"Sorry, Ange." I sling an arm around her. "Christian and I have a lot of catching up to do."

A flicker of worry passes over her face, but it's gone so fast I wonder if I imagined it. "Well, I think it's rude," she says.

"Okay, okay. No mind-melding. I get it."

"At least not until I learn to do it too. Which will be soon. I've been practicing," she says.

11

"No doubt," he says.

I catch the laughter in his eyes, bite back a smile. "So, have you met your roommate yet?" I ask him.

He nods. "Charlie. He wants to be a computer programmer. Married to his Xbox. How about you?"

"Her name's Wan Chen, and she's premed and extremely serious about it," I report. "She showed me her schedule today, and it made me feel like a total slacker."

"Well, you are a total slacker," Angela points out.

"So true."

"What about your roommate?" Christian asks Angela. *Poor defenseless thing,* he adds silently, which makes me snicker.

"I have two roommates—lucky, lucky me," says Angela. "They're total blondes."

"Hey!" I object to her tone on the subject of blondes.

"And they're complete fuzzies. One's a communications major—whatever that means—and one is undecided."

"There's nothing wrong with being undecided." I glance at Christian, a tad embarrassed about my undecidedness.

"I'm undecided," he says. Angela and I stare at him, shocked. "What, I can't be undecided?"

"I assumed you'd be a business major," Angela says.

"Why?"

"Because you look really stellar in a suit and tie," she says with false sweetness. "You're pretty. You should play to your strengths."

He refuses to rise to the bait. "Business is Walter's thing. Not mine."

"So what is your thing?" Angela asks.

"Like I said, I haven't decided." He gazes at me intently, the gold flecks in his green eyes catching the light, and I feel heat move into my cheeks.

"Where is Walter, anyway?" I ask to change the subject.

"With Billy." He turns and points at the designated parent section of the quad, where, sure enough, Walter and Billy look like they're deep in conversation.

"They're a cute couple," I say, watching Billy as she laughs and puts her hand on Walter's arm. "Of course I was surprised when Billy called me this summer to tell me that she and Walter were getting married. I did not see *that* coming."

"Wait, Billy and Walter are getting married?" Angela exclaims. "When?"

"They got married," Christian clarifies. "July. At the meadow. It was pretty sudden."

"I didn't even know they liked each other," I say before Angela can deliver the joke I know she's cooking up about how Christian and I are now some kind of weird brother and sister, since his legal guardian has married my legal guardian.

"Oh, they like each other," Christian says. "They're trying to be discreet, for my sake, I guess. But Walter can't stop thinking about her. Loudly. And in various states of undress, if you know what I mean."

"Ugh. Don't tell me. I'm going to have to scrub my brain with the little bit I saw in her head this week. Is there a bear-skin rug at your house?"

"I think you just ruined my living room for me," he says with a groan, but he doesn't mean it. He's happy about the Billy-Walter situation. He thinks it's good for Walter. Keeps his mind off things.

What things? I ask.

Later, he says. *I'll tell you all about it. Later.*

Angela lets out an exasperated sigh. "Oh my God, you guys. You are totally doing it again."

After the orientation speeches, them telling us how proud we should be of ourselves, what high hopes they have for our futures, the amazing opportunities we'll have while we're at "the Farm," as they call Stanford, we're all supposed to head back to our dorms and get acquainted with one another.

This is the point when they tell the parents to go home.

Angela's mom, Anna, who's been her intensely quiet self, sitting in the backseat of my car reading her Bible for the entire thousand-mile trip, suddenly bursts into tears. Angela is mortified, red-cheeked as she escorts her sobbing mother out to the parking lot, but I think it's nice. I wish my mom were here to cry over me.

Billy gives me another one of those encouraging shoulder squeezes. "Knock 'em dead, kid," she says simply, and then she's gone, too.

I pick a comfy sofa in the lounge and pretend to study the patterns on the carpet while the rest of the students are saying their own tearful good-byes. After a while a guy with short, dyed-blond hair comes in and sits across from me, sets a hefty stack of folders on the coffee table. He smiles, reaches out to shake my hand. "I'm Pierce."

"Clara Gardner."

He nods. "I think I've seen your name on a couple of lists. You're in B wing, right?"

"Third floor."

"I'm the fee here in Roble," he says.

I stare at him blankly.

"P-H-E," he explains. "It stands for peer health educator. Kind of like the doctor of the dorm. I'm where you go for a Band-Aid."

"Oh, right."

He's looking at my face in a way that makes me wonder if I have food on it.

"What? Do I have the words *clueless freshman* tattooed across my forehead?" I ask.

He smiles, shakes his head. "You don't look scared."

"Excuse me?"

"Freshmen usually seem pretty terrified, first week on campus. They wander around like lost little puppies. Not you, though. You look like you've got things all under control."

"Oh. Thanks," I say. "But I hate to tell you, it's an act. Inside I'm a nervous wreck."

15

I'm not, actually. I guess next to fallen angels, funerals, and forest fires, Stanford feels like a pretty safe place. Everything's familiar here: the California smells of exhaust and eucalyptus trees and carefully landscaped roses in the air, palm trees, the Caltrain noise in the distance, the same old varieties of plants that I grew up with outside the windows.

It's the other stuff that scares me: the dark, windowless room in my vision, what's going to happen in that place, the bad thing that's happened before I end up hiding there. The possibility that this is going to be my entire life: one vague, terrifying vision after another, for the next hundred years. That's what's scary. That's what I am trying very hard not to think about.

Pierce writes a five-digit number on a Post-it and holds it out. "Call me if you need anything. I'll come running."

He's flirting, I think. I take the Post-it. "Okay."

Just then Angela bustles in, running her hands down the sides of her leggings like she's wiping off her mother's emotions. She stops short when she sees Pierce.

She doesn't look scared, either. She looks like she's come to conquer.

"Zerbino, Angela," she says matter-of-factly when Pierce opens his mouth to greet her. She glances at the folders on the table. "Have you got something in that pile with my name on it?"

"Yeah, sure," he says, flustered, and rummages through the folders until he lands on *Z* and a packet for Angela. Then he fishes one out for me. He gets up. Checks his watch. "Well, nice to meet you, girls. Get comfortable. We'll probably start our getting-to-know-you games in about five minutes."

"What's that?" Angela gestures to my Post-it as he walks away.

"Pierce." I stare at his retreating back. "Anything I need, he'll come running."

She shoots a glance at him over her shoulder, smiles thoughtfully. "Oh, really? He's cute."

"I guess."

"Right, I forgot. You only have eyes for Tucker still. Or is it Christian now? I can never keep track."

"Hey. Like, ouch," I say. "You're being awfully rude today."

Her expression softens. "Sorry. I'm tense. Change is hard for me, even the good changes."

"For you? No way."

She drops into the seat next to mine. "You seem relaxed, though."

I stretch my arms over my head, yawn. "I've decided to stop stressing about everything. I'm going to start fresh. Look." I dig around in my bag for the rumpled piece of paper and hold it up for her to read. "Behold, my tentative schedule."

Her eyes quickly scan the page. "I see you took my advice and enrolled in that Intro to Humanities class with me. The Poet Re-making the World. You'll like it, I promise," she says. "Interpreting poetry's easy, because you can make it mean pretty much whatever you want it to mean.

It will be a cakewalk kind of class."

I seriously doubt that.

"Hmm." Angela frowns as she reads farther down. "Art history?" She quirks an eyebrow at me. "Science, Technology, and Contemporary Society? Intro to Film Studies? Modern Dance? This is kind of all over the place, C."

"I like art," I say defensively. "It's simple for you, since you're a history major, so you take history classes. But I'm—"

"Undecided," she provides.

"Right, and I didn't know what to take, so Dr. Day told me to enroll in a bunch of different classes and then drop the ones I didn't respond to. But look at this one." I point to the last class on the list.

"Athletics 196," she reads above my finger. "Practice of Happiness."

"Happiness class."

"You're taking a class on happiness," she says, like that has got to be the most total slacker class in the universe.

"My mom said I was going to be happy at Stanford," I explain. "So that's what I intend to be. I'm going to find my happiness."

"Good for you. Take charge of yourself. It's about freaking time."

"I know," I say, and I mean it. "I'm ready to stop saying good-bye to things. I'm going to start saying hello."

2

BAND RUN

That night I wake up at two in the morning to somebody pounding on my door.

"Hello?" I call out warily. There's a jumble of noise from outside, music and people shouting and frantic footsteps in the hall. Wan Chen and I both sit up, exchange worried glances, and then I slide out of bed to answer the door.

"Rise and shine, dear freshmen," says Stacy, our RA, in a chipper voice. She's wearing a neon-green plastic circle around her neck and rainbow clown hair. She grins. "Put your shoes on and come out front."

Outside we're met by a scene that seems straight out of those bad acid trips you see in the movies: the Stanford marching band in what appears to be mostly their underwear and glow-in-the-dark necklaces and bracelets and stuff, rocking their respective instruments, trumpets blaring, drums beating, cymbals crashing, the school mascot in his big green pine tree costume zooming around like a crazy man, a bunch of half-dressed, partially glowing students jumping and bumping and whooping and laughing. It's incredibly dark, like they've turned out the streetlights for the occasion, but I search for Angela and spot her looking supremely annoyed, standing next to two blond girls—her roommates, I assume. I weave my way over to them.

"Hi!" Angela yells. "You have bed hair."

"This is insane!" I shout, combing through my hair with my fingers, with little success.

"What?" she screams.

"Insane!" I try again. It's so unbelievably loud.

One of Angela's roommates gapes and points behind me. I turn to see a guy wearing a Mexican-style wrestling mask that covers his entire face. A shiny gold wrestling mask. And nothing else.

"My eyes, my eyes!" Angela shrieks, and we all start giggling hysterically, and then the song is over, and we can hear again, and they're telling us to run.

"Run, little freshmen, run!" they scream, and we do, like a herd of confused, stampeding cattle in the dark. When we finally stop, we're at the next dorm over, and the band starts up again, and pretty soon another crowd of bleary and baffled freshmen begins to filter out of the doors.

I've lost Angela. I look around, but it's too dark and the crowd is too big to find her. I make out one of her roommates standing a few feet away from me. I wave. She smiles and pushes her way over to me like she's relieved to see a familiar face. We bob halfheartedly to the music for a few minutes before she leans over and yells next to my ear, "I'm Amy. You're Angela's friend from Wyoming?"

"Right. Clara. Where are you from?"

"Phoenix!" She hugs her sweatshirt tighter around her. "I'm cold!"

Suddenly we're moving again. This time I make it a point to stay close to Amy. I try not to think about how this feels eerily similar to my vision in some ways, running around in the dark, not knowing where I'm going or what I'm going to end up doing. It's supposed to be fun, I know, but I find this whole thing a bit creepy.

"Do you have any idea where we are?" I pant out to Amy the next time we stop.

"What?" She can't hear me.

"Where are we?" I yell.

"Oh." She shakes her head. "No clue. I'm guessing they're going to make us run all the way across campus."

I remember how on the tour they told us that Stanford has the largest campus of any university in the world aside from one in Russia.

It could be a long night.

There's still no sign of Angela or the other roommate, who Amy tells me is named Robin, so Amy and I stick together and dance and laugh at Naked Guy and shout out a conversation the best we can. In the next half hour here's what I find out about Amy: we were both raised with single mothers and little brothers, we're both thrilled that tater tots are served at breakfast in the Roble dining hall every morning and horrified at how tiny and claustrophobic the shower stalls in the bathrooms are, and we both suffer from annoyingly unruly hair.

We could be friends, I realize. I could have made my first new friend at Stanford, just this easily. Maybe there's something to this making-us-run thing.

"So what's your major?" she asks as we're jogging along.

"Undecided," I answer.

She beams. "Me too!"

I'm liking her more and more. But then disaster strikes. As we come up on the next dorm, Amy stumbles and falls. Down to the pavement she goes, all flailing arms and legs. I do my best to make sure she doesn't get trampled by the ever-growing stream of scrambling freshmen, then drop to the sidewalk next to her. It's bad. I can tell just by looking at her white face and the way she's clutching her ankle.

"I stepped wrong." She groans. "God, this is embarrassing."

"Can you stand up?" I ask.

She tries, and her face gets even whiter. She sits back down heavily.

"Okay, that's a no," I deduce. "Don't go anywhere. I'll be right back."

I mill around looking for someone who seems even a little bit helpful and miraculously spot Pierce at the edge of the crowd. Time to put his "dorm doctor" skills to good use. I run over to him and touch him on the arm to get his attention. He smiles when he sees me.

"Having fun?" he yells.

"I need your help," I yell.

"What?" he yells.

I end up taking him by the hand and dragging him over to Amy and pointing at her ankle, which is starting to swell. He spends several minutes kneeling beside her, gently holding her ankle between his hands. Turns out that he's premed.

"It's probably a sprain," he concludes. "I'll call someone to give you a ride back to Roble, and we'll get it elevated and put some ice on it. Then you should go to Vaden—the student clinic—in the morning, get an X-ray. Just hang in there, all right?"

He walks off to find somewhere quieter to use his phone. The band finishes its song and moves on, leading the crowd away from us in a rumble of feet. Finally I can hear myself think.

Amy starts to cry.

"I'm so sorry," I say, sitting down next to her.

"It doesn't hurt that much," she sniffles, wiping at her nose with the back of her sweatshirt. "I mean, it hurts—a lot, actually—but that's not why I'm crying. I'm crying because I did something so totally stupid like wear flip-flops when they told us to put on shoes, and this is only the first week of school. I haven't even started classes yet, and now I'm going to be hopping around on crutches, and everyone's going to label me as that klutzy girl who hurt herself."

"Nobody will think less of you. Seriously," I say. "I bet there are plenty of injuries happening tonight. It's all pretty crazy."

She shakes her head, sending a tumble of wild blond curls over her shoulders. Her lip quivers. "This is not how I wanted to start things," she chokes out, and buries her face in her hands.

I glance around. The group has moved far enough away that we can only faintly hear them. Pierce is standing next to the building with his back to us, talking into his cell. It's dark. No one's around.

I lay my hand gently on Amy's ankle. She tenses, like even this light touch is hurting her, but doesn't lift her head. Through my empathy I can feel the hurt in her, not only the way she's mentally beating herself up over how she's already ruined her reputation, but the physical part, too, the way the ligaments in her ankle are pulled away from the bone. It's a bad injury, I know instantly. She could be on crutches all semester.

I could help her, I think.

I've healed people before. My mom after she was attacked by Samjeeza. Tucker after our post-prom car accident last year. But those times I had the full circle of glory around me, the whole shebang, light emanating from my hair, my body glowing like a lantern. I wonder if there's a way to localize the glory to just, say, my hands, to channel it fast so that nobody will notice.

I clear my head, glad for the relative quiet, and focus my energy on my right hand. Just the fingers, I think. All I need is glory in my fingers. Just once. I concentrate on it so hard that a bead of sweat moves along my hairline and drips down onto the concrete, and after a few minutes the very tips of my fingers start to glow, dimly at first and then more brightly. I press my hand firmly to Amy's ankle. Then I send the glory out of me like a trickle of light spreading from me to her, not too much or too fast but hopefully enough to do some good.

Amy sighs, then stops crying. I sit back, watching her. I can't tell if what I did helped at all.

Pierce comes back over, looking apologetic. "I can't find anyone to come get you. I'll have to run and get my car, but it's on the other side of campus, so it will take a while. How are you doing?"

"Better," she says. "It doesn't hurt as much as before."

He kneels down next to her again and examines her ankle. "It looks better, actually, not as swollen. Maybe you just twisted it. Can you try to walk?"

She gets up and gingerly puts her weight on her injured foot. Pierce and I watch as she limps a few steps, then turns back to us. "It feels okay now," she admits. "Oh my God, am I a drama queen or what?" She laughs, her voice full of relief.

"Let's get you back to your room," I stammer out quickly. "You still need to put some ice on that, right, Pierce?"

"Absolutely," he says, and we get on either side of her and walk her slowly back to Roble.

"Thanks for helping me out tonight," Amy says to me after she's situated in her room with her foot wrapped tightly in an Ace bandage, propped on a stack of pillows with a bag of ice pressed to her ankle. "I don't know what I would have done without you. You're a lifesaver."

"You're welcome," I say, and I can't help a gloaty smile.

I did help her, I think later when I've gone back to my room. The sun is almost up, but Wan Chen isn't back yet. I lie on my tiny twin bed and stare at the water damage on the ceiling panels. I want to sleep, but I've still got too much adrenaline in my system from using my power out in the open like that. But I did it. *I did it,* I keep thinking, over and over and over again. I healed that girl. And it felt amazing. It felt right.

Which gives me another crazy idea.

"I think I might want to go premed."

Dr. Day, the academic adviser for Roble Hall, looks up

from her computer. She has the grace not to look too surprised that I've burst into her office and informed her that I am contemplating becoming a doctor. She simply nods and takes a minute to pull up my schedule.

"If you're considering premed, which is typically a straight biology or human biology major, we should get you enrolled in Chem 31X," she says. "It's a prerequisite for most of the other biology courses, and if you don't take it this fall, you'll have to wait until next fall to start the core classes you'll need."

"Okay," I say. "I like chemistry. I took College Prep Chemistry last year."

She looks at me from over the top of her glasses. "This course can be a little hard-core," she warns me. "The class meets three times a week, and then there's a biweekly discussion session led by a teaching assistant, plus another couple hours a week in the lab. The entire biology track can be fairly high intensity. Are you ready for that?"

"I can handle it," I say, and an excited tremor passes through me, because I feel oddly sure about this. I think about how good it felt when Amy's ankle was righting itself under my hand. Being a doctor would put me in contact with the people who need healing the most. I could help people. I could fix the broken things in this world.

I smile at Dr. Day, and she smiles back.

"This is what I want to do," I tell her.

"All right, then," she says. "Let's get you started."

Everybody takes the news that I've gone premed in a different way. Wan Chen, for instance, who's premed herself, reacts like I'm suddenly competition. For a few days she doesn't say more than two words to me, maneuvering around our tiny dorm room in chilled silence, until she realizes that we're both in that insanely hard chemistry class and I'm pretty good at chemistry. Then she warms up to me fast. I hear her tell her mother on the phone in Mandarin that I'm a "nice girl, and very smart." I make an effort not to smile when I hear her say it.

Angela instantly loves the idea of me as a doctor. "Very cool" are her exact words. "I believe we should use our gifts, you know, for good, not just sit on them unless we're required to do some angel-related duty. If you can stomach all the blood and guts and gore—which I totally couldn't, but kudos to you, if you can—then you should go for it."

It's Christian who doesn't think it's a good idea.

"A doctor," he repeats when I tell him. "What brought this on?"

I explain about band run and Amy's miraculously healed ankle and my subsequent aha moment. I expect him to be impressed. Excited for me. Approving. But he frowns.

"You don't like it," I observe. "Why?"

"It's too risky." He looks like he wants to say something else, but we're standing on the crowded sidewalk outside

28

the Stanford Bookstore, where I've bumped into him while coming out with my armload of poetry collections for my humanities class and a giant ten-pound textbook entitled *Chemistry: Science of Change*, which is what prompted this conversation. *You could get caught using glory,* he says in my head.

Relax, I reply. *It's not like I'm going to go around healing people right this minute. I'm looking into it as a possible career path, that's all. No big deal.*

But it feels like a big deal. It feels like my life finally has a—for lack of a better word—purpose, one that isn't all about being an angel-blood but makes use of the angel-blood part of me, too. It feels right.

He sighs.

I get it, he says. *I want to help people, too. But we have to lie low, Clara. You're lucky that this girl you healed didn't see what you did. How would you have explained that? What would you do if she was going around campus telling everybody about your magical glowing hands?*

I don't have an answer for him. My chin lifts. *But she didn't notice. I'll be careful. I would only use glory when I thought it was safe, and the other times, I'd use regular medical stuff. Which is why I want to become a doctor. I have the power to heal people, Christian. How can I not use it?*

We stand there for a minute, locked in a silent argument about whether or not it's worth the risk, until it becomes clear that neither of us is going to change our mind. "I have to go," I say finally, trying not to pout. "I have a set of problems on quantum mechanics to work through, if you think that's not too dangerous for me to tackle."

"Clara . . . ," Christian starts. "I think it's great that you found a direction to go in, but . . ." *All it would take is one slip,* he says. *The wrong person seeing you, one time, and then they could figure out what you are, and they'd come after you.*

I shake my head. *I can't spend my entire life being afraid of the black-winged bogeymen. I have to live my life, Christian. I won't be stupid about glory, but I won't sit around and wait for my visions to happen in order to do something with it.*

At the word *visions* a new worry springs up inside him, and I remember that there was something he promised to tell me. But I don't want to hear about it now. I want to sulk.

I shift my heavy load of books to the other arm. "I've got to run. I'll catch you later."

"Okay," he says stiffly. "See you around."

I don't like the feeling that's hanging like a dark cloud over me as I walk back to my dorm.

That it doesn't matter what I said about not wanting to be afraid. That I'm always, in some form or another, running away from something.

3

WHITE PICKET FENCE

This time someone else is with me in the blackness, another person's breathing shuddering in and out somewhere behind me.

I still can't see anything, can't determine where I am, even though this is like the umpteenth time I've had the vision. It's dark, as always. I am trying to keep quiet, trying not to move—not to breathe, even—so I can't exactly explore my surroundings. The floor is slanted down. Carpeted. There's the faint scent of sawdust in the air, new paint, and this: the hint of some distinctly masculine smell, like deodorant or aftershave, and now the breathing. Close, I think. If I turned and reached out, I could touch him.

There are footsteps above us: heavy and echoing, like people descending a set of wooden stairs. My body tenses. We'll be found. Somehow I know this. I've seen it a hundred times in my visions. I'm seeing it right now. I want to get it over with, want to call the glory, but I don't, on the off chance that it won't happen this time. I still have hope.

There's a noise from behind me, strange and high-pitched, like maybe a cat yowl or a birdcall. I turn toward the sound.

There's a moment of silence.

Then comes a burst of light, blinding me. I flinch away from it.

"Clara, get down!" yells a voice, and in that wild, scuffling moment I instantly know who's with me—I'd recognize his voice anywhere—and I find myself vaulting forward, upward, because some part of me knows that now I have to run.

I wake to a ray of sunshine on my face. It takes me a second to place where I am: dorm room, Roble Hall. Light pouring through the window. The bells of Memorial Church in the distance. The smell of laundry detergent and pencil shavings. I've been at Stanford for more than a week now, and this room still doesn't feel like home.

My sheets are tangled up in my legs. I must have really been trying to run. I lie there for a minute taking deep breaths from the abdomen, trying to calm my racing heart.

Christian's there. In the vision. With me.

Of course Christian's there, I think, still peeved with him. He's been in every other vision I've had, so why stop now?

But there's some kind of comfort in that.

I sit up and glance over at Wan Chen, who's asleep in the bed on the other side of the room, snoring in little puffs. I free myself from the sheets and pull on some jeans and a hoodie, fight my hair into a ponytail, trying to keep quiet so I don't wake her.

When I get outside there's a large bird sitting on a lamp-post near the dorm, a dark shape against the dawn-gray sky. It swivels to look at me. I stop.

I've always had a complicated relationship with birds. Even before I knew I was an angel-blood, I understood that there was something off about the way birds went quiet whenever I passed by, the way they followed me and sometimes, if I was oh-so-lucky, dive-bombed me, not in an unfriendly way, really, but in an I-want-to-see-you-closer sort of way. One of the hazards of having wings and feathers yourself, I suppose, even if they're hidden most of the time: you attract the attention of other creatures with wings.

One time when I was having a picnic in the woods with Tucker, we looked up and our table was surrounded by birds—not just the common camp-robber jays that try to get the food you're eating, but larks, swallows, wrens, even some kind of nuthatch Tucker said was extremely rare, all hanging out in the trees around our table.

"You're like a Disney cartoon, Carrots," Tucker teased me. "You should get them to make you a dress or something."

But this bird feels different, somehow. It's a crow, I think: jet-black, with a sharp, slightly hooked beak, perched on top of the post like a scene straight from Edgar Allan Poe. Watching me. Silent. Thoughtful. Deliberate.

Billy said once that Black Wings could turn into birds. That's the only way they can fly; otherwise their sorrow weighs them down. So is this bird an ordinary crow?

I squint up at it. It cocks its head at me and stares right back with unblinking yellow eyes.

Dread, like a trickle of ice water, makes its way down my spine.

Come on, Clara, I think. It's only a bird.

I scoff at myself and walk quickly past it, hugging my arms to my chest in the cold morning air. The bird squawks, a sharp, jarring warning that sends prickles to the back of my scalp. I keep walking. After a few steps I peer back over my shoulder at the lamppost.

The bird is gone.

I sigh. I tell myself that I'm being paranoid, that I'm just creeped out because of the vision. I try to put the bird out of my mind, and start walking again. Fast. Before I know it, I'm across campus, standing under Christian's window, pacing back and forth on the sidewalk because I don't actually know what I'm doing here.

I should have told him about the vision before, but I was too upset that he rejected my being-a-doctor idea. I should have told him before that, even. We've been here for almost two weeks, and neither one of us has talked about visions or purpose or any of the other angel-related stuff. We've been playing at being college freshmen, pretending that there's nothing on our plates but learning people's names and figuring out which rooms our classes are held in and trying not to look like complete morons at this school where everybody seems like a genius.

But I have to tell him now. I need to. Only it's——I check my phone——seven fifteen in the morning. Too early for the guess-what-you're-in-my-vision conversation.

Clara? His voice in my head is bleary.

Oh crap, sorry. I didn't mean to wake you.

Where are you?

Outside. I——Here . . . I dial his number.

He answers on the first ring. "What's up? Are you okay?"

"Do you want to hang out?" I ask. "I know it's early. . . ."

I can actually hear him smiling at the other end of the line. "Absolutely. Let's hang out."

"Oh, good."

"But first let me put some pants on."

"You do that," I say, glad he can't see me totally blushing at the idea of him in boxers. "I'll be right here."

He emerges a few minutes later in jeans and a brand-new Stanford sweatshirt, his hair rumpled. He restrains himself from hugging me. He's relieved to see me after our argument at the bookstore a week ago. He wants to say he's sorry. He wants to tell me that he'll support me in whatever I decide to do.

He doesn't have to say any of this out loud.

"Thanks," I murmur. "That means a lot."

"So what's going on?" he asks.

It's hard to know where to begin. "Do you want to get off campus for a while?"

"Sure," he says, a spark of curiosity in his green eyes. "I don't have class until eleven."

I start walking back toward Roble. "Come on," I call over my shoulder. He jogs to catch up with me. "Let's take a drive."

Twenty minutes later we're cruising around Mountain View, my old hometown.

"Mercy Street," Christian reads as we pass through downtown looking for this doughnut shop I used to go to where the maple bars are so good it makes you want to cry. "Church Street. Hope Street. I'm sensing a theme here. . . ."

"They're just names, Christian. I think someone had a laugh putting city hall on Castro between Church and Mercy. That's all." I check my mirrors and find myself unprepared for the glimpse of his gold-flecked eyes gazing at me steadily.

I glance away.

I don't know what he expects of me now that I am offi-cially single. I don't know what I expect of myself. I don't know what I'm doing.

"I'm not expecting anything, Clara," he says, not looking at me. "If you want to hang with me, great. If you want some space, I get that too."

I'm relieved. We can take this "we belong together" thing slow, figure out what that really means. We don't have to rush. We can be friends.

"Thanks," I say. "And look, I wouldn't have asked you to hang out with me if I didn't want to hang out with you." *You're my best friend,* I want to say, but for some reason I don't.

He smiles. "Take me to your house," he says impulsively. "I want to see where you lived."

Awkward conversation officially over. Obediently I make a right toward my old neighborhood. But it's not my house. Not anymore. It's somebody else's house now, and the thought makes me sad: someone else sleeping in my room, someone else at the kitchen window where Mom always used to stand watching the hummingbirds flit from flower to flower in the backyard. But that's life, I guess. That's being a grown-up. Leaving places. Moving on.

The sun is coming up behind the rows of houses when we get to my street. Sprinklers cast nets of white mist into the air. I roll the window down and drive with my right hand, let my left hand drag through the cool air outside. It smells so good here, like wet cement and fresh-cut grass, the aroma of bacon and pancakes wafting between the homes, garden roses and magnolia trees, the smells of my life before. It's surreal, passing along these familiar tree-lined streets, seeing the same cars parked in the driveways, the same people headed off to work, the same kids walking to school, only a little bigger than the last time I saw them. It's like time has stopped here, and these past two years and all the crazy stuff that went down in Wyoming never took place.

I park the car across the street from my old house.

"Nice," Christian says, gazing out the open window at the big green two-story with blue shutters that was my home-sweet-home for the first sixteen years of my life. "White picket fence and everything."

"Yeah, my mom was a traditionalist."

The house, too, looks exactly the same. I can't stop staring at the basketball hoop that's set up over the garage. I can almost hear Jeffrey practicing, the cadence of the ball hitting the cement, his feet shuffling, his exhaled breath as he jumps and puts the ball through the hoop, the way the backboard thumps and the net swishes, and Jeffrey hissing, "Nice," between his teeth. How many times did I do my homework with that sound in the background?

"He'll turn up," Christian says.

I turn to look at him. "He's sixteen, Christian. He should

be home. He should have someone taking care of him."

"Jeffrey's strong. He can handle himself. You really want him to come home and get arrested and all that?"

"No," I admit. "I'm just . . . worried."

"You're a good sister," he says.

I scoff. "I messed everything up for him."

"You love him. You would have helped him if you'd known what he was going through."

I don't meet his eyes. "How do you know? Maybe I would have blown him off and kept on obsessing about my own thing. I'm good at that."

Christian catches his breath, then says more firmly, "It's not your fault, Clara."

I wish I believed him.

Silence falls over us again, but this time it's weightier.

I should tell him about the vision. I should stop stalling. I don't even know why I'm stalling.

"So tell me," he says, leaning his elbow on the edge of the window.

Thus I rattle off every detail I can remember, ending with my revelation that it's him there with me, him in the dark room. Him yelling for me to get down.

He's quiet for a while after I'm done. "Well. It's not a very visual type of vision, is it?"

"No, it's pretty much darkness and adrenaline, at this point. What do you think?"

He shakes his head, baffled. "What does Angela say?"

I shift uncomfortably. "We haven't really talked about it."

He looks at my face, his eyes narrowing slightly. "Have you told anybody else?" He reads my guilty expression. "Why not?"

I sigh. "I don't know."

"Why haven't you told Billy? That's the entire reason she became your guardian, you know, to help you through stuff like this."

Because she's not my mom, I think.

"Billy just got married," I explain. "I didn't want to spill my depressing guts all over her on her honeymoon, and Angela, well, she had her own thing going on in Italy."

"What thing?" he asks, frowning.

I bite my lip. I wish I could tell him about Phen.

"Who's Phen?" Christian asks with a hint of a smile, able to pick that much out of my head. "Wait, wasn't he the angel who told Angela about the Black Wings all those years ago?" His eyes widen as they meet mine. "*He's* the mysterious Italian boyfriend?"

It's official. I suck at keeping secrets, especially from him.

"Hey! No mind reading! I can't talk about it!" I sputter. "I promised."

"Then stop thinking about it," he says, which is like someone telling you not to think of an elephant, which of course is the first image that pops into your brain. "Whoa. Angela and an *angel*. What's this about the gray wings?"

"Christian!"

"He's not a Black Wing, is he?" Christian looks genuinely worried, the way he always does whenever the topic of Black Wings comes up. They killed his mother, after all.

"No, he's not—" I stop myself. "I would have told you if— Christian!"

"Sorry," he mutters, but he's not very sorry at all. "So, uh . . . back to your vision. And why you kept it to yourself this long. Because that, I'm pretty sure, you are allowed to tell me."

I'm relieved to be off the subject of Angela, although the vision stuff is not any easier to talk about. I sigh.

"I didn't tell you because I didn't want to be having a vision," I confess. "Not right now."

He nods like he understands, but I get a flicker of pain from him.

"I'm sorry I didn't say something about it earlier," I say. "I should have."

"I didn't tell you mine, either," he says. "For basically the same reason. I wanted to be a regular college student for a little while. Act like I have a normal life." He gazes up through the windshield into the peach-colored sky. A vee of ducks is cutting its way across the horizon, heading south. We watch the birds ride the air. I wait for him to start talking again.

"It's ironic," he says. "You've been having a vision of dark, and I've been having a vision of light."

"What do you mean?"

"All I can see is light. I don't know where I am. I don't know what I'm supposed to be doing. Just light. It took me a few times to figure out what it is."

I'm holding my breath. "What *what* is?"

"The light." He looks over at me. "It's a sword."

My mouth drops open. "A sword?"

"A flaming sword."

"Shut the front door," I gasp.

He does his laugh/exhale thing. "At first all I could think was, How great is this? I'm wielding a flaming sword. A *sword* made of *fire*. Awesome, right?" His smile fades. "But then I started thinking about what it could mean, and when I told my uncle about it this summer, he completely freaked out. He started me doing push-ups on the spot."

"But why?"

"Because obviously I'm going to have to fight." He clasps his hands together behind his neck and sighs.

"Who?" I'm almost afraid to ask.

"I have no idea." He drops his hands, his smile mournful as he looks at me. "But Walter is trying to make sure that I'm prepared for whoever it is." He shrugs.

"Wow," I say. "I'm sorry."

"Yeah, well, we're kidding ourselves if we think we're ever going to be allowed to lead normal lives, aren't we?" he says.

Silence. Finally I say, "We'll figure it out, Christian."

He nods, but there's something else that's bothering him, a grief that reverberates through me and makes me look up to meet his eyes. Then I know without having to ask that Walter's dying and that it's the one-hundred-and-twenty-years rule.

"Oh, Christian. When?" I whisper.

Soon. A few months, is his best guess. He doesn't want me to be there, he says silently, because he doesn't think he'll be able to say it out loud. It hurts him so much, Walter telling him to stay away, the idea that he might never get to spend time with him again. *He doesn't want me to see him like that.*

I understand. At the end my mom was so weak she couldn't even walk to the bathroom. That was one of the worst parts of it, the indignity of it all. Her body giving out. Giving up.

I scoot over and slip my hand into his, which startles him. The familiar electricity passes between us, making me feel stronger. Braver. I rest my head on his shoulder. I try to comfort him the way he's always managed to comfort me.

I'm right here, I tell him. *I'm not going anywhere. For what it's worth.*

"Thanks."

"Forget all the gloom-and-doom stuff," I say after a while. "Let's just live a little."

"Okay. Sounds like a plan."

I pull away, glance at the clock on the dashboard. Seven forty-five—plenty of time, I think. I know something that will make us both feel better.

"Where are we off to now?" Christian asks.

"You'll like it," I say, starting the car. "I promise."

An hour later I park the car near the visitor center at Big Basin Redwoods State Park and hop out.

"Follow me," I say, and head off beneath the towering trees toward the Pine Mountain Trail.

I'm surprised that I remember the way, but I do. I remember like it was yesterday. It's shaping up to be a sunny day, but it's cool in the shadow of the giant redwoods. There aren't any other hikers along the path, and I get the eerie sense that Christian and I are the only two people on earth, like somehow we've wandered back into a time before the dawn of man, and any moment now a woolly mammoth is going to step out of the trees to confront us.

Christian stays a few steps behind me as we hike, a quiet appreciation for the beauty of this place rolling off him. He doesn't hesitate when we reach Buzzards Roost and have to do a bit of rock climbing. Within moments we're at the top of the ridge, gazing across the valley of enormous trees, blue coastal mountains in the distance, the gleam of the ocean barely visible beyond them.

"Wow," he breathes, turning in a slow circle, taking it all in.

"That's what I said, the first time." I sit down on a boulder, lean back to soak in the sun. "This is where my mom brought me to tell me about the angels, when I was fourteen. She said it was her thinking spot, and now that I live here again, I think it could be mine, too. I'm supposed to find a thinking spot for happiness class. A safe zone, the professor calls it."

"How's happiness class going, by the way?"

"Okay, so far."

"Are you feeling happy?" he asks with the hint of a smirk.

I shrug. "The professor says that happiness is wanting what you have."

Christian makes a thoughtful noise in the back of his throat. "I see. Happiness is wanting what you have. Well, there you go. So what's the problem, then?"

"What do you mean?"

"Why is the class only okay?"

"Oh." I bite my lip, then confess. "Every time I meditate, I start glowing."

His mouth opens. "Every time?"

"Well, not every time *now*, since I figured out how it works. Every time that I do it the way you're supposed to—empty my mind, focus on the present; you know, *just be*, remember?—whenever I actually get into it, then boom. *Glorified*."

He gives a disbelieving chuckle. "So what do you do?"

"I spend the first five minutes of every class trying *not* to meditate while all the other students are trying *to* meditate." I sigh. "Which is not conducive to the whole stress-relief thing."

He laughs, a full-blown, delighted kind of laugh, like he finds the whole thing hilarious. It's a great sound, warm, spine-tingly, and it makes me want to laugh too, but I only smile and shake my head sadly like, *What else can I do?*

"Sorry," he says. "But that's too funny. All last year you stood up on the stage at the Pink Garter and you tried so hard to achieve glory, and you couldn't, and now you have to work to hold it back."

"That's what we call irony." I get to my feet, brush dirt off my jeans. "All right. Not that I don't enjoy chatting with you, Christian, but I didn't bring you up here to talk."

He squints up at me. "What?"

I take off my hoodie and toss it down next to him.

Now he really looks confused. I turn my back to him and summon my wings, stretch them over my head, flex. When I glance over at him again, he's standing, staring with a kind of yearning admiration at my feathers, which gleam white in the sun.

He wants to touch them.

"Clara——" he says breathlessly, and takes a step forward, and reaches out.

I leap off the rock. The wind rushes me, cold and greedy, but my wings open and carry me up and up. I sweep out and away from Buzzards Roost, skimming the trees, laughing. It's been forever since I've flown. There's nothing on earth that makes me feel happier than this.

I circle back. Christian's still on the rock, watching me. He's taken off his jacket. He unfolds his gorgeous white and black-speckled wings, steps to the edge of the rock, and looks down.

"Are you coming or what?" I call.

He grins, then lifts off the top of the rock in two powerful beats of his wings. My breath catches. We've never flown together before, not like this, not in the light of day, unimpeded, without there being something terrible we were flying away from or something scary we were flying toward. We've never flown for fun.

He zips by me, so fast all I see is a streak against the blue of the sky. He's a better flier than I am, more gifted at it, more practiced. He hardly has to flap his wings to stay aloft. He simply flies, like Superman, cutting through the air.

Come on, slowpoke, he says. *Get the lead out.*

I laugh and start after him.

Today it's just us and the wind.

4

THE LABYRINTH

That night I dream of Tucker and me, riding Midas on a forest trail. I'm sitting behind him, my legs pressed against his as the horse shifts under us, my arms draped loosely around his chest. My head is filled with the smell of pine and horse and Tucker. I'm completely relaxed, enjoying the sun on my shoulders, the breeze in my hair, the feel of his body against mine. He is all things warm, and good, and strong. He is mine. I lean into him, press a kiss to his shoulder through his blue plaid shirt.

He turns to say something, and the brim of his Stetson hits me in the face. I'm surprised; I lose my balance and nearly slide off the horse, but he steadies me. He takes the hat off, looks at me with his golden-brown hair all askew, eyes impossibly blue, and laughs his husky laugh, which makes goose bumps jump up all along my arms.

"This isn't working." He reaches up and transfers the hat to my head, grins. "There. Much better on you." He angles his face to kiss me. His lips slightly chapped but gentle, tender on mine. His mind full of love.

In this moment I know I'm dreaming. I know it isn't real. Already I can feel myself waking up. I don't want to wake up, I think. Not yet.

I open my eyes. It's still dark, a lamp outside spilling a watery silver light through our open window, a crack of gold under the door, soft shadows cast by the furniture. I'm filled with a strange feeling, almost like déjà vu. The building is eerily quiet, so I know without looking at my clock that it must be pretty late, or early, however you want to look at it. I glance over at Wan Chen. She sighs in her sleep, turns over.

The dream is unfair, I think. Especially since I had such a good time with Christian this morning. I felt connected with him, like I was finally where I was supposed to be. I felt right.

Dumb dream. My stupid subconscious is refusing to face facts: Tucker and I are over. Done.

Dumb brain of mine. Dumb heart.

There's a light tapping sound, so faint I think I might have imagined it. I sit up, listening. It comes again. All at once I realize that it was the knocking that woke me.

I throw on my sweatshirt and tiptoe to the door. I unlatch it and open it a crack, squint into the brightness of the hall.

My brother is standing outside my door.

"Jeffrey!" I gasp.

I probably should play it cool, but I can't. I throw my arms around him. He stiffens in surprise, the muscles in his shoulders tense as I hang on to him, but then finally he puts his hands on my back and relaxes. It's so good to be able to hug him, to know that he is solid and safe and unharmed, that I almost laugh.

"What are you doing here?" I ask after a minute. "How did you find me?"

"What, you think I couldn't track you down if I wanted to?" he says. "I thought I saw you today, and I guess I missed you."

I pull back and look at him. He seems bigger, somehow. Taller, but leaner. Older.

I grab him by the arm and haul him downstairs into the laundry room, where we can talk without waking everybody up.

"Where have you been?" I demand after the door closes behind us.

He's been expecting this question, of course. "Around. Ow!" he says when I punch him in the shoulder. "Hey!"

"You little twerp!" I yell, punching him again, harder this time. "How could you take off like that? Do you have any idea how worried we've been?"

The next time I go to hit him, he catches my fist, holds me back. I'm surprised by how strong he is, how easily he stops the blow.

"Who's 'we'?" he asks, and when I don't understand what he means, he clarifies: "Who was worried?"

"Me, you idiot! And Billy, and Dad——"

He shakes his head. "Dad didn't worry about me," he says, and in his eyes I see that angry gleam I'd almost forgotten, his fury at Dad for leaving us when we were kids. For not being there. For lying. For representing everything in his life that feels unfair.

I put my hand on his arm. His skin is cold, clammy, like he's come from walking around outside in damp weather or flying through clouds. "Where have you been, Jeffrey?" I ask, calmly this time.

He fiddles with the buttons at the top of one of the washing machines. "I've been doing my own thing."

"You could have told us where you were going. You could have called."

"Why, so you could convince me to be a good little angel-blood? Even if I ended up getting arrested?" He turns away, his hands shoved in his pockets, and scuffs at a spot on the carpet with his shoe. "It smells good in here," he says, which strikes me as such a ridiculous attempt to change the subject that it gets a smile out of me.

"You want to do some laundry? It's free. Do you even know how to do laundry?"

"Yes," he says, and I picture him at a Laundromat some-place, frowning at a washing machine as he separates whites from darks, about to do his very first load of laundry on his own. For some reason the image makes me sad.

It's funny that all this time, all these months, I've wanted to talk to him so much I've had imaginary conversations with him, thinking about what I'd say when I saw him again. I wanted to grill him. Chastise him. Convince him to come home. Sympathize over what he's going through. Try to get him to talk about the parts of his story that I don't under-stand. I wanted to tell him that I love him. But now that he's here, I can't think of what to say.

"Are you going to school somewhere?" I ask.

He scoffs. "Why would I do that?"

"So you're not planning on graduating from high school?"

His silver eyes go cold. "Why, so I can get into a fancy college like Stanford? Graduate, get a nine-to-five job, get married, buy a house, get a dog, bang out a couple of kids—what would our kids be, anyway, thirty-seven-and-a-half percent angel-blood? Think there's a Latin term for that?—and then I'd have the Angel-American dream and live happily ever after?"

"If that's what you want."

"It isn't what I want," he says. "That's what humans do, Clara. And I'm not one."

I struggle to keep my voice neutral. "Yes, you are."

"I'm only a fourth human." He looks up at me like he's gazing into me, inspecting my humanness, too. "That's a pretty small piece of the pie. Why should it define me?"

I cross my arms over my chest, shiver even though it's not cold. "Jeffrey," I say quietly. "We can't just run away from our problems."

He flinches, then pushes past me for the door. "It was a mistake coming here," he mutters, and I wonder, *Why did he come here? Why did he want to see me?*

"Wait." I start after him, catch his arm.

"Let go, Clara. I'm done playing games. I'm done with all of it. I'm not going to have anyone else tell me what to do, ever again. I'm going to do what I want."

"I'm sorry!" I stop, take a breath. "I'm sorry," I try again, more quietly. "You're right. It's not my place to boss you around. I'm not——"

Mom, I think, but the word doesn't come out. I let go of his arm and take a couple steps back. "I'm sorry," I say again.

He looks at me hard for a minute like he's deciding how much to tell me.

"Mom knew," he says finally. "She knew that I was going to run away."

I stare at him. "How?"

He scoffs. "She said a little bird told her."

It sounds exactly like something Mom would say. "She was kind of infuriating, wasn't she?"

"Yeah. A real know-it-all." He smiles the raw-hurt kind of smile. It breaks my heart.

"Jeffrey——" I want to tell him about heaven then, about seeing Mom, but he doesn't let me.

"The point is, she knew," he says. "She even kind of prepared me for it."

"But maybe I could——"

"No. I don't need you messing up my life right now." He looks embarrassed, like he just caught on to how rude he sounds. "I mean, I have to make it on my own, Clara. All right? But I'm okay. That's what I came to tell you. You don't have to worry. I'm fine."

"Okay," I murmur, my voice suddenly thick. I clear my throat, get a hold of myself. "Jeffrey——"

"I've got to get back," he says.

I nod like it totally makes sense that he would have somewhere he needs to be at five in the morning. "Do you need money?"

"No," he says, but he waits while I sprint up to my room to get my wallet, and he takes some when I give it to him.

"If you need anything, call me," I order him. "I mean it. Call me."

"Why, so you can boss me around?" he says, but he sounds good-natured about it.

I walk him to the front door. It's chilly outside. I worry that he's not wearing a coat. I worry that the forty-two dollars

I gave him won't be enough to keep him safe and fed. I worry that I'll never see him again.

"Now's when you let go of my arm," he says.

I make my fingers release.

"Jeffrey, wait," I say as he starts to walk away.

He doesn't stop walking, doesn't turn back. "I'll call you, Clara."

"You'd better," I yell after him.

He rounds the corner of the building. I wait for all of three seconds before I run after him, but when I get there, he's gone.

That stupid crow is hanging out at my happiness class, perched on a branch right outside the window, watching me. I'm supposed to be meditating right now, which means I have to sit and look like I'm chilling with the sixty or so students who are spread out in various meditative positions on the floor, letting go of all my worldly thoughts and whatnot, which I can't do because if I did I'd start glowing like a tanning bed. I'm supposed to have my eyes closed, but I keep opening them to see if the bird is still there, and it is every time I check, looking straight at me through the glass with those bright yellow eyes, taunting me, like, *Oh yeah, what are you going to do about it?*

It's a coincidence, I think. It's not the same bird. It can't be. It looks like the same bird, but then, don't all crows look alike? What does it want?

This is clearly putting a major kink in my quest for inner peace.

"Excellent job, everyone," says Dr. Welch, stretching his arms over his head. "Now let's take a few minutes to write in our gratitude journals, and then we'll start the discussion."

Go away, I think at the bird. *Don't be a Black Wing. Just be a stupid bird. I don't want to deal with a Black Wing right now.*

It cocks its head at me, caws once, and flies off.

I take a deep breath and let it out. I'm being paranoid, I tell myself again. It's only a bird. It's only a bird. Stop wigging yourself out.

I am grateful that meditation time is over, is what I write in my journal. Just to be snarky.

The guy sitting next to me looks over, sees what I've jotted onto my paper, and smirks.

"I'm not good at it, either," he says.

If only he knew. But I smile and nod.

"You're Clara, right?" he whispers. "I remember you from that stupid introductory game we played on the first day."

Dr. Welch clears his throat and looks pointedly at the two of us, which means, *You're supposed to be grateful right now. Not talking.*

The guy grins and turns his notebook slightly so I can see what he's writing. *I'm Thomas. I'm grateful that this class is pass/ fail.*

I smile and nod again. I already knew his name. I've been privately referring to him as Doubting Thomas, since he's always the first one to question everything Dr. Welch says. Like last week, for instance, Dr. Welch said that we have to stop chasing after material things and work to be content with ourselves, and Thomas's hand shot up, and he said something like, "But if we all sat around content with exactly where we were in life, nobody would strive for excellence. I want to be happy, sure, but I didn't come to Stanford because I wanted to find happiness. I came because I want to be the best."

Humble, this guy.

My phone vibrates, and Dr. Welch looks over again. I wait a few minutes before I sneak it out of my pocket. There's a text from Angela asking me to meet her at Memorial Church.

After class I book it down the main stairs of Meyer Library, where happiness is held, and Thomas calls after me. "Hey, Clara, wait!" I don't have a lot of time for this, but I stop. I scan the skies nervously for the mysterious crow, but I don't see anything out of the ordinary.

"Um, do you——" Thomas pauses, like he's forgotten what he was going to say now that he's got my attention. "Do you want to get something to eat? There's this place behind Tresidder that makes these amazing chicken burritos. They put in rice and beans and *pico de gallo*——"

"I can't. I'm meeting somebody," I interrupt before he can really get going on the burritos. Which are incredibly tasty—it's true. But I *am* meeting someone, and besides that, I really do not want to go out with Doubting Thomas. That much I know.

His face falls. "Some other time, then," he says, and shrugs one shoulder like it's no big deal, but I feel a prickle of wounded pride coming off him, a "who does she think she is" kind of vibe, which makes me feel immediately less guilty for turning him down.

Angela's text—*C, meet me at MemChu. 5:30 p.m. Important*—has me jogging through the archways of the arcade, my footsteps echoing on the checkered stones. Her vision is going to take place here at Stanford, after all—it's the entire reason we all ended up here—so *important* could be pretty darn monumental. I check my watch—five thirty-five—and canter across the quad, not slowing as I often do to take in the sight of the church, its gleaming golden mosaics at the front, the Celtic cross perched at the apex on the roof. I shove my shoulder against the heavy wooden door and step inside, pause for a minute in the vestibule to let my eyes adjust to the dimness within.

I don't immediately see Angela among the scattering of students who are gathered here, most of them walking slowly in an indiscernible pattern at the front of the sanctuary. I wander down the red-carpeted aisle toward them, past the rows of mahogany pews, my skin prickling at the depictions of angels everywhere, in the stained-glass windows, in the mosaics on both sides of me, in the space between the arches on the ceiling: angels everywhere, gazing down, always with their wings unfurled behind them. One of them is probably Michael, I think. All I have to do to find my dad is go to church.

I spot Angela. She's with the others, walking inside a circle at the top of the steps at the front. Something's laid out on the floor like an enormous rug, deep blue with white patterns on it, a kind of path that goes in loops. She doesn't see me. Her lips are pursed in concentration, and then they move like she's saying something, but I don't hear a sound outside of the shuffling of feet, the whisper of clothing as people walk. She stops in the center of the circle, bends her head for a long moment, her hair obscuring her face, then starts up again, walking slowly, her arms swinging by her sides.

My empathy surges to life. I can feel them all, every single one of the people inside the circle. There is a girl on my left who's homesick. She misses the big city, her family's walk-up in Brooklyn, her two little sisters. A guy who's stopped in the center wants desperately to ace his first calculus test. Another guy is wondering about a blonde in his film-studies class, whether she thinks he has good taste in movies, whether she likes him, and then he feels guilty for thinking about such things in a church. Their emotions and the entwined thoughts are like wafts of air hitting me in the stillness of this place—hot and cold, fear and loneliness and hope and happiness—but I get a sense that it's all emptying out, as if the feelings cluttering their brains are slowly being drawn into the circle like water swirling down a drain.

And above the rest of them I feel Angela. Focused. Full of purpose. Determination. Seeking the truth with the persistence of a guided missile.

I take a seat in the front pew and wait, lean forward onto my knees and close my eyes. I have a sudden memory of Jeffrey as a kid, back when we went to church when I was little, falling asleep in the middle of a sermon. Mom and I had a hard time trying not to laugh at him, all slumped over like that, but then he started snoring, and Mom poked him in the ribs, and he jolted upright.

What? he whispered. *I was praying.*

I stifle a laugh, remembering that. *I was praying.* Classic.

I open my eyes. Someone is sitting next to me putting on shoes: a pair of boots, beat-up and black with ratty laces. Angela's. I look over at her. She's wearing a baggy black sweatshirt and purple leggings, a little grungier than usual, no makeup, not even the normal black around her eyes. She's got that same look on her face that she got last year when she was trying to figure out what college to go to: a mix of frustration and excitement.

"Hi," I start to say, but she shushes me, gestures to the door. I follow her out of the church, glad for the fresh air on my face, the sudden sun, the breeze that shifts the fronds in the palm trees at the edge of the quad.

"Took you long enough to get here," Angela says.

"What is that thing anyway, in the church?"

"It's a labyrinth. A knockoff of one, anyway. It's made of vinyl so they can roll it up and move it around. It's patterned after these huge stone labyrinths they have in churches in Europe. The idea is that walking in circles can free the mind so that you can pray."

I arch an eyebrow at her.

"I was thinking about my purpose," she says.

"Does it work? Was your mind freed?"

She shrugs. "At first I thought it was pointless, but I've been having a hard time concentrating lately." She clears her throat. "So I tried it, and after a while I got this amazing clarity. It's weird. It just steals over you. Then I figured out that I could make the vision come to me this way."

"Make the vision come? On purpose?"

She scoffs. "Of course on purpose."

Knowing this instantly makes me want to go back inside and try it. Maybe I'd get more than that little bit of darkness. Maybe I'd figure my vision out. But there's another part of me that shudders at the thought of going to the pitch-black room voluntarily.

"So. Why I texted you," Angela says, her shoulders tense. "I have the words."

I stare at her. She throws her hands up in exasperation.

"The words! The words! All this time—I mean, for years, C—I've been seeing this place in my visions, and I know I'm supposed to say something to somebody, but I never hear myself say the words. It's been driving me crazy, especially since I got here and I know it's going to happen pretty soon—within the next four years, I'm guessing anyway. I'm supposed to be a messenger, at least that's what I thought, but I never knew the message, until now." She takes a breath, sighs it out. Closes her eyes. "The words."

"So what are they?"

She opens her eyes, her irises a flash of eager gold.

"The seventh is ours," she says.

Okay. "So what does that mean?"

Her face falls, like maybe she was expecting me to know the answer and share it with her. "Well, I know that the number seven is like the most significant of all the numbers."

"Why, because there are seven days in a week?"

"Yes," she says, completely straight-faced. "Seven days in a week. Seven notes on the music scale. Seven colors in the spectrum."

She is seriously obsessed with this. But I guess that comes as no real surprise. It's Angela.

"Huh. So your vision is brought to you by the number seven," I joke. I can't help but think of *Sesame Street*. This episode is brought to you by the number twelve and the letter *Z*.

62

"Hey, C, this is serious," she says. "Seven is the number of perfection and divine completion. It's God's number."

"God's number," I repeat. "But what does it mean, Ange? 'The seventh is ours'?"

"I don't know," she confesses, frowning. "I have considered that it might be an object of some kind. Or a date, I suppose. But . . ." She grabs my hand. "Here, come with me."

She pulls me across the quad again, essentially retracing the route I used to get here, all the way out into the arcade, where there's a group of black statues, a replica of Rodin's *Burghers of Calais*, six mournful-looking men with ropes around their necks. I don't know the history or what doom they're supposed to be going toward, but they're clearly walking to their deaths, which I've always found weird and unsettling to run into in the middle of Stanford's bustling campus. Kind of a downer.

"I see them, in my vision." Angela pulls me past the burghers, until we're standing at the top of the steps looking out at the Oval and beyond it Palm Drive, the long street that's lined with giant palm trees and marks the official entrance to the university. The sun is setting. Students are playing Frisbee in the grass wearing shorts and tank tops, sunglasses, flip-flops. Others are stretched out under trees, studying. Birds are singing, bicycles whirring by. A car makes its way around the circle with a surfboard strapped to the roof.

Ladies and gentlemen, I think: October in California.

"It happens here." Angela stops and plants her feet. "Right here."

I look down. "What, you mean where we're standing?"

She nods. "I'm going to come from that direction." She points to the left. "And I'm going to climb up these five little steps, and there's going to be someone waiting for me, right here."

"The man in the gray suit." I remember her telling me.

"Yes. And I'm going to tell him, 'The seventh is ours.'"

"Do you know who he is?"

She makes an irritated noise in the back of her throat, like I am bursting her "guess how brilliant I am" bubble by bringing up something that she doesn't know. "It feels like I recognize him, in the vision, but he's got his back to me. I don't ever see his face."

"Ah, one of those." I think back to the days when I had my first vision, the forest fire, the boy watching it, and it was frustrating as all get-out that I could never see what he looked like. It took me a while to get used to seeing Christian from the front.

"I'm going to find out, obviously," she says, like it's not important. "But it's happening. Right here. This is the place."

"Very exciting," I say, which is what she wants to hear.

She nods, but there's something troubled in her expression. She chews on her lip, then sighs.

"Are you okay?" I ask.

She snaps out of it. "Right here," she says again, like this spot has magical properties.

"Right here," I agree.

"The seventh is ours," she whispers.

On the way back to Roble we cut through the Papua New Guinea Sculpture Garden. In among the tall trees there are dozens of sculpted wooden poles and large stone carvings done in the native style. My eye goes right to a primitive version of *The Thinker*, a man bent over with his huge head framed in his hands, wearing a contemplative expression. Perched on top of his head is a large black crow. As we approach, it pivots to look at me. Caws.

I stop walking.

"What is it?" Angela asks.

"That bird," I say, my voice dropping in embarrassment at how silly this is going to sound. "This is like the fourth time I've seen it since I got here. I think it's following me."

She glances over her shoulder at the bird. "How do you know it's the same bird?" she asks. "There are a lot of birds here, C, and birds act weird around us. That's kind of a given."

"I don't know. It's just a feeling, I guess."

Her eyes widen slightly. *You think Samjeeza might have followed you here?* she asks silently, which startles me. I forgot that she can speak in my mind. *Do you feel sorrow?*

I feel instantly dumb that I never thought to feel for

sorrow before. Usually around Sam the sorrow overwhelms me without me having to seek it out. I gaze up at the bird, slowly open the door of my mind, and wait to be flooded with Samjeeza's sad, sweet despair. But before I can discern anything beyond my own anxiety, the bird squawks, almost in a mocking way, and flaps off through the trees.

Angela and I stare after it.

"It's probably just a bird," I say. A shudder passes through me.

"Right," she says, in a voice that conveys she doesn't believe that for a second. "Well, what can you do? I guess if it's a Black Wing, you'll find out soon enough."

I guess so.

"You should tell Billy about it," Angela says. "See if she has any, I don't know, advice for you. Maybe some kind of bird deterrent."

I want to laugh at her choice of words, but for some reason I don't think it's so funny. I nod. "Yeah, I'll call Billy," I say. "I haven't checked in with her for a while."

I hate this.

I'm sitting on the edge of my bed with my cell in my hand. I don't know how Billy will react to the news that I'm possibly seeing a Black Wing, but there's the high likelihood she'll say I should run away—that's what you do when you see a Black Wing, we've all been taught over and over and over again.

You run. You go to someplace hallowed. You hide. You can't fight them. They're too strong. They're invincible. I mean, last year when Samjeeza started showing up at my school, the adults went full lockdown on us. They got scared.

I might have to leave Stanford, is what that would mean.

My jaw clenches. I'm tired of being scared all the time. Of Black Wings and frightening visions and failure. I'm sick of it.

It makes me think of when I was a kid, maybe six or seven, and I went through a scared-of-the-dark phase. I'd lie with the covers clutched up to my chin, convinced that every shadow was a monster: an alien come to abduct me, a vampire, a ghost about to lay its chilly dead hand on my arm. I told my mom I wanted to sleep with the lights on. She humored me that way, or let me sleep in her bed, curled against the security of her warm, vanilla-scented body until the terror faded, but after a while she said, "It's time to stop being afraid, Clara."

"I can't."

"You can." She handed me a spray bottle. "It's holy water," she explained. "If anything scary comes into this room, tell it to go away, and if it doesn't go away, spray it with this."

I seriously doubted that holy water would have any effect on aliens.

"Try it," she dared me. "See what happens."

I spent the next night muttering, "Go away," and spraying shadows, and she was right. The monsters disappeared. I made them go away, just by my refusal to be afraid of them. I took control of my fear. I conquered it.

That's how I feel right now, like if I just refuse to be afraid of the bird, it'll go away.

I wish I could call Mom instead of Billy. What would she say to me, I wonder, if I could magically go to her, if I could run downstairs to her room in Jackson the way I used to and tell her everything? I think I know. She'd kiss me on the temple, the way she always did, and smooth the hair away from my face. She'd draw a quilt around my shoulders. She'd make me a cup of tea, and I'd sit at the kitchen counter and I'd tell her about the crow, and about my vision of the darkness, how I feel inside it, about my fears.

And here's what I'd want her to say: *It's time to stop being afraid, Clara. There's always going to be danger. Live your life.*

I turn the phone off and set it on my desk.

I won't let you do this to me, I think at the bird, even though it's not present at the moment. *I'm not scared of you. And I'm not going to let you drive me away.*

5

I REALLY WANT A CHEESEBURGER

The days start zipping by, October leaning toward November. I get caught up in the busyness of school, the "Stanford duck syndrome," which is where it appears like you're swimming calmly, but under the water you're furiously kicking. I go to class five days a week, five or six hours a day. I study roughly two hours for every hour I spend in class. That's at least seventy-five hours a week, if you do the math. Then once you subtract sleeping and eating and showering and having sporadic visions of me and Christian hiding in a dark room, I'm left with about twenty hours to hit the occasional party with the other Roble girls, or get my Saturday afternoon coffee with Christian, or go snack shopping with Wan Chen, or go to the movies or the beach or learn how to play Frisbee golf in the Oval. Jeffrey's also calling me every once in a while, which is a huge relief, and we've been having an almost-weekly breakfast together at the café where Mom used to take us when we were kids.

So there's not much time to think about anything but school. Which suits me just fine.

I keep seeing the crow around campus, but I do my best to ignore it, and the more times I see it and nothing happens, the more I believe what I keep telling myself: that if I don't engage it, everything will be fine. It doesn't matter if it's Samjeeza or not. I try to act like everything's normal.

But then one day Wan Chen and I are coming out of the chemistry building, and I hear somebody call my name. I turn around to see a tall blond man in a boxy brown suit and a black fedora—I'm thinking circa 1965—standing on the lawn. An angel. There's no denying that.

He also happens to be my dad.

"Uh, hi," I say lamely. I haven't seen or heard from him in months, not since the week after Mom died, and now *poof.* He appears. Like he walked off the set of *Mad Men.* With a bicycle, bizarrely enough, a pretty blue-and-silver Schwinn that he takes a minute to lean against the side of the building. He jogs over to where Wan Chen and I are standing.

I pull myself together. "So . . . um, Wan Chen, this is my dad, Michael. Dad, my roommate, Wan Chen."

"Pleased to meet you," Dad rumbles.

Wan Chen's face goes greenish, and she says that she's got another class to get to, and promptly takes off.

Dad has that effect on humans.

As for me, I am filled with the sense of deep abiding happiness I always get when I'm around my father, a reflection of his inner peace, his connection with heaven, his joy. Then, because I don't like feeling emotions that are not my own, even the good ones, I try to block him out.

"Did you bike here?" I ask.

He laughs. "No. That's for you. A birthday present."

I'm surprised. Never mind that my birthday was in June, and it's November. I can't remember ever receiving a birthday gift from Dad in person. In the past he usually sent something extravagant in the mail, a card stuffed with cash or an expensive locket or concert tickets. Money for a car. All nice things, but it always seemed like he was trying to buy me off, make up for the fact that he'd abandoned us.

He frowns, an expression that's not quite natural on his face. "Your mother arranged the presents," he confesses. "She knew what you'd want. She was also the one who suggested this bicycle. She said you'd need it."

I stare at him. "Wait, you mean it was *Mom* who sent all that stuff?"

He nods in this half-guilty way, like he's admitted to cheating on the good-father test.

O-kay. So I was actually getting presents from my mom when I thought I was getting presents from my absentee father. That is messed up.

"What about you? Do you even have a birthday?" I ask, for lack of something better to say. "I mean, I always thought your birthday was July eleventh."

He smiles. "That was the first full day I got to spend with your mother, the first day of our time together. July the eleventh, 1989."

"Oh. So you're like twenty-three."

He nods. "Yes. I'm like twenty-three."

He looks like Jeffrey, I think as I scrutinize his face. They have the same silver eyes, the same hair, the same golden tone to their skin. The difference is that while Dad is literally as old as the hills, calm, at peace with everything, Jeffrey is sixteen and at peace with nothing. Out there "doing his own thing," whatever that means.

"You saw Jeffrey?" Dad asks.

"Don't read my mind; that's rude. And yes, he came to see me, and he's called me a couple times, basically because I think he doesn't want me to look for him. He's living around here somewhere. We're going out to Joanie's Café tomorrow. That's the only way I can get him to spend time with me—offer free food—but hey, whatever works." I have a stellar idea. "You should come with us."

Dad doesn't even consider it. "He won't want to talk to me."

72

"So what? He's a teenager. You're his father," I say, and what I don't say, but what he probably hears me think anyway, is *You should make him go home.*

Dad shakes his head. "I can't help him, Clara. I've seen every possible version of what could happen, and he never listens to me. If anything, my interference would make things worse for him." He clears his throat. "Anyway, I came here for a reason. I've been given the task of training you."

My heart starts beating fast. "Training me? For what?"

Something in his jaw works as he considers how much to disclose. "I don't know if you know this about me, but I am a soldier."

Or the leader of God's army, but okay, let's be modest. "Yeah, I kind of did know that."

"And swordplay is a specialty of mine."

"Swordplay?" I say this too loudly, and the people walking by flash us alarmed looks. I lower my voice. "You're going to train me to use a sword? Like . . . a flaming sword?"

But that's Christian's vision, I think immediately. Not mine. Not me, fighting.

Dad shakes his head. "People often mistake it for a flaming sword, from the way the light ripples, but it's made from glory, not fire. A glory sword."

I can't believe I'm hearing this. "A glory sword? Why?"

He hesitates. "It's part of the plan."

"I see. So there's a definite plan. Involving me," I say.

"Yes."

"Is there a copy of this master plan written down that I could take a peek at? Just for a minute?"

The corner of his mouth lifts. "It's a work in progress. So, are you ready?" he asks.

"What, *now?*"

"No time like the present," he says, which I can tell he thinks is a joke. He goes over to retrieve the bicycle, and together we meander slowly back toward Roble.

"How's school, by the way?" he asks, like any other dutiful dad.

"Fine."

"And how's your friend?"

I find it bizarre that he's asking about my friends. "Uh—which one?"

"Angela," he says. "She's the reason you came to Stanford, isn't she?"

"Oh. Yeah. Angela's doing okay, I think."

The truth is, I haven't hung out with Angela since that day at MemChu, almost three weeks ago. I called her this past weekend and asked if she wanted to go to the new gory slasher film that came out on Halloween, and she blew me off. "I'm busy" is all she said. She's also not interested in going to parties or even poetry readings, which I assumed she'd be all over, or doing much of anything besides going to class, and even in our Poet Re-making the World class she's been oddly quiet and nonopinionated. Lately I've seen

74

more of her roommates than I have of Angela: Robin is in my art history class on Mondays and Wednesdays and a lot of times we get coffee after, and Amy and I always seem to show up in the dining hall for breakfast at the same time, where we sit together and chat up a storm. It's through them that I know that Angela's either been hanging out at the church or holed up in their room, glued to her laptop or reading big intimidating-looking books or scribbling away in her good old black-and-white composition notebook, wearing sweats most days, sometimes not even bothering to shower. Clearly something more intense than usual is going on with her. I figure it's her purpose heating up—her obsession with the number seven, the guy in the gray suit, all that jazz.

"I always liked Angela," Dad says now, which startles me because as far as I know, he only met her that one time. "She's very passionate in her desire to do what is right. You should look out for her."

I make a mental note to call Angela as soon as I have a minute. We've reached Roble by this point, and Dad stands looking at the building with its ivy-covered facade while I park the bike on the rack outside.

"Do you want to see my room?" I ask a bit awkwardly.

"Perhaps later," he says. "Right now we need to find a place where we won't be disturbed."

I can't think of anywhere better than the basement of the dorm, where there's a study room with no windows. People mostly use it to make phone calls when they don't want to bother their roommates. "It's the best I can do on short notice," I say, as I lead Dad down there. I unlock the door and hold it open for him to see.

"It's perfect," he says, and goes right in.

I'm nervous. "Should I stretch out or something?" My voice echoes strangely in this claustrophobic little room. It smells in here, like dirty socks, sour milk, and old cologne.

"First we should decide where you would like to train," he says.

I gesture around us. "I'm confused."

"This is the starting point," he says. "You must decide the ending point."

"Okay. What are my options?"

"Anywhere," he answers.

"The Sahara desert? The Taj Mahal? The Eiffel Tower?"

"I think we'd make quite a spectacle practicing sword-play at the Eiffel Tower, but it's up to you." He grins goofily, then sobers. "Try somewhere you know well, where you'll be comfortable and relaxed."

That's easy. I don't even have to think about it for two seconds. "Okay. Take me home. To Jackson."

"Jackson it is." Dad moves to stand in front of me. "We will cross now."

"And what is crossing, exactly?" I ask.

"It's . . ." He searches for the words, finds them. "Bending the rules of time and space in order to move from one place to another very quickly. The first step," he adds dramatically, "is glory."

I wait for something to happen, but nothing does. I look at Dad. He nods his head at me expectantly.

"What, *I'm* going to do it?"

"You've done this before, haven't you? You brought your mother back from hell."

"Yes, but I didn't know what I was doing."

"Brick by brick, my dear," he says.

I swallow. "What, I'm like building Rome now? Maybe we should start with something smaller." I close my eyes, try to center myself in the now, try to stop thinking, stop processing, just be. I listen to my breath drag in and out of my body, try to empty myself, forget myself, because only then can I reach that quiet place inside me that's part of the light.

"Good," Dad murmurs, and I open my eyes to glory's golden wash around us.

"In this state," he says, "you have access to anything you ask for. You must simply learn how to ask."

"Anything?" I repeat skeptically.

"If you ask and you believe, yes. Anything."

"So if I really wanted a cheeseburger, like right now . . ."

He laughs, and the sound echoes around us like a chorus of bells. His eyes are molten silver in this light, his hair gleaming.

"I suppose I've had stranger requests." He holds out his hand, and something golden brown appears in it. I take it. It's like bread, only lighter.

"What is it?" I ask. Because it's so not a cheeseburger.

"Taste it."

I hesitate, then take a bite. It explodes on my tongue, like the best buttery croissant I've ever had, almost melting in my mouth, leaving a faint aftertaste of honey. I scarf down the rest, and afterward I feel completely satisfied. Not full. But content.

"This stuff is amazing," I say, resisting the urge to lick my fingers. "And you can produce this out of thin air, anytime you want?"

"I ask, and it comes," he says. "But now, focus. Where were we?"

"You said that in glory we can access anything."

"Yes. That is how one passes between heaven and earth, and how it's possible for me to travel from one place on earth to another. One time to another."

I get momentarily excited. "Are you going to teach me how to move through time, too?"

I like the idea of giving myself an extra hour to study for exams, or finding out who's going to win the Stanford-Berkeley game before it happens. Or—a lump jumps up in my throat—I could go to see Mom. In the past.

Dad frowns. "No."

"Oh," I say, disappointed. "Not part of the plan, huh?"

He puts his hand on my shoulder, squeezes gently. "You will see your mother again, Clara."

"When?" I ask, my voice suddenly hoarse. "When I die?"

"When you need it most," he says, ambiguous as ever.

I clear my throat. "But for now, I can what, *cross* to wherever I want to go?"

He takes my hands in his, looks into my eyes. "Yes. You can."

"That could come in extremely handy when I'm running late for class."

"Clara." He wants me to be serious now. "Crossing is a vital skill. And it's not as difficult as you might think to achieve," he says. "We are all connected, everything that lives and breathes in this world, and glory is what binds us."

Next thing he'll be talking about the Force, I know it.

"And every place has a piece of that energy, as well. A signature, if you will. So to move from here to there, you must first connect to that energy."

"Glory. Check."

"Then you must think of the place you wish to go. Not the location on a map, but the life of that place."

"Like . . . the big aspen tree in my front yard in Jackson?"

"That would be ideal," he says. "Reach for that tree, the power it's generating from the sun, the roots stretching themselves out in the earth, drinking, the life of the leaves. . . ."

For a minute I'm hypnotized by the sound of his voice. I close my eyes, and I can see it so clearly: my aspen tree, the leaves starting to turn colors and drop, the movement of the chilly autumn wind through the branches, the whispering as it stirs the leaves. It actually makes me shiver, imagining it.

"You're not imagining it," Dad says. "We're here."

I open my eyes. Gasp. We're standing in my front yard under the aspen tree. Just like that.

Dad lets go of my hands. "Well done."

"That was me? Not you?"

"All you."

"It was . . . easy." I'm shocked by how simple it was, such an impossible-sounding thing as going almost a thousand miles in the literal blink of an eye.

"You're very powerful, Clara," Dad says. "Even for a Triplare, you're remarkable. Your connection is strong and steady."

This makes me want to ask him a dozen questions, like, *If that's true, why don't I feel more, I don't know, religious? Why aren't my wings whiter? Why do I have so many doubts?* Instead I say, "Okay, let's do this. Teach me something else."

"With pleasure." He takes off his hat and suit jacket and lays them carefully on the porch railing, then goes to the house and returns with Mom's kitchen broom, which he promptly snaps into two pieces like it's a strand of uncooked spaghetti. He holds out one half to me.

"Hey," I gasp. I know it shouldn't be a big deal, but I connect the broom with Mom dancing around the kitchen, sweeping theatrically, mock singing "Whistle While You Work" in her most nasally high-pitched Snow White voice. "You broke my broom."

"I apologize," he says.

I take my half of the broom, narrow my eyes suspiciously on his face. "I thought this was about glory swords."

"Brick by brick," he says again, raising his half of the broom, which is the end with the bristles on it. He brushes it behind my calves, and I jump. "First let's work on your stance."

He teaches me about balance, and angles, and anticipating the moves of my opponent. He teaches me to use the strength of my core rather than the muscles of my arm, to feel the blade—er, broom—as an extension of my body. It's like dancing, I realize very quickly. He moves, and I move in response, keeping time with him, staying light, quick, up on the balls of my feet, avoiding his blows rather than blocking them.

"Good," he says at last. I think he might even be sweating.

I'm relieved because this fighting thing isn't too difficult. I thought it might be one of those things like flying, where I totally sucked for a while, but I pick it up pretty quickly, all things considered.

I guess I'm my father's daughter.

"You are," Dad says with pride in his voice.

On the other hand, while part of me is all glowy and sweaty and proud that this is going so well, another part finds it crazy. I mean, who uses swords anymore? It feels like theater to me, like play, trouncing around the backyard whacking at my dad with a stick. I can't imagine it as something dangerous. I'm holding this broom like a sword, and half the time I want to bust out laughing it's so ridiculous.

But underneath it all, the idea of really wielding a weapon, trying to cut someone with it, totally freaks me out. I don't want to hurt anybody. I don't want to fight. Please don't let it be that I have to fight.

The thought makes me miss a step, and Dad's section of the broomstick is at my chin. I look up into his eyes, swallow.

"That's enough for today," he says.

I nod and drop my piece of broom into the grass. The sun is going down. It's getting dark now, and cold. I hug my arms to my chest.

"You did well," Dad says.

"Yeah, you said that already." I turn away, kick at a fallen pinecone.

I hear him come up behind me. "Sometimes it's difficult to be the bearer of a sword," he says gently.

Dad's known for being tough, the guy who's called in whenever some big baddie needs a slap-down. Phen talked

82

about him like he was the bad cop in the "good cop/bad cop" scenario, the one who smacks the criminals around. In the old artwork Michael's always the stern-faced angel hacking up the devil with a sword. His nickname is the Smiter, Phen said. That job would definitely suck. But when I try to peek inside Dad's mind, all I get is joy. Certainty. An inner stillness like the reflection on the surface of Jackson Lake at sunrise.

I glance over my shoulder at Dad. "You don't seem too conflicted about bearing a sword."

He reaches down and picks up my half of the broom, holds the pieces together for a few seconds, then hands the broom back to me in one piece. My mouth drops open like a kid at a magic show. I run my fingers over the place where it was jagged, but I find it perfectly smooth. Not even the paint is marred. It's like it was never broken.

"I'm at peace with it," he says.

Together we turn and walk back toward the house. Somewhere off in the trees I hear a bird singing, a bright, simple call.

"Hey, I was wondering. . . ." I stop and work up the guts to bring up something that's been in the back of my mind ever since he mentioned the word *sword*. "Would it be okay if Christian trained with us?" His gaze on me is steady and curious, so I go on. "He's having a vision of using a flaming—I mean glory—sword, and his uncle's been training him some, but his uncle's not going to be around much longer, and I think it would be nice—I mean, I think it would be useful for both of us—if you trained us together. Could that be part of the plan?"

He's quiet for such a long time I'm sure he's going to say no, but then he blinks a few times and looks at me. "Yes. Perhaps when you're home for Christmas break, I'll train you together."

"Great. Thank you."

"You're welcome," he says simply.

"Do you want to come in?" I say at the edge of the porch. "I think I can scrounge up some cocoa."

He shakes his head. "Right now it's time for the next part of your lesson."

"The next part?"

"You remember how to cross?"

I nod. "Call the glory, think of the place, click your heels together three times and say, 'There's no place like home.'"

"I've seen that movie," he says. "One of your mother's favorites. We watched it every year."

Us too. Thinking about it makes a sudden tightness in my throat. *WOO*, she called it. She read the book to me out loud every night before bed when I was seven, and when we were finished, we watched it on DVD, and we sang the songs together, and we tried to do that walk they do when they're on the yellow brick road, stepping over each other's legs.

No more *WOO* with Mom, ever.

"So now what?" I ask Dad, refusing to let myself get choked up again.

He grins, a wicked grin, even though he's an angel. "Now you get yourself home."

And just like that, he vanishes. No glory or anything. Just *fft*. Gone.

He expects me to cross back to California on my own.

"Dad? Not funny," I call.

In answer, the wind picks up and sends a bunch of red aspen leaves into my hair.

"Great. Just great," I mutter.

I put the broom in the hallway, near the door, in case we need it again. Then I wander back into the yard and summon a circle of glory. I check my watch and determine that Wan Chen's going to be in class for another hour, so I close my eyes and concentrate on my room, the lavender bedspread, the small desk in the corner that is always messy with papers and books, the air conditioner in the window.

I can picture it all perfectly, but when I open my eyes, I'm still in Jackson.

Dad told me to focus on something living, but we don't even own a houseplant. Maybe this isn't going to be so easy after all.

I close my eyes again. There's the smell of mountain snow on the air. I shiver. I would have brought a coat if I'd known I was going to be in Wyoming today. I'm a wuss about cold.

You're my California flower, I remember Tucker saying to me once. We were sitting on the pasture fence at the Lazy Dog, watching his dad break in a colt, the leaves in the trees red just like they are today. I started shivering so hard my teeth actually began to chatter, and Tucker laughed at me and called me that—his delicate California flower—and wrapped me in his coat.

All at once I become aware of the smell of horse manure. Hay. Diesel fuel. A hint of Oreos.

Oh no.

My eyes fly open. I'm in the barn at the Lazy Dog. I haven't gone to my home.

I've gone to Tucker's.

I'm so startled I lose the glory. And right that minute Tucker comes whistling into the barn carrying a bucket of horseshoes. He sees me, and the tune fades from his lips. He promptly drops the bucket, which lands on his foot, which makes him jerk his foot up and start hopping on the other one.

For a long minute we just stare at each other. He stops hopping and stands with his hands shoved in his pockets, wearing a flannel shirt that's one of my favorites, blue plaid, which makes his eyes so beautiful. I flash back to the last time I saw him, almost six months ago, Yellowstone and the brink of a waterfall and a kiss that meant good-bye. It feels like it happened a lifetime ago, and at the same time like it happened yesterday. I can still taste him on my lips.

He frowns. "What are you doing here, Clara?"

Clara. Not Carrots.

I don't know how to answer him, so I shrug. "I was in the neighborhood?"

He snorts. "Isn't your neighborhood about a thousand miles southwest of here?"

He sounds mad. Something in my gut twists. Of course he has all sorts of reasons to be mad at me. I'd probably be furious if the situation were reversed. I hid things from him. I pushed him away when all he wanted was to be there for me. Oh yeah, and I almost got him killed, let's not forget. And I kissed Christian. That was the kicker. Then I had to go and break his heart.

He rubs the back of his neck, still frowning deeply. "No, seriously, what are you doing here? What do you want?"

"Nothing," I say lamely. "I . . . came here by accident. My dad's teaching me how to move through time and space, something he calls crossing, which is like teleporting yourself to where you want to go. He thought it would be hilarious to leave me to get home all by myself, and when I tried, I ended up here."

I can tell by his face that he doesn't believe me. "Oh," he says wryly. "Is that all? You teleported."

"Yeah. I did." I'm starting to get irritated, now that I'm finally over the shock of seeing him again. There's something about his expression, a wariness that instantly rubs me the wrong way. The last time he looked at me like that was after we first kissed, right here in almost exactly this spot, when I lit up with all my happy glory and he knew I was something otherworldly. He's looking at me like I'm some strange unearthly creature, something not human.

I don't like it.

"You can mess with *time*, huh?" he says, rubbing his neck. "Think you could go back about five minutes and warn me about dropping the bucket of horseshoes? I think I might have busted one of my toes."

"I can fix it," I say automatically, stepping forward.

He takes a quick step back, puts a hand up to stop me. "With your glory thing? No, thanks. That always makes me want to puke."

It hurts, him saying that. It makes me feel like a freak.

So he's decided to go with the old reliable Tucker-the-jerk routine. And what I extra-triple-hate about this is that I know he's not a jerk, not even a little bit of a jerk, but he's putting on his jerk hat special for me because I've hurt him, and because he wants to keep me at a distance, and because it makes him angry to see me here.

"So you were trying to get back home to California," he says, putting a heavy emphasis on the words *home* and *California*. "And you ended up here. How'd that happen?"

I meet his eyes, and there's a question in them that's

different from the one he asked.

"Bad luck, I guess," I answer.

He nods, bends to pick up the scattered horseshoes at his feet, then straightens. "Are you going to stay out here all night?" he asks, the very definition of surly. "Because I have chores to do."

"Oh, by all means, don't let me keep you from your chores," I retort.

"Horse stalls won't muck themselves." He grabs a shovel and offers it to me. "Unless it'd make your little heart go pitter-pat to get to work on a real-live working ranch."

"No, thanks," I say, stung that he'd treat me like a city slicker after everything. I feel a flash of despair. Then anger. This is not how I imagined it would be, seeing him again. He's making it difficult on purpose.

Fine, I think. If that's how he wants it.

"I can go right now," I say, "but to do that I'll have to use glory, so you might want to step outside for a minute. I'd hate to make you puke all over your nice boots."

"Okay," he says. "Don't trip on your way out."

"Oh, I won't," I say, because I can't think of a witty come-back, and I wait until he slips out of the barn before I summon glory and will myself anywhere but here.

6

HOOKING UP

One thing's for certain: my brother can eat. It's like he has a hollow leg, and all that food gets crammed in there: four pancakes now, three scrambled eggs, hash browns, a side of wheat toast, three strips of bacon, three links of sausage, and a pitcher of orange juice. I'm feeling kind of sick to my stomach just watching him.

"What?" he says when he catches me staring. "I'm hungry."

"Clearly."

"This is good. All I ever get to eat these days is pizza."

Ah, a Jeffrey tidbit. That's what this breakfast is all about. Crumbs that he occasionally throws me. Clues. From which I am piecing together a picture of his life.

"Pizza?" I say all nonchalant. "What's up with pizza?"

"I work at a pizza joint." He pours more syrup on his final pancake. "That smell gets into everything." He leans forward like he wants me to sniff him. I do, and sure enough, I get a definite whiff of mozzarella and tomato sauce.

"What do you do there?"

He shrugs. "Run the cash register. Bus tables. Take phone orders. Make pizza, sometimes, if we're short a cook. Whatever needs to be done. It's a temporary gig. Until I figure out what I really want to do."

"I see. Is this pizza joint around here?" I ask slyly. "Maybe I'll stop in and order something. Give you a big tip."

"Nuh-uh," he says. "No way. So. What's been going on with you?"

I put my chin in my hand and sigh. A lot's been going on with me. I'm still in a kind of disbelieving shock over seeing Tucker. I'm also still obsessing over the idea that somewhere in the near future I'm going to have to use a sword—me, who's never particularly thought of myself as the Buffy the Vampire Slayer type. Me, fighting. Possibly for my life, if my vision is any solid indication.

"That good, huh?" Jeffrey says, studying my face.

"It's complicated." I consider telling him about my training session yesterday, but I think better of it. Jeffrey has a sore spot when it comes to Dad. Instead I ask, "Do you still have visions?"

His smile vanishes. "I don't want to talk about that."

We stare each other down for a minute, me unwilling to let the subject drop so easily, him not wanting to go into it because he's decided to ignore his visions. He's not on God's payroll anymore, is how he feels. Screw the visions. He still feels a pang of bone-deep guilt every time he thinks about his last vision, which didn't turn out so well.

But deep down he also does want to talk about it.

He finally looks away. "Sometimes," he admits. "They're useless, though. They never make sense. They just tell you things you don't understand."

"Like what?" I ask. "What do you see?"

He readjusts his baseball cap. His eyes get distant, like he's seeing his vision happening in front of him. "I see water, lots of it, like a lake or something. I see somebody falling, out of the sky. And I see . . ." His mouth twists. "Like I said, I don't want to talk about it. Visions only get you in trouble. Last time I saw myself starting a forest fire. You tell me how that's any kind of divine message."

"But you were brave, Jeffrey," I say. "You proved yourself. You had to decide whether to trust your visions, whether to trust the plan, and you did. You were faithful."

He shakes his head. "And what did it get me? What did I become?"

A fugitive, he thinks. A high school dropout. A loser.

I reach across the table and put my hand on his. "I'm sorry,

Jeffrey. I'm really, really, ridiculously sorry, for everything."

He pulls his hand away, coughs. "It's fine, Clara. I don't blame you."

This is news, since the last time I checked, he was all about blaming me.

"I blame God," he says. "If there even is such a thing. Sometimes I feel like we're all chumps, doing stuff from these visions just because somebody told us to, in the name of a deity we've never even met. Maybe the visions have nothing to do with God, and we're just seeing the future. Maybe we're all just perpetuating the myth."

Those are some big words coming from my brother, and for a minute I feel like I'm sitting at the table with a stranger making somebody else's argument. "Jeffrey, come on. How can you—"

He holds up his hand. "Don't give me the religious talk, okay? I'm fine with the way things are. I am currently avoiding all large bodies of water, so my vision won't be a problem. We're supposed to be talking about you now, remember?"

I bite my lip. "Okay. What do you want to know?"

"Are you dating Christian, now that you're—" He stops himself again.

"Now that I'm broken up with Tucker?" I finish for him. "No. We hang out. We're friends. And beyond that, we're figuring stuff out."

We're more than friends, of course, but I don't know

what *more* really means.

"You should date him," Jeffrey says. "He's your soul mate. What is there to figure out?"

I almost choke on my orange juice. "My soul mate?"

"Yeah. Your other half, your destiny, the person who completes you."

"Look, I'm a complete person," I say with a laugh. "I don't need Christian to complete me."

"But there's something about you two, when you're together. It's like you fit." He grins. Shrugs. "He's your soul mate."

"Whoa, you have got to stop saying that." I can't believe I'm having this conversation with my sixteen-year-old brother. "Where'd you even hear that term, anyway—*soul mate?*"

"Oh, come on. . . .You know, people say that sort of thing."

My eyes widen as I feel the flutter of embarrassment from him, the image of a girl with long, dark hair, ruby red lips, smiling. "Oh my God. You have a girlfriend."

His face goes a charming shade of fuchsia. "She's not my girlfriend. . . ."

"Right, she's your soul mate," I croon. "How'd you meet her?"

"I knew her before we moved to Wyoming, actually. She went to school with us."

My mouth drops open. "Get out! So I probably know her, then. What's her name?"

He glares at me. "It's no big deal. We're not dating. You don't know her."

"What's her name?" I insist. "What's her name, what's her name? I could go on like this all day."

He looks mad, but he wants to tell me. "Lucy. Lucy Wick."

He's right; I don't know her. I sit back in the booth. "Lucy. Your soul mate."

He points a warning finger at me. "Clara, I swear. . . ."

"That's great," I say. Maybe this will turn him around, give him something positive to think about. "I'm glad you like someone. I felt bad when—"

Now it's my turn to stop myself. I don't want to dredge up his ex or that horrifying scene in the cafeteria last year when he dumped her in front of the entire school. Kimber was clearly not his soul mate. She was a cute girl, though. Nice, I always thought.

"Kimber was the one who called the police on me, I think," he says. "I guess I shouldn't have told her I started the fire." I open my mouth to bombard him with questions, but he doesn't let me get them out. "No, I didn't tell her what I am. What we are. I only told her about the fire." He scoffs. "I thought she would think it was badass or something."

"Oh, she did. She really did."

We're quiet for a minute, and then we both start laughing quietly.

"I was kind of an idiot," he admits.

"Yeah, well, when it comes to the opposite sex, it's hard to keep your head on straight. But maybe that's just me."

He nods, takes another drink of OJ. Looks at me hard.

"I've been thinking a lot about Tucker," Jeffrey says then, which catches me off guard. "It's not fair to him, what happened. I've been putting some money aside. It won't be a lot. But something. I was kind of hoping you'd give it to him, once I get it together."

I don't fully understand. "Jeffrey, I—"

"It's to help buy a new truck, or put a down payment on one. A new trailer, a saddle, trees to plant on his land." He shrugs. "I don't know what he needs. I just want to give him something. To make up for what I did."

"Okay," I say, although I don't know if it will work for me to be the one who gives it to him. Last night between Tucker and me did not go well. But Tucker has a right, I remind myself, to be mad at me. And I never even apologized for what I did. I never tried to make it right. "I think that's a great idea," I tell Jeffrey.

"Thanks," he says, and I can see in his eyes how he knows it isn't enough, given all he's taken from Tucker, all we've taken, but he's trying to make amends.

Maybe my brother's going to turn out okay, after all.

After breakfast I head back to Stanford, full of carbs and deep thoughts. I plan to have a nice, low-key kind of day, maybe take a nap, get started writing a paper I've been procrastinating on all week. But I run into Amy as I pass by the Roble game lounge, and she ropes me into a game of table hockey. She rants about how the administration has canceled the Full Moon on the Quad—which is where students meet up around midnight on the night of the full moon and kiss each other while a local band plays romantic music in the background, basically a ritualized-and-thereby-socially-acceptable, well-lit make-out session—because they're afraid we're going to spread mono all over campus.

"I don't see how they can stop us, though," she's saying. "I mean, there's still going to be a full moon and the quad's still going to be there and we're still going to have our lips."

I nod and grumble agreeably about how unfair it is, but I could care less. I'm still ruminating on the conversation at breakfast: Jeffrey with a new set of opinions and a new love interest and a new vision.

"Well, I think it's kind of gross," Amy says. "Don't you?"

"Yeah."

"He's so much older than she is."

I have no idea what she's talking about. "Wait, who's older?"

"You know. The guy Angela's hooking up with."

I stare at her. The puck clatters into my goal. "*What?* What guy?"

"I can't remember his name, but he's definitely older. A

senior, probably. Oh my god, what is his name—I know this!" Amy scoffs at herself in disgust. "I swear, my brain is so crammed full of random facts for my philosophy exam on Monday that it can't hold any more information. Seriously, it's on the tip of my tongue. Starts with *P*."

I feel immediately guilty that I didn't call Angela last night after my dad told me to watch out for her. My mind whirls. Why would Phen come here? What could he want? What happened to *we're just friends* and *we know it's impossible for us to be together* and *it's temporary* and all that other crap he fed to Angela this summer? I know I probably shouldn't be butting into Angela's love life—not again, anyway—but this is seriously bad. Phen claims that he's not on the side of evil, but he's definitely not, from what I saw this summer, on the side of good. Angela deserves something better. I've always thought so.

"Pierce!" Amy bursts out, relieved. "That's it."

Hold up. "Pierce? The PHE? That's who you think is involved with Angela?"

"That's the guy," she confirms. "The one who helped me with my ankle that time. He's a senior, right?"

This I do not believe. Angela's all wrapped up in her purpose right now, even more obsessed than usual, it seems. No way would she take time out to mess around with some random guy. Something is wrong, I think. Something weird is going on.

"Why do you think Angela's been hooking up with Pierce?" I grill Amy.

"Well, because she's been going out all of a sudden, like almost every night. And two nights this week she didn't come back to the room at all, and Robin saw her this morning coming out of his room," Amy reports. "Hair all messed up. Not wearing her shoes. Same clothes she was wearing the night before. Post-hookup, definitely."

My mind whirls some more. It's like a Category 5 hurricane inside my brain.

"Pierce is the dorm doctor," I say after a minute. "Maybe Angela wasn't feeling well."

"Oh," Amy says. "I didn't think of that. She has been looking kind of worn-out lately." She shrugs. "I guess she could have been sick."

"See, let's not jump to conclusions. There could be another explanation," I say, but I can tell Amy doesn't buy it.

I don't buy it, myself. Angela's not sick. I know this better than anyone.

Angel-bloods don't get sick.

"What are you so upset about?" Christian asks later when I fill him in on the Angela situation. We're sitting in the CoHo (the Stanford Coffeehouse) drinking coffee, our usual Saturday afternoon ritual. "What, Angela's not allowed to hook up with anybody?"

I really, really wish I could tell him about Phen.

"I think it's a good thing if Angela's seeing somebody," Christian goes on to say. "Maybe it will help her get out of her own head a little."

I take a sip of my latte. "It's not like her, that's all. She's been acting weird for weeks, but this—a guy, staying out all night—is really not like her."

But then, come to think of it, maybe it is like her. That's what happened in Italy. Once she reconnected with Phen, she pretty much disappeared every night, sneaking back to her grandmother's house in the mornings before anybody else woke up.

"Angela dated guys back in Jackson," Christian reminds me.

I shake my head. "Not so much. She went to parties sometimes. And prom. But she never even kissed anybody, she told me. She said boys were a complete waste of time and energy."

Christian's dark eyebrows furrow, and I can feel him remembering that one party back in eighth grade where they played spin the bottle and he and Angela went out on the back porch and kissed. Then his eyes meet mine and he knows that I know he's remembering this, and his face starts to get red.

"It wasn't anything," he mutters. "We were thirteen."

"I know," I say quickly. "She said it was like kissing her brother."

Christian stares into his coffee cup. Finally he says, "If you want to find out what's going on with Angela, you should ask her."

"Good idea." I pull out my cell and dial Angela's number for like the twentieth time today, put it on speaker so Christian can hear as it goes straight to voice mail. "I'm busy right now," Angela's voice says in the recording. "I may or may not call you back. Depends on how much I like you."

Beep.

"Okay, okay," Christian says as I hang up. "I don't know what to tell you. It's a mystery."

I let out a frustrated breath. "I'll see her in class Tuesday," I say. "Then we'll get to the bottom of this."

"Tuesday is three days away—you sure you can wait that long?" Christian asks playfully.

"Shut up. And anyway, it's probably nothing. I bet you ten bucks it has to do with her purpose, not some guy. Something about 'the seventh is ours.'"

"'The seventh is ours'?"

"It's what Angela says in her vision. She's been driving herself crazy trying to figure out what it means. She keeps going to the church to make herself have the vision, but she hasn't got much beyond the location on campus where it's going to happen and 'the seventh is ours,' at least not that she's told me lately."

"That's cryptic." Christian's eyes are thoughtful. "Wait,"

he says, officially catching up. "What's this about church? Angela makes herself have the vision? How?"

I tell him about the labyrinth and Angela's theory that it will, under the right circumstances, induce visions. Christian sits back in his chair and stares at me like I've told him that the moon is made of cheese. Then he presses his fingers to his eyes as if he has a sudden headache.

"What?" I ask him.

"You never tell me anything, you know that?" He drops his hand and looks at me accusingly.

I gasp. "That is not true. I tell you loads of stuff. I tell you more than anybody. I mean, I didn't blab to you about this thing with Angela, but it's Angela, and you know how she is."

"How she is? What happened to 'there are no secrets in Angel Club'?"

"You never agreed to that," I point out. "You had the biggest secret of us all, and you never breathed a word."

"Is there anything else I don't know?" he asks, ignoring my very good point about his blatant hypocrisy. "Besides the stuff with this Phen guy that you can't tell me about?"

"I saw my dad," I say. "But this only happened yesterday, okay? I was going to tell you today. Right now, as a matter of a fact. See, I'm telling you."

Christian pulls back, surprise all over his face, his mind reeling with it in a way that makes me feel surprised all over again by what happened. "Your dad? Michael?"

"No, my other dad, Larry. Yes, my dad, Michael. He said he's been given"—I inflate my voice to sound all authoritative and official—"the task of training me. We went back to my house and spent a couple hours in the backyard whacking each other with broomsticks."

"You were in Jackson yesterday?" Christian looks dazed. He's in that phase where he's repeating everything I say because he can't process it fast enough. "Training?" he says. "Training you to what?"

I become aware that we're sitting in a public place and we shouldn't be openly discussing any of this. I shift to talking in his mind. *To use a sword.*

His eyes widen. I look away, sip the last dregs of my cold coffee. The enormity of what I just told him—that I'm going to be expected to use a sword, too, to fight, maybe even to kill somebody—is really settling in for the first time.

This is the part where my life becomes all apocalyptic, I think.

Which sucks, quite frankly. I remember how good it felt to help Amy that night, to use my power to fix her ankle even the little bit that I did. How happy I was with the idea that I could use my power to heal hurts and right wrongs. Now it all feels like a silly pipe dream. I'm going to fight. Possibly die.

You were right, I say bleakly. *We're never going to be allowed to live normal lives.*

103

I'm sorry, Christian says. He wishes something better for me, something easier.

I shrug it off. *It's what we're supposed to do, right? Maybe that's our purpose, to become fighters. That makes sense, if you think about it. Maybe it's what all the Triplare are meant for. We're like warriors.*

Maybe, Christian says, although I can sense that he doesn't want to accept this any more than I do.

Oh. And I asked my dad if you could train with us, since you've been seeing yourself wielding a sword in your vision (the sword's made of glory, not flame, by the way), and he said yes, probably around winter break. FYI.

He gives an incredulous laugh at the idea that he could be taking lessons from the archangel Michael. "Wow," he says out loud. "That is—thank you."

"At least we can do this together," I say, reaching across the table and laying my hand on his, which sends that familiar spark between us.

We belong together. The words come to mind immediately, and this time, instead of fighting the idea or worrying about what it might mean, I accept it. Whatever our fate is, we're clearly in it together. Through thick and thin.

Come hell or high water, he adds in my mind.

I smile. *Preferably high water, right? I have no intention of going to hell.*

Agreed. He slides his fingers up through mine so we're clasping hands. I get a nervous quivery sensation in the pit of my stomach. "In the meantime," I say to get back to the topic at hand, remembering what my dad said about watching out for Angela, "let's figure out what's going on with Angela. Maybe we can help her."

"If she'll let us."

"True, that." I check my watch. "I should go. I've got a paper to write on *The Waste Land* by Tuesday. Worth twenty percent of my grade, so no pressure there."

He squeezes before he lets go of my hand. "Thanks for hanging out with me this afternoon. I know you're busy."

"Christian, there's nobody on earth, seriously, who I'd rather hang out with than you," I tell him, and it's absolutely true. Whatever we are—soul mates, friends, whatever— there's that.

It isn't until later that I realize I didn't tell him about seeing Tucker. But then, I think, he really wouldn't want to know.

I take a detour on the way back to the dorm to check out Memorial Church on the off chance that I might find Angela there. The church is empty. I make my way up the center aisle to the front of the sanctuary, where the labyrinth is still laid out on the altar. There's a sign posted that says, SILENCE, PLEASE, WHILE VIEWING THE CHURCH. Somebody right outside is trimming the hedges with a weed whacker, but it still feels quiet in this place, a stillness that transcends noise.

Angela's obviously not here, but I don't leave yet. I stand

looking at the twisting paths of the labyrinth.

What the heck, I think. I'll give it a try.

I take a minute to read the pamphlet about the labyrinth, which I find in a small woven basket in the front pew. *Does life have you wandering aimlessly in circles?* it reads. *Embark on a personal journey that's stood the test of time for thousands of years.* I slip my shoes off and position myself at the starting point, then begin to walk. The hems of my jeans scuff against the fabric on the floor. I try to make myself slow down and take deep breaths, the way I learned in happiness class: cleansing breaths from the belly. *As you enter the labyrinth,* the pamphlet says, *let go of the details of your life; shed thoughts and distractions. Open your heart and quiet your mind.*

I do my best, but part of me is already tensing, bracing for the vision, the blackness of the room, the terror I feel. I keep walking, trying to clear my head, the way I always do to call glory, which is coming so easily these days. You'd think this would be easy, too, but for whatever reason, maybe because having the vision is a bit like being slapped in the face, it's not the same.

I reach the center of the pattern. I'm supposed to stop here and pray. *Receive,* the pamphlet says.

I bow my head. I've never learned how to talk to God. The concept seems as far away for me as making a personal phone call to the president of the United States or having a conversation with the Dalai Lama. Which is ironic, I know. I have angel blood in my veins, the strength of the Almighty worked right into my cells, God's intent for me, His plan. Whenever I call glory, I feel that power, that connection to everything that Dad talks about, the warmth and joy and beauty that I know must be where God is. But I don't know how to communicate in words with that presence. I can't.

I look up, and there are angels all around, and I feel their eyes on me, solemn and questioning. *What are you doing?* they ask. *What is your purpose?*

"What is my purpose?" I whisper back at them. "Show me."

But the vision doesn't come.

I wait five minutes, which feels like longer, then sigh and make my way back through the pattern the way I came, faster this time. This is where the pamphlet tells me I'm supposed to enter the third stage: *Return. Join with a higher power, come together with the healing forces at work in this world.*

I'm so not feeling the healing forces.

I put my shoes on, suddenly exhausted and cranky and frustrated by my failure to connect. I better get back and start working on that nap, I think. The paper can wait. So much for finding Angela. So much for figuring out my vision.

So much for clarity.

The vision hits me as I'm biking home. It's cloudy and chilly out—not Wyoming cold by any stretch of the imagination, but still cold enough to make me want to get warm and cozy under the covers. So I'm biking pretty fast, hurrying, when I suddenly find myself in the dark room.

This time it's happening further along in the vision than it's ever happened before. The noise, that high-pitched sound that echoes around us, is still ringing in my ears. It's giving us away, I realize. It's drawing their attention.

There's the flash of light, as blinding as always.

"Get down!" Christian yells, and I dive for the floor, roll out of the way as he comes from behind me swinging a sword, a flaring, bright, beautiful blade, which he raises over his head and brings down hard. There's a clashing sound like nothing I've ever heard before, worse than nails on a chalkboard, and then a curse and a low laugh. I scramble backward until my back hits something hard and wooden, my heart pounding. It's still so dark in here, but I can make out Christian fighting, his light slicing the air around him, trying to get at the dark figures closing in on him.

Figures, I realize, plural. Two dark figures. He's fighting them two to one.

Stand up, I tell myself. *Stand up and help him.*

I jump to my feet, my knees shamefully wobbly.

"No," Christian yells. "Get out of here. Find a way out!"

There's no way out without you, I think, but I don't have time to form the words because, without warning, somebody else yells, "Look out!" and I'm back on the sidewalk at Stanford, where I'm about to crash my bicycle.

* * *

There's no avoiding it. I swerve wildly but hit the half wall of a brick bicycle ramp. My bike stops. I keep going, soaring over the ramp, hitting the ground hard, bouncing off the pavement, then sliding on my back across the sidewalk and into a juniper bush.

Ouch.

I lie there for a minute with my eyes closed, sending a silent, sarcastic *thank you so much for that* in the skyward direction.

"Are you all right?"

I open my eyes, and there's a guy kneeling over me. I recognize him from my happiness class, a tall guy with shoulder-length brown hair, brown eyes, glasses. My scrambled brain reaches for his name.

Thomas.

Excellent. I've biffed it big time in front of Doubting Thomas.

He helps me crawl out of the juniper bush.

"Whoa, you really bit it there. Do you need me to call an ambulance?" he asks.

"No, I think I'm okay."

"You should really watch where you're going," he says.

He's so nice, too.

"Yeah, I'll try that next time."

"You have a cut." He points to my cheek. I touch the spot gingerly, come away with a smear of blood. I must have hit hard. I don't typically bleed.

"I have to go," I say quickly, getting to my feet. My jeans are a mess, split at the knee, a raw-looking scrape showing through on one side. I should get out of here now, before my wounds miraculously heal themselves right in front of this guy and I have some serious explaining to do.

"Are you sure you're okay? I can take you to Vaden," he offers.

"No, I'm fine. It probably looks worse than it is. I need to go home." I grab my bike from where it's fallen, the front wheel still spinning. When I set it upright, I discover that the frame is badly bent.

Crap.

"Here, let me help you," Thomas says, and nothing I say works to get rid of him. I limp along, mostly because I know I should be limping, and he walks beside me, carrying my bicycle on one shoulder and my backpack on the other. It takes us forever to get to Roble, and by the time we arrive, I'm pretty sure both the cut on my face and the scrape on my knee have mended. I hope he's not terribly observant.

"Well, this is me," I say lamely. "Thanks." I grab my backpack from him, stick the bike on the rack, not bothering to lock it, and turn to go into the building.

"Hey, wait," Thomas calls after me. I stop. Turn back.

"Do you want to . . ." He hesitates.

"I don't need to go to the health center, really," I say.

He shakes his head. "I was going to say, do you want to go out with me tonight? There's this party at the Kappa house. If you're feeling up to it."

Sheesh. There's no discouraging this guy. I must look better right now than I think I do.

He stuffs his hands in his pockets but maintains eye contact. "I've been trying to ask you all semester. So here's my opportunity, right? Now that I've officially rescued you."

"Oh, wow. No," I blurt out.

"Oh. You have a boyfriend, right?" he asks. "Of course you do."

"No, not really . . . I mean I . . . My life is complicated right now . . . I can't . . . I'm sure you're great, but . . . ," I somehow manage to get out. "I'm sorry."

"Well, can't hurt to ask, right?" He reaches into his pocket and pulls out a business card. He hands it to me. *Thomas A. Lynch,* it reads. *Physics major at Stanford University. Tutor in math and sciences.* Then it lists his cell number.

"If you change your mind about the party, call me, or just show up," he says, and without another word he turns and walks away.

Wan Chen is playing Farmville on Facebook, her great weakness. She glances up from her laptop when I come in, her eyebrows drawing together in a little befuddled frown as she takes in the pieces of juniper bush in my hair, my dirt-and-blood-stained jacket, my torn jeans.

111

"It's been that kind of day," I say before she can get the question out. I go to the sink and start washing the blood and gunk off my face.

"Hey, did you hear that your friend Angela is hooking up with the PHE?" Wan Chen calls out to me.

Sigh. I so cannot wait until Tuesday.

As soon as I finish cleaning myself up, I call Angela. No answer.

"Angela Zerbino, don't make me hunt you down, because I will," I say into the phone. "Call. Me. Back."

I'm busy, she texts a few minutes later. *Chill. I'll catch up with you later.*

I wait an hour, then head down to second-floor A wing and knock on Angela's door. Robin answers. "Oh, hey, Clara," she says cheerfully. She's wearing a blue-and-white zebra-print strapless polyester top over a short white mini; her hair is curled big and parted down the middle. She looks like she's ready to hit the town, back in 1978 or so.

"I'm looking for Angela," I tell her.

Robin shakes her head. "I haven't seen her since this morning." She looks around, then leans toward me and whispers conspiratorially. "She spent the night with Pierce."

"Yeah, I heard," I say, irritated. "You probably should stop with the rumor spreading, since you don't know squat about Angela."

Robin immediately flushes. "Sorry," she says, and seems

112

so genuinely ashamed of herself that I feel bad for putting the smackdown on her.

"You look like Farrah Fawcett," I observe. She recovers somewhat and manages a smile.

"We're all going over to a seventies party at the Kappa house tonight," she explains. "Do you want to come?"

This is the party Thomas invited me to, and he's going to be there, and if I show up he'll probably think I'm interested. But then I think about my options: (a) staying in my room on a Saturday night slogging away on a paper about T. S. Eliot's *The Waste Land*, which will be impossible because I will be distracted because I can't stop thinking about Dad and Tucker and Jeffrey and Angela and Pierce and Christian and my vision, and (b) . . . who am I kidding? No way I'm going to do that. I need to get out.

"Sure," I say to Robin. "Let me find my platform shoes."

7

RUM AND COKE

The party's in full swing when I arrive with Robin, one Bee Gees song after another blasting out from the windows, strobe lights going back and forth in the living room, and I'm pretty sure I spot a disco ball over the dining room table.

This is going to be fun. And loud. And maybe exactly what I need.

"Hey, gorgeous!" says the frat boy who opens the door. "Where have you been all my life?"

He makes us put our keys into a huge pickle jar by the front door and introduces us to a guy in a Vegas-style white Elvis Presley costume who, should we wish to leave, will be the judge of whether or not we're fit to drive.

"Nice outfit," I tell him, although I'm not sure how it

relates to the theme of the party, except that I think Elvis died in the seventies.

"Why, thank you. Thank you very much," he drawls.

Somehow I knew he was going to say that.

Of course almost the first person I spot in there is Thomas, swaying under the disco ball, wearing a flowered satin button-down shirt that shows his spotty chest hair. He brightens when he sees me, waves me over. So I go.

"You changed your mind," he says.

"Yep. So here I am," I say. "Thanks for helping me out before."

"You don't look like you needed it," he says, his eyes searching my face for the scratches and scrapes that were there last time he saw me, like two hours ago.

Whoops. I forgot about that.

"I told you it wasn't bad," I try to explain. "I have a few bumps and bruises on my legs is all, nothing serious. Nothing that a little makeup can't hide."

"You look great," he says, his eyes now roaming down my body, stopping on my legs.

"Thanks," I say, uncomfortable. It was hard to go full-blown seventies on such short notice, but fortunately Robin had a bright orange polyester halter dress as a backup to the blue zebra-print. It's mildly itchy.

"Do you want to dance?" Thomas asks.

That's when I discover that I don't really know how to dance to disco. We get some laughs out of it, anyway, trying to do the John Travolta thing.

"So what's your major?" he asks me, the college equivalent of "what's your sign?"

"Biology," I answer. I already know that his is physics.

"You want to be a biologist?"

"No," I laugh. "I want to be a doctor."

"Aha," he says, like he's figured out something important about me. "Did you know that over half of the incoming freshmen at this school consider themselves premed? But only like seven percent of them end up taking the MCAT."

"I did not know that." I must look tense, because Thomas laughs.

"Sorry, I didn't mean to depress you," he says. "Let me get you a drink."

I open my mouth to tell him that I'm not twenty-one, but of course he must know that. The only time I've ever had alcohol at a party was that summer with Tucker. Ava Peters's house. He made me a rum and Coke.

"What's your order?" Thomas asks me. "They have pretty much everything. I bet you're a martini type of girl, am I right?"

"Uh, rum and Coke," I say, because I know I was able to handle that okay that night without getting even a little tipsy. I want to be able to drive home.

"Rum and Coke it is," he says, and away he goes to the kitchen.

I look around. Off in a back room I can hear people chanting somebody's name. There's another group around the dining room table, dipping stuff into fondue pots, and dancers going wild under the disco ball, people holding shouted conversations in corners, the occasional couple making out on the stairs and against the wall. I spot Amy on the couch in front of the TV, with a bunch of people playing some sort of drinking game that involves watching *That Seventies Show*. I wave, and she waves back enthusiastically.

Thomas returns with my drink.

"Cheers." He knocks his plastic cup dully against mine. "To new adventures with new people."

"To new adventures." I take a big drink, which burns all the way down my throat and settles like a pool of lava in my stomach. I cough.

Thomas pats me on the back. "Uh-oh, are you a lightweight?"

"This is rum and Coke? Nothing else?" I ask.

"One part rum, two parts Coke," he says. "I promise."

It doesn't taste anything like the drink I had at the party with Tucker. And now, almost two years later, I realize why. Tucker never put any rum in my rum and Coke.

That little stink.

That overly protective, impossible, infuriating, and utterly sweet little stink.

In that moment I miss him so much my stomach hurts. Or

that could be the rum. There's a loud cheer from the people in the back room.

"Christian! Christian! Christian!" they're chanting.

I push forward through the crowd until I'm standing in the doorway of the back room, arriving in time to see Christian chug a large glass of dark brown liquid. They cheer again when he's done, and he grins and wipes his mouth on the sleeve of his white polyester suit.

The girl sitting next to him leans over to whisper something in his ear, and he laughs, nods at her.

My stomach clenches.

Christian looks up and sees me. He stands up.

"Hey, where are you going?" says the girl who's sitting on the other side of him, pouting prettily. "Christian! Come back here! We still have to get through another round."

"I've had enough," he says, not quite slurring, but not sounding like himself, either.

I don't have to touch his mind to know he's drunk. But underneath the haze of alcohol I can feel that he's upset about something. Something that's happened since I saw him this afternoon.

Something he wants to forget.

He brushes his hair out of his eyes and crosses the room to me, walking in a mostly straight line. I back up to let him get through the door, but he puts his hand on my bare arm and pulls me into the corner. His eyes close momentarily as the current of energy passes through us; then he leans toward me until his nose is almost touching mine, his breath surprisingly sweet considering the nasty stuff I watched him drink. I want to be casual about this—it's a party, after all, drinking happens, and yeah, there were girls in that room fawning all over him, but he's fire hot, and he's smart and funny and well-spoken. And he's not my boyfriend, I remind myself. We've never actually been out on a date. We're not together.

Still, his touch sends a flock of rabid butterflies careening around my stomach.

"I was just thinking about you," he says, his voice rough, his pupils so big they make his eyes look black. "Dream girl."

My face is getting hot, both from what he's saying and what he's feeling right now. He wants to kiss me. He wants to feel my lips again, so soft, so perfect to him—he wants to carry me out of this stupid noisy house to somewhere where he can kiss me.

Whoa. I can't breathe properly. He leans in. "Christian, stop," I whisper the moment before his mouth touches mine.

He pulls away, breathing heavily. I try to retreat a little, put some space between us, but I run into the wall. He takes a step forward, closing the distance, and I put my hand on the center of his chest to keep him back, for which I get another electric zap, like fireworks going off against a dark sky.

"Let's go outside," I suggest breathlessly.

"Lead the way," he says, and walks behind me, his hand

on the small of my back as I head toward the door, burning through the fabric of my dress. We're about halfway there when we literally bump into Thomas, who I realize I simply walked away from with no explanation the minute I heard Christian's name.

"I was looking for you," Thomas says. He looks at Christian and, more importantly, at Christian's hand, which has moved down to my hip. "Who is—"

"Hey, you're Doubting Thomas!" Christian says, suddenly jovial.

Thomas looks over at me, startled. "Is that what you call me? Doubting Thomas?"

"It's affectionate, really," Christian says, and as Thomas looks, well, doubtful, and hurt, Christian claps him on the shoulder and moves us past him. "You have a nice night."

Something tells me that Thomas isn't going to ask me out again.

I'm relieved for the cool air that greets us when we make it outside. There's a bench on the porch, and I steer Christian over to it. He sits, then abruptly puts his face in his hands. Groans.

"I'm drunk," he says, his voice muffled. "I'm sorry."

"What happened to you?" I sit down next to him, reach to put my hand on his shoulder, but he sits up.

"Don't touch me, okay? I don't think I can handle it like this."

I fold my hands in my lap. "What's wrong?" I ask.

He sighs, runs his palms over his hair. "You know how you said Angela could make herself have the vision by walking in that thing at the church? Well, I did it. I went there."

"I went there, too," I gasp. "We must have just missed each other."

"Did you have the vision?"

"Yes. I mean no, not at the church. But later, I had it." I swallow. "I saw you with the sword."

"Fighting?" he asks.

"Fighting two people."

He nods grimly. "I think we're having the same vision. Did you see who I was fighting?"

"It was too dark. I couldn't tell."

We take a minute to process this, which is hard with the Bee Gees blaring out at us, "Somebody help me, somebody help me, yeah."

"That's not all," Christian says. "I saw you."

Hopefully he didn't see the part where I was cowering against the wall, trying and failing to summon the courage to get up.

He shakes his head. "No, you were . . ." His voice is raspy, like his throat is dry, and, absurdly, he wishes that he could get another drink.

Dread boils over me. "I was what?"

"You were hurt."

He puts his hand on my wrist and shows me what he saw. My own face, tearstains on my cheeks, my hair loose and tangled around my shoulders. My lips pale. My eyes glazing over. The front of my shirt covered in blood.

"Oh" is all I can think to say.

He thinks I was dying.

He licks his lips. "I don't know what to do. I only know that when I'm there, in that room, wherever it is, I have one overwhelming thought. I have to keep you safe." Something works in his throat. "I would lay down my life to protect you, Clara," he says. "That's what I feel. I'd die to protect you."

We don't talk as I drive him home. I walk him up the stairs and into his room, past Charlie, who's sprawled on the futon playing his Xbox. I guide Christian over to his bed.

"You don't need to take care of me," he protests as I pull back the covers and sit him down on the mattress. "I was stupid. I just wanted to escape for a minute. I thought—"

"Shut up," I say gently. I pull his shirt over his head and toss it in the corner, then go to the minifridge and find him a bottle of water. "Drink." He shakes his head. "Drink."

He downs almost the entire bottle, then hands it back to me.

"Lie down," I tell him. He stretches out on the mattress, and I go to work removing his shoes and socks. He stares up at the ceiling for a minute, then groans.

"I think this is the first time I've ever had a real headache. I feel like—"

"Shh." I cast a glance at Charlie over my shoulder. He's faced away from us, his fingers punching the buttons on the Xbox controller passionately. I turn back to Christian.

"You should sleep," I tell him. I stroke his hair away from his face, my fingers lingering near his temple. He closes his eyes. I move my hand to his forehead, and peek again at Charlie, who's as oblivious as ever.

Then I call the glory to my fingers and send the tiniest bit of it into Christian.

His eyes open. "What did you just do?"

"Does your head feel better?"

He blinks a few times. "The pain's gone," he whispers. "Completely gone."

"Good. Now go to sleep," I tell him.

"You know, Clara," he sighs sleepily as I get up to leave. "You should be a doctor."

I close the door behind me, then take a minute to lean against the wall and catch my breath.

It's funny. Here I've been seeing this dark room for months, and I know something bad has happened right before Christian and I end up there, hiding, and I know it's not going to do any good for us to hide, and I know that this whole vision could be life or death. Those people, whoever they are, want to kill us. I've sensed that from the beginning.

But I don't think I ever truly considered that I might die.

Okay, God, I cast upward at breakfast Sunday morning, nibbling at a dry piece of toast while the bells of Memorial Church chime in the background. *Give me a break. I'm eighteen years old. Why put me through all of this, the forest fire and the visions and the training, if I'm going to kick the bucket, anyway?*

Or maybe this is a punishment. For not fulfilling my purpose the first time.

Or maybe it's some kind of ultimate test.

Dear God, I write in my notebook as I'm sitting in chemistry class on Monday morning listening to a lecture on the laws of thermodynamics. *I don't want to die. Not now. Sincerely, Clara Gardner.*

Please, God, I plead when I'm up at three a.m. on Tuesday morning trying to dash off my *Waste Land* paper. *Please. I don't want to die. I'm not ready. I'm scared.*

"Oh yeah?" says T. S. Eliot. "I will show you fear in a handful of dust."

Angela doesn't show up for the Poet Re-making the World. Doesn't turn in the paper. Which means, according to the rules in the syllabus, that she can't pass the class.

The idea sends a chill through me. Angela Zerbino: straight-A student, high school valedictorian, school-geek extraordinaire, lover of all things poetical, is going to fail her first college poetry course.

I've got to find her. Talk to her. Right freaking now. I'll do whatever it takes.

The minute class is over, I call Amy. "Do you know where Angela is?" I ask.

"She was in the room, last time I saw her," she tells me. "Why? Is something going on?"

Oh, something's going on.

I sprint all the way back to Roble, but stop short when I reach the building. Because a crow is perched on the bike rack again.

"Don't you have somewhere better to be?" I ask it.

No reply, except it hops from the rack to one of the bikes. My bike, as a matter of fact.

I don't want bird poo on my bike, broken or not. I take a few steps forward, waving my arms at it. "Go away. Get out of here."

It cocks its head at me, but doesn't otherwise move.

"Go on."

I'm directly in front of it now. I could touch it if I wanted to, and it doesn't budge. It stares at me calmly and holds its ground. Which is when I know—or maybe I've always known, and haven't wanted to admit to myself—that this is not a regular old crow.

It's not a bird at all.

I open my mind then, like cracking open a door, ready to push it closed again at any moment. I can feel him, that particular flavor of sorrow I know so well. I can hear that sad

125

music, the way I used to hear it calling me last year from the field behind the school grounds, a melody of *this is all that I am, when I was so much more; I'm alone, alone now for good, and I can never go back, never go back, never go back.*

I wasn't being paranoid. It's Samjeeza.

I take a step back, slam the door in my mind so hard it gives me an instant headache, but a headache's better than the sorrow by a long shot.

"What are you doing here?" I whisper. "What do you want?"

I know I felt sorry for him last year, I did; I knew how much he'd cared about my mom, even in his twisted-up way, and I'd taken pity on him that day in the cemetery. Even now I don't fully understand what came over me. I just walked over there and gave him my mother's bracelet, and he took it, and he didn't try to hurt us and we all got home safe and sound. But that doesn't make him any less dangerous. He's a fallen angel, aligned with the powers of dark. He's almost done me in on two separate occasions.

I force myself to stand up straight, look him in his wide yellow eyes.

"If you're here to kill me, then do it already," I say. "Otherwise I've got stuff I've got to do."

The bird shifts and then, without warning, takes off, straight at me. I yelp and duck and prepare to, I don't know, have my head separated from my shoulders or something, but he breezes past me over my shoulder, so close he brushes my cheek with his feathers, up and away, into the cloud-darkened sky.

Standing outside her dorm room in A wing, I try to call Angela again, and I can hear her phone ringing from inside. She's home. It's a miracle.

I pound on the door.

"Come on, Ange. I know you're there."

She opens the door. I push my way inside before she can protest. A quick glance around reveals that the roommates aren't here. Which is good, because it's about to get ugly.

"Okay, what is going on with you?" I demand to know.

"What do you mean?"

"What do you mean, what do I mean?" I cry. "You've been dodgy. The whole dorm is talking about how you're involved, in a horizontal-type way, with Pierce. He's the PHE, you know, the dorm doctor. He lives on the first floor. Blondish, shortish, scruffyish—"

She gives me an amused look and closes the door behind me, locks it. "I know who he is," she says with her back to me. "And yes, we're together. Involved, if that works better for you, in a horizontal-type way."

My mouth drops open.

I owe Christian ten bucks.

Angela puts a hand on her hip. I notice that she's got a wet washcloth slung over one shoulder. She's wearing sweats, an oversize Yellowstone National Park T-shirt with a trout on the front, her hair braided in a long, single plait down her back, no shoes or socks, and no polish on her fingers or toes. Under the fluorescent lights of our room, her skin has a blue cast to it, lavender shadows under her eyes.

"Are you okay?" I ask.

"I'm fine. Tired, is all. I was up all night working on my Eliot paper."

"But you weren't in class——"

"I got an extension," she explains. "Things have been crazy lately, and I've been so swamped that I've fallen way behind. I spent all weekend trying to catch up with everything."

I squint at her. She's lying, I sense vaguely. But why?

"Are *you* okay?" she asks. "You look a little wild-eyed."

"Oh, well, let's see: My dad showed up saying that he wants to train me to use a glory sword. Because I'm apparently going to have to fight for my life at some point. And oh yes, I'm having a vision where someone is trying to kill me, which works well with Dad's theory that I should sharpen up my glory sword. And if that's not enough, Christian's having the same vision, except in his vision he doesn't see me holding a glory sword. He sees me all weak and covered with blood. So maybe I'm going to die."

She stares at me in horror.

"This is what happens when you don't return my phone calls," I say, flopping down on her bed. "All the proverbial

128

crap hits the proverbial fan. Oh, and I just saw the bird again, and I felt his sorrow this time, and it's definitely Samjeeza. So yay, right?"

She leans against the door frame like all that bad news has knocked the air out of her. "Samjeeza? Are you sure?"

"Yep. Pretty sure."

There's a sheen of sweat on her forehead, a greenish tinge to her skin.

"Hey, I didn't mean to scare you," I say, sitting up. "I mean, it's not good, but——"

"Clara——" She stops and presses the washcloth to her mouth, inhales deeply, closes her eyes for a minute. And she goes even greener.

All thoughts of Samjeeza fly out of my head.

"Are you . . . sick?"

I've never been sick, truly sick, a day in my life. Never had a cold, the flu, never got food poisoning, never had a fever or an ear infection or a sore throat. And neither has Angela.

Angel-bloods don't get sick.

She shakes her head, closes her eyes.

"Ange, what is going on? Stop saying everything's fine and spill."

She opens her mouth to say something, but suddenly she groans and rushes out into the hall and two doors down to the bathroom, where I hear the unmistakable sounds of her throwing up.

I creep to the bathroom door. She's in a stall crouched in

front of the toilet, clutching the sides with white-knuckled hands, shivering.

"Are you okay?" I ask softly.

She laughs, then spits into the bowl, gets a wad of toilet paper, and blows her nose. "No. I am definitely not okay. Oh, Clara, isn't it obvious?" She pushes her hair out of her face and glares at me with fierce, shining eyes. "I'm pregnant."

"You're—"

"Pregnant," she says again, the word echoing off the tile. She stands up and brushes herself off, pushes past me and back to her room.

"You're—" I try again, following her.

"Knocked up. Yes. A bun in the oven. Preggers. With child. Expecting. In the family way." She sits down on the bed, stretches her back, and lifts her shirt.

I stare at her belly. It's not huge, not so much that I would have noticed it if she weren't pointing it out, but it's gently rounded. There's a faint black line that stretches from her belly button down. She stares up at me with tired eyes, and I feel in that moment that she's about an eyelash away from crying. Angela Zerbino, on the edge of tears.

"So," she says softly. "Now you know."

"Oh, Ange . . ." I keep shaking my head, because there's no way that this could be true.

"I've already talked to Dr. Day, and three or four people in administration. I'm going to see if I can make it through

130

winter quarter, since I'm not due for a while, and then take a leave of absence. They tell me that it won't be any problem. Stanford will be here when I decide to come back; that's the policy when it comes to these types of situations." She gives me a look that's trying hard to be brave. "I'm going to go back to Jackson and live with my mom. It's all worked out."

"Why didn't you tell me?" I breathe.

She lowers her head, rests her hand lightly on her belly. "I guess I didn't want to tell you because I didn't want you to look at me the way you're looking at me right now. Telling people makes it real."

"Who's the father?" I ask.

Her expression smoothes itself in perfect composure again. "Pierce. We had this night a couple months ago, just something that happened, and we've been kind of on again/ off again since then."

She's lying. I can feel it like she has a neon sign that says LYING flashing over her head.

"You think people are going to believe that?" I ask.

"Why wouldn't they?" she asks sharply. "It's the truth."

I sigh.

"For one thing, Ange, you can't really get away with lying to me. I'm an empath. And secondly, even if I wasn't an empath, Pierce is the PHE."

"What does that have to do with anything?" She's not looking at me now.

131

"He's the guy who gave out the safe-sex pamphlets during orientation. He's got a dorm's worth supply of condoms stashed in his room. And——"

She pulls her shirt back down. "Get out," she says, almost a whisper.

"Ange, wait."

She stands up and crosses to the door, holds it open for me. "I don't need this from you right now."

"Ange, I only want to hel——"

"Sounds like you've got your own stuff going on," she says, still not looking at me. "You should worry about that."

"But what about your purpose?" I say. "What about 'the seventh is ours' and the guy in the gray suit?"

"Don't talk about my purpose," she says fiercely between clenched teeth.

Then she shuts the door in my face.

I wander to the Old Union in a daze, sink to a bench next to the Claw fountain in White Plaza. I sit there, staring at the falling water, until the sun is much lower in the sky. People are all around me, coming and going from the CoHo on their search for coffee. I don't hear them. I only hear the fear in Angela's voice.

I'm pregnant.

This is how Christian finds me, dazed and silent on the bench. He takes one look at me and drops to his knees in front of me, peers up into my face.

"Clara?" *Clara? What's wrong?*

I blink, look into his worried green eyes. Should I tell him?

I don't have a choice. He can read the shocked thought like I'm shouting it. His mouth drops open.

"She's . . ." He can't even finish the sentence.

My eyes burn. *What is she going to do?* I keep thinking. *What is she going to do?*

Christian puts his hand over mine.

"Clara," he says quietly. "I think it's time you told me about what happened in Italy."

So I tell him. I tell him about how, this one night in Rome, on the metro, of all places, we ran into this guy, and Angela totally freaked just looking at him. How she sneaked away that night to see him, and didn't come home until morning. How he turned out to be Phen, the mentor angel she'd told me about before, but he was clearly more than her mentor. I tell Christian about how Angela desperately wanted me to like Phen, but I just couldn't. I saw Phen for what he was—a gray soul, weary with the world. How I didn't think he could truly love her, but Angela loved him, and acted like she didn't love him, so she could keep seeing him and call it casual.

"So what do you think?" I ask Christian when I'm done with the story.

He shakes his head. "I think this changes everything."

8

WHEN I MET YOUR MOTHER

It's a few weeks later, winter break, and I'm standing next to Christian, holding his hand as we watch Walter's coffin being lowered into the ground. Snow is coming down, thick and heavy, blanketing Aspen Hill Cemetery. The circle of faces around us is familiar, all members of the congregation: Stephen, the pastor; Carolyn, who was my mother's nurse; Julia, who's an all-around pain in the butt, if you want my opinion, but at least she's here; and finally I settle on Corbett Phibbs, the old Quartarius who was my high school English teacher, who looks especially somber, his hands folded as he gazes into the grave. He must not be that far away from this fate himself, I think. But then he glances up at me and winks.

"Amen," Stephen says. The crowd of mourners starts to

clear out, everybody headed home in case the storm (because it's December in Wyoming) becomes a blizzard, but Christian stays, so I stay.

The snow, I'm pretty sure, is Billy's doing. She's standing on the other side of me, wearing a long white parka that makes the shining black of her hair look like spilled ink down her shoulders, and the snow is swirling around her, drifting down as she stares at the hole before us with an anguish in her eyes that makes me want to hug her. The snow's her way of crying. It's hard to see her this way when normally she's so strong and steady, so quick to make a joke to break the tension. At my mother's funeral she smiled every time she met my eyes, I remember, and I was oddly comforted by that, as if Billy smiling was proof that nothing truly bad had happened to my mom. Just a little death, is all. A change of location.

But this is her husband.

They start to fill in the grave, and she turns away. I reach out and touch her shoulder. The sharp, aching chasm of her grief opens up in my mind. *So little time,* she thinks. *For all of us.*

She sighs. "I need to get out of here."

"Okay. See you at the house?" I ask. "I can make us some dinner."

She nods and hugs me, a stiff hug.

"Billy—"

"I'll be all right. See you later, kid." She strides off through the snow, leaving a trail of dark tracks behind her, and after she's gone, the snow lets up.

Christian doesn't say anything as the men work to fill in the hole. A muscle moves in his cheek. I step closer, until our shoulders touch, and I will my strength to flow into him the way his came into me the day we buried my mother.

I wish I'd known Walter better. Or at all. I don't know if more than three sentences ever passed between us. He was a hard man, always guarded, and he never quite warmed up to me or to the idea that I was involved in Christian's vision. But Christian loved him. I can feel that, Christian's love, his hurt now that Walter's gone, his sense of being alone in the world.

You're not alone, I whisper in his mind.

His hand tightens in mine. "I know," he says out loud, his voice hoarse with the tears he's holding back. He smiles and looks at me, his eyes dark and red-rimmed. He reaches to brush snow out of my hair.

"Thank you for coming here with me," he says.

A bunch of trite responses spring to mind—*you're welcome, don't mention it, no problem, it's the least I can do*—but none of them feel right, so I simply say, "I wanted to come."

He nods, glances briefly at the white stone bench beside his uncle's grave that serves as his mother's headstone. He takes a deep breath, and lets it out. "I should get out of here, too."

"You want me to go with you?" I ask.

"No. I'll be all right," he says, and for a moment there's the shimmer of tears in his eyes. He turns away, then pauses and turns back. He smiles in a sad way and gazes straight into my eyes. "This is going to sound weird and inappropriate, probably . . . but will you go out with me, Clara?"

"Out where?" I ask stupidly.

"On a date," he says.

"What, you mean now?"

He laughs like he's embarrassed. "God," he says, then covers his face with his hands. "I'm going home." He uncovers his face and smiles at me sheepishly. "But maybe when we get back to school. I mean it. An official date."

A date. I flash back to prom two years ago, the way it felt to stand in the circle of Christian's arms while we danced, enveloped by his smell, his warmth, gazing up into his eyes and feeling like I'd finally broken through with him, that he was finally seeing me.

Of course, that was before Kay had a meltdown and Christian opted to take her home instead of me.

He sighs. "I'm never going to live that down, am I?"

"Probably not."

"So that's a no, then?"

"No."

"No?"

"I mean no, it's not a no. It's a yes. I will go out with you." I don't even need to think about it. With us it's always been forest fires and formal dances and funerals. Don't we deserve something normal for once? And it's been more than six months since I broke up with Tucker. It's time, I decide, to give this thing with Christian a shot.

"I'm thinking dinner and a movie," he says.

"I'd love to go to dinner and a movie."

And now we suddenly don't know what to say to each other, and my heart is beating fast, and the men are shoveling the last layer of earth over Walter Prescott.

"I'm going to——" I point up the hill toward my own mother's grave, a simple marble headstone under the aspens.

He nods, then shoves his hands in his pockets and makes his way down toward his truck. I watch him drive away. When he's gone, I climb the hill, pausing on the concrete stairs that I saw so often in my vision last year. The cemetery seems different to me now, in the snow: uglier, colder, a gray, deserted place.

I stand for a few minutes, looking at my mother's grave. There's a smudge of dirt on the top corner of the headstone, and I rub at it with my gloved hand, but I can't get it to come clean.

Some people go to cemeteries to talk to the person who died. I wish I could do that, but the minute the words *Hi, Mom* come out of my mouth, I feel stupid. She's not here. Her body, maybe, but I don't really want to think about her body here, under the earth and snow. I know where she is now. I saw her in that place, walking into the sunrise, making her way from the outer edge of heaven. She's not here, in that box, under the ground.

I wonder if, when I die, I'll be buried here, too.

I walk to the chain-link fence at the edge of the graveyard, stare past it into the snow-filled forest beyond. I feel something then, a familiar sadness, and I know who has joined me.

"Come out," I call. "I know you're there."

There is a moment of silence before I hear footsteps in the snow. Samjeeza emerges from the trees. He stops a few feet from the fence, and a sense of déjà vu washes over me. I throw up a mental wall between us, blocking him from my mind. We stare at each other.

"Why are you here, Sam?" I ask. "What do you want?"

He makes a small noise in the back of his throat. He has one hand in the pocket of his long leather coat, and I wonder if he's fingering the bracelet I gave him, my mother's bracelet, the only thing he has left of her.

"Why did you give it to me?" he asks after a long moment. "Did she ask you to?"

"She told me to wear it to the cemetery."

He bows his head. "The first time was in France," he says. "Did she ever tell you?" He smiles and glances up, something alive in his eyes. "She was working at a hospital. The moment I saw her, I knew she was something special. She had the divine handprint all over her."

So that's it, I think. He wants to tell me about my mother.

I should stop him, tell him I'm not interested, but I don't. I'm curious to know what happened.

He moves closer to the fence, and I hear the faint crackle of his gray electricity running through the metal. "One day she and the other nurses went to a pond at the edge of the town to swim in their undergarments. She was laughing at something one of the other girls said, and then she felt my eyes on her and looked up. The other girls saw me too, and made a dash for their clothing on the shore, but she stayed where she was. Her hair was brown then, because she dyed it, and short for a woman's, just at the chin, but I loved the way it curled against her neck. She walked up to me. She smelled like cloud and roses, I remember. I was frozen there, staring, feeling so strange, and she smirked and reached into my front pocket, where I always kept a packet of cigarettes for the look of it more than anything, and she took one and put the package back and said, 'Hey, Mister, make yourself useful and give me a light, will you?' It took me a moment to realize that she wanted me to light her a cigarette, but of course I didn't have a lighter, and I said so, and she said, 'Well, a fat lot of good you are then, aren't you?' and turned and left me."

He seems charmed by the memory, but I don't like it. That isn't the mother I know, this saucy cigarette-smoking brunette that he seems so enthralled with.

"It was a while before I could get her to talk to me again. And longer still before she let me kiss her—"

"Why do you think I would want to hear this?" I interrupt.

The corner of his mouth quirks up in a sly smile. "You're very much like her, I find."

A cold draft of air slips up my sleeves and along my arms, and I pull my coat tighter around me. I'm safe for the moment, on this side of the fence. Hallowed ground. But I will have to leave it sometime.

"Tell me a story about her," he says. "Something small." He gazes at me calmly with his gold eyes. "Something new."

I take a nervous breath. "This is why you're stalking me? For stories?"

"Tell me," he says.

My thoughts scramble for something to offer him. Of course I have so many memories of my mother, random ones and stupid ones, times I was mad at her because she'd suddenly stopped being my best friend and turned into my mother, set boundaries for me, punished me when I crossed them, tender moments when I knew she loved me more than anything else in the world. But I don't want to share any of these stories with him. Our stories don't belong to him.

I shake my head. "I can't think of anything."

His gaze darkens.

He can't hurt me here, I tell myself. He can't get me. But I'm still trembling.

"All right," he says, like I'm being selfish but it can't be helped; I'm partially human, after all. His tone changes, becomes casual. "Maybe you'll feel like it on another occasion."

I seriously doubt it.

"Did you ever find out the secret? Whatever it was your mother was keeping from you?" he asks, like we're talking about the weather.

I fight to keep my face neutral, to keep my mind carefully under wraps, my tone as casual as his as I say, "I don't know what you mean."

He smiles. "You did find out," he says. "Otherwise you wouldn't be trying so hard to keep me at bay."

So he knows I'm blocking him. I wonder if he can read me anyway, if he can hear my heart's crazy rhythm, the quick intake of my breath, my fear like a sour smell oozing from my pores.

I shake my head helplessly. This was a bad idea, talking to him. Why did I think that I could handle him?

I turn to leave.

"Wait," he says before I make it more than a few steps. "You don't need to be afraid of me, little bird," he says, walking up behind me as closely as the fence will allow. "I won't harm you."

I stop, my back to him. "You're like the leader of the Watchers, right? Isn't it your job to try to harm me?"

"Not anymore," he says. "I was . . . demoted, if you will, from that title."

"Why?" I ask.

"My brother and I, we had a difference of opinion," he says carefully, "regarding your mother."

"Your brother?"

"He's the one you should truly fear."

"Who is he?" I ask.

"Asael."

The name sounds familiar. I think Billy mentioned him once.

"Asael seeks the Triplare," Samjeeza continues. "He's always fancied himself a collector, of beautiful women, of powerful men, of angel-bloods, especially those with a higher concentration of blood. He believes that whoever controls the Triplare will have the advantage in the coming war, and thus he is determined to have them all. If he finds out what you truly are, he won't rest until you either submit to his will or he destroys you."

I turn, the words *if he finds out what you truly are* resonating in my head. "This is all very interesting, Sam, but I have no clue what you're talking about. My mother's secret"—I force myself to look into his eyes—"was that she was dying. And that's old news now."

At the word *dying* he gives out a pulse of despair that I feel even through the emotional wall I've erected between us, but his demeanor doesn't change. In fact, he smiles.

"Oh, what a tangled web we weave, when first we practice to deceive," he says.

"Whatever."

I'm in a bind now, I realize. I don't have a ride. I rode here with Billy, and I intended to fly home, but he could always turn into a bird and come after me.

"I had my suspicions about you from the beginning, of course," he continues smoothly, like I didn't try to brush him off. "I couldn't understand what had happened that day in the forest. You resisted me more than you should have. Somehow you made the jump back from hell to earth. You summoned glory. You bested me." He shakes his head like I'm an impertinent but charming little girl.

"My mom did it," I say, hoping he'll believe it.

"Your mother was many things," he says. "She was beautiful, she was strong, she was full of fire and life, but she was, for all that, a mere Dimidius. She could not cross between worlds. Only a Triplare would be capable of that."

"You're wrong." I try but can't quite keep the waver out of my voice.

"I'm not," he says softly. "Michael is your father, isn't he? That lucky bastard."

He just keeps talking, and the more he babbles on, the more I risk giving everything away.

"Okay, well, this has been lovely, really it has, but it's cold and I've got someplace else to be." I turn my back on him one more time and move away from the fence, deeper into the cemetery.

"Where's your brother now, Clara?" he calls after me. "Does he know about his proud lineage?"

"Don't talk about my brother. Leave him alone. I swear—"

"You don't have to swear, dear. I have no interest in the boy. But then, like I said, there are others who'd find his parentage fascinating."

I think he's trying to blackmail me. I stop.

"What do you want?" I glare at him over my shoulder.

"I want you to tell me a story."

He's crazy. I throw my hands up in frustration and stalk off through the snow.

"All right," he says, chuckling. "Another time."

I know without having to look back that he's turned into a bird.

"Caw," he says to me, mocking, testing me.

Crazy freaking angels! I'm suddenly so mad I'm on the edge of tears. I kick at the snow under my feet, uncover a patch of wet, black earth, pine needles, rotting leaves, dead grass, bits of gravel. I bend and pick up a small stone, smooth and dark, like it belongs at the bottom of a river somewhere. I turn it over in my hand.

"Caw," says Samjeeza the crow.

I hurl the rock at him.

It's a good throw, the kind that would get me on Stanford's women's softball team in a heartbeat. It's more than human, that throw. It cuts through the air like a bullet, over the fence and straight at the meddlesome Black Wing. My aim is true.

But it doesn't hit him.

The rock shoots past the branch, which is now empty, and

145

falls silently into the snow on the forest floor. I'm alone again.

For now.

I'm looking forward to building a great big fire in the living room fireplace, making something to eat for Billy and me, and maybe putting up some Christmas decorations, calling Wendy to see if she wants to go to a movie or something. I need some normal time. But first I stop at the grocery store.

Which is where, in the middle of the baking aisle, I run into Tucker.

"Hi," I breathe. I curse my stupid heart for how it leaps when I see him standing there in a white tee and holey jeans, holding a basket with green apples, a lemon, a package of butter, and a bag of white sugar in it. His mom must be making a pie.

He looks at me for a minute as if deciding whether or not to bother talking to me. "You're awful dressed up," he says finally, taking in my coat and the black dress and the knee-high black boots, the way my hair is done up in a loose chignon at the crown of my head. His mouth twists into a mocking smile. "Let me guess: you're magically teleporting to some fancy Stanford party, and you lost your way?"

"I came from a funeral," I say tightly. "At Aspen Hill."

Right away his face sobers. "Whose?"

"Walter Prescott's."

He nods. "I heard about that. A stroke, wasn't it?"

I don't answer.

"Or not a stroke," he surmises. "He was one of your people."

My people. Nice. I start to walk away, because that's the wise thing to do—just leave, don't engage with him—but then I stop, turn back. I can't help myself. "Don't do that," I say.

"Don't do what?"

"I know you're mad at me, and I understand why you would be, I get it, I do, but you don't have to be like that. You're like the kindest, sweetest, most decent guy that I know. Don't be a jerk because of me."

He looks at the floor, swallows hard. "Clara . . ."

"I'm sorry, Tuck. I know that might not be worth much, me saying it. But I'm sorry. For all of it." I turn to walk away. "I'll stay out of your way."

"You didn't call," he says before I can flee.

I blink up at him, startled. "What?"

"This summer. When you got back from Italy, before you went to California. You were home for two weeks, right? And you didn't call. Not once," he says with accusation in his voice.

That's what he picks to be mad about?

"I wanted to," I say, which is true. Every day I thought about calling him. "I was busy," I say, which is a lie.

He scoffs, but the anger fades from his face, becomes a

kind of resigned frustration. "We could have hung out some, before you had to go."

"I'm sorry," I murmur again, because I don't know what else to say.

"It's just that . . . I thought maybe we could be . . ." His throat works for a minute before he gets the word out. "Friends."

Tucker Avery wants to be my friend.

He looks so vulnerable right now, staring at his boots, his ears slightly red under his tan, his shoulders tight. I want to reach over and put my hand on his arm. I want to smile and say, *Sure. Let's be friends. I would love to be your friend.*

But I have to be strong. I have to remember why we broke up in the first place: so that he could have a life where he wouldn't be attacked by a fallen angel at the end of a date, where he could kiss his girlfriend without her literally lighting up like a sparkler on the Fourth of July, where he wouldn't be constantly kept in the dark. He needs someone normal. Someone who will age when he ages. Someone he can protect the way a man protects his woman, and not the other way around. Someone not me. I mean, five minutes ago I was being blackmailed by a Black Wing, for heaven's sake. I'm being hunted by a fallen angel who means to "collect" me. I'm going to have to fight. Possibly die.

I take a deep breath. "I don't think that's a good idea."

He looks up. "You don't want to be friends."

148

I try to meet his eyes. "No. I don't."

For once I'm glad he can't read my mind the way Christian does. He'd see how much I think about him, how I dream about him, how even after all this time apart my heart still aches to see him, touch him, hear his voice. He'd see that we can't be friends. He'd see that every minute I'm with him I want his arms around me. I remember his lips on mine. I'll never, *never*, be able to see him as a friend.

It's better this way, I repeat to myself. It's better this way. It's better this way. He has to live his life, and I have to live mine.

His jaw tightens. "All right," he says. "I get it. We're done. You're moving on."

Yes, I need to say to him. But I can't make my lips form the word.

He nods, flexes his hands like he wants his cowboy hat to put on now, but he doesn't have it. "I should go," he says. "I have chores to do back at the ranch."

He moves to the end of the aisle, then stops. There's something else he wants to tell me. My breath hitches in my throat.

"Have a nice life, Clara," he says. "You deserve to be happy."

My hands clench into fists as I watch him walk away.

So do you, I think. So do you.

9

BACK, BACK, YOU FIEND

"You're distracted, Clara," Dad says. "You need to focus."

I lower my part of the broom, panting. My shoulder smarts from where Christian just whacked me. We've been sparring in my backyard in Jackson in ankle-deep snow for the past half hour, and so far it's been pretty even. I hit him; he hits me. Although that last hit was a doozy.

Christian looks at me with guilt in his gold-flecked eyes.

"Are you okay?" he asks quietly. "I'm sorry."

"I'm fine. We agreed not to pull our punches, and I left you an opening, so you should go for it." I rotate my arm in its socket, wince, then roll my head from side to side, stretching. "Can we take a break for a minute? I could use a breather."

Dad frowns. "We don't have time for that. You must practice."

This is our fifth training session together—me, Dad, and Christian—and every time Dad seems more tense, like we're not making enough progress. He's been working us like crazy all week, but winter break is almost over, and we won't have as much free time to train once we go back to school. We should have moved on from brooms and mops by now. We should be wielding the real deal.

"I thought there's no such thing as time for you." I'm trying not to whine. "Come on. I need hot chocolate. My feet are freezing."

Dad sighs, then strides across the yard to stand between Christian and me. He puts a hand on the back of my neck right under the hairline, then does the same to Christian. I don't have time to ask what he's doing before I feel a jolt in my stomach and the world dissolves into a bright white light, and when it fades we're standing on a beach. It looks like the set of a deserted-island movie, all perfect white sand and blue water, nobody around but a few curious seagulls.

"Holy crap, Dad," I gasp. "Try warning us next time."

"Now," he says, clapping his hands together. "Again."

We take off our boots and socks, strip off our jackets, and toss them down on the sand. Dad stands on the water's edge a ways off and crosses his arms to watch us. I lift my broom and approach Christian, who drops into a defensive posture. Sand squishes between my toes.

"So," Christian says, like we're having a laid-back conversation instead of trying to beat each other to a pulp. "How's Angela?"

"She's all right. She's speaking to me again, at least." I thrust. He parries. "I had dinner at her house a couple nights ago, and we talked some. At least she gave me the version of the story she wants everyone to believe." He swings; I block. "She's going to be in my lit class this quarter—did I tell you? We're reading Dante. That should be a barrel of laughs."

"I saw her in the square yesterday, eating a double-decker ice cream cone in twenty-degree weather," Christian says. "She gave me guff just like her normal old self. Only . . . bigger."

"Oh, come on, she's not that big. You can hardly tell."

"What is she now, like six months along?"

I see an opening and take a whack at his leg, but he moves too fast. I stumble past him and whip around barely in time to deflect a blow meant for my hip. I push him away.

"That depends on which story you believe." I wipe at a strand of hair that's sticking to my face. "If Pierce is the father, that would make her like four months, tops. But she told me that she's due in March, which would make her six. The math doesn't add up. Six months means she got pregnant in Italy. So the baby has to be Phen's."

"But she won't admit that Phen's the father, not even to you?" Christian asks.

"No way—she says it's Pierce. She even told Pierce that he's the father, which means that he is now completely freaked out. He's offered to help, but Angela won't let him do anything for her. He's a decent guy. Too bad he's not the father."

Christian frowns. "So Angela's going to stick it out through winter quarter?"

I brush his ribs with the broom, and he jumps back. "Yep. But then she's going on a leave of absence, or something," I tell him. "Indefinitely."

"But what about her purpose? That takes place at Stanford, doesn't it?"

"She doesn't want to talk about her purpose. It's like she's stopped believing in it, or she's decided not to care, or she's too busy focusing on this baby thing right now." I stumble, and Christian gets a solid hit to my thigh. "Ow! Hey, not so freaking hard!"

He pauses, lowers his broom. "But I thought we agreed—"

I charge him, taking advantage of his lowered weapon. "Back, back, you fiend!" I scream, and he laughs as I disarm him, his broom flying into the water. He sinks to his knees, the end of my broom at his throat. He grins, lifts his hands in the air.

It's good to see him smiling. It's been a rough couple weeks for him, being home in his empty house, constantly reminded of Walter and the stuff they used to do together.

"Surrender," I intone gravely.

"Death first," he yells, then barrels into me, catching me around the middle and dragging me to the sand.

"No, stop," I scream, struggling as he throws a leg over mine. "No tickling! There's no tickling in sword training. Christian!" I laugh helplessly.

"That's enough," Dad says suddenly.

Christian and I pause to look at him. I think we both forgot he was there. He is not amused, either. Christian gets off me and pulls me to my feet, brushing sand off his shirt. Dad hands him back his broom.

"Again," he says.

"Sheesh, you're such a drill sergeant," I snicker. "Lighten up."

Dad's eyes spark. "This is not gym class," he says.

"I never was too fond of gym," I joke.

Which is, of course, the wrong thing to say. "This is life and death, Clara. I expected better from you. I expected you to take it seriously."

I stare at the sand. I've been trying hard not to obsess about the image of myself covered in blood, dull-eyed, that occasionally flashes through Christian's mind along with a wave of anxiety.

"She deals with tension by making jokes," Christian says quietly. "She gets that it's serious."

The fire leaves Dad's eyes. He lets out a breath. "I'm sorry," he says, which shocks the crap out of me. "Let's take a break."

We sit in a line on the shore, watching the waves. I look

154

over at Christian and smile, send him a mental hug to assure him I'm okay, because at the moment he's considering giving the archangel Michael a piece of his mind.

"In some ways," Dad says to Christian, "I am just her father."

"Here's what I don't get," Christian says after a minute. "All my life, since my uncle first told me about Black Wings, he told me to run. He told me it wouldn't do me any good to try to fight them—they're too powerful, too fast, too strong. You can't kill them. Run, he always said."

"Mom said that, too," I chime in.

"It's true," Dad says. "In a one-on-one battle with an angel, you won't prevail. It's not only about the power and the speed and the strength. It's experience. We've been grappling with one another a long, long time." He seems sad at the idea. "And you've only just begun to fight."

"So what's the point?" Christian asks. "If we can't fight a Black Wing and succeed, why did my uncle try to teach me? Why are you teaching us to use the glory sword?" He shakes his head. "I know I see myself wielding one in the vision. But why? Why, if I can't win?"

"Black Wings are unlikely to harm you directly," Dad says. "They're still angels, after all, and to hurt someone on the side of good goes against our design. It would cause even a Black Wing a great deal of pain. That's why they prefer to use minions to inflict any physical damage."

"Minions?" I repeat.

"Angel-bloods," he says. "Black Wings do their evil work through the Nephilim. And the Triplare are the most powerful of the Nephilim."

"So in the vision we're fighting other angel-bloods," Christian concludes.

Dad nods.

I relate what Samjeeza said to me in the cemetery about Asael.

"Yes," Dad says. "Asael is very dangerous. Perhaps the most dangerous and wholly evil of the Black Wings, other than Satan himself. Without pity. Without hesitation. He takes what he wants, and if he sees you, if he knows what you are, he will take you. He has killed or enslaved many, if not most, of the Triplare."

"Are there a lot of Triplare?" I ask tremulously.

"No," Dad says. "There are very few of you. In fact there are never more than seven Triplare walking the earth at the same time. And at the moment Asael is in possession of at least three."

"Seven," Christian says, almost to himself. "So there's you, me, and Jeffrey . . . that only leaves one more."

Seven Triplare. Seven.

I meet Christian's eyes. We have the same thought at the same moment.

The seventh is ours.

"Angela's baby," I realize. "Because Phen *is* the father."

Dad scowls. "Phen." He says the name like it's a swear word. "Disgusting, cowardly creatures, the ambivalent. Worse than the fallen, in many ways." His eyes are so fierce it's a tad scary. "They have no conviction at all."

"I'll tell her on the drive back to California," I say to Christian when we're back at my house in Jackson, sitting on the couch in the living room in front of a roaring fire, drinking raspberry tea, which is making me miss my mother. "The sooner she knows, the better."

He stares into the flames. "Okay. You want to meet on Tuesday night at the CoHo, since we're going to miss Saturday?"

"Of course." I bite my lip. "And I thought, maybe, if you're up to it, you and I could start jogging in the mornings. I know we're supposed to be training for the glory sword, but it could be good to brush up on our running, just in case."

"Just in case," he echoes. "Yeah, I'd like that. Every morning?"

"Yeah. Let's say six thirty." I shudder at the thought of getting up so early, but it's for a good cause. Like, possibly extending my life expectancy.

"All right," he says with a smile. "Just remember that it was your idea."

"I will. So tell me what your schedule this quarter's like."

"Nothing too exciting. My craziest class is going to be structural engineering."

I cock my head at him. "Structural engineering? That sounds serious." I narrow my eyes at him suspiciously. "Are you picking a major?"

He does his laugh/exhale thing. "I'm thinking about architecture."

"You want to be an architect? When did this happen?"

"I like building things. I was killer with Lincoln Logs as a kid." He shrugs. "It makes a kind of sense, so I thought I'd go for it, try it out, tackle all the math and physics and drawing and see if at the end of all that I still like the idea."

He's not looking directly at me, but I can tell he's watching to see how I'll react. Whether I'll think it's silly, to be going toward something so heavy as architecture, whether I'll laugh picturing him in a suit and a hard hat with a roll of blueprints under his arm.

I think it's hot. I jostle my shoulder into his. "That's amazing. It sounds . . . perfect."

"What about you?" he asks. "Still going strong on premed?"

"Yep. I'm taking a biochemistry class called Genomics and Medicine, which I'm pretty sure is going to blow my mind."

"What else?" he asks. "No more happiness?"

I sigh. "No more happiness. Just the normal prereqs and premed and, uh, some PE class."

He catches my attempt to slide that by him. "Clara, what

PE class?" He fishes it out of my mind. "You're taking fencing? That's cheating."

"Hey, nobody ever said that we can't train on our own time."

He sits back, looks at me like I'm more devious than he thought. "I'm going to sign up for that class, too. When is it?"

"Monday and Wednesday, one to two p.m."

He nods like it's all settled, then. "So we'll run in the mornings, and spar in the afternoons."

"Okay."

"And don't make plans for next weekend," he adds.

I look up at him. "Why not?"

The corner of his mouth lifts. He pins me with a gaze that would turn any red-blooded girl's legs to jelly. "I am taking you out. On a date. Before things get crazy."

My heart beats faster. "Dinner and a movie," I remember.

"Friday night," he says. "I'll pick you up at seven."

"Seven," I repeat with a stupid quiver in my voice. "Friday."

He goes to the door and starts putting on his coat.

"Where are you going?"

"Home. I have to prepare," he says.

"For Friday?"

"For everything," he replies. "I'll see you at the Farm."

"You're speeding," Angela says.

I don't have to check the speedometer to know she's right.

I'm nervous about how she's going to take the whole "maybe the seventh is your baby" thing. We've driven all day, about to find a hotel for the night, and still I haven't worked up the nerve to broach the subject.

"I didn't know you had a speeding problem," she remarks. "You're usually a decent driver, when you're not crashing into angels, that is. You're a rule follower."

Which of course she makes sound like an insult. "Gee, thanks."

She returns to the parenting magazine she's reading. She's been researching this baby thing with the same kind of passion she usually reserves for angel stuff. What she keeps stashed under her pillow lately is a dog-eared copy of *What to Expect When You're Expecting*. And a three-hundred-year-old tome that has a passage about a woman giving birth to a Nephilim. Just a little light reading.

"So, how was your break?" she asks, and smiles suggestively. "Did you get to blow off some steam with Christian?"

I ignore her obvious innuendo. "We spent some time at the beach."

She gazes at the window wistfully, where outside the sky has darkened to a deep, beguiling blue; her hands rest on the swell of her stomach. I wonder when the last time was, when she did anything but worry.

"Ange, we need to talk."

"We could talk about why you're not with Christian," she suggests.

"How about we not talk about that, but say we did?"

"What's the holdup, C?" she continues like she didn't hear me. "He's hot, he's hot for you, he's available, and wait, hold on . . ." Her golden eyes widen theatrically. "Aren't *you* available now?"

I hate that I'm blushing.

"And let's not forget that he's your destiny. Your purpose or whatever. Your guy. So make out with him already. *Just be*, with him. In a horizontal sort of way, like you said."

"Thank you, Angela," I say wryly. "This is so illuminating."

"Sorry," she says, although she's clearly not in the least bit sorry. "I get annoyed watching the two of you torture yourselves."

Here I started out determined to talk about her, and we're talking about me. I let her change the subject for the moment, but I'm determined to get back around to this whole baby situation.

"We're not—" I sigh. "It's complicated. We don't want to be together because somebody told us that we have to be."

"And by 'somebody' you mean God, right?"

Of course it sounds insanely arrogant of me, insisting on a relationship on my own terms, when she puts it like that.

"It's not so complicated," she says. "You want to be together all on your own. It's obvious, especially for him. Don't tell me you haven't noticed the way he looks at you, like he'd kiss the ground you walk on if he thought it would win you over."

"I know," I admit softly. "But—"

161

"But you're still hung up on the cowboy."

I check my mirrors. "I don't want to bounce out of one relationship and right into another. Christian and I have time to become whatever it is that we're meant—that we decide to be."

"You don't want him to be your rebound," she says thoughtfully. "How very adult of you."

"Thanks. I'm trying, here." I change lanes, then speed up to pass a motor home that's moseying along the freeway.

"But maybe you don't have time," she says, the first time she's acknowledged what I told her about my vision. "And it's been months since you ended it with Tucker, hasn't it?" she points out.

Okay, that's it. Enough discussion about me. "So how come you get to mandate that we don't talk about your love life and then jump straight into talking about mine? That hardly seems fair," I say.

Her whole body tenses. "I don't have anything to say about Pierce. He's a sweet guy."

"I'm sure he is. But you're not in love with him. And he's not the father of your baby, right?"

She scoffs. "Come on, C. We've been over this."

"I get why you're saying that he is," I tell her. "I understand, really, I do. I don't know if it's the best thing to do to Pierce, but I get it. You're protecting your baby. The way my mom tried to protect Jeffrey and me by letting us think my dad was of the regular deadbeat variety."

She looks into her lap. She's determined not to admit it. Not to anybody. She made a promise to herself, a commitment to the idea of Pierce as the baby daddy, and she's not going to break that for anybody. Not even for me. It's safer that way.

"Okay, fine, be that way," I say.

I'll have to let her figure it out herself. But there's nothing wrong with me helping.

I turn on the radio, and we listen without talking for a while, both of us deep in thought. I come up with a new approach. "Hey, you remember how I kept seeing that bird around campus, and it turned out to be Samjeeza?"

"Yes," she says lightly, relieved because she thinks I'm changing the subject. "What happened with him, anyway? Is he still stalking you?"

"I threw a rock at him a few weeks ago, and I haven't seen him since."

"You threw a rock at a Black Wing?" she says, impressed. "Whoa, C."

"I was mad. It was probably a mistake. He knows I'm a Triplare, and maybe I pissed him off enough that he'll decide to tell Asael about me."

Angela freezes. "Asael. Who's that?"

"The big bad Watcher, apparently. He collects the Triplare. Apparently there are only seven of us at any given time, and he wants to own the entire boxed set," I rattle off like it's common knowledge.

"Seven of you . . . ," she repeats.

She's finally getting it. "My dad said that there are never more than seven Triplare to walk the earth at any given time, and Asael wants them all. Christian said something about that once, too—seven Triplare, something Walter told him." I look over at her. "What is it with the number seven, right? But like you said, it's God's number."

"The seventh," she whispers. She gazes down at her stomach. "The seventh is ours."

"Now we're on the same page," I tell her, and speed up.

When I get back to Stanford, the first thing I do is try to find my brother. What Samjeeza said about Jeffrey—*where's your brother, Clara?*—bugs me, and I don't want to wait for him to call me to hang out. Part of me just wants to see him. Plus he should know about the seven-Triplare thing. So I take matters into my own hands and start Googling pizza places in or around Mountain View—let's call it a hunch that Jeffrey's hanging out in or near our old hometown. After all, that first time he showed up at my dorm room he said he thought he'd seen me, and that was the day I took Christian to Mountain View before we went to Buzzards Roost.

It turns out that there are three pizza joints in Mountain View, and Jeffrey works at the third one I check—right next to the train station, on Castro Street.

He's not thrilled to see me when I come barging into his life. "What are you doing here?" he asks when I appear at the counter and sweetly ask for a Diet Coke.

"Hey, can't a girl miss her brother?" I ask. "I need to talk to you. Do you have a minute?"

"All right, fine. Hey, Jake, this is my sister," he tells a huge Latino guy behind the counter, who kind of grunts and nods. "I'm going on break." He guides me to a table in the far front corner, under the window, and sits down across from me. "Do you want a pizza?" he asks, and hands me a menu. "I get a free one every day."

"Dream job, huh?" I look around at the huge frescoes of different vegetables painted on the orange wall behind Jeffrey's head: a giant avocado, four big tomatoes, an enormous green pepper. This isn't quite what I pictured when Jeffrey told me he worked in a pizza joint. The place is small, narrow, but in a cozy way, with warm peach-colored tile on the floors, simple tables lined up on either side of the room, the kitchen open behind the counter, clean and shining with stainless steel. It's more upscale and organic than your average pizzeria.

Jeffrey looks tired. He keeps blinking and rubbing at his eyes.

"You alive over there?" I ask.

He smiles wearily. "Sorry. Late night."

"Working?"

"Playing," he says, his smile amping up into a grin.

That doesn't sound good. "Playing what?" I ask, and I'm guessing that the answer isn't going to be Xbox.

"I went to a club."

A club. My sixteen-year-old brother is tired because he was out late at a club. Awesomesauce. "So, let me see your fake ID," I say, trying to play it cool. "I want to see how good it is."

"No way." He takes the menu from me and points at a pizza called the Berkeley vegan. "This one's gross."

"Well, let's not have that, then." I look down at the paper placemat-menu. "How about we try this one?" I say, pointing to pizza called the Casablanca.

He shrugs. "Fine. I'm kind of sick of all of them. Whatever sounds good to you."

"Okay. So come on, let me see the ID."

He folds his arms across the table. "I don't have a fake ID, Clara. Honest."

"Oh, right. You're going to one of those superawesome clubs that don't require an ID," I say sarcastically. "Where's that, because I am totally going."

"My girlfriend's dad owns the club. He lets me in. Don't worry. I don't drink . . . much."

Oh, how comforting, I think. I actually have to bite my lip to keep myself from going all nagging-older-sister on him.

"So you're calling her your girlfriend now, huh?" I say. "What's her name again?"

"Lucy." He takes a minute to run to the back and put in our order. "Yeah, we're like, together now."

"And what's she like, other than being the daughter of some guy who owns a club?"

"I don't know how to describe her," he says with a shrug. "She's hot. And she's cool."

Typical guyspeak, about as vague as possible.

He smiles, thinking about her. "She's got a wicked sense of humor."

"I want to meet her."

He smirks, shakes his head. "I don't think that's a good idea."

"Why not? What, you think I'd embarrass you?"

"I *know* you'd embarrass me," he says.

"Oh, come on. I'll behave, I promise. Bring her to meet me sometime."

"I'll think about it." He stares out the window, where a group of teenagers is walking down the sidewalk, purposely bumping into one another, laughing. He watches them as they pass by, and I get a sad vibe off him, like he's looking at the life he used to have. Without meaning to, he's made himself grow up. He's being an adult. Taking care of himself.

Going clubbing.

He clears his throat. "So what did you come to talk to me

about?" he asks. "You need advice on the love life again? Did you hook up with Christian yet?"

I roll my eyes. "Ugh. Why does everyone keep asking me that? And you're my little brother. That sort of thing is supposed to disgust you."

He shrugs. "It does. I'm disgusted, really. So did you?"

"No! But we are going on a date on Friday night," I admit with reluctance. "Dinner and a movie."

"Ah, so maybe Friday . . . ," he teases.

I want to smack him. "That's the kind of girl you think I am?"

Another shrug. "I was there that morning you snuck home after spending the night over at Tucker's. You can't play all innocent with me."

"Nothing happened!" I exclaim. "I fell asleep, is all. Sheesh, you're worse than Mom. Not that my innocence or lack thereof is any of your business," I continue quickly, "but Tucker and I, we couldn't . . . you know."

His forehead rumples up in confusion. "You couldn't what?"

He never was the sharpest knife in the drawer. "You know," I say again, with emphasis.

Comprehension dawns on his face. "Oh. Why?"

"If I got too . . . happy, I started to glow, and then Tucker kind of got sick. That whole glory-terrifies-humans thing. So." I start rearranging the packets of crushed red pepper on the table. "That's what you have to look forward to, I guess."

Now he really does look weirded out. "O-kay."

"That's why it's hard to have relationships with humans," I say. "Anyway, that's not what we need to discuss." I swallow, suddenly nervous about how he'll take this idea of mine. "I've been training with Dad."

His eyes narrow, immediately cautious. "What do you mean, training?"

"He's been training me to use a glory sword. Me and Christian both, actually. And I think you should come with us, next time."

For a minute he stares at me with guarded eyes. Then he looks at his hands.

I keep babbling. "That sounds fun, right? I bet you'd do great."

He scoffs. "Why would I want to learn how to use a sword?"

"To defend yourself."

"Against who, an angel samurai? This is the twenty-first century. We have something called guns now."

Jake comes out and puts a steaming pizza on the table. He looks grouchy. Jeffrey and I wait in silence as he sets plates in front of us.

"Is there anything else I can get you?" Jake asks sarcastically.

"No, thank you," I say, and he stalks off, and I lean across the table and whisper, "To defend yourself against Black

Wings." I tell Jeffrey about my talk with Samjeeza in the cemetery, including the fact that Samjeeza specifically asked about him, the way I keep seeing Samjeeza as a crow around campus, the things Dad said about the seven, er, *T-people* and how if we're going to fight anybody, it's probably going to be them. "So Dad's teaching me. And I know he'd want to teach you, too."

"T-people?"

I stare at him pointedly until he says, "Oh."

"So what do you think? Will you come? It could be like Angel Club, except without Angela, because she's . . . busy."

He shakes his head. "No, thanks."

"Why not?"

"I'm not going to learn to fight. That's just playing the game. It's not for me."

"Jeffrey, you're like a champion fighter. You're a linebacker. You're the district mid-class wrestling champ. You're—"

"Not anymore." He stands up, gives me a look that says very clearly that he's done talking about it. "Enjoy the pizza. I have to get back to work."

10

DINNER AND A MOVIE

"You should go black," Angela says.

I turn around, startled to see her standing behind me at the mirror. She points at the dress I'm holding in my left hand.

"The black," she says again.

"Thanks." I hang up the other dress. "Why does it not surprise me that you would choose black?" I tease. "Goth girl."

She walks stiffly over to Wan Chen's bed and sits, helps herself to a bottle of peppermint-scented lotion Wan Chen keeps next to the bed, and starts rubbing it into her feet. I try not to stare at her belly. Just in the last few days she's kind of popped. With the dark, baggy clothes and the way she always hunches her shoulders lately, she's still able to hide that she's pregnant if she wants to. Not for long, though. Pretty soon there's going to be a baby.

A baby. The idea still seems too crazy to be true.

I step into the bathroom and change into the dress, the very definition of the little black dress, sleeveless and form-fitting and cut to the knee. Angela was right. It's perfect for a date. Then I go over to the mirror that hangs on the back of my closet door and contemplate whether I should pull my hair up or leave it down.

"Down," Angela says. "He loves your hair. If you leave it down, he'll want to touch it."

Hearing her say it that way, as if I'm preparing myself like a plate of food to be served up for Christian, only increases the anxiety I feel about this whole situation. Everything I do to get ready for this date boils down to the same thing: Will Christian like it? Will he like my perfume? My strappy shoes? My hair? The necklace I chose, a tiny silver bird's wing that glints against the hollow of my throat? *Will he like it?* I ask myself each time, and then I have to ask myself if I want him to like it.

I pull my hair out of the ponytail and let it fall freely down my back. There's a sharp knock at the door, and I run to open it. Christian's standing in the hall wearing khakis and a blue dress shirt, sleeves rolled to the elbows. He smells like Ivory soap and shaving cream.

He holds out a bouquet of white daisies. "For you."

"Thank you," I say, which comes out as a squeak. I clear

my throat. "I'll put these in some water."

He follows me inside. I rummage around for something to use as a vase, but the best I can find is a Big Gulp cup. I fill it with water and set the flowers on my desk.

Christian glances at Angela sitting on Wan Chen's bed, scribbling away in her black-and-white composition note-book. "Hello, Angela," he says.

"Hi, Chris," she says, but she doesn't stop writing. "Clara said I could crash here while you were out tonight. I need to get away from my roommates. They're treating me like an episode of *16 and Pregnant*. So. You brought flowers. Very smooth."

"Yeah, I try," he says with a smirk. He looks at me. "You ready?"

"Yes." I fight the urge to tuck my hair behind my ears. "Bye," I say to Angela. "Wan Chen will be back from her astronomy thing around midnight. You might want to get off her bed before then."

She waves her hand at me dismissively. "Go," she says. "Get swept off your feet already."

When we're both situated in his truck, Christian puts the key in the ignition, but he doesn't start it. Instead he turns to me.

"This is a date," he says.

"Oh, good," I say, "because I was wondering, what with the flowers and all."

"And as a date, there are certain ground rules we need to go over."

Oh boy. "Okay," I laugh nervously.

"I will be paying for all of our activities this evening," he begins.

"But—"

He holds up his hand. "I know that you are a modern, liberated, independent woman. I respect that, and I understand that you are capable of paying for your own meal, but I will still be paying for the movie, and then for dinner, and whatever else. Okay?"

"But—"

"And even though I'm paying, it doesn't mean that I expect anything from you. I want to treat you tonight, and that's all."

It's cute that he's blushing.

"All right," I fake-grumble. "You'll pay. Anything else?"

"Yes. I'd like us to steer clear of all angel-related topics tonight, if you don't mind. I don't want to hear the word *angel*, or *purpose*, or *vision*, or any of our other special terminology. Tonight I want us to simply be Christian and Clara, two college students on a date. How's that sound?"

"Sounds good," I say. More than good, even. It sounds perfect.

It was a great idea in theory, not talking about angel stuff, but what it really means is that an hour later, sitting in the dimly lit auditorium before the movie begins at this amazing little indie film theater in Capitola, we're running out of things to talk about. We've already been through how the first week of winter classes went, and the gossip going around Stanford, and our favorite movies. Christian's is *Zombieland*, which surprises me—I would have pegged him as a profound type, like *The Shawshank Redemption*.

"*Shawshank*'s good," he says. "But you can't beat the way Woody Harrelson kills zombies. He takes such joy in it."

"Uh-huh," I say, making a face. "I've always found zombies to be the least threatening of the scary monsters. I mean, come on. They're slow. They're brain-dead. They don't plot evil or try to take over the world. They just—" I put my arms out in front of me and give him my best zombie groan. I shake my head. "So not scary."

"But they just. Keep. Coming," Christian says. "You can run, you can kill them, but more of them always pop up, and they never stop." He shudders. "And they try to eat you, and if you get bitten, that's it—you're infected. You're doomed to become a zombie yourself. End of story."

"Okay," I concede, "they're *kind of* scary," and now I'm vaguely disappointed that we're not here to watch a zombie movie.

"Next time," Christian says.

"Hey, I have a new rule for our date," I suggest with a cheerful grin. "No mind reading."

"Sorry," he says quickly. "I won't do it again." He sounds so serious all of a sudden, embarrassed like I've caught him looking down the front of my shirt, that I have no choice but to throw a piece of popcorn at him.

"You'd better not," I say.

He smiles.

I smile.

And then we sit in silence, munching popcorn, until the lights dim and the screen flickers to life.

Afterward he drives me to the beach. We have dinner at Paradise Beach Grille, this little upscale place on the shore, and after dinner we take our shoes off and walk along the sand. The sun set hours ago, and the light of the moon is playing off the water. The ocean gently shushes us, lapping at our feet, and we're laughing, because I have admitted that my favorite movie is *Ever After*, this old and completely cheesy retelling of the Cinderella story where Drew Barrymore tries and fails to master an English accent. Which is embarrassing, but there it is.

"So, how am I doing?" he asks after a while.

"Best date ever," I answer. "Good movie, good food, good company."

He takes my hand. His power and mine converge, the familiar heat sparking between us. A cool breeze picks up and blows my hair, and I toss it back over my shoulder. He glances at me out of the corner of his eye, then looks away, out at the water, which gives me a chance to look at him.

It's awkward to call a guy beautiful, but he is. His body is lean but strong, and he moves with such grace——like a dancer, I think, although I would never tell him that. Sometimes I forget how beautiful he is. His gorgeous gold-flecked eyes.

Those thick dark eyelashes any girl would kill to have, his serious eyebrows, the finely chiseled angles of his cheekbones, the full, expressive lips.

I shiver.

"Are you cold?" he asks, and before I can answer, he takes off his jacket, the black fleece jacket, and pulls it around me. I am immediately enveloped by his smell: soap and cologne, a whiff of cloud, like he's been flying. I flash back to the first time I wore his jacket, the night of the fire, when he put it around my shoulders. It's been over a year since that night, but the vision still lingers bright in my mind: the burning hillside, the way Christian said, *It's you,* the way it felt when he took my hand. It never actually happened that way, but it feels like a memory.

It's you, he said.

"Thank you," I say to him now, my voice faltering.

"You're welcome," he says, and picks up my hand again.

He doesn't know what else to say. He wants to tell me how beautiful I am to him, too, how I make him feel like the best, strongest version of himself, how he wants to tuck my runaway hair behind my ear and kiss me, and maybe this time I'd kiss him back.

Now I'm the one cheating.

I let go of his hand.

It doesn't matter, he says into my mind. *I don't mind you seeing what's inside me.*

My breath catches. I have to stop being such a chicken,

I think. It's not that I'm afraid of him, exactly, because if there's one person in this world who makes me feel safe, it's Christian, but I'm scared to let go, to let what's between us really happen. I'm afraid to lose myself.

"You won't lose yourself," he whispers.

Now we're clearly both cheating.

I won't? I ask silently.

Not with me, he says. *You know who you are. You won't let anyone take that away.*

He loves that about me. He loves—

He pulls me closer and looks into my eyes. My heart careens wildly in my chest. I close my eyes, and his lips touch my cheek near my ear.

"Clara," he says, my name is all, but it sends a tremor through me.

He draws back, and I know he's going to kiss me, any second now, and I want him to, but in that moment, his lips inches from mine, I suddenly see Tucker's face. Tucker's blue eyes. Tucker's mouth a breath away from mine.

Christian stops, his body going rigid. He sees what I see. He pulls away.

I open my eyes. "I—"

"Don't." He rakes his hand through his hair, stares off at the water. "Just . . . don't."

He hates me. I would hate me about now, too.

"I don't hate you," he says sharply. Sighs. "But I wish you would get over him."

"I'm trying."

"Not hard enough." His eyes are flinty when he looks at me this time. He's not used to chasing girls; they've always chased him. He's certainly not used to being someone's second choice. The thought makes him clench his jaw.

"I'm sorry," I say. He deserves so much better than this.

He shakes his head and starts back up the beach toward the road. I trail after him, struggling to put my shoes on as I go.

"Wait," I say. "Let's not go yet. It's still early. Maybe we can—"

"What would be the point?" he interrupts. "You think we should brush it off and try to pretend it didn't happen? I'm not built that way." He sighs again. "Let's just go."

I hate the idea of the silent drive back to Stanford. "I can get home by myself," I say, taking a step back. "You go. I'm sorry."

He stares at me, hands shoved in his pockets. "No. I should—"

I shake my head. "Good night, Christian," I say, and then I close my eyes and call the glory and send myself away.

I mean to go to Buzzards Roost, someplace quiet, where I can think, but when the glory fades and my eyes adjust, I find myself in an enclosed space in pretty much pitch black. I almost have a panic attack right there, but then I think this can't be my vision, my doom, because I left Christian behind. I stumble forward, arms outstretched, feeling at the floor with my feet, breathe out a sigh when I find that it's not slanted. I encounter the wall, rough and wooden, and attempt to walk along it in slow, shuffling steps. I run into something like a row of rakes leaning against the wall, which fall to the floor with a very loud crash. I hurry to set them upright again, then figure, *Screw it,* and call the glory to light my way.

I hold up my hand and concentrate on drawing the glory inside it, the way Dad says you do with the glory sword, but right now I'm thinking lantern, not blade. I'm impressed with myself when I'm able to shape a glowing ball in my hand, which feels so warm and alive it makes my fingers tingle. Ah, glory, I think, so useful—the power of the Almighty when you need a weapon, but also doubles as a handy flashlight.

I look around. I'm in a barn. A very familiar barn.

Crap.

I head for the door, passing the horse stalls on the way out. Midas nickers a greeting at me, his ears tilted forward, his eyes on me and the glowing ball in my hand, strangely unafraid of my light. Maybe he thinks he's seen it all already.

"Hi, handsome," I say to him, reaching with my free hand and stroking his velvety nose. "How are you, big boy? Do you miss me?"

He leans down and blows a wet, hay-scented breath onto my neck, then gently nips my shoulder.

"Hey, cut it out," I laugh.

Suddenly the barn floods with light. Midas backs away from me and whinnies in alarm. I spin around to find myself at the business end of a shotgun. I yelp and lift my hands in immediate surrender, my glory ball instantly dissipating.

It's Tucker.

He blows out an exasperated breath. "Good grief, Clara! You scared me!"

"*I* scared *you*?"

He lowers the gun. "That's what you get for sneaking into people's barns in the middle of the night. You're lucky it was me that heard you and not my dad; otherwise you might be missing your head about now."

"I'm sorry," I blurt out. "I didn't mean to come here."

He's still wearing his flannel pajama bottoms under an oversize tan work coat. He sets the gun against the wall and goes to Midas, who's throwing his head back and kicking at the door.

"Horses don't like surprises," he says.

"Obviously."

"It's okay, buddy," he says, and reaches in the coat pocket and produces a handful of what look to be candies. Midas immediately steps forward, snuffling, and Tucker feeds them to him.

"Do you always carry candy around with you in case of emergencies?" I ask.

"He likes jelly beans," he says with a shrug. "We've kind of been letting him have as many as he wants, too. He's getting chubby." He strokes Midas's neck, then looks over at me. "You want to feed him?"

"Sure," I say, and he hands me some.

"Keep your hand flat," Tucker instructs. "Or you might lose a finger."

Midas jerks his head up and moves around impatiently as I step forward. Then he drops his nose into my palm and slurps the jelly beans right up, munching them noisily.

"It tickles," I laugh.

Tucker smiles, and I reach for another handful in his pocket, and for a minute things feel normal between us, like we haven't had all that sniping and awkwardness and telling each other good-bye.

"You look nice," he says, looking at me appraisingly, at my curled hair and makeup, his gaze flickering over the hemline of my little black dress, my pretty sandals and painted nails, up to the black fleece jacket, which I'm still wearing around my shoulders. "Not a funeral, this time."

"No." I don't know what else to say.

"A date."

I'm tempted to lie, to say that I was out with a bunch of people, no biggie, nothing special, but I'm bad at lying, and Tucker's really good at spotting a fib. "Yeah. A date."

"With Prescott," he concludes.

"Does it matter?"

"I guess not." He pats Midas on the nose, then turns and scuffles away a few steps. The look on his face is killing me, like he's trying so hard to act like he doesn't care, but I know him.

"Tucker—"

"Nah, it's all right," he says. "I guess I should have expected him to make his move, now that we're over and done. So how'd it go?"

I stare at him wordlessly.

"Well, it can't have gone too well, or you wouldn't have ended up here at the end of the night."

"That," I say carefully, "is none of your beeswax, Tucker Avery."

"Well, you're right about that," he says. "We've got to move on, don't we? But the way I see it, there's one big thing getting in the way of us doing that."

My breath catches. "Oh yeah? What?"

He looks at me coolly. "You keep showing up."

He has a point.

"Look—" we say at the same time. He sighs.

"You go," I say.

He scratches at the back of his neck. "I wanted to tell you that I'm sorry I've been so testy with you. You were right. I've been a jerk."

"You were surprised. And you're right. I'm invading your space."

He nods. "Still, it's no excuse. You're not the worst thing that could pop up unexpectedly into my life."

"Oh great. I'm not the *worst* thing."

"Nope."

We laugh, and it feels good, laughing. It feels like old times. But then I think, Maybe I *am* the worst thing that could pop up in his life. He's looking at me with a flicker of longing in his eyes that I recognize all too well, and it sends a dart of fear for him all though me. I can't let myself get close to him. I'm not good for him. Plus, I might not even make it through this year.

"Your turn," he says.

"Oh." I find I can't tell him what I was thinking. I point my thumb behind me at the open barn door. "I was going to say that I should go."

"Okay."

He looks confused when I don't move. Then amused. "Oh, right. You want *me* to leave."

"You can stay. Only, the glory . . ."

"That's all right." He smiles with his dimples, then moseys past me toward the door. "Maybe I'll see you around, Carrots."

No, you won't, I think grimly. I have to stop this. I can't keep coming here. I have to stay away.

He called me Carrots.

Angela's still in the same position she was in when I left her, scribbling away on Wan Chen's bed. She stares at me for a minute after I materialize in the room.

"Wow," she says. "You were right when you said it was like

beaming yourself in *Star Trek*. That is pretty cool."

"I'm getting better at it," I admit.

"How did your date——" she starts to ask, then gets a look at my face. "Oh. It didn't go well."

"No, it didn't go well," I say, kicking off my shoes and lying on my back on my bed.

She shrugs. "Men."

"Men."

"If we can send one man to the moon, why can't we send them all there?" she says.

I'm tired and can't help but laugh at her joke.

"That's why I don't bother with men," she says. "I don't have the patience."

Right. She doesn't deal with mere mortals, she means.

"It's Phen," she says then.

"The father, you mean?"

She starts like my question surprises her, then hesitates for a split second before she says, quietly, "Yes. But you already knew that."

"Uh, yeah."

"But it's also Phen in my vision," she goes on to say. "The man in the gray suit. It's Phen."

Shock ripples through me. "Are you sure?"

She nods enthusiastically. "I can't believe I didn't recognize him before. All those times I had the vision, but I didn't think it was about me."

"Yeah, visions can be tricky that way."

185

"I wasted so much time feeling sorry for myself," she says. "I thought, since this happened"—she nods at her baby bump—"that I'd wrecked everything. But I didn't. It was supposed to happen this way. It was meant to be."

I turn over onto my stomach. "So what are you supposed to do?"

"I'm supposed to tell him about our baby," she says. "The seventh is ours."

This strikes me as a very bad idea, given all I know about Phen. He's just not trustworthy, for all his charm. But Angela's not going to want to hear that right now. She doesn't listen to reason when it comes to Phen.

"Okay, let's say that you're right—" I start slowly.

"Of course I'm right," she says.

"Of course you're right," I agree. "But how does Phen know to come? How will he know to meet you there?"

"That's easy. I sent him an email."

I try to get my head around the idea of an angel with a Gmail account. "But Ange—"

"He'll come, and I'll tell him," she says firmly. "Don't you see what this means, Clara?"

I don't.

"It means," she says serenely, curving her arm around the crook of her swollen belly, "that everything is going to be okay."

I highly doubt that. But for once, I hope she's right.

11

ONE STEP FORWARD, TWO STEPS BACK

I'm in the dark again. Hiding.

I'm crying. No doubt about it this time. My face is wet. Strands of my hair stick to my cheeks. Tears gather under my chin and drip down. Something's happened that I can't get out of my brain, but I only understand it in terms of sounds: a strangled moan, a sob, a few whispered words.

God help me.

I put my hand over my mouth to keep from screaming. The Clara that is me in the future feels helpless. Useless. Lost. The Clara that is me now doesn't know where I am. I only know the darkness. The fear. The sound of voices coming. The smell of blood.

It's no use hiding. They'll find me. My fate has already been decided. I just have to wait for it all to play out. I have to be brave, I think, and face it.

God help me, I think, but I feel so very little faith that God will.

I come to under a tree. There's something hard poking me under my back, and I feel for it: the book I was reading before the vision got me. I glance around to see if anybody saw me go comatose in the grass, but nobody, as far as I can tell, is looking. I wipe at my eyes. Crying again. Panicky, my heart drumming, my palms sweating, with what feels like one big knot in my stomach.

I've got to figure this vision out before I drive myself crazy.

I take out my phone and stare at Christian's name in my contact list for a long time before I sigh and put it back into my backpack. Christian hasn't said two words to me for more than a month, not even in fencing class. His pride is wounded. I get that. I'd be mad too if I'd been about to kiss him, to lay my heart on the line like that, and he went and thought about another girl.

I pick up my book, flip to the page I was on before my brain took a quick trip to the future. It's a novel, one of the epic dystopians that's so popular these days. I'm liking it—it puts things into perspective. Sure, I might have occasional visions of doom, a mysterious, soul-crushing pain in my heart, a premonition of death, but at least I'm not scrounging the post-apocalyptic countryside looking for shelter, my only friend a three-eyed mutated dog that I'll have to eat later in order to survive nuclear winter.

Of course, a mutated dog would be a step up from my friend situation at the moment. On top of Christian not speaking to me, Jeffrey hasn't called, and Angela's too busy trying to orchestrate her purpose and her everything's-going-to-be-fine meeting with Phen to even notice I'm alive. Amy and Robin have been batty since they figured out that Angela has a bun in the oven, and all they want to do when we get together is talk about how tragic and surprising it is that Angela's in this position, and what is she going to do, anyway? Even Wan Chen's been acting aloof since she found out, like pregnancy is something that might be catching.

I sigh again, try to remember the kind of thing I would write in my gratitude journal, which, to be truthful, I haven't picked up since fall quarter ended.

I have a good life, I remind myself. There are plenty of people who love me.

They're just not around at the moment.

I hear the squawk of a crow directly over my head. I peer up into the branches of the tree, and, sure enough, there's Samjeeza gazing down at me.

Every single time I see him, no matter how brave I try to be about it, how casual, it's like getting splashed with ice water. Because every single time, I wonder if he's decided to kill me. And he could, with the littlest flick of his wrist, I think. He could.

"Don't you have better things to do than follow me around?" I ask, trying to keep my tone saucy.

The bird cocks his head, then flutters down from the branch to land in the grass beside me. The sad melody of his sorrow twines itself around my mind, making my chest tight with the regret he's feeling.

Meg, he thinks, my mother's name and nothing more, but there's a world of memory and pain in the word. Longing. Guilt. *Meg.*

I shut him out. "Go away," I whisper.

Suddenly he's a man, unfolding from the body of the crow, expanding, in the blink of an eye.

"Geez!" I scramble backward, up against the trunk of the tree. "Don't do that!"

"No one is looking," he says, like what I'm really concerned about at this moment is whether anybody saw me talking to a bird and what that might do to my sterling reputation.

I'm torn between the desire to run—hightail it straight to Memorial Church, the nearest hallowed ground I can think of—or to suck it up and hear what he's going to say this time.

I glance over at the church, which is all the way across the quad. It's too far.

"How can I help you, Sam?" I ask instead.

"I took your mother dancing once," he says, starting up again on his stories. "She wore a red dress, and the band played 'Till We Meet Again,' and she put her head down on my chest to hear my heart beating."

"Do you even have a heart?" I ask, which is foolish of me to say, and maybe even a little mean, but I can't help it. I don't like the idea of him and my mother that way. Or any way, really.

He's offended. "Of course I have a heart. I can be wounded, the same as any man. She sang to me that night, as we danced. 'Smile the while you kiss me sad adieu. When the clouds roll by I'll come to you,'" he sings, and his voice isn't half bad.

I know the song immediately. Mom used to sing it when she was doing some mundane task, like folding laundry or washing dishes. It's the first time I've ever recognized my mother in this mysterious Meg of his.

"She smelled like roses," he says.

She did.

He takes the silver charm bracelet out of his pocket and holds it in his palm. "I gave this to her on her doorstep, right before we said good night. All that summer I would leave charms for her to find. This one"—he fingers a charm shaped like a fish—"for that first time I saw her at the pond." He touches the horse. "This one for when we rode through the French countryside after the hospital where she worked was bombed."

He caresses the tiny silver heart with a single ruby at its center, but doesn't tell me about that one. But I know what it means.

That's the point of all this, I guess. He loved her.

He still loves her.

His hand closes around the bracelet, and he returns it to his pocket.

"What year was that?" I ask him. "When you danced?"

"1918," he says.

"You could go back there, right? Can't angels travel through time?"

His eyes meet mine, resentful. "Some angels," he says.

He means the good ones. The ones who can access glory. Who are still on God's good side.

"Will you tell me a story now?" he asks me softly. "About your mother?"

I hesitate. Why do I feel sorry for him?

Maybe, supplies my pesky inner voice, because he loves someone he can't have. And you can relate.

I tell my inner voice to shut it. "I don't have any stories for you." I get up, brush grass off my jeans, and gather my stuff. He stands up, too, and I'm horrified to realize that the grass underneath where he was sitting is brown and crisp. Dead.

He really is a monster.

"I have to go."

"Next time, then," he says as I turn to walk away.

I stop. "I don't want there to be a next time, Sam. I don't know why you're doing this, what you want from me, but I don't want to hear any more."

"I want you to know," he says.

"Why? So you can rub it in my face that you had a

supposedly passionate love affair with my mother?"

He shakes his head, the two layers of him, body and soul, form and formless, blurring with the motion. And then I realize: He wants me to know because there's no one else to share it with. No one else cares.

"Good-bye, Sam."

"Until next time," he calls after me.

I walk away without looking back, the image of my mom wearing a red dress, a silver charm bracelet tinkling against her wrist, singing and smelling of roses, bright in my head.

"So tomorrow's it," Angela informs me. We're doing her laundry in the Roble laundry room, me helping since it's getting harder and harder these days for Angela to bend down, the noise of the churning washer and dryers the perfect mask for a secret conversation about destiny. Which is apparently happening tomorrow.

"How do you know?" I ask her.

"Because that's when I told him to meet me," she says, "in the email."

"How do you know he got the email?"

"He replied and said he'd come. And because that's what happens. He comes because I see him there."

This is circular logic, but I go with it. "So you're going to just march up to him and say, 'The seventh is ours.'" This idea worries me. A lot. I've been going over and over the scenario in my head, and I can never imagine it turning out well. It's not just Phen's wings that are gray, but his soul—his very being. And Angela always gets kind of crazy when it comes to him. He's bad news, in my opinion.

Angela catches her bottom lip in her teeth for a few seconds, the first sign of real nervousness that I've seen since she put the whole seventh thing together. "Something like that," she says.

I do believe her when she says it's her vision. So it must be destined to happen, right?

I don't know. I never did figure out why Jeffrey had a vision of starting a forest fire and then saving someone from the same fire. Or why I was supposed to meet Christian in the forest that day. Or what I was doing at my mom's funeral.

Ours is not to reason why, I suppose. Ours is but to do or—well, crap.

"And then what?" I ask. "You tell him, and then—"

"He and I will deal with this thing"—she rests her hand lightly on her belly—"together."

I mull this over. Does she think that she'll tell him and then they all—nineteen-year-old college student, thousands-of-years-old gray-souled ambivalent angel, and bouncing bundle of Triplare joy—will be a happy family? I guess stranger things have happened, but still . . .

She reads the doubt on my face.

"Look, C, I'm not expecting a fairy-tale ending here. But this is my purpose, don't you see? This is what I was put on this earth to do. I have to tell him. He's . . ." She takes a quick breath, like this next thing she's about to say takes all her courage. "He's the father of my child. He deserves to know."

I'm familiar with that gleam of certainty in her eyes. Her faith in the vision, and how she feels in the vision, her faith in the way things work. I felt that way myself once, not long ago.

"If this is a test of some kind, my moment of spiritual decision," she says, "then I choose to tell him the truth."

"So tomorrow. Big day," I say, like, I get it. I understand.

She smiles. "Big freaking day. Will you come with me, C?"

"To see Phen? I don't know, Ange. Maybe this is between you and him." Last time I had one-on-one interaction with Phen, I sort of told him to leave Angela alone, that she deserved better than he could offer her. And he called me a hypocrite and a child. We're not exactly best buds, Phen and me.

Angela leans against the dryer. "You're going to come with me," she says matter-of-factly. "You're always there, in my vision."

I had forgotten all about that. Or maybe I thought she made that bit up so that she could coerce me into coming to Stanford with her. "Right. And where am I, exactly, in this vision?"

"Like two steps behind me, most of the way. For moral support, I think." She bats her eyes and pouts at me.

All of a sudden this feels like a test for me, too. As an angel-blood who's supposed to believe in the visions. As her friend.

"All right, all right. I'll be there, two steps behind," I promise.

"I had a feeling you were going to say yes," she says gleefully.

"Yeah, don't push your luck."

She reaches into her back pocket and pulls out a sheet of wrinkled paper, unfolds it for me. It's an ultrasound.

"You went to a doctor?" I ask. "I would have gone with you, if I'd known."

She shrugs. "I've been a bunch of times. I wanted to make sure it was okay." She corrects herself: "He. It's a boy."

I stare at the picture, part of me stunned that this is really a tiny person growing inside my friend. It's grainy, but I can clearly make out a profile, a tiny nose and chin, the bones that make up the baby's arm. "Are they sure? That it's a boy?"

"Pretty sure," she says with a smirk. "I think I'm going to name him Webster."

"Webster, like after the dictionary? Hmm, I like it." I hand the picture back to her.

She looks at it for a long moment. "He was sucking his thumb." She refolds the paper and puts it back in her pocket. The dryer beeps that it's done, and she starts pulling clothes out and into the basket.

"I'll take that," I offer, and she slides the basket over to me.

When we're back in her room, folding, she suddenly says, "I don't know how to be a mother. I'm not very . . . maternal."

I fold a shirt and lay it across her bed. "My guess is that nobody knows how to be a mother until they become one."

"He's going to be so special," she says softly.

"I know."

"Phen will know what to do," she says, like a mantra she's repeating to herself. "He'll know how to protect him."

"I'm sure he will," I say to reassure her, but I have my doubts about Phen. I've seen inside him, and *paternal* is not a word that springs to mind.

I knock on Christian's door. He's sweating when he opens it, wearing a white tank top and sweat pants, a towel slung around his neck. He's surprised to see me. He wishes I'd called first.

"But you're not returning my calls," I say.

His jaw tightens.

"You're still mad at me, and I think that's reasonable, considering. But we need to talk."

He pushes the door open for me, and I move past him into his room. I look immediately in the direction of the TV for Charlie, but he's not here.

"We need to discuss Angela," I say.

He doesn't answer. Involuntarily, it seems, his eyes move to a framed photograph on his dresser, a black-and-white snapshot of a woman swinging a small dark-haired boy up in the air. The picture's a little blurry, since they're both in motion, but the boy is unmistakably Christian, Christian at four or five years old, I'm guessing. Christian and his mom. Together. Happy. They're both laughing. I can almost hear it, looking at them. I can almost feel it. Joy. And it makes me sad to think that he lost her when he was so young. And now Walter, too.

I turn to look at him. He's standing with his arms crossed over his chest, closed off in every way. "You know, if we're going to have a conversation, you're going to have to speak to me. With words, and stuff," I say.

"What do you want me to say? You ditched me, Clara."

"I ditched you?" I repeat incredulously. "That's what you're mad about? You were the one who wanted to leave."

"I don't want to be mad at you about the other thing," he says, not meeting my eyes. "You can't control that."

Sometimes he's so understanding it bugs me.

"But then you disappeared on me," he says, and I hear the hurt in his voice. "You left."

"I'm sorry," I say, and I mean it.

"Where did you go?" he asks. "I came by your dorm later, to apologize for what I said, or maybe for how I said it, anyway, and Angela said you weren't back yet."

I stare up at him, caught.

He closes his eyes and frowns like I am causing him physical pain. "That's what I thought."

I wonder if it'll make him feel any better to know that my conversation with Tucker that night didn't go much better than my conversation with him.

He opens his eyes. "It might."

Good grief. Men.

Moving on. "Okay, as much fun as this is, I didn't come here to talk to you about us," I tell him. "I came to tell you about Angela."

"Has she had the baby?" he asks, concerned. "What is she going to do?"

"She hasn't had the baby," I say. "Yet. But tomorrow she's going to talk to Phen about it."

Christian goes rigid. "She's going to tell him about the baby?"

"Well, she's going to tell him that he's the father. That's her plan, anyway."

"Bad idea," he says, shaking his head like this is the worst idea ever. "She shouldn't be telling anybody about the seventh. Especially not Phen."

"He's not good news," I admit. "He's not . . . happy. But I guess we'll see. Angela is dead-set on this. I'll call you tomorrow after I get back."

His brows draw together. "Wait. You're going with her?"

"She asked me to go. Well, she told me I was going, and so I am."

His mouth twists into a disapproving line. "You should stay out of it."

"It's her purpose. Besides, Phen's already met me, so it's not like I'd be giving anything away, here. I'm going to be there for moral support."

"No way." His green eyes are frosty. "It's too risky. He's an angel. He could figure out what you are."

"He's not evil, technically speaking. . . ."

Christian scoffs. "You heard what your dad said about ambivalent angels. He's worse than the Black Wings, he said. They don't have any allegiance to anybody." He grabs me by the shoulders like he wants to shake some sense into me, but all he says is "We can't go parading ourselves around in front of ambiguous angels."

"Ambivalent," I correct him. "And I was thinking a marching-band uniform and a baton."

"Don't joke about this," he says. "I'm serious."

I try to step back, but he's holding me tightly.

"Don't go," he says. "Be cautious, for once in your life."

"Don't boss me around," I say, shaking him off.

"Don't be an idiot."

"Don't call me names." I head for the door.

"Clara, please," he pleads, his anger dissolving.

I stop.

"All my life . . . well, all my life since my mom died, my uncle warned me about this exact sort of thing. Don't reveal yourself, to anyone. Don't trust anyone."

"Yeah, yeah, don't talk to strange angels." This would not be the best time to tell him about my little chat with Samjeeza this afternoon. And so I don't. "I'm there in her vision, Christian."

"You, of all people, should know that things don't always happen the way they do in the visions," he says.

That's a low blow.

"Clara," he starts in, "I've seen you in my vision, too. What if this is what's going to——?"

I hold up my hand. "I think we've talked enough."

I'm going to be there with Angela tomorrow. Where I'm supposed to be. Two steps behind. No matter how it turns out.

And so it comes to pass that at fifteen minutes to noon, February 13, a day that Angela herself picked to be her destiny, she and I set off from Roble to meet an ambivalent angel. She's dressed up for the occasion, wearing a purple maternity camisole with lace at the hem, fitted jeans with a band around the belly instead of a zipper, a cream knit sweater that brings out the glow in her skin and the blue tint to her black hair. She'd even put on makeup, not her usual heavy eyeliner and dark lips, but a simple coat of mascara and rose-tinted lip balm. It's warm weather for February, and Angela's pink-cheeked and sweating under her layers of clothing, but she moves with a spring in her step that's surprising for a girl in her condition. She looks healthy and vibrant and beautiful.

"I never paid attention to this part," she huffs as we walk. "In the visions, I never thought about how I was feeling—physically, I mean. I can't believe I never noticed this." She gestures to her ballooning belly. "Or how my center of gravity has shifted way down. Or how I have to pee."

"Do you want to stop?" I ask. "Find a bathroom?"

She shakes her head. "I can't be late."

The closer we get to the steps from her vision the lighter she feels, almost bursting into glory she's so excited, her skin definitely glowing, her eyes alight with purpose.

"There he is," she whispers suddenly, clutching at my hand.

There he is. Standing in the courtyard with his back to us, wearing a gray suit just as she described. What guy wears a suit to a meeting with his former girlfriend, I wonder? He's looking at the burghers, whose downcast, mournful faces seem even more in contrast to the bright, sunny day, the flowers blooming all around the courtyard, the sun shining, the birds singing.

Birds. I glance around nervously. I hadn't thought about birds.

Angela hands me her purse. "Here I go," she says.

"I'm right behind you," I promise, and trail her to the bottom of the steps.

She takes her time approaching Phen. The cut of her sweater parts in the middle, exposing her swollen belly, which pushes at the edge of her camisole like she's swallowed a basketball, even though she's not that big. I see her take a quick breath at the last step, and I can't tell if it's her sudden nervousness or my own that I'm feeling now.

She touches his shoulder, and he turns.

It's definitely Phen. She was right on that count.

"Hello," she says breathlessly.

"Hello, Angela," he says, all charming smiles. "It's good to see you." He leans over and gives her a kiss on the mouth. I try not to think about the gray-souled creature that's hiding in that attractive body of his.

"How are you?" she asks, like this is all about him.

"I'm better, for seeing you," he says.

Um, gag me.

"You're a vision," he says. "I could paint you, right now."

Here it comes. Her hands close into fists briefly, then release. "I'm better for seeing you, too," she says, and pulls away from him, gazes down, and pushes the folds of her sweater back, rubbing her hand over her belly. His smile fades as his eyes travel down the length of her body. I swear that even from here I can see the color leave his face. I strain to hear their voices.

"Angela," he gasps. "What happened to you?"

"You happened to me," she says with a smirk in her voice, but then gets serious. "It's yours, Phen."

"Mine," he breathes. "Impossible."

"Ours," she says, and I can't see her face from here, but I think she's smiling that serene, hopeful smile that's so not the normal Angela—so open, so vulnerable. She puts her hand on his shoulder again, rests it there this time, looks up into his shocked dark eyes, and says, clearly, "The seventh is ours."

A chill passes through me. Out of the corner of my eye I think I see the flutter of black wings, but when I look I don't see anything. I turn my attention back to Phen. He reaches out and places his hand on her belly, his eyes still incredulous, and for a few seconds I think it's all going to be okay, like Angela said. He's going to take care of her. He's going to protect them both.

But then the control over his human form slips, and I catch a flash of that gray soul of his. He looks wildly around, like it's not safe to be seen in public with her. His gaze glances off me with only a flicker of recognition. I wouldn't have to be an empath to pick up on the naked fear in his eyes, pure and undiluted. He's terrified.

"Phen, say something," Angela says urgently.

He looks up into her face. "You shouldn't have told me," he murmurs without emotion. "I shouldn't be here."

"Phen," she says, alarmed, her fingers gripping his suit jacket. "I know it's a shock. It was a shock for me too, trust me. But it was supposed to happen, don't you see? This is my vision, my purpose. I've been seeing this moment since I was eight years old. It's you, Phen. We're allowed to be together. We're *supposed* to be together."

"No," he says. "We're not."

"But I love you." Her voice breaks on the word *love*. "My heart's been yours ever since I first saw you in the church. You love me, too. I know you do."

"I can't love you," he says firmly, and she flinches. "I can't protect you, Angela. You should not have told me. You shouldn't tell anyone else."

"Phen," she pleads. She reaches into her pocket to pull out the ultrasound, like a picture of the baby might make him change his mind, but he catches her hand in his and closes her fingers around the paper before she can open it. He gazes up into her eyes, lifts his other hand to her face, his fingers brushing her cheek, and for a split second he looks torn.

Then he disappears. No good-bye. No *Sorry, but you're on your own, honey.* He's just gone.

I rush up the stairs as Angela sinks to her knees.

"It's okay," I'm saying over and over again, like saying it will make it true.

She gazes at me with unshed tears in her eyes. Her hands are shaking when I help her to her feet, but she won't let me support her. She's acutely aware of other students watching us, so she lifts her head and starts to walk in her awkward way back the way we came. I try to put my arm around her, to help take some of the weight, but she shakes me off.

"I'm fine," she says then, in almost a monotone. "Let's go."

Back at Roble she moves around like a zombie, taking her clothes off and dropping them on the floor until she's only wearing her camisole and panties.

Amy comes in, bearing an armload of books. I grab her by the arm and turn her around, push her back out into the hall. "You should come back later," I tell her.

"But I have to——"

"Like maybe tomorrow. Get out."

Amy looks horribly offended. I shut the door and turn to Angela.

Suddenly she laughs as if this whole thing is terribly funny, like Phen has played some hilarious trick on her. She brushes her bangs out of her face, smiles the most awful, heartbroken smile. "Well, that didn't go the way I thought it would."

"Oh, Ange."

"Let's not talk about it. I'm fine."

She gets into bed and pulls the covers up to her chin. Outside, the birds are still singing, the sun is still shining, but inside her I feel everything go dark. I sit at the edge of her bed. I don't say anything, because everything I think of sounds completely stupid.

"We agreed from the beginning that we weren't going to talk about love." She rolls over and puts her back to me, to the wall. "I should have remembered that," she adds, her voice thin, straining with the force of acting like this isn't killing her. "It's fine. I'm fine with it. I understand."

If she says the word *fine* any more, I think my head will explode. I stare at her back, where her shoulders are all tensed up.

"No. It's not fine," I say. "This is his responsibility too. He should be there for you. He should have stepped up."

"He's an angel," she says, already making excuses for him. "It's the same thing as what happened with your dad. I see that now. He can't be with you all the time. He can't protect you. It's the same."

It is so not the same, I think. My dad married my mother. He was there for my birth, my first steps, my first words.

He took care of us, even if it was only for a little while. But I don't say that.

"Ange." I put my hand on her shoulder.

"Don't touch me," she says sharply. "Please . . . I don't want you to read me right now."

She starts to cry. There's no shutting it out. Her humiliation hits me like a punch to the gut. Her embarrassment. Her fear. Her misery. *Of course he doesn't love me,* she thinks. *Of course he doesn't.*

I lie down beside her and put my arms around her, hug her awkwardly from the back as she sobs. Tears run down my face as I feel it with her. For a minute I can't breathe, I can't think—I just hang on.

"It will be okay," I tell her shakily, and I mean it. It hurts her now, but it's better this way, I think. "You're better off without him."

She sits up, pulling away from me, and takes a deep, shuddering breath, then uses the sheet to wipe her eyes. As quickly as she lost it, she collects herself.

"I know," she says. "It'll be fine."

After a while she lies back down. My heart aches for her, but I don't dare reach out again. I listen to her breathing become steadier, deeper, until I think she's fallen asleep. But then she speaks.

"I don't want to be here anymore," she says. "I want to go home."

12

THE RIGHT ROAD LOST

The next day Angela Zerbino officially drops out of Stanford University. Her mom shows up two days later and packs her stuff in boxes, which I help load in the car, and I stand on the sidewalk watching them drive off. Angela rests her head against the window, closes her eyes, and rides away. She doesn't look back.

The visions start coming more often after this, all through February and the beginning of March, at least once or twice a week. I split my time between studying for school and preparing myself, in whatever capacity I can, to go into the dark room and whatever fate awaits me there. I buy a notebook and start to document each vision when I see it, trying to get the details down, but I don't get much other than the shock and the terror, the juxtaposition of dark and light, the silhouette of Christian ablaze with glory, shouting at me, "Get down!" and fighting off the black shapes that mean to kill us, and almost every time now I run up against the moment where I know I should help him, I must draw my own sword and fight my own fight. That's my moment of truth, my purpose, but I never stay in the vision long enough to know how I handle it.

I guess that's still to come.

Things between Christian and me are strained, but we're back to meeting every morning on a path that circles Lake Lag and running up to the Dish, an enormous radio telescope that juts out from the foothills. It's a nice trail, pretty, through small wooded glades and rolling green hills, up to a spot where on clear days we can see all the way to San Francisco Bay. We understand that there is something going on that is larger than us, and we talk, all business at first, about Angela and our visions, but slowly our conversations give way to our thoughts on the freshman scavenger hunt or articles in the Stanford paper, my medicine and his building designs. And things get better between us.

One morning we cross paths with a mountain lion on the trail. It stops and stares at us with wide golden eyes, a deep rumble coming from somewhere inside, a surprise and anger I can feel from ten feet away.

"Go away," I tell it sternly in Angelic, like *Shoo!* and it turns right around and disappears into the high grass.

"How'd you know to do that?" Christian asks me, astonished, laughing, and I tell him how I happened upon a grizzly bear with two cubs once, and all it took was Angelic and a little bit of glory to turn her away. I don't tell him that I was with Tucker when it happened, and that it was the incident that convinced Tucker that I was indeed something supernatural. Which led to our moment in the barn, and the first time we ever kissed.

I like you, Clara, Tucker said. *I really like you. . . . I just wanted you to know. . . . I don't think you want to be with Christian Prescott. . . . He's not your type.*

Oh, and I suppose you're my type, right?

I suppose I am.

I clamp down on the memory, the words and the way he said them, all rough-edged and cocky, reeling me in like a fish on his line. I close myself off so that Christian doesn't look into my head and see Tucker. I put him out of my mind.

"That's amazing," Christian says. "You're an animal whisperer."

I nod, smiling. I can tell by looking at his face that he didn't catch me thinking about Tucker.

It feels like a small victory in the war between me and myself.

* * *

210

In March I go to see my brother. I haven't seen him since that first day back from winter break. I miss him. I stand for five minutes sneaking peeks at him through the window of the pizza place on Castro. He looks unhappy, I decide, watching him move between tables, stack the dirty plates, slide a dishcloth over the tables, and reset the silverware. He hardly seems awake, shuffling from one table to the next, not looking up, just: stack the dishes, put them in a tub, carry the tub back to the kitchen, wipe the table, reset.

I might have sneaked back to Palo Alto right then, content to know where he is and that at least he isn't in the clutches of a Black Wing, when a girl with long dark hair brushes by me on the street and goes into the restaurant, and something about her makes me pause. She says Jeffrey's name, and he looks up at her and smiles—holy crap, really smiles, something I haven't seen him do since the day Mom admitted she was dying.

This must be Lucy, the girl who's stolen my little brother's wounded heart.

Of course now I have to stay and watch them.

She slides into an empty booth in the far corner, puts her back against the wall, and tucks her legs under her like this is her preordained spot. She's pretty, maybe part Asian or Polynesian, with straight black hair that falls down her back in a single shiny sheet, delicate eyebrows, and dark, heavily lined eyes. Jeffrey immediately picks up the pace and finishes the remaining tables. Then he disappears into the kitchen for a minute and returns with a tall dark glass of what looks to be iced tea. She smiles at him. He wipes his hand on his white apron and slides into the booth across from her.

I wish I could hear what they are saying. But I can't, so I make it up.

"Oh, Jeffrey," I say out loud for Lucy as I watch them talk. "You look so strong when you lift those dish tubs. Your muscles are so spectacular."

"Well, thank you, little lady. I do have fantastic muscles."

She reaches across the table and touches his arm. "Can I feel your bicep? Ooh. So manly."

"I also happen to think you're hot. And cool. You're a walking contradiction, baby," I say for him. A man passes behind me on the sidewalk, and I clear my throat and step away from the window. When I look up again, they're holding hands across the table. Jeffrey's laughing, really laughing, his face all flushed, his silver eyes bright.

Aw. She makes him happy. The job might make him miserable, but this girl makes him smile.

He's all right. I should go.

But as luck would have it, right at that very moment a family in the restaurant gets up to leave, and Jeffrey glances over, past them, and those bright eyes spot me before I can duck out of the way. His mouth opens, and then Lucy turns to look at me, too, and through the glass I catch the word *sister*, and the word *annoying*, and he jumps to his feet.

I take off down the sidewalk toward my car.

"Hey, Clara!" Jeffrey calls before I get there. "What are you doing?"

I spin back around. "I wanted to make sure you were okay. You haven't called in months."

He stops a few feet away from me and crosses his arms over his chest like he's cold.

"I keep telling you, I'm fine." Something flickers in his eyes: a decision, albeit a reluctant one. "Do you want to come back with me? I can scrounge you up some free pizza."

"Well, you know I can't say no to free pizza."

"My girlfriend's in there," he tells me as we walk back to the restaurant together.

"She is? I didn't notice," I say with mock innocence.

He rolls his eyes. "Don't humiliate me, okay? No stories about me as a kid. Promise."

"All right," I say, with a little pout. "No stories about how when you were three you pooped on the neighbor's lawn."

"Clara!"

"I'll be good."

He opens the door for me. Lucy is still sitting where she was, her eyes curious. She smiles as we approach the table.

"Luce, this is my sister, Clara," Jeffrey mumbles by means of a formal introduction. "Clara, Luce."

"Hi," I say, and give her a little wave, which makes Jeffrey give me a warning look like I'm already making him look bad.

"Jeffrey's told me a lot about you," Lucy says as I slide into the booth and Jeffrey gets in beside me.

"Good things, I hope."

She raises a perfectly defined eyebrow at me and her smile becomes something sassier. "For the most part," she says.

"Hey, I gotta work," Jeffrey says, and hops up. "Moroccan pizza?" he directs at Lucy.

"You know what I like," she says.

He smiles, all sheepish, and goes off to the kitchen. Then it's just me and the new girlfriend.

"Jeffrey told me you go to Stanford," she says.

"Yep. Guilty as charged."

"That's hard-core," she says. "I never liked school. I was *so* happy when I graduated."

"Graduated?" I'm unable to keep the surprise out of my voice. "When did you graduate?"

"Two years ago," she answers nonchalantly. She shudders. "I was so glad to get out of that hellhole."

That would make her what, twenty?

"So, do you live around here?" I ask, while I ponder how weird it feels that my brother's girlfriend is older than me.

"Yes and no," she says. "My father owns a tattoo parlor on El Camino, and I like to hang out there, and the guys who work there have a pizza thing, so I come by here fairly often."

"Wait, I thought Jeffrey said that your dad owned a club."

"That too." She smiles. "He has his fingers in a lot of pies."

I've never understood that expression. It has always seemed vaguely disgusting to me.

"So there's a tattoo parlor in Mountain View? I don't think I remember that from when I lived here," I say.

"He opened it few years ago," she says. "Business is good. People are more open now to the idea of ink as a way of expressing themselves."

I scan her for tattoos. She's wearing a metallic-silver shirt/dress and black leggings, black boots, dangly silver earrings. No tattoos, though. She does have a very interesting ring, a silver snake with ruby eyes curled around her right index finger. There's something about her that reminds me vaguely of Angela—maybe the eyeliner or the dark nail polish.

Jeffrey returns to the table and sits by her side, scans both of our faces before he asks, "So what were you talking about?"

"I was telling her about my dad's tattoo shop," Lucy says.

He looks at her adoringly. "That place is awesome."

She nudges his shoulder. "Show her what you got."

He shakes his head. "No."

"You got a tattoo?" I say, my voice a little louder than usual.

"Show her," Lucy urges.

He grunts and rolls up the sleeve of his shirt to reveal a line of Sanskrit characters circling his forearm.

"That is so hot," Lucy says, and Jeffrey beams. "It says——"

"'I control my destiny,'" I read off his skin, then close my eyes briefly. Whoops. She's probably going to think it's odd that I can read Sanskrit.

"The words were her idea," Jeffrey says. "I'm saving up for some real art next time."

"Next time?" I'm trying to stay calm here. No high school diploma and a bunch of ink already. Sweet.

"Yeah, I'm thinking a bird on my shoulder, like a hawk or something."

"Maybe a raven," she suggests.

I fake-check my watch. Time to retreat and recoup, figure out how to handle this. "You know, actually, I should go. I have finals coming up, and I have to seriously cram." I slip out of the booth, extend my hand to Lucy. "It was great meeting you."

"Likewise," she says. Her hand in mine is cool and soft, perfectly manicured, and her mind is playful, full of a kind of gleeful mischief. She's enjoying that she's got me off balance.

I pull my hand away. "Walk me to my car?" I ask Jeffrey.

"I really shouldn't——"

"It will take two minutes," I insist.

We make our way down the street in silence until we reach my car. I turn to face him. Stay calm, I tell myself. Keep it cool. Don't freak out on him yet.

He sees the look on my face. "Clara, don't be mad."

"You got a *tattoo*?"

"It's fine."

"God, I hate that word. This is anything but fine. You're going to clubs, getting tattoos, drinking, and hanging out with an older girl."

"She's not that much older," he protests.

"It's illegal!" I am light years away from cool. I close my eyes and rub my forehead, take a breath, open them. "All right, Jeffrey, enough's enough. You should come home now."

"You haven't listened to a thing I've told you, have you?" he says. "I was never home in Wyoming. Never."

I stare at him wordlessly, stung by the idea that home wasn't where we were. Where I was.

"I am home," he says. "Here."

I'm struck by the horrible feeling that I've lost him and that there's no way for me to ever get him back. Not without Mom.

"Did you tell Lucy that you're a . . ." My voice wavers. "T-person?"

His chin lifts. "I told her everything. It's okay. I can trust her."

I start screaming at him again—another epic fail in the keeping-it-cool department. "Didn't you learn anything from Kimber?"

He shakes his head. "Lucy's not like that. She's good with the paranormal stuff. She accepts me for what I am. We even talk about religion sometimes. She's so smart, and she's read all these books . . . if you'd step off with the judgment, you'd see that she's the perfect girl for me."

"So she's where you're getting all this crap about there being no God and—"

"It's not cr—"

"You are such a tool! This is reckless, even for you. You're putting us all in danger. Don't you get that? Don't you understand that people could get hurt, maybe even killed, if you don't keep what you are a secret?"

His eyes blaze in a way that reminds me of Dad.

"You're not my mother," he says.

"Don't you think I know that? Mom would freak—"

"So quit trying to act like her," he jabs at me. "I have to go back."

He turns to go.

"Hey! We are not done talking about this!"

"It's my life," he roars at me. "For the last time, stay the hell out of it!"

He stomps up the street and disappears into the restaurant. I get in the car and slam my hands down on the steering wheel.

I wish for Mom so badly that I can't breathe. My eyes blur.

Nothing in my life is going even remotely right.

Shakily, I reach for my phone. I sigh, and press number two on speed dial.

"It's me," I say when Christian picks up. "I need you."

* * *

He's sitting on the floor, his back against my dorm door, when I arrive. We don't speak until we get inside, but the second the door closes behind us, he puts his arms around me, about a millisecond before I seriously start to cry.

"It's okay," he murmurs against my hair.

Wan Chen makes a throat-clearing noise from where she's sitting at her desk.

"I think I'll go get some dinner," she says, slipping past us without meeting my eyes.

I find a tissue, blow my nose hard. "I'm sorry. I don't know why I'm so emotional. Maybe I'm overreacting just a tad."

"Tell me," he says.

"It's Jeffrey." I start welling up again. But between the sniffles I manage to tell him everything.

"I don't know what to do!" I exclaim. "He won't listen to me, and I have a bad feeling about his girlfriend. Maybe I'm being unfair, judgmental, like he said, but you should have seen the way she had him wrapped around her little finger. 'You know what I like. . . .' Gag me. And she was all super smug like, 'You're in college? Yuck, I hate school.' Where does she get off? And hello, she's like twenty and he's six-freaking-teen. And she's filling his head with nonsense, I can just tell." I finally run out of breath. "I sound like a crazy person, don't I?"

He doesn't smile. "You sound scared."

I slump into my desk chair. "What should I do?"

He goes to the window and looks out, thoughtful. "There's not much you can do. Unless . . ."

I wait, but he doesn't finish the sentence. "Unless what?"

"You could call the police."

"On her?"

"On him. About the fire. You could tip them off to where he works."

I stare at him, dumbfounded.

"He'll get arrested, but it would get him away from her. He'd be safe," he says.

"Safe."

"Safer. He'd have to go back to Jackson. To juvie, maybe, for a while. But it might straighten him out."

"I don't think I could do that to him," I say after a minute. I can't betray him that way. He'd hate me forever. "I can't."

"I know," Christian says. "I was just putting it out there."

Jeffrey doesn't call me after that, but then what did I expect? I think about going back to the pizza place to apologize, but something tells me (namely, Christian tells me) that I would probably end up making things worse. *Let him cool down,* Christian says. *Let you cool down.*

Christian and I are miraculously back to normal, back to deep conversations over coffee, racing each other on our morning jogs, laughing as we thrust and parry at each other in fencing class, everything like it was before our date. Well, almost. There's always this moment at the end of our times hanging out together, as we're saying good-bye, when I know he wants to ask me out again. To try again. To woo me. Because he thinks that's part of his purpose.

But he's decided to let me make the first move, this time. The ball's in my court. And I don't know if I'm ready.

Which brings us to late March, and the end of winter quarter, a few days before we're out for spring break. I'm about to sit down for my lit class final exam, when I get the following text:

Water broke. Do NOT come to the hospital. I'll call you later.

Angela's in labor.

I have a pretty hard time concentrating on my test. I keep thinking about her face when she said, *I don't know how to be a mother,* her face after Phen disappeared and left her standing in the courtyard, the way the fire in her seemed to burn out right before my eyes. When I talk to her lately she always sounds sleepy, and she always says that she's fine, gives me some little detail about how she's preparing for the baby—took a Lamaze class, bought a bassinet, stocked up on diapers—but she's not her fierce and fiery self. She thinks her life is ruined. Her purpose over with, irrelevant. Lost.

I check my phone after I turn in my final, but there's no update.

Is he here yet? I text. I try not to think too much about all that might entail.

She doesn't answer.

About an hour later I'm pacing around my dorm, chewing my fingernails, when Christian knocks on my door.

"Hey, I finished my last final. Do you want to grab some sort of celebratory dinner?" he asks.

"Angela's in labor!" I burst out.

I almost laugh at the aghast look on his face.

"She texted me a few hours ago, and I don't know if it's happened already or not. She told me not to come to the hospital until she called me, but . . ."

"You're going to go anyway, aren't you?"

"I'll stay in the waiting room or something but . . . yeah. I want to go." I put on a coat, because it's March in Wyoming and probably still freezing. "Do you want to come with me?"

"You mean, you'd take us both to Wyoming? You can do that?"

"I don't know. I've never tried to bring anybody along with me before." I hold my hand out to him. "Dad does it, though. Want to try?"

He hesitates.

"The waiting room. Not the delivery room," I emphasize.

"All right." He takes my hand, and my blood positively boils with our shared power and the anticipation I'm feeling. Zapping us should be no trouble at all.

"Okay, give me your other hand." I face him, both of our hands joined. He gasps when I summon the glory around us.

"It's that easy for you, isn't it?"

"Glory? I'm getting better at it. How about you?"

He looks at his feet, gives me a half-embarrassed smile. "It's not that easy. I can do it, but it usually takes me a little while. But I can't cross. That is way beyond me still."

"Well, glory's easier when I'm with you," I say, and am rewarded by his eyes lighting up. "Let's go." I close my eyes, think of my backyard in Jackson, the aspen trees, the sound of our babbling brook. The light around us intensifies, red behind my eyelids. Then fades.

I'm not holding Christian's hand anymore.

I open my eyes.

Tucker's barn.

Gack, maybe it's a good thing I didn't succeed in bringing Christian. I whip out my phone.

Sorry, I text him. *Want to try again? I can come back.*

It's okay. I'll get home the traditional way. See you in a couple days. Say hello to Angela for me.

I look up to see Tucker staring at me from the hayloft.

I'm gone before he has time to form a greeting.

I find Angela in the recovery part of the maternity wing, dressed in a faded blue-and-white hospital gown, staring out the window. The baby's a few feet away in a plastic bassinet on wheels, wrapped up tightly in a blanket so he looks like a little burrito, sleeping, a tiny blue cap on his head that doesn't quite cover his thatch of thick, black hair. WEBSTER

223

says a printed card at the end of the tub. His face is all purple and splotchy, swollen around the eyes. He kind of looks like he was just in a boxing match. And lost.

"He's adorable," I whisper to Angela. "Why didn't you text me?"

"I was busy," she says, and there's a hollow quality to her voice that makes my heart sink, a terrible dullness in her eyes.

I sit down in a chair near the bed. "So it was pretty bad, huh?"

She shrugs, using only one shoulder like she's too tired to use both. "It was humiliating, and terrifying, and it hurt. But I survived. They say I can go home tomorrow. We, I mean. We can go home."

She stares out the window again. It's a nice day, blue sky, fluffy clouds moving past the glass.

"Good," I say, for lack of something better. "Do you need me to—"

"My mom can handle it. She's out getting more supplies right now. She'll help me."

"I'll help you too," I say. "Seriously. I'm all done with finals. I have almost two weeks off." I lean forward and put my hand on hers.

She's feeling such despair that it makes my chest hurt.

"I don't know anything about babies, but I'm here for you, okay?" I gasp against the pain.

She pulls her hand from under mine, but her eyes soften slightly. "Thanks, C."

"I don't think I ever told you how much I admire you for how you're handling all this," I say.

She scoffs. "Which part? For the way I lied to everybody about who the father is? For the way I put all my hopes in a silly vision? For how stupid I was to let it happen in the first place?"

"Um, none of the above. For going through with this, even though you're scared."

Her lips tighten. "I couldn't give him away to some stranger, not ever knowing what would happen to him."

"That's brave, Ange."

She shakes her head. *Maybe not,* she says in my head. *Maybe he would have been safer away from me. With a human family. Maybe he would have been better off. Maybe I'm being selfish.*

The baby starts making a grunting noise, twisting in the blanket he's wrapped in. He opens his eyes, golden like hers, and starts to cry, a thin, reedy-sounding wail. The sound sends a prickle down my spine. I jump to my feet.

"Do you want me to hand him to you?" I ask.

She hesitates. "I'll page the nurse." She presses a button on the frame of her bed.

I go to the side of the bassinet and look in. He's so tiny. I don't think I've ever seen anything so small and new. I've never even held a baby before, other than Jeffrey, I guess, and I don't remember that.

"I don't want to break him," I confess to Angela.

"Me either," she says.

225

But we're saved by Anna, who comes into the room a few steps ahead of the nurse. She sweeps right in and lifts the baby, cooing, holds him to her shoulder, but he doesn't stop crying. She checks his diaper, which is apparently fine. This is clearly a relief to Angela.

"He's hungry," Anna reports.

Angela looks tense. "Again? He just fed like an hour ago."

"Do you want to try to nurse him again?" the nurse asks.

"I guess." She holds out her arms, and Anna gives her the baby; then Angela looks at me like, *Sorry to be rude, but I'm about to flash my breasts here.*

"I'll be . . . out," I say, and duck into the hall. I head down to the gift shop and buy her some yellow flowers in a vase that's in the shape of a baby boot. I'm hoping she'll think it's funny.

When I get back, Anna's holding the baby again, and he's quieted down. Angela is lying with her eyes closed, her breathing shallow. I set the flowers on the windowsill and gesture to Anna that I'm going.

She nods, but walks with me to the door.

"Do you want to hold him?" she whispers.

"No, I'm good to look and not touch. He's beautiful, though," I say, even though that might be a stretch.

She gazes down at him with adoration in her eyes.

"He's a miracle," she says. Her eyes flicker over to Angela. "She is frightened now. It was the same for me. But she'll understand, soon enough. That he's a gift. She'll realize that she's been blessed."

The baby yawns, and she smiles, readjusts the blue cap on his head. I inch toward the door.

"Thank you for being here," she says then. "You're a good friend. Angela is lucky to have someone like you."

"Tell her to call me," I say, unnerved as usual by the steady intensity of Anna's dark, humorless eyes on me. "I'll be around."

When I get in the elevator, I hold the door for a couple with a baby dressed in what looks like a pink jumpsuit with ladybugs embroidered on the feet. They're both—the mother in a wheelchair with the baby in her arms, the father standing behind her—focused entirely on the baby, their bodies turned toward her, their eyes not leaving her tiny face.

"We're taking her home," the father tells me, proudly.

"Congratulations. That's epic."

The orderly who's pushing the wheelchair looks at me all suspicious. The mother doesn't even seem to hear me. The baby, for her part, thinks that the elevator is the most fascinating thing, like, ever. She decides the appropriate reaction to this wonderful magic box that takes you somewhere different from the place that you started in is a sneeze.

A sneeze.

You'd think she'd recited the alphabet, for all the excitement this action stirs up in her parents.

"Oh my goodness," says the mother in a high, soft voice, bending her face close to her baby's. "What was that?"

The baby blinks confusedly. Then sneezes again.

Everybody laughs: the mother, the father, the orderly, and me, for good measure. But I'm watching the way the father puts his hand gently on the back of his wife's shoulder, and how she reaches up briefly to touch his hand, love passing between them as simply as that, and I think, Angela won't get this. She won't leave the hospital this way.

It makes me remember a quote from today's exam. From Dante. *Midway upon the journey of life, I found myself in dark woods, the right road lost.*

I know what he means.

13

A SUNDAY SCHOOL LESSON

"A glory sword is more than a simple weapon," Dad's saying. "I have talked about a sword being an extension of your arm, imagining that it's part of you, but a glory sword is more than a metaphor. The glory *is* part of you; it grows from the light inside you, that energy, that connectedness to the power that governs all life."

We're on the deserted beach again, because he decided that place is less distracting for us to train than my backyard in Jackson. It's dusk. Christian and I are sitting near the waterline, our toes buried in the sand, while Dad gives us a mini lecture on the composition of glory and its many uses.

And here I thought I was on spring break. We've been

training every day since we got back to Jackson. At least today we're hitting the beach.

Dad continues. "There is nothing, not on earth, or in heaven, or even in hell, that can overcome that light. If you believe this, then the glory will shape itself into anything that you need."

"Like a lantern," I say.

"Yes. Or an arrow, as you've also seen. But the most effective form is a sword. It's quick, and powerful, sharper than any two-edged blade, piercing even to the dividing of soul and spirit, and of the joints and marrow, a discerner of the thoughts and intents of the heart."

Now he's gone all poetic on us.

I remember how Jeffrey reacted to the idea of a glory sword. "What about a glory gun?" I ask. "I mean, this is the twenty-first century. Maybe what we should really be trying to shape is a glory semiautomatic."

"Which would require you to create what, a glory stock and barrel, a firing mechanism, glory gunpowder, glory shells and bullets?" Dad questions, his eyes amused.

"Well, it sounds dumb when you put it that way. I guess a sword is good."

Dad makes a face. "I think you'll find the sword more useful than anything else. And tasteful."

"An elegant weapon, for a more civilized age," I joke.

He doesn't get it, but my geekiness makes Christian smile, which counts for something.

"Why?" Christian asks suddenly. "Why would a sword be more useful, I mean?"

"Because the enemy uses a blade as well," Dad says, his eyes serious. "Fashioned from their sorrow."

I sit up straighter. "A sword made of sorrow?" I try not to think about Christian's vision, about the blood on my shirt, about how scared I am, like every minute, that what he's seeing is my death. But I haven't worked up the courage yet to ask Dad for his interpretation of the future.

"Typically it's shorter, more like a dagger. But sharp. Penetrating. And painful. It injures the soul as well as the body. It's difficult to heal," Dad says.

"Well that's . . . great," I manage. "We have a glory sword. They have a sorrow dagger. Yay."

"So you see why it's so important that you learn," he says.

I get up, brush sand off my shorts. "Enough talk," I say. "Let's try it."

About an hour later I drop back down to the sand, panting. Christian is standing next to me with the most beautiful blade of glory in his hand, perfect and shining. I, on the other hand, have made a glory lantern a few times, a glory arrow of sorts (more like a glory javelin, but it'd do the trick in a pinch, I think, which is not *nothing*, I point out), but not a glory sword.

Dad is frowning, big time. "You're not concentrating on the right things," he says. "You must think of the sword as more than something physical that you can hold in your hand.

You must think of it as truth."

"I thought you said it wasn't a metaphor."

"I said it was more than a metaphor. Let's try something else," he suggests. The sun is fully down now, shadows stretching across the ground. "Think of something you know, absolutely, to be true."

I say the first thing that comes to mind. "I know I'm your daughter."

He looks pleased. "Good. Let's start there. Think about the part of you that knows that fact. That feels it, in your gut. Do you feel it?"

I nod. "Yes. I gut-feel it."

"Close your eyes."

I do. He steps up beside me and takes my wrist in his hand, stretches my arm out in front of me. I feel him draw glory around us. Without being asked, I bring my own to meet it, and his glory and my glory combine, his light and mine making something greater, something brighter. Something powerful and good.

"You are my daughter," he says.

"I know."

"But how do you know you're my daughter? Because your mother told you so?"

"No, because . . . because I feel a connection between us that's like . . ." I don't have the right word for it. "Something inside me, like in my blood or whatever."

"Flesh of my flesh," he says. "Blood of my blood."

"Now you're getting weird."

He chuckles. "Focus on that feeling. Believe that simple truth. You are my daughter."

I focus. I believe. I know it to be true.

"Open your eyes," Dad says.

I do, and gasp.

Right before my eyes is a vertical bar of light. It's definitely glory, that light, a rippling mix of golden warmth and cool silver, the sun and moon combined. I can feel its power moving through me. I glance down at my outstretched arm, watch the glory curl around my elbow, down my forearm, to where I'm grasping the light like it has a kind of handle; then I sweep my gaze up the length again, to the tip, and it seems to have an edge to it. A point.

Yep. It's a sword.

I look over at Christian, who grins and gives me a mental thumbs-up. Dad lets go of my wrist and steps back, admiring our handiwork.

"Beautiful, isn't it?" he says.

"Yeah. Now what do I do with it?"

"Whatever you want," he says.

"Do I have to be careful with it? Can I cut myself?"

Dad responds by forming his own glory sword and swinging it at Christian, so fast that he doesn't even have time to move, let alone duck out of the way, before the sword cuts through him. I bite back a scream, sure I'm about to see my best friend cut in half, but the blade passes through like a sunbeam cutting through clouds. Christian stands there totally shocked, his own glory sword abruptly gone from his hand, then looks down at his stomach. A long section of his T-shirt flutters to the ground, cleanly severed. But there's not a scratch on his body.

"Holy . . ." Christian lets out a breath. "You could warn a guy before you attack him like that. I liked that shirt."

"If you were a Triplare," Dad says matter-of-factly, "you'd be dead."

I frown. "He is a Triplare."

"One of theirs, I mean," Dad clarifies. "Those with the dark wings."

"So we can't hurt each other?" I ask. "I mean, if we spar with glory swords, they'll pass through like that?"

"As long as you are aligned with the light, glory will not harm you," Dad answers. "It is part of you, after all."

Christian's chewing on his bottom lip, which is not like him. "My wings aren't all white," he confesses, meeting Dad's eyes. "They have black specks. What does that mean?"

"It happens when a child is born from a white-winged mother and one of the Sorrowful Ones," Dad says thoughtfully. "It's a mark the Black Wings leave to identify their Triplare children."

"But our wings are a reflection of our souls, right?" I ask, confused. "You're saying that Christian's father marked his soul?"

Dad doesn't answer, but his grim look says it all.

Christian looks like he's going to be sick to his stomach.

Time for some stress relief, I think.

I move my arm slowly back and forth, watch the way the light lingers in the air, trailing my movement. It's almost dark now, the sky a deep navy, and the sword against it reminds me of sparklers on the Fourth of July. On an impulse I write my name with it. *C. L. A. R. A.*

"Come on," I say to Christian. "You try."

He recovers himself and focuses until a bright blade appears in his hand, then starts writing his own letters in the air. We start to goof around, turning circles, making patterns, then taking swipes at each other's exposed arms and legs. Just as Dad said, the blades pass right through. The warmth and power of the glory makes me a bit giddy, and I keep laughing as I maneuver the sword. For a minute I forget about the visions. There's nothing that can touch me, with this. Nothing to fear.

"I'm glad you understand now," Dad says, and there's relief in his voice. "Because this is our last session."

Christian and I both drop our arms and look at him, startled. "The last session?" I repeat.

"Of your training," he says.

"Oh." I lift the sword again. My heart is suddenly heavy, and the sword dims in my hand, flickers. "Will we be—will I be seeing you around?"

"Not for a long while," he says.

The sword goes out. I turn to him, stricken, fearful that I haven't been taught enough. I've learned so much in this small amount of time: how to fly better, how to fight, how to cross and transport others, which has already come in handy when I need to get Christian and me to the beach on our own, how to almost instantaneously call glory and shape it, and use it more efficiently for healing. He's also taught us to speak to each other in our minds one-to-one, so that we can talk silently without being heard by anyone else, not even angels, which I'm sure every now and then he regrets doing, when it's clear that Christian and I are talking about him behind his back. It's been harder work than any of my courses at Stanford, but I've loved the training, truth be told, as scared as it makes me feel. It's brought me closer to my dad, more a part of his life. It's made me feel closer to Christian. But I don't feel ready for any kind of Black Wing–Triplare battle. He didn't even teach us to use the actual glory swords until today. "How long?"

He puts his hand on my shoulder. "You've got some trials ahead of you, I'm afraid, and I can't help you. I can't interfere, as much as I'd like to."

That doesn't sound good. "Any more hints you'd like to give me?"

"Follow your vision," he says. "Follow your heart. And I'll be with you again soon."

"But I thought you said not for a long while—"

He smiles almost embarrassedly. "It's a matter of perspective."

He turns to Christian. "As for you, young man, it's been a pleasure getting to know you. You have a fine spirit. Take care of my daughter."

Christian swallows hard. "Yes, sir," he says.

Dad turns back to me. "Now, try again with the sword, on your own this time."

I close my eyes and try again, going through the steps carefully, and it works. The sword fills my hand. Dad draws his own, and we all spend a little more time there, just a little more time, together on the beach, Christian and Dad and I, writing our shining names onto the air.

"I heard about Angela," Wendy says as we walk out of the Teton Theatre in Jackson a few days later. I called her, like I promised, asked her to hang out, and since I picked her up it's been like old times, her and me joking around, shooting the breeze, and I've done an admirable job, I must say, of not showing that I think about Tucker every single time that I see any of his expressions cross her face.

Sometimes it really sucks that they're twins.

"What did you hear?" I ask her.

"That she had a baby."

"Yep, she did, a boy," I say a bit guardedly. I'm protective when it comes to the subject of Angela and her baby. Maybe because I feel like they don't have anybody else to protect them, and there is so much in this world that they might need protecting from, starting with the nasty gossip that's surely going around about them in Jackson. Word here travels fast.

"That's tough," Wendy says.

I nod. Last time I called Angela, I could hear Web wailing the whole time in the background, and she said, "What do you want, Clara?" all monotone, and I said, "I'm calling to see how you are," and she said, "I'm a clueless teen mom whose baby never stops freaking crying. I'm covered in milk and puke and crap, and I haven't had more than two hours of sleep in a week. How do you think I am?" And then she hung up on me.

She obviously hasn't come around to seeing how she's blessed.

"She'll get through it," I say to Wendy. "She's smart. She'll figure it out."

"I never thought she'd be the kind to . . ." Wendy trails off. "Well, you know. She's not exactly the motherly type."

"She has her mom to help her," I say.

We head toward the square, where the antler arches greet us at the four corners. I think about how long ago it feels since I first came here and stood under one of those arches, when my hair started to glow and my mom decided we needed to dye it. Just to get me by until I learned to control it, she'd said, and I'd laughed and said something like, *I'll learn to control my hair?* and it had felt crazy, saying that. Now I can control it. If my hair started to glow at this moment, I'm fairly certain I'd be able to put it out pretty quick, before anybody noticed.

I've grown up, I think.

We walk into the park and take a seat on a bench. In one of the trees over our heads there's a small dark bird staring at us, but I refuse to look closely enough to see if it's a bird or a particularly annoying angel. I haven't been seeing as much of Sam these days, only twice since February, and neither time he spoke to me, although I'm not sure why. I wonder if I offended him, last time. I take a sip of the soda I got for the movie. Sigh.

"It's nice to be back," I say.

"I know," Wendy says. "You haven't talked much about what's going on with you. How's Stanford?"

"Good. Stanford is good."

"Good," she says.

"Stanford is great, actually."

She nods. "And you're going out with Christian Prescott?"

I nearly spit out my soda. "Wendy!"

"What? I'm not allowed to ask you about your love life?"

"What about your love life?" I counter. "You haven't said anything about that."

She smiles. "I'm dating a guy named Daniel; thanks for

239

asking. He's studying business communications, and we were in the same English composition class last fall, and I helped him with some of his papers. He's cute. I like him."

"I bet that's not all you helped him with," I tease.

She doesn't take the bait. "So what's going on with you and Christian?"

I'd rather have my teeth pulled than have this conversation, her staring at me expectantly with her version of Tucker's hazy blue eyes.

"We're friends," I stammer. "I mean, we've been on a date. But . . ."

She quirks an eyebrow at me. "But what? You've always liked him."

"I do like him. He makes me laugh. He's always there for me, whenever I need him. He understands me. He's amazing."

"Sounds like a match made in heaven," she says. "So what's the problem?"

"Nothing. I like him."

"And he likes you?"

My cheeks are getting hot. "Yes."

"Well." She sighs. "It's like my daddy always says. You can lead a horse to water, but you can't make him drink."

I don't know what she means, but I have the distinct feeling that she's getting at something Tucker-related. I laugh like I get it, and look off across the street, where there's a sudden flurry of noise and movement. Some kind of show is being put on. They've blocked off part of the road, and a number of costumed guys are standing in the middle of it, shouting something about how the notorious Jackson gang has robbed a bank in Eagle City.

"What is this?" I ask Wendy.

"You've never seen this before?" she asks incredulously. "Cowboy melodrama. One of the other great things about this town. Where else on earth can you go and witness a good old-fashioned Wild West shoot-out? Come on, let's go have a look."

I follow her across the street toward the action. The cowboy actors are quickly drawing a crowd from the tourists on the boardwalk. I can't hear what they're saying, but I notice that the actors all tote rifles or pistols.

Wendy turns to me. "Fun, right?"

"Consider me entertained." I turn, laughing, pressed in by the people around me, when suddenly I see Tucker farther up the boardwalk, coming out of what appears to be the Ripley's Believe It or Not! museum, another place I've never been to even though I've considered Jackson my home for more than two years. He's smiling with his dimples out, his teeth a flash of white against his tanned face. I can hear the faint sound of his laugh, and I can't help it, it makes me smile to hear it. I love his laugh.

But he's not alone. Another second and Allison Lowell, the girl from the rodeo, the girl who was one of his dates at prom the year I went with Christian, the girl who's had a giant crush on him pretty much her whole life, follows Tucker out of the building, and she's laughing too, her long red hair in a fish-tailed braid over her shoulder, peering up at him exactly the way I know I used to look at him. She puts her hand on his arm, says something else to make him smile. He folds his arm around her hand, like he's escorting her somewhere, always the perfect gentleman.

Shots ring in the air. The crowd laughs as one of the villains staggers around melodramatically, then dies and lies twitching.

I know how he feels.

I should go. They're coming this way, and any second he's going to see me, and there isn't even a word for how awkward that's going to be. I should go. Now. But my feet don't move. I stand like I've been frozen, watching them as they walk along together, their talk easy, familiar, Allison glancing over at him from under her lashes, wearing a western-style shirt with those vees on the shoulders, tight jeans, boots. A Wyoming girl. His type of Wyoming girl, specifically.

I can't stop thinking about how much better she'd be for him than I am.

But I also kind of want to tear her hair out.

They're close now. I can smell her perfume, light and fruity and feminine.

"Uh-oh," I hear Wendy say behind me, noticing them at

last. "We should—" *Get out of here,* she's about to say, but then Tucker glances up.

The smile vanishes from his face. He stops walking.

For all of ten long seconds we stand there, in the middle of the crowd of tourists, staring at each other.

I can't breathe. Oh man. Please don't let me start crying, I think.

Then Wendy pulls on my arm, and my feet magically work again, and I turn and run—oh yes, I'm that dignified—and I'm about three blocks away, around the corner, before I slow down. I wait for Wendy to catch up to me.

"Well," she says breathlessly. "That was exciting."

She's not talking about the gunfight.

We take the long way getting back to my car. When we're both seat-belted in, ready to go, she suddenly reaches and takes the keys out of the ignition.

"So you're still in love with my brother," she says, and when I try to grab the keys, she adds, "Oh no, we're going to talk about this."

Silence. I fight the humiliating urge to cry again.

"It's okay," she says. "Let's get it all out in the open. You still love him."

I bite my lip, then release it. "It doesn't matter. I've moved on, and he's moved on. Clearly he's with Allison now."

Wendy snorts. "Tucker is not in love with Allison Lowell. Don't blow stuff out of proportion."

"But—"

"It's you, Clara. You're the only one, from the first day he saw you. He looks at you exactly the same way my daddy looks at my mom."

"But I'm not good for him," I say miserably. "I have to let him go."

"And how's that working out for you?"

"We're not meant to be," I murmur.

This gets another snort. "That," she says, "is a matter of opinion."

"Oh, so it's your opinion that Tucker and I, that we—"

"I don't know." She shrugs. "But I do know that he loves you. And you love him."

"I'm at Stanford. He's here. You said yourself that long-distance relationships don't work out. You and Jason—"

"I didn't love Jason," she says. "Plus, I didn't know what I was talking about." She sighs heavily. "Okay, so I probably shouldn't be telling you this. I know I shouldn't be telling you this, as a matter of fact. He'd kill me. But Tucker applied to college this year. And he's going, in the fall."

"What? Where?"

"UC Santa Clara. You see, don't you, why this is important?"

I nod, stunned. UC Santa Clara just so happens to be in my part of California.

My heart is in my throat. I try to swallow it down. "You suck."

Wendy puts her hand on mine. "I know. It's my fault, partly. I kind of threw you two together that summer with the boots."

"You really did."

"You're my friend, and I want you to be happy, and he's my brother, and I want him to be happy, too. And I think you could make each other happy, if you'd give it a real chance."

If only it were so simple.

"I think you should talk to him again, that's all," she says.

"Oh yeah? And what should I say?"

"The truth," she says solemnly. "Tell him how you feel."

Fantastic, I think. I'm crying over Tucker. Not very women's lib of me, I know. It goes against everything I believe about myself, all that my mother taught me—that I am strong, that I am capable, that I don't need a man to make me happy—but here I am, all curled up on the couch in the fetal position, an uneaten bowl of microwaved caramel popcorn on the floor by my feet, sobbing into the cushions because all I wanted was to watch a stupid movie to get my mind off things and all Netflix has lined up for me is romantic comedies.

I'm replaying that moment on the boardwalk over and over, Allison Lowell looking up at Tucker, her brown eyes all doe-like and alluring and crap, and how she touched him the way I've touched him. How she smiled.

And he smiled back at her.

But he's also apparently going to college about twenty miles from me. The possibility of that, Tucker nearby, expands into an aching, hopeful, confused mess in my soggy brain.

He might want for us to be together.

I might want for us to be together.

But nothing else has changed, has it? I'm still me, still a T-person, still Little Miss Glowworm, still having creeptastic visions that I might not survive, and if I do survive, I'm still meant for someone else. He's still him, funny, warm, gorgeous, kind, perfectly normal and yet so extraordinary, but when I kiss him too enthusiastically, I make him sick. Because he's human. And I'm not, mostly. When he's eighty, I'll look like I'm thirty. It's not right.

Except Dad told me to follow my heart.

Is this what he meant?

I blow my nose. I wish Angela were here to tell me to take a chill pill already, to kick my butt back to okay again, but that part of our friendship seems long gone. She's not going to be in the mood to discuss boy issues. She'd probably kill for my easy little problems right now. *So you still have a thing for the cowboy,* I can imagine her saying. *Big whoop.*

Which starts a whole new round of tears for me, because not only is my heart all confused and broken again, but I am totally, indisputably alone.

My cell rings. I sniffle and answer.

"Hey, you," Christian says softly.

"Hey."

He hears that something's not quite right with my voice. "Did I wake you?"

I sit up, wiping at my eyes. "No. I was about to watch a movie."

"Do you want some company?" he asks. "I could stop by."

"Sure," I say. "Come over. We could watch zombies."

Zombies would be excellent. I scroll through the menu looking for anything zombie, and I feel moderately less devastated and worn-out.

There's a knock on the door, and I think, Well, that was fast, but then I freeze.

Five syncopated raps.

Tucker's knock.

Crap.

He knocks again. I stand in the hall and contemplate how quietly I can sneak out the back door and fly away. But I don't know if I can fly when I feel this way, and Christian will be here any minute.

"I know you're in there, Carrots," he calls through the door.

Double crap.

I go to the door and open it. I hate that I look like I've been crying, my eyelids puffy, my skin all blotchy. I force myself to meet his gaze.

"What do you want, Tucker?"

"I want to talk to you."

Cue the casual I-could-care-less shrug, which I don't quite pull off in a convincing way. Still, I have to get points for trying. "Nothing to talk about. I'm sorry I interrupted you on your date. This isn't a good time, actually. I'm expecting—"

He puts his hand on the door when I try to close it.

"I saw your face," he says.

He means earlier. I stare at him. "I was surprised, that's all."

He shakes his head. "No. You still love me."

Trust Tucker to just come right out and say it.

"No," I say.

The corner of his mouth lifts. "You are such a bad liar."

I take a few steps back, lift my chin. "You really should go."

"Not going to happen."

"Why do you have to be so pigheaded?" I exclaim, throwing my hands in the air. "Fine." I turn away from the door and let him follow me inside.

He laughs. "Back at you."

"Tucker! I swear!"

He sobers. He takes his hat off and puts it on the hook by the door. "The thing is, I've tried to stop thinking about you. Believe me, I've tried, but every time I think I've got a handle on my heart, you pop up again."

"I will work on that. I will try to stay out of your barn," I promise.

"No," he says. "I don't want you to stay out of my barn."

"This is crazy," I say. "I can't. I'm trying to do—"

"What's right," he fills in. "You're always trying to do what's right. I love that about you." He comes closer, too close now, stares down at me with that familiar heat in his eyes.

Then he says it. "I love you. That's not going away."

My heart flies up like a bird on wings, but I try to clobber it back down. "I can't be with you," I manage.

"Why, because of your purpose? Because God told you so? I want to see that written down somewhere, I want to see it decreed, that you, Clara Gardner, can't love me because you're part angel. Tell me where it says that." He reaches behind him, and to my shock he pulls what looks to be a Bible out of the waistband of his jeans. "Because I want to read you this."

He opens it, thumbs through to find the right passage.

"Whoever does not love does not know God, because God is love. See, right there in black and white."

"Thank you for the Sunday school lesson," I say. "Don't you find it a little silly that you're quoting the Bible to somebody like me, who receives divine instructions straight from the source? Tucker, come on, you know it's more complicated than that."

"No, it's not," he says. "It doesn't have to be. What we have, that's divine. It's beautiful and good and right. I feel it. . . ." He presses his hand to his chest, over his heart. "I feel it all the time. You're in here, part of me. You're what I go to bed thinking about and what I wake up to in the morning."

The tears start to slip down my face. He makes a noise in the back of his throat and crosses the room toward me, but I stumble back.

"Tuck. I can't," I breathe.

"I like it when you call me Tuck," he says, smiling.

"I don't want you to get hurt."

Sudden understanding dawns in his eyes. "That's what this breaking-up business was all about for you, wasn't it? You thought I was going to get hurt. You pushed me away to protect me. You're still pushing." He shakes his head. "Losing you, that's the worst kind of hurt there is."

He reaches out and touches a strand of my hair, tucks it behind my ear, then backs off a little, tries a different approach. "Hey. How about this? You're home for a couple more days, right? I'm home, as usual." I see the news of his college situation rise up in his mind, but for some reason he doesn't tell me about it. "Let's go fishing. Let's climb a mountain. Let's try again."

I've never wanted anything so much.

He sees the uncertainty on my face. "I should have fought for you, Clara, even if I would have had to fight you to fight for you. I should never have let you go."

I close my eyes. I know that any minute now he's going to kiss me, and my resistance is going to melt away completely.

"It wasn't your fault," I whisper. And then, out of self-protection more than anything else, I bring the glory. I don't warn him or anything. I don't damp it down. I bring it. The room fills with light.

"This is what I am," I say, my hair ablaze around my head.

He squints at me. His jaw juts out a little in pure stubbornness. He stands his ground.

"I know," he says.

I take a step toward him, close the space between us, put my glowing hand against his ashen cheek. He starts to tremble. "This is what I am," I say again, and my wings are out now.

His knees wobble, but he fights it. He puts his hand at my waist, turns me, pulls me closer, which surprises me.

"I can accept that," he whispers, and holds his breath, and leans in to kiss me.

His lips brush mine for an instant, and an emotion like victory tears through him, but then he pulls away and glances toward the front door. Groans.

Christian is standing in the doorway.

"Wow," Tucker says, trying to grin. "You really know how to cramp a guy's style."

His legs give out. He falls to his knees.

My light blinks off.

Christian's clutching a DVD copy of *Zombieland* in one hand, the other hand clenched into a fist at his side. His expression is completely shut down.

"I guess I'll come back later," he says. "Or not."

Tucker's still catching his breath on the floor.

I follow Christian to the door. "He just came over. I didn't mean for you to—"

"See that?" he finishes for me. "Great. Thanks for trying to spare my feelings."

"I was trying to prove a point to him."

"Right," he says. "Well, let me know how that turns out."

He turns toward the door, then stops, the muscles in his back tensing. He's about to say something really harsh, I think, something he won't be able to take back.

"Don't," I say.

Dizziness crashes over me. I hear a strange whooshing sound, like wind in my ears, accompanied by the distinct smell of smoke. Christian turns, his face all scrunched up like he's confused by what he sees in my head. He looks suddenly worried.

That's when I pass out.

The black room is filling up with smoke.

I jolt into future Clara in the exact instant that the darkness explodes into light, and in that moment I understand: This light's not glory. It's fire. A fireball streaks over my shoulder and strikes the wall somewhere off to the side, behind me. Then Christian screams, "Get down!" and I drop just in time for him to literally leap over my body, his glory sword out and bright and deadly, blinding me. Everything's a jumble of black-and-white flashing: Christian and the figures circling him, the swift movement of his blade against the dark. I scramble backward until my back hits something solid, glance over my shoulder to see what's happening with the fire.

The flames lick up the side of the room, igniting the velvet curtains like tissue paper. This place is going to be an inferno in about five minutes. My heart's hammering, but I swallow and push myself to my knees, then to my feet. I have to help Christian. I have to fight.

No, he says in my mind. *You've got to find him. Go.*

The high-pitched noise comes again, thin and reedy, frightened. Smoke chokes me, the air in here close and hot and heavy in my lungs, but inexplicably I turn away from Christian and what I think must be the exit and stumble toward the fire, coughing, my eyes watering.

I hit the edge of something hard and wooden right at chest level, hard enough to knock the wind out of me if I had any wind in me to begin with. I figure out what the barrier is at the same time that my eyes finally decide to adjust.

It's a stage.

I look around wildly to confirm what I already know, but it's so crazy obvious I can't believe I never figured this out before. It all falls neatly into place: the slanted floor of the auditorium, the ghosts of white tablecloths along the front, the rows of metal-backed seats. The velvet curtains and the smell of sawdust and paint.

We're in the Pink Garter.

And in that instant, I figure out what the noise is.

It's a baby crying.

"Clara!"

I open my eyes. Somehow I ended up on my living room floor, and I don't quite know how. Two sets of eyes are staring down at me, one blue and one green, both insanely worried.

"What happened?" Tucker asks.

"It was the black room," Christian says, not a question.

"It was the Garter." I struggle to sit up. "I need my phone. Where's my phone?"

Tucker finds it on the coffee table and brings it to me, while Christian helps me over to the couch. I still feel out of breath.

"There's going to be a fire," I tell Christian.

Tucker makes a disbelieving noise. "Oh, great."

I dial Angela's number. It rings and rings, and each second that ticks by where she doesn't pick up makes the sense of dread in my stomach grow stronger. But then, finally, there's a click and a faint hello on the other end.

"Angela!" I say.

"Clara?" She sounds like she's been sleeping.

"I just had my vision again, and the black room is the Garter, Angela, and the noise I hear—do you remember me telling you?—that noise, which is what gives us away, it's a baby. It's got to be Webster. You need to get out. Now."

"Now?" she says, still half-awake. "It's nine o'clock at night. I just got Web to sleep."

"Ange, they're coming." I can't help the frantic squeak in my voice.

"Okay, slow down, C," Angela says. "Who's coming?"

"I don't know. Black Wings."

"Do they know about Web?" she asks, starting to comprehend some of what I'm saying. "Are they coming for him? How would they know?"

"I don't know," I say again.

"Well, what do you know?"

"I know something terrible is going to happen there. You have to leave."

"And go where?" she asks, still not fully getting it. "No. I can't go anywhere tonight."

"But Ange—"

"How long have you been having the vision? Almost a year? There's no need to rush off all panicked and clueless. We'll think it through."

"The vision was different tonight. It was urgent."

Her voice hardens. "Well, sometimes the visions are like that, aren't they? And you think you know what they mean, but you don't." She sighs like she realizes that she's taking her issues out on me, and she's sorry. "I can't go running off in the middle of the night on a whim, C. I have Web to think about now. We need a plan. Come to the Garter in the morning, and we'll talk about your vision, okay? Then I'll decide where to go from there."

There's a high-pitched wail in the background. The sound of it makes the hairs on the back of my neck stand on end.

"Oh, great. You woke him up," she says, annoyed. "I have to go. I'll see you in the morning."

She hangs up on me.

I stare at the phone for a minute.

"What was that all about?" Tucker asks from behind me. "What's going on?"

I meet Christian's eyes, and he knows what I'm thinking. "We can take my truck," he says.

We start moving toward the door. "We'll go over there and I can put my hand on her and try to show her what I see. Maybe she'll be able to receive it. We'll make her understand. Then we'll pack her and the baby up and take them to a hotel." I sling my coat over my shoulder.

"Wait, what?" Tucker follows us out onto the porch. "Hold on, Carrots. Explain this to me. What's happening?"

"We don't have time." I look at Tucker over my shoulder as I'm dashing away, and I say, "I have to go; I'm sorry," and then I climb up into Christian's pickup and we take off, spraying the gravel in the driveway, off to Jackson, and I get the sinking feeling that the trials my dad was telling me about are really about to begin.

14

ABANDON ALL HOPE

Just before we get to town, I get a text from Angela: *trp dr*, it says, and I don't know what that means, but it makes my bad feeling get worse. Then when we arrive at the Garter, we find the front door open a crack. Christian and I both stiffen at the sight. We know that Anna Zerbino keeps this place locked up extra tight in the off hours, ever since an incident last year when a group of drunken tourists broke in and stole a bunch of costumes out of the dressing rooms and went gallivanting in chaps and petticoats all over town. Christian toes the door open enough for us to pass through, and we creep into the front lobby. The room is empty. He takes a moment to inspect the door, but there's nothing to suggest violence. The lock is intact.

I cross the lobby to the red velvet curtain that separates the front of the house from the auditorium and push it aside. The lights are off. The theater is a pit of blackness straight out of my worst fears, and I can't look at it for more than a few seconds before I have to turn away.

Upstairs there's the sound of a muffled voice, a dragging noise like a chair scraping across the floor.

I glance uncertainly at Christian like, *What should we do?*

He gestures with his head toward the back corner, where there's a staircase that goes to the second floor. We take the stairs slowly, careful not to make any noise. At the top we stop and listen. This door is closed, a ribbon of bright light glowing beneath it.

I'm tempted by the ridiculous urge to knock, like maybe if I act normal, things will be normal. I'll knock, and Anna will answer it all serious and ask us what we're doing here at this late hour, but then she'll take us back to Angela's room, and Angela will look up from where she's sprawled on her bed, reading, and she'll say, *Really, you guys? You're really so paranoid that you couldn't wait until morning?*

I could knock, and then there wouldn't be anything evil on the other side of that door.

Christian shakes his head slightly. *What do you feel?* he asks.

I open my mind. The minute I lower my defenses—which I wasn't even aware I had up—sorrow floods me, a deep penetrating pain, so fierce it makes me gasp for air. I lean against the wall and try to delve inside the suffering, to identify its source, but all I get is an image of a woman's body floating facedown in the water, her dark hair spreading out around her head. The angel—oh yes, definitely an angel—is not Samjeeza, that much I know. His sorrow is different from Sam's, angrier, a rage caught up in an agony that's centuries old and still red hot, but it's also more controlled than Sam's, less self-pitying, like he's channeling his emotions into something else: a purpose. A desire to destroy.

There's a Black Wing, I say to Christian silently, careful to keep the words flowing only between us, the way Dad taught us to do. *Grade-A sorrow. That's about all I can get—it overwhelms everything else. What about you? Can you tell what somebody's thinking in there?*

There are at least seven people in that room, he says, closing his eyes. *It's hard to sift through.*

"I told you that you're not welcome here," a voice says suddenly, low and frightened. "I want you to leave."

"Come now, Anna," responds another voice—an older man, from the sound of it, with the slight lilt to his speech that Dad has. "Is that any way to treat an old friend?"

"You were never my friend," Anna says. "You were a mistake. A sin."

"Oh, a sin," he says. "I'm flattered."

"I rebuke you," Anna says. "In the name of Jesus Christ. Begone."

This annoys him. "Oh, don't be so dramatic. This isn't about you."

"Then what is it about?" This from Angela, steady and crazy calm considering there's a Black Wing in her living room. "What do you want?"

"We've come to see the baby," he says.

Christian and I exchange troubled glances. *Where is Webster?*

"My baby?" Angela repeats, almost stupidly. "Why?"

"Penamue would like to see the wee thing, as would I. I'm the grandfather, after all."

Holy crap, I think. Phen's here. And . . . does that mean that the other angel is Angela's father?

"You are nothing to him, Asael," Anna spits out. "Nothing."

At the name *Asael* my brain floods with every piece of information I've gathered about this guy over the past year: the collector, the big bad who would stop at nothing to recruit or destroy all of the Triplare from this world, the brother who usurped Samjeeza as the leader of the Watchers. *Very dangerous,* I can practically hear my father saying. *Without pity. Without hesitation. He takes what he wants, and if he sees you, if he knows what you are, he will take you.* I want to run, that's my instinct—run, run down the stairs and out the door and not look back—but I clench my teeth and stay right where I am.

"He's not here," Angela says, like she's only irritated at this intrusion and not terrified out of her mind. "You could have simply called, Phen, and I would have told you that. You didn't have to make the trip all this way."

Asael laughs. The sound makes my skin crawl. "We could have called," he repeats, amused. "Where is the baby, then, if not here?"

"I gave him away."

"You gave him away? To whom?"

"To a nice couple in a profile I picked at the adoption agency, who desperately wanted a kid. The dad's a musician; the mom's a pastry chef. I liked the idea that he'd always have music and good food."

"Hmm," Asael says thoughtfully. "I believe that Penamue was under the impression that you were going to keep the child. Isn't that right?"

"Yes," answers a voice I wouldn't have recognized as Phen's if I didn't know it was him speaking. He sounds like he has a bad cold. "She told me she was keeping it."

"Him," Angela corrects. "And I changed my mind, after it was clear that you were going to bail on me." She can't keep the bitterness out of her voice. "Look, I'm not the maternal type. I'm nineteen years old. I go to Stanford. I have a life. Being strapped with a kid's the last thing I want. So I gave him to some people who'd take care of him."

I can't see, but I can imagine Angela standing there, that carefully blank expression she gets when she's hiding something, her hip pushed out a bit to one side, her head cocked like she can't believe she's still having this oh-so-boring conversation. "So it looks like you wasted your time," she adds. "And mine."

There's a moment of silence. Then Asael starts to clap, slowly, so loudly I flinch every time his hands strike each other.

"What a performance," he says. "You're quite the actress, my dear."

"Believe me or don't," she says. "It doesn't matter to me."

"Search the apartment," Asael says, an untroubled calm to his voice, like still water on the lake, which doesn't reveal the turmoil under the surface. "Look in all the nooks and crannies. I believe the baby is here, somewhere."

I hear people moving away from us, down the hall, and then the noise of tossing furniture and breaking glass. Anna starts to whisper to herself, soft and desperate, something that I vaguely recognize as the Lord's Prayer.

We should do something, I send to Christian.

He shakes his head again. *We're outnumbered. There are two full angels, Clara, and your dad said we wouldn't be able to beat even one of them in a head-to-head fight. Then add in a few what I am betting are Triplare. We wouldn't stand a chance in there.*

I bite my lip. *But we have to help Angela.*

He shakes his head. *We should figure out where Web is. That's what Angela would want us to do,* he says. I can feel his desire to run away, the way he's been conditioned to in this situation, and I can feel his fear, almost panic at this point, rising in him. He's not afraid for himself. He's afraid for me. He wants to put me in his truck and drive far away from here. He knows if we stay it will all play out like his vision, which ends with me covered in blood, staring up at him with glassy eyes. He can't let that happen.

Now it's my turn to shake my head. *We can't just leave Angela.*

"He's not here. I told you," Angela says.

"You are mine," Asael says in a harder voice, starting to lose patience. The floor creaks under his weight as he takes a step toward her. "You are blood of my blood, flesh of my flesh, and that baby belongs to me as well. The seventh is *mine*. I will have it."

"Him," she corrects again softly.

The others return.

"There's no baby," a woman's voice reports. "But there's a crib in one of the back rooms." Then they start tearing apart the kitchen, dumping out drawers, throwing things on the floor for good measure.

Anna's praying gets louder.

"Enough," Asael says, his voice calm again. "Tell us where he is."

"He's gone," Angela says, her voice wavering. "I sent him away from here."

"Where?" Asael asks again, less patiently. "Where did you send him?"

She doesn't answer.

"Angela," rasps Phen. "Please. Tell him. Just tell him, and he will let you go."

Asael makes an amused sound in the back of his throat. "Oh, Penamue, you really do care for her, don't you? How droll. I would never have imagined, when I sent you to check up on my long-lost daughter in Italy, that you'd lose your little gray heart. But I suppose I understand. I do. She's so young, isn't she? So new, like a tender green sprout pushing up out of the earth."

I get a flash of the floating woman again, him carrying her this time, his face pressed against her white, pulseless neck.

"So," Asael continues, "do as your lover bids you. Tell us where you've taken the baby."

"No."

He sighs. "Very well. I don't enjoy having to employ this particular tactic, but . . . Desmond, hold her mother for a moment?"

Footsteps. Anna stops praying as she's yanked away from Angela. Then she starts up again: "Your kingdom come, your will be done, on earth as it is in heaven. . . ."

"Amen. I do hope He's listening to all this," Asael says. "Now, then, tell me what I want to know, or your mother will die."

I hear Angela's sharp intake of breath. I cast a desperate glance at Christian, my mind whirling. What can we do?

"It's quite the dilemma," Asael says. "Your mother or your son. But consider this: If you tell us where to find the infant, I promise you that he'll be safe from harm. He'll want for nothing. I will raise him as my own child."

"Yeah, well, I'm your child," Angela says. "And that's not working out so great."

He gives a startled laugh at her back talk. "Then be my daughter, as these two lovely girls have been—your sisters, you know. I will give you a room in my house, a place at my table, by my side."

"In hell, you mean," she says.

"Hell's not so bad. We're free there. The angels are kings, and you could be a princess. And you could remain with your child."

"Don't do it," Anna says.

"Come with me, and we'll let your mother go unharmed, for the rest of her life," Asael promises.

"No. Remember what I taught you," Anna murmurs. "Don't worry about me. They can murder my body, but they can never harm my soul."

"Are you so sure about that?" Asael asks. "Olivia, come here, dear. Perhaps we should educate her. This"—he pauses briefly—"is a very special kind of knife. I call it *Dubium Alta*— the great doubt. The blade causes grievous injury, I'm afraid, to both body and soul. If I say the word, my girl Olivia here will cut your soul to ribbons. I think she'll rather enjoy it."

"Lead us not into temptation——"

"Olivia," he prompts.

I don't hear the one called Olivia move, but suddenly Anna gives a long, agonized cry.

"Mom," whispers Angela, as Anna dissolves into ragged sobs.

I taste blood I'm biting my lip so hard. Christian's hand comes down on my arm, tight enough to hurt.

No, he says.

I'll call glory, I say, *and we'll run to them, before they can——*

I feel him going through the possible scenarios, but none of them work, none of them will end the way we want them to, with all of us together and safe. *It's no use,* he says. *They're too fast. Even with surprise on our side, there are too many of them. They're too strong.*

"And deliver us from evil," Anna pants out finally.

"She's a bit like a broken record, isn't she? Olivia, sweetheart . . ."

Anna cries out again.

"Stop," Angela says. "Stop hurting her!" She takes a deep breath. "I will take you to Web—to the baby."

"Excellent," Asael almost purrs.

"No, Angela," Anna pleads weakly, like speaking is almost too much for her.

"You have to promise me that he'll be taken care of, that he'll be safe," Angela says.

"I give you my word," Asael agrees. "Not a hair on his head will be harmed."

"All right. Let's go, then," she says.

Christian starts pulling me down the stairs.

But Asael sighs. "I wish I could believe you, my dear."

"What?" Angela's confused.

"You have no intention of taking us to your son. I hate to think of the wild goose chase you'd lead us on."

"No, I swear—"

"You'll give me what I want," he says almost cheerfully. "Eventually. A few hours in hell and you'll be drawing me a map to the child, I think." His voice hardens. "All right, Olivia. I'm tired of playing games."

"Wait!" Angela says desperately. "I said I would—"

Someone gags—a muffled cough, choking.

"Mom!" Angela's crying, struggling against someone's arms. "Mom! Mom!"

Anna whispers hoarsely, "God help me," and falls heavily to the floor.

I can smell her blood.

God help me.

"Mom," whimpers Angela. "No."

The reality of what's happened breaks over me like a tidal wave. We've waited too long, too afraid to take action. We've let this happen. We've let them kill her.

"Let's go," Asael says.

They move swiftly toward the door, giving Christian only seconds to drag me down the stairs before we're seen. There's not enough time to make it across the lobby and out into the street. He pulls me inside the auditorium, moving us blindly into the dark.

For a few minutes I stand in the blackness, quaking, my eyes going in and out of focus, my stomach cramping, yet at the same time I feel strangely disconnected from my body, like I'm seeing myself from a distance. From a vision, maybe. My vision.

Anna is dead. Angela is being taken to hell. And there's nothing I can do about it.

The group comes down the stairs, Phen first, from the little I can see through the two-inch slit in the velvet curtains, then Angela being flanked by two identically dressed dark-haired girls. I don't see their faces, but something about them strikes me as young, about my own age, maybe even younger. Angela's face as she passes is shocked; tears gleam on her cheeks. She keeps her eyes down. Then a guy I've never seen before saunters by—the one called Desmond, I assume—and finally a man in a black suit who looks enough like Samjeeza that from a distance I doubt I could tell them apart. He raises a hand, and everybody stops in the middle of the lobby.

"You two," he says. "I want you to stay and clean up."

"Clean up?" repeats one of the girls in almost a whine. "But Father—"

"Burn the place," he says.

"But how are we supposed to get back?" asks the other.

"Just take care of it," he says irritably.

Desmond snickers, and one of the girls hits him hard in the chest. He lifts his fist to retaliate, but Asael stops him, laying a hand on his shoulder in a paternal manner, then turns to Angela and grabs her gently at the back of the neck. He smiles. Leans close to her ear. Whispers, "This, my child, is where you must abandon all hope."

They vanish.

The first girl makes a disgusted sound, kicks a booted foot against one of the brass poles that holds up a line of velvet rope. It topples to the floor with a resounding crash. "Why do we always get the crap jobs?"

I expect Phen to disappear too, now that his dirty work is done, but he stays. He comes to the theater entrance and pulls back the curtain, forcing Christian and me to slink even farther into the belly of the auditorium, deeper in shadows, crouching among the seats.

"All the world's a stage," Phen says absently, like he's talking to himself. "And all the men and women merely players."

"What are you talking about?" one of the girls asks him. Their voices are exactly the same, like they're twins or something, although one of them is wearing a bunch of glinting silver bracelets that occasionally jangle together when she moves. From the sound of it they're breaking open the cash register at the refreshments counter and scooping out the change.

"I think Father's done with you," she says to Phen. "You can go back to your little hidey-hole in Rome. Unless you'd give us a ride home? Would you? That would be so sweet of you."

"All the world's a stage," he murmurs, seeming not to hear her. "A stage."

He turns, letting the curtain drop, and we're plunged back into utter darkness.

"Oh, come on," the girl purrs, "we'll make it worth your while."

No answer. He's gone.

"Jerk," Evil Twin One mutters. "Where's the next train station? Like five hundred miles from here, I bet. Dumb hick town."

"You have to admit, though, Phen's sexy," teases Evil Twin Two. "I wouldn't have minded doing him a favor."

"Just because he's in a hot body doesn't mean he's not an old man inside," Evil Twin One retorts.

"That's right; I forgot," says Evil Twin Two, obviously chewing on something, probably candy from under the counter. "You only go for younger guys."

"Shut up. Come on, let's get this over with," Evil Twin One says.

It's quiet for a minute. My heart drums in my ears, hard

and fast. Then I catch the first whiff of smoke in the air.

This is it.

I know how this is going to happen. I've seen it too many times to count. But even so, in the real-life moment, knowing all that I do, I hold on to the hope that they'll just leave now. I hear them jangling toward the door, and I think, They'll leave this time, and then we can get out of this black hole that's got us. I'll run upstairs, and Anna will still be alive, and I'll heal her. We'll find Web. Everything will be okay, somehow.

But then, as always happens, there's the high-pitched cry, muffled and frightened. And I remember.

Web's in here with us. Somewhere in this darkness.

Behind me I feel Christian tense like a coiled spring.

"What's that?" one of the twins says. "Shh. Be quiet."

As if on cue, the crying abruptly stops. The silence in its wake is deafening. I hold my breath.

Then the curtains part, sending a beam of light down the middle of the auditorium.

"Something's in there. Get the light." They scuffle along the wall.

"I can't find the stupid switch."

The first one laughs. "Watch this."

The fireball arcs over my head and strikes the back edge of the left wall, which ignites instantly. I'm blinded by the light.

Christian doesn't wait for them to see us. "Get down!"

he yells, his glory sword like a flare in his hand. I dive for the aisle, which is awkward since it's slanted. I bang my chin hard and then lie flat as Christian leaps over me, bringing his blade down hard on an evil twin's black dagger. The sorrow blade crackles and splits, but the girl has another one in her hand before the first has fully disintegrated. She lunges down at him, swiping at his legs, but he moves aside. The other girl hisses and tries to move in on his flank.

"Who are you?" She darts in, and he easily deflects her blow, shatters her dagger.

"Concerned. Citizen," he gets out between lunges.

They haven't even seen me.

I scramble backward until my back hits a chair. I watch Christian dodge another strike from the second twin, moving faster than I've ever seen him move. Suddenly he veers sideways into the first twin and turns and hurls her into the second one. They stagger but recover quickly, advancing. One hops over a row of seats, then another, attempting to get behind him, but he retreats, keeping them in front of him. They remind me of snakes, I think dazedly, their movements fluid, purposeful, synchronized.

The fire's spread to the heavy curtains at the edge of the stage now, filling the room with thick black smoke that boils in the rafters overhead. The baby starts to cry again, louder this time, angrier. The twins turn toward the sound.

Christian pivots to stand between them and the direction

the cry is coming from. He's amazing with the sword, whirling and cutting, keeping them at bay almost like a dance, so much more than I ever saw in our training together. There's a fierceness in him that's breathtaking to behold. But he's tiring. I can see that, too.

I need to get up, I think. I need to draw my own sword, and help him.

I get my legs under me and shakily rise to my feet.

No, get back, Christian says in my mind. *I'll hold them off. Find the baby.*

Web. My shell-shocked brain struggles to focus. I need to get Web.

I stumble up onto the stage and beyond it, backstage into one of the tiny dressing rooms on the side. There's fabric everywhere, rolls of it lying around, costumes. I paw through them but don't hit anything solid like a baby. I try to listen for the crying, but it's stopped again.

"Web!" I call, even though he obviously can't answer me. "Web, where are you?"

Over to the other side of the stage I go, to another dressing room, but it's empty. The fire is on this side, and I can literally feel its heat growing. There's a snapping sound above me, and one of the lenses from a stage light crashes to the floor, making me scream. It's dark back here, too freaking dark to see anything.

"Cry, Web, cry," I call. I hear Christian shout out in pain

from somewhere above me, near the door to the lobby. I have to do something.

I stagger into the middle of the stage. I don't see the bright arc of Christian's sword or the shadows of the twins anymore. The lobby is completely engulfed in flames. There's not much time left before I won't be able to breathe or see or fight my way out of here.

But I can't leave here without Web.

And then I remember the trapdoor. Angela showed it to us once, when we were bored during Angel Club. It's a space under the stage only big enough for a person to fit, meant for moments in a play when the character should magically disappear.

trp dr

Angela was trying to tell me where he was.

I dash over to the spot and start tearing at the floorboards, then reach deep down into the dark beneath, coughing on account of the growing smoke, and my fingers touch something soft and warm and alive.

I pull out a bundle wrapped in a blanket.

Web.

I don't take time to get reacquainted. I snug his body into my shoulder and turn and head straight for the back door, which lets out into the alley behind the building.

Christian, I think. *I have him. I'm getting out.*

But before I make it three steps, I find my path blocked by the twins.

I take a stumbling step back.

They're my brother's girlfriend. At least, one of them is.

"Lucy," I say, blinking at them in confusion.

"Clara Gardner," says the one with the jangling bracelets, her dark eyes widening in astonishment. "Oh my God." She smiles. "What a coincidence, me stumbling upon you here, of all places. Clara, I'd like to introduce you to my sister, Olivia," she says, like we've bumped into each other at the country club.

She killed Anna, I think. That girl just killed my friend's mother.

"Charmed, I'm sure," says Olivia, although she's clearly not charmed. "Give us the baby," she says. "It's over."

I glance over my shoulder, back at the auditorium. Where is Christian?

"Oh, we took care of your friend, although he did put up a pretty good fight," Lucy says offhandedly. "Now hand us the baby. If you give it to us right now, I promise it'll be quick when I kill you."

My throat closes in despair at the idea that Christian is lying in the dark below us somewhere, dead or dying, his soul laid bare. I clutch Web to my chest. He's being so quiet—too quiet, I think—but I can't worry about that at the moment.

"Give me the baby," Lucy says.

I shake my head.

She sighs like I am really wrecking her day. "I'm going to enjoy gutting you." The black dagger appears in her hand. I

sense a kind of humming noise from it, a vibration that reso-
nates all through me. She steps closer to me. "I just adore
your brother, you know." She laughs. "He's the best boyfriend
I've ever had. So attentive. So sexy. It's going to be terrible
when he finds out his sister died. So tragically too—a fire.
He's going to need so much TLC to get him through it."

She's trying to goad me, I realize dully, but nothing in me
rises to fight her. I don't have long now. Out of the corner
of my eye I see Olivia start to move in on me from the side.
They're backing me to the edge of the stage. Even if I could
fight them, I'd never be able to keep them both at bay. Not
with Web in my arms.

They're closing in for the kill.

I need to summon glory, I think. I don't know if it will
keep them back the way it will for Black Wings, but I need to
try. It's my only shot.

I close my eyes.

I try to empty myself.

Focus.

Every other time I've asked it, truly asked it, the light has
come to me—that day in the forest with my mother, when
I fought Samjeeza; the night of the car accident after prom;
any time I've truly needed it, it's been there like it was waiting for the moment to literally shine. But there's no glory
anywhere inside me right now, or if there is, I can't feel it. I
can't access it.

All I feel is dark. Because I'm going to lose this battle. Christian's seen it.

I am going to die.

No, comes Christian's voice in my mind. *No, you aren't.*

Tears spring to my eyes. *You're not dead,* I say stupidly.

I need you to do what I tell you, exactly when I tell you to. Okay? Okay.

I hear the sound of sirens in the distance.

"Give. Us. The baby." Olivia is close enough now that she could easily stab me. She lifts the dagger.

"Go. To. Hell," I say between clenched teeth. Maybe there is some fire left in me, after all.

Lift Web up over your head! Now! Christian shouts in my mind, and I don't think, I just do as he asks, I lift the baby, and Christian leaps up from the orchestra pit onto the stage, and his glory sword is a blinding spray of light as it passes through me from shoulder to hip. I can feel it slicing through my clothes, but when it touches my skin, there's only warmth.

"No!" someone calls out.

Dazed, I lower Web back to my shoulder, and that's when I see Lucy—the one with the bracelets—standing a few feet away, her face a mask of rage and disbelief, screaming in this ragged, animal-like agony.

And Olivia falls at my feet, dead.

Cut almost in half by Christian's glory sword.

"I will kill you!" Lucy screams, staring at me with bulging, grief-filled eyes, the black dagger clutched in her fist.

But Christian is with me now, beside me, sword in hand, and the sirens are getting closer. Any minute and this place will be crawling with firefighters.

Lucy glances toward the exit. "I swear I will kill you, Clara Gardner." A tear makes its way down her face, dangling on her chin for a few seconds before it drops. "And I'll make sure you suffer first," she says, then turns and runs up the aisle of the theater, bursting through the smoke and flame and out onto the street.

I can hear her sobbing as she runs.

I don't look at Olivia. I can't. I turn away, bile rising in my throat as I realize that I'm covered in her blood, my shirt soaked with it, my shoulders and arms splattered.

I used to think of this place as being so safe, I think. A place for all of us to talk and be ourselves. A magic place.

Now it's burning down around us. It's gone.

Angela is gone.

Slowly I become aware of Christian standing in front of me, panting, pressing his shirt to his ribs.

"Are you okay?" he asks, squeezing my shoulder. "Did I hurt you?"

"No," I answer to both questions, then see that he's bleeding. "You're cut."

"I'll survive," he says. At the same moment, we hear shouted voices in the lobby. "We have to get out of here. Now."

We hurry toward the back exit and into the alley behind the theater. Cool night air hits my skin, my lungs, and I can breathe again.

"We have to fly," Christian says. He unfolds his wings, the black speckles standing out on his white feathers like ink spilled on paper in the dark.

My heart is so heavy with dread and shock, with sadness for Anna, with fear for Angela, with Olivia's death, that I know flight isn't possible. I shake my head at Christian. "I can't."

He looks down at the ground for a minute, thinking, then nods solemnly and retracts his wings. "Okay. We'll circle around and get my truck. It's a better plan, anyway. All right?"

I nod.

"You've got him?" Christian asks.

I gaze down into Web's round little face. He looks up at me with wide amber eyes. Angela's eyes. He coughs. I pull him tighter to me.

"I've got him," I say, and then we're running, running, through the smoky streets of Jackson.

Christian's hand trembles as he puts the keys in the ignition. Then his jaw tightens and the truck rumbles to life and we peel away from the curb. Neither of us says anything for a while, the only sound the gunning of the engine. I want to tell him that he's driving too fast, that the last thing we need is to get pulled over, what with us all bloody and a baby in the front seat, but I don't have the heart. He's doing the best he can.

"Where are we going?" I ask as he turns onto the road that will lead us out of town.

"I don't know," he says. "The girl, the one who I didn't—" He stops talking for a minute and takes a shallow breath, like he's trying not to puke. "She'll probably call for reinforcements. I don't know how long it will take her to get to hell and back."

"Lucy," I murmur.

He glances over at me sharply. "How do you know her name?"

"She's Jeffrey's girlfriend."

If it's possible for his face to go any stonier, it does. "And she knows who you are? She knows your name?"

"Yes."

"Then we can't go home," he says, as if that settles it.

I fight down a wave of panic. "Why? It's hallowed ground; your place and mine both are. It'd be safe there."

He shakes his head. "The hallowed-ground thing works on Black Wings, not Triplare." He takes a deep breath. "We have to go," he says slowly, deliberately, because he knows this is going to upset me. "They'll be hunting you. They'll be after the baby, too. We have to get far away from here."

"But Angela—"

"Angela would want us to keep Web safe," he says.

I know he's right, but there's a finality I feel in this moment, like if we go now, if I leave this place, we'll never come back. We'll always be running. We'll always be scared.

"Clara, please," he says softly. *We'll figure something out. But right now I need you to trust me. I need you safe.*

I swallow, hard, and nod. Christian lowers his head for a second, relieved, then reaches under his seat and pulls out a faded road atlas. He opens it to a map of the United States and lays it across the dashboard.

"Close your eyes and put your finger down on a spot," he says. "And that's where we'll go."

I squeeze my eyes shut and touch my finger to the page.

I wonder if I will ever see Tucker again.

We drive through the night. In the morning we pull over at a rest stop to clean up and then Christian goes into Walmart for some new clothes, a car seat, and baby supplies. He surprises me by unlocking the silver box in the bed of his truck to reveal an escape kit straight out of an action movie: a bunch of documents, birth certificates, fake driver's licenses, something that looks like insurance paperwork, and the biggest pile of cash I've ever seen.

"My uncle," he says by way of explanation. "He could see into the future—not just his own, sometimes, but for others.

He always said someday I'd have to run."

His uncle was a bit extreme. But then, here we are. Running.

I try to fix Web a bottle of formula, but he won't drink it. He takes one good look at me now that it's light and starts crying. Hard. Nothing I do seems to help. I am not his mother. *Where is my mother?* I can practically feel him wondering. *My grandmother? What have you done with them?*

"You should try to get some rest," Christian says after we pull back out onto the highway and Web, lulled by the vibrations of the road, finally goes back to sleep.

There's no possibility of that. Whenever I close my eyes, I'm back in that stairwell listening to somebody kill my friend's mother. I'm in the dark room waiting to be killed myself. I'm watching someone die right in front of me. Instead I reach into my pocket and take out my cell and call Billy for like the tenth time since we fled Jackson.

She doesn't answer, which makes me all kinds of paranoid that somehow Lucy has gotten back to hell by now and rallied some evil army of the undead and has already been to my house looking for me, possibly stumbling over an unsuspecting Billy. I keep imagining it like a scene out of a horror film, where Lucy is standing in front of the answering machine, laughing wickedly as she hears my voice trying to warn Billy.

"Hi, Billy, this is Clara," I say into the phone, my voice cracking on my own name. "Call me. It's important."

"I'm sure she's fine," Christian says after I hang up. "Billy can take care of herself."

I think about the blood. The sound of Olivia's body hitting the stage.

"It's okay, Clara," Christian murmurs. "We're safe."

I turn to look out the window. We're passing a ridge full of wind turbines: tall white windmills, their propellers whirling round and round, cutting the air. The clouds leave shadows as they move between the sun and the earth, like dark creatures roaming the land.

Will we ever be safe again? I wonder.

Christian takes one hand off the wheel and reaches for mine. He rubs his thumb across my knuckles, and it's supposed to comfort me the way it always does. It's supposed to fill me with his strength.

But all I feel is weak.

15

PLAYING HOUSE

The place I pointed to on the map ends up being Lincoln, Nebraska. When we get there, we find a hotel. The clerk at the front desk, a round, kind-looking woman in her late fifties, smiles at us like we're a married couple and leans over the desk to get a peek at Web.

"Oh my, he's a tiny one," she says. "How old?"

"Nine days," I answer, suddenly nervous, and her expression clearly reflects that she thinks nine days is too soon for me to be traveling with a baby, but that's not her business.

"We're visiting the in-laws," Christian says, putting his arm around my waist and pulling me to him like he can't stand for us to be six inches apart. "It's not the best arrangement, staying in a hotel, but what can we do? She doesn't get along with my mother."

How easily he jumps into this role: devoted husband, sleep-deprived father.

"Believe me, I understand," says the lady almost slyly. "We have those rolling port-a-cribs. Do you need one?"

"Yes, thank you. You're a lifesaver," he answers, and I swear she blushes when he turns on that high-wattage smile of his. He keeps his arm around me as we walk out of the lobby, but as we wait for the elevator, his face goes grim again.

We get Web settled in the port-a-crib next to the bed, and he goes right back to sleep. I guess babies sleep a lot at his age. I 411 the number for the pizza place in Mountain View, hoping to talk to Jeffrey, although who knows what I would say to him. How do you break it to your brother that his girlfriend's a homicidal black-winged Triplare and she's just vowed to kill me?

"He's not here," Jake says when I ask for Jeffrey. "It's his day off."

"Well, can you tell him to call me?" I say, and he makes a noncommittal noise and hangs up.

I don't know what else to do.

Christian insists that I take the first shower. I stand under the scalding spray and scrub my skin until it's raw, getting off the last of Olivia's blood. As I stand in front of the steam-wiped mirror combing out my hair, my own face seems to accuse me.

Weak.

You didn't try to save Anna, or to stop them from taking Angela. You didn't even try.

Coward.

You spent all these hours training to use a glory sword, because your father told you that you'd need it, but when the moment came, you couldn't even draw it.

Gutless.

I grip the comb so hard my knuckles turn white. I don't meet my eyes again until my hair is done.

When I open the door, Christian is sitting cross-legged on the single queen bed, staring at the painting on the wall, a picture of a large white bird with long legs and a stripe of red on the top of its head, spreading its wings, its toes touching the water, although I can't be sure whether it's taking off or touching down.

Failure, I think, remembering my inability to so much as conjure my wings at the Garter. Even at something as simple as flying. I've failed.

Christian looks at me. I clear my throat and gesture that it's his turn to use the bathroom. He nods and gets up and brushes past me, his movements stiff and jerky, like his muscles have only now caught up with all the hell he's put them through in the last twenty-four hours.

I sit on the bed and listen to the shower running, to Web's breathing, to the clock ticking on the nightstand, to my own stomach growling. After about five minutes the water stops abruptly, the shower curtain rips aside, hurried foot-steps cross the bathroom floor, running, and then there's the sound of the toilet lid banging and of Christian throwing up. I jump to my feet and go to the door, but I'm afraid to open it. He won't want me to see this. I lay my hand on the smooth painted wood of the door frame and close my eyes as I hear him retch again, then groan.

I knock, lightly.

I'm okay, he says, but he is not okay. I've never felt him less okay.

I'm coming in, I say.

Give me a minute. The toilet flushes.

When I go in exactly sixty seconds later, he's standing at the sink with a towel wrapped around his waist, brushing his teeth. He unwraps a glass from the tray on the counter and fills it with water, takes a swig and swishes it, spits.

His eyes when they meet mine in the mirror are ashamed.

Failure. He feels it, too.

I look away, inadvertently gazing down at his body, and that's when I see the jagged wound in his side.

"It's not as bad as it looks," he says as I gasp. "But I probably shouldn't have showered without tending to it first, because it's opened up again."

It doesn't matter what he says—it's bad, a deep nine-inch gash from the top of his left rib to his hip, black on the edges like the sorrow dagger burned him as it cut.

"We need to get you to a hospital," I say.

He shakes his head. "And say what, exactly? That I was attacked by a pair of evil twins who cut me with a knife made of sadness?" He winces as I make him lean over the counter so I can get a better look. "It will heal. It should have closed already. I normally heal faster than this."

"It's not a normal cut." I look up at him. "Can I try to fix it?"

"I was kind of hoping that you would."

I have him sit on the edge of the counter, and I stand in front of him. My mouth is dry with sudden nerves, and I lick my lips and try to concentrate.

Focus.

Strip away everything, all the thoughts, the feelings, the silent accusations, and burrow down to my core. Forget what's happened. What all I've failed to do. Just be.

Call the glory.

A few minutes later I glance up at Christian apologetically, sweat shining on my forehead. He rests his hand on my shoulder to help, to add his strength to mine, and I try again to bring the light.

Again, I fail.

Web wakes up and starts screaming like somebody poked him.

"I'm sorry," I say to Christian.

"It'll come back to you," he says.

I wish I had his certainty. "We can't leave the wound like

this. This needs professional care."

He shakes his head again. "If you can't fix it with glory, we'll have to do it the old-fashioned way. I'm sure they have a sewing kit around here somewhere."

Now I'm the one who's queasy. "Oh no. You should see a doctor."

"You want to be a doctor, Clara," he says. "How about you start now?"

After the hard stuff is done, he falls into a deep sleep, thanks in part to the little bottle of hotel whiskey he drank before I started sewing him up. I can't help but feel that the world is ending, that this is just the first act of something horrible to come, and I curl up next to him.

I watch Web sleeping in his crib. His breathing seems labored and uneven, and it scares me. I lie on the bed on my stomach with my feet dangling over the side and observe his tiny chest moving up and down, afraid that it will suddenly stop, but it doesn't. He keeps on breathing, and pretty soon, exhausted, I fall asleep.

I'm woken up by my cell phone ringing. For a minute I'm completely disoriented. Where am I? What am I doing here? What's happened? Web starts crying, and Christian mumbles something and swings out of the bed, groans and clutches his side like he forgot he was hurt, but stumbles over to pick Web up.

I find the phone. It's Billy.

"Oh, Billy, I've been so worried. Are you okay?"

"Am *I* okay?" she exclaims. "What happened to *you*?"

I tell her. After I finish, she stays quiet for a few minutes. Then she says, "This is bad, kid. The Garter is all over the news. They're reporting that Anna and Angela Zerbino are dead, the victims of arson."

"Wait," I interrupt. "They think Angela's dead?"

But then I get it. The firemen would have found two bodies in the Garter: Anna and Olivia, and Olivia is nearly the same height and weight as Angela. They're sisters, if Asael is to be believed, and I think he is. It's a natural assumption for the authorities to make. I wonder how long it will take for them to figure out their mistake.

"The congregation is also reporting sightings of several suspicious-looking figures lurking in Jackson and the surrounding area, poking around where they shouldn't be," continues Billy. "Corbett even spotted a couple of them skulking around the house. They're definitely looking for you. Where are you?"

"Nebraska."

"Oh, lord."

"We didn't know where to go, so we picked somewhere random," I say defensively. It might not be the most glamorous place in the world, sure, but it's also not anywhere that anybody would think to look for us.

"Are you all right?" Billy asks. "No one's hurt?"

I look at Christian. He's standing by the window, holding Web flat against his chest and talking to him in a low murmur. He turns and meets my eyes.

"We're alive," I answer. "I think that's pretty good, considering."

"Okay, listen," Billy says. "I want you two to sit tight for a few days. I'll call an emergency meeting of the congregation, and we'll see if we can come up with some kind of plan. Then I'll call you. You good with that?"

"Yeah. Sit tight. We can do that."

"You did the right thing, getting out of here," she says. "I want you to be extremely careful. Don't call anybody else. I mean it. No one. Don't be friendly with anybody. I will feel a whole lot better knowing that I'm the only one who knows where you are. I'll call you as soon as we have a plan of action."

A plan of action sounds so good I want to cry.

"Take care of that baby, kid," she says. "And take care of yourself." She sighs heavily, then adds, "Sometimes he was so annoying."

"Who?" I ask.

"Walter. He said this would happen. Infuriating man always had to be right."

We lie low for a few days. We move to a nicer hotel, one where we have a full kitchen and dining area and living room space, two bedrooms so we can shut the door and watch TV while Web naps. We fall into something of a routine: Web wakes up and starts crying. We play rock, paper, scissors to determine who gets to change his diaper. We attempt to convince him to take a bottle of formula. We try different brands and different types of bottles, but he chokes and sputters and looks generally pissed that Angela is nowhere to be found, and eventually he drinks about two ounces of the stuff. We worry that it's not enough. After he eats, he pukes. He starts crying again. We clean him up. We rock him, talk to him, sing, turn up white noise on the television, ride the elevator up and down, take him for long drives in the truck, jiggle and soothe and plead, but he cries for hours and hours, usually in the middle of the night.

I'm sure the other guests of the hotel are loving us.

At some point he falls asleep again. Then we tiptoe around, clean ourselves up, brush our teeth, chow down whatever leftovers are in the fridge—we memorize the takeout menus of all the local restaurants, which in Nebraska are a lot of steak houses. I change the dressing on Christian's wound, which refuses to heal. I try to call the glory. I fail. We talk about anything but what happened at the Garter that night, even though we both know that's all we can think about. We sit like zombies on the couch watching random shows. And then, too soon, always too soon, Web wakes up and we start the whole thing over.

I'm starting to understand why Angela was cranky.

Still, there are nice moments, too. Funny stuff happens, like once when Web pees on Christian's T-shirt during a diaper change, right smack on the Coldplay logo, and Christian just nods all calm and says, "So what are you saying, Web?" We laugh until our sides hurt over that one, and it's good, laughing. It eases the tension.

On the fourth night, as we're sitting there on the couch after I've spent the past hour pacing around with Web yelling in my ear, Christian reaches over and draws my feet into his lap and starts massaging them. I bite back a laugh, because I'm ticklish, then a groan at how good it feels. It's nice, the feeling that we're with each other in this, that we're partners and we're going to make it through somehow.

"I think I've gone deaf," I say, a running joke between us every time Web suddenly stops crying and falls asleep.

"When did Billy say she'd call, again?" Christian replies, another joke we've been telling often, and I laugh.

But something inside me squirms uncomfortably, because all of this feels like a scene we're acting out of someone else's life with someone else's kid, and all we're doing here is playing house.

Christian's fingers go still against my ankle. He sighs.

"I'm beat." He gets up and crosses to the bedroom where Web is sleeping. "I'll take the first shift. Good night, Clara."

"Good night."

He goes into his room and shuts the door. I flip channels

for a while, but nothing good's on. I turn the TV off. It's early, only nine o'clock, but I wash my face and dress for bed. I check on Web one last time. I lie down.

I dream of Tucker. We're in his boat on Jackson Lake, stretched out on a blanket in the bottom of the boat, tangled up in each other's arms, soaking up the sun. The way things used to be. I'm completely at peace, my eyes closed, almost asleep but not quite. I press my face into Tucker's shoulder and breathe him in. He plays with the short, fine curls at the base of my neck—the baby hair, he calls it. His other hand moves up from my hip to that tender spot below my arm.

"Don't you tickle me," I warn, smiling against his skin.

He laughs like I dared him and drags his fingers over the back of my arm, feather lightly, sending a jolt all down my body. I bite his shoulder playfully, which gets another laugh out of him. I raise my head and gaze into his warm blue eyes. We both try to look serious, and fail.

"I think we should stay here, Carrots," he says. "Forever."

"I totally agree," I murmur, and kiss him. "Forever sounds good."

A shadow passes over us. Tucker and I look up. A bird sails overhead, a huge crow, larger than an eagle, bigger than any other bird I've ever seen. It turns in a slow circle high above us, a blot against the blue sky.

Tucker turns to me with worry in his eyes. "It's only a bird, right?"

I don't answer. Dread moves like ice freezing in my veins as another bird joins the first, circling, weaving through the air above us. Then another joins, and another, until I can't keep track. The air seems colder, like the lake could freeze beneath us. I can feel the birds' eyes on us as they turn, the circle tightening.

"Clara?" Tucker says. His breath comes out in a puff of cloud.

I stare upward, my heart pounding. They're waiting for the right moment to swoop down, to tear into us with their sharp beaks and claws. To rip us apart.

They're waiting.

The way vultures will circle a thing that's dead or dying. That's how they're looking at us.

"Oh, well," says Tucker, shrugging. "We always knew this was too good to last."

The next morning, Christian and I do dishes. We're standing shoulder to shoulder at the sink, me washing, him drying, when he says out of the blue, "There's something I need to tell you."

"Okay," I say warily.

He goes out of the room for a minute, and when he comes back, he's holding a black-and-white composition notebook.

Angela's journal.

"You went back," I say, astonished.

He nods. "Last night. I flew back to the Garter. I found it in a trunk in her bedroom that didn't burn."

"Why?" I gasp. "That was so dangerous! Billy said there are Black Wings there, looking. You could have been——"

Caught. Killed. Taken off to hell. And I would never have known what happened to him.

"I'm sorry," he says. "I didn't want her journal to fall into the wrong hands. I mean, who knows what Angela wrote about us in here? Or about the congregation? And I just wanted to . . . do something. I have so many questions. I thought maybe this would give us some answers. I was up all night reading it."

"So did you find what you were looking for?" I ask softly, not sure whether to be furious at him for taking such a risk or relieved that he came back unharmed.

His mouth twists. "There's a lot of stuff in there. Research. Poems. A detailed account of all Web's soiled diapers. A list of songs Anna sang him to get him to sleep. And Angela's thoughts, how she felt about things. She was tired, and angry, and scared, but she wanted what was best for Web. She was making plans."

And now she won't get to carry any of them out, I think. I don't know exactly where Angela is, not exactly, but I do know something of hell. It's cold and colorless. Bleak. Full of despair. I get a tightness in my chest, imagining Angela in that place, the hopelessness she must feel. The pain.

"And there was a last entry, written down fast," Christian says. "She got a text from Phen that night. He warned her that the Black Wings were coming. She only had a minute to hide Web, but Phen gave her that minute."

So Phen's not all bad, is what he's saying. But somehow that doesn't make me feel much better about him. Because he was the one who got her in this mess to begin with.

"Anyway," Christian says. "I wanted to tell you."

He holds the journal out to me, an offering, but I don't take it. I don't know how I feel about reading her diary now that she's gone. That's her private stuff.

"I'll put it on the nightstand," he says. "If you want to read it."

"No, thanks," I reply, although I'm curious.

We go back to doing dishes, silent now, each of us lost in our own thoughts. Christian's thinking about the journal, something that Angela must have written, something about Web and family. After a while he says, "Do you ever think about that day in the cemetery?"

He means do I ever think about the kiss. Do I ever think about *us*.

I don't think I can handle this conversation. Not right now. "You're the mind reader. You tell me," I joke weakly.

But the truth is, yes, I think about it. When we're walking

together and he naturally takes my hand. When he looks up at me across the table at dinner, laughing at a joke I've told, his green-gold eyes all bright. When we pass each other on the way to the bathroom, his hair wet from the shower, his tank top clinging to him damply, the smell of his shaving gel wafting off him. I think about how easy it would be to accept this life. To be with him.

I think about what it would be like to go into the same room at the end of the night. I do. I think about it. Even if that makes me feel like a bad person, because he's not the only guy I think that way about.

"It's clean," he observes, and gently takes the dish I've been vigorously scrubbing.

"I think about it," he says after a minute.

He's not going to let it go.

"Do you think you would have done it all on your own?" I ask.

He stares at me, surprised at my question. "On my own?"

"Well, kissing me was part of your vision, so you knew what was going to happen. You said, 'You're not going to go,' when I wanted to leave. Because you knew I would stay. You knew you would kiss me, and I would let you."

Something works in his throat. He drops his head, a curl of hair falling into his eyes, and gazes into the sink like there's some mysterious answer to be found in the soapy dishwater.

"Yes, I kissed you in a vision," he says finally. "But it didn't turn out the way I thought it would."

"What do you mean?"

"I thought . . ." I feel his disappointment then, his embarrassment, his wounded pride.

"You thought if we kissed, we'd be together," I say for him.

"Yes. I thought we'd be together." He shrugs. "Not my time, I guess."

He's waiting. He's still waiting. He's given up everything for me. His entire life. His future. Everything, because he wants to keep me safe. Because he believes, in his heart, that he's my purpose and I'm his.

"For the record, it was on my own." He tucks the dish towel into the handle of the refrigerator, then steps closer to me. "I wanted to kiss you," he murmurs. "Me. Not because of some vision I saw. Because of you. Because of what I feel."

The words hang between us for a second, and then he leans in, strokes my cheek with the back of his hand, and kisses me, gently, without pressure. He keeps his lips against mine for a long moment, brushing softly. Heat rises between us. Time slows. I see the future he imagines: always together, always there for each other. We are partners. Best friends. Lovers. We travel the world together. We build a life with each other, minute by minute, hour by hour, day by day. We raise Web as our own, and if trouble comes knocking, we face it. Together.

We belong together.

He pulls away. His eyes search mine, the flecks of gold like sparks, asking me a question.

"I . . . ," I start, but I have no idea how I'm going to answer. I want to say yes, but something's stopping me.

My cell phone starts to ring.

He sighs. "Answer it," he says. "Go on."

I answer the phone.

"All right, kid," Billy says, not even bothering with a greeting. "It's time to come in. Can you be in the meadow by Friday night?"

I look at Christian. Should we go back to Wyoming? It's safe here, where nobody knows where to find us. Web's safe here. We could stay.

"Sure, why not?" he says, too lightly. "What have we got to lose?"

So much, I think then. There is still so very much to lose.

16

CLARA LUX IN OBSCURO

As far as I can tell, every single member of the congregation is gathered around the campfire by the time we arrive in the meadow on Friday night, and when we step into the circle, me cradling Web in my arms, everyone goes quiet.

I've never seen so many worried faces.

"Well," says Stephen, after a minute. Apparently he's the master of ceremonies at tonight's event. "Have a seat, both of you."

Great. No small talk, no *good to see you in one piece*—straight to the interrogation.

People scoot to make room for us at the front of the circle, and we hunker down in the grass. I pull the blanket more tightly around Web, like that will shield him from all the curious stares he's getting. He reaches a tiny hand out in the direction of the fire, his golden eyes reflecting the light.

"Before we open this up for discussion," Corbett Phibbs says, stepping forward, "we'd like to hear what happened, in your own words. That way we'll all be sure to understand."

I let Christian tell it. I struggle to keep my face passive as I listen to him relate the events without embellishment, the way we talked about on the drive over, without getting too much into the gritty details. Christian keeps it simple: We showed up. Asael wanted Angela's baby. He told one of his minions to kill Anna Zerbino, then left, taking Angela, leaving the others to burn the place. We found where Angela had hidden Web, fought our way out of the Garter, and fled. The bare bones of what happened.

After that the congregation peppers us with some questions Christian doesn't know how to answer. "How did Asael know about the baby?" and "How did Angela know to hide the baby before the Black Wings arrived?" and, finally, "How did you fight them off?"

"With a glory sword," Christian replies, which makes them collectively gasp. I guess how to wield a glory sword isn't common knowledge among them. "My uncle taught me."

The first of the lies we plan to tell tonight.

It sucks not being wholly honest with the congregation, but if there's anything that Christian and I have had ingrained in us by our parents, it's that we should never admit to being Triplare. Not to anyone. We don't even want to let on that we know the Triplare exist. That's why Corbett asked us to tell our story this way, so we can spin it the way we need to, without revealing ourselves, or Web. Only Corbett and Billy know the truth.

"So the girl's body they found in the Garter isn't Angela," someone confirms. I locate the source of the voice: Julia. The voice of dissent every time we had a meeting last year. Not my favorite person.

"No. Asael took Angela," Christian answers.

"Why? What would he want with her?" Stephen asks.

"She's his daughter," Christian says. "At least, that's the way he was talking. Like he'd been keeping tabs on her."

My throat closes briefly. Asael had been using Phen to keep tabs on Angela. All that time, all of what she felt for Phen, all that she thought she knew about him, was a lie. He was following orders. He didn't seem to enjoy following them, but that doesn't change the truth. She was a job to him.

If I thought Stephen's expression was serious before, it's apocalyptically serious now.

"I see," he says. "And who is the father of Angela's child?"

"Some guy at school," I reply quickly. Lie number two.

Stephen frowns. "Some guy?"

"His name's Pierce. He lives in our dorm. But it doesn't matter who the father is," I say, my voice louder than usual.

"We need to find Angela. We need to get her back. Web needs her. So I'm really hoping you've got some awesome kind of plan."

Silence. Even Corbett looks uncomfortable for a minute.

"We do have a plan," he says gently. "But it involves the baby, not Angela."

"What do you mean? How can it involve the baby and not Angela?" I hug Web tighter to me.

"We think it might be best if you give the baby to Billy. She's agreed to care for him, guard him, and protect him, perhaps indefinitely. Until there are further developments."

"Further developments?" I exclaim. "What does that mean?"

"Clara," Christian murmurs. "Calm down. They're doing their best."

"What, you don't care?" I challenge. "Angela's one of us. She's been kidnapped. Aren't we even going to try to get her back?"

"It's not that we don't care," Billy says. She's been quiet up to now, sitting behind the fire, stirring the embers with a stick. "It's that we don't have the power to save her. From what you've told us"—her eyes meet mine across the fire, meaning *from what you've told me*—"it sounds like they took her to hell."

I knew that. They took her to hell, and I did nothing to stop them.

I clear my throat. "Well, then, we have to get her out of there."

Corbett shakes his head sadly. "We can't get into hell. Even if we had the ability to move between dimensions, it'd be impossible to find her. Hell is as vast as the earth, or so we believe. You couldn't hope to locate Angela without some kind of guide, some idea of where to go."

"A guide. Like an angel?" I ask.

Corbett scratches at his beard. "A real, full-blooded angel could do it. But none of us here know any of those."

My dad could help us, I think, but he said he was going away for a while. He said I'd have to make it on my own. He said he couldn't help me.

We're going to have to find some other way.

"We think the two of you have been so brave, and faced so much," Billy says as my mind churns with this new information, and the congregation murmurs their agreement. "You did everything you could, and we'll do everything we can to help you now. I volunteered to take Web because I thought it'd take some of the burden off you."

"But what would we do? If we gave Web to you, where would we go?" Christian asks.

Billy nods like she was expecting the question. "We've had some disagreements about that, but the majority of us think that you should remain in hiding. We could funnel you to one of our sister outposts, anywhere in the world." She sighs like the idea totally depresses her.

My hope turns to a leaden ball of dread in the pit of my stomach. "You're saying we can't go back. To our old lives. Ever."

Her smile is sympathetic. "We can't make that decision for you. But yes, that's what I'm saying. The general consensus is that it's not safe for you to go back to California."

So that's it. No more Stanford. No more dreams of becoming a doctor. No more normal life. We're going to be expected to start over.

"I think the baby should stay with us," Christian says. "We're doing fine with him."

"But won't the Black Wings be looking for a couple with a baby?" Julia says from the circle.

Shut up, Julia.

"I don't care," Christian says fiercely. "Web stays with us."

Because we're already a family, he feels. Because we're responsible for him. Because it's the least we can do, for Angela.

There's not much to say after that, and the meeting is adjourned. Billy and Christian and I cross through the tall grass toward the trail that leads back to the truck, a sleeping Web snuggled up against Christian's chest in a baby carrier that someone in the congregation gave us. It's always full summer here no matter what the season outside, and I try to take a moment to enjoy the sweet air, the smell of grass and fresh water and summer wildflowers. The sky, unsullied by clouds. The stars wheeling bright over our heads.

I'm dragging my feet, literally. Something inside me doesn't want to leave this place. It's like I'm waiting for something else to happen.

I stop walking.

"What?" Christian asks. "What's the matter?"

I can't make myself go any farther. I'm crying. All this time, since the night the Garter burned, since everything fell apart, part of me has been numb. Silent. Paralyzed. But now I'm crying buckets.

"Oh, kid," Billy says, enveloping me in her arms, rocking me. "Just breathe. It's going to be all right, you'll see."

I don't see. How can it be all right, if we're going to leave Angela in hell? I pull away and wipe at my eyes, then start bawling all over again. I thought we'd find a solution to our problems here. I thought I'd finally be able to do something about what happened that night at the Garter. To save Angela. But here I am, giving up. Going back into hiding. Running away.

I'm a coward. A failure. Weak.

"Clara," Christian says. "You're the strongest person I know."

"You don't have to shoulder all this by yourself," Billy says. "I'm here for you, kid. And this guy's sure here for you." She jerks her chin at Christian. "We're all on Team Clara, everybody in this meadow, every single one of us in your corner, even Julia." She grimaces, and I stifle a laugh that comes out as a sob. "Sure, things are dark right now. Put us one-on-one against the Black Wings, we're all weak. We're scared. We're easily defeated. But together we're a force to be reckoned with."

I nod, dry my eyes on my shirt, and try to smile. It's not fair of me to expect too much from the congregation. They've tried to help us in every way they could. They even offered to send a couple scouts to look for Jeffrey this week, to warn him, but I didn't think he'd listen to any of them.

"We've got to lean on each other," Billy says, squeezing me.

"Thanks." I shift my weight to lean heavily against her, and she laughs.

"That's my girl. Now come on. Let's get you two on the road." She keeps her arm around me as we walk to the edge of the meadow. "You call me," she says, at the point where we're supposed to say good-bye. "Anytime, day or night. I mean it. I've got your back."

"Wait," I say. I turn to Christian. *I want to join the congregation,* I say, and I don't know why it embarrasses me to tell him, but it does. *Officially, I mean,* I clarify, since it seems like, in some ways, I've been a member of this group all along.

I've been thinking about this for the entire fourteen-hour drive from Nebraska. Longer than that, even. I've thought about becoming a member of the congregation since the first time I came to this meadow. Mom and I had a talk about it. I asked her, "So will I be expected to join the congregation now?" and she smiled and said it was something I would have to decide for myself.

"It's not something to be done lightly," she said. "It's a great commitment, you understand, binding yourself to these people, to this cause, for life."

"Commitment?" I repeated. "Well, when you put it like that, maybe I'll wait."

She laughed. "When the time is right, you'll know," she said.

It feels like the time is right.

Do you mind waiting? I ask Christian.

No, of course not, he says. He understands. He joined the congregation last year, but he doesn't often talk about why.

I did it because I wanted to be part of them, he says. *I know on the outside they might seem like a bickering, badgering, half-dysfunctional family, but underneath all that, they're trying to do the right thing. They're fighting on the side of good, in every way they know how.*

He's remembering the way they came together after his mother was killed. Protected him. Comforted him. Stopped by with meals so he didn't starve while his uncle learned how to cook for a ten-year-old vegetarian. They became his family, too.

I turn to Billy, who's been waiting patiently for me to say

something out loud. "I don't know the rules, if I have to be invited or perform some special task or something, but I want to join the congregation. I want to fight on the side of good." My voice wobbles on the word *fight*, because I can't fight. I've already proven that. But this isn't a fight with glory swords they're talking about. Christian's right—it's family, the only family I have left. I need to do something. I need to stand for something tangible and good, the way my mother did. I need to try. "Can I do that, before I go?"

"You bet," she says, and she takes me to find Stephen. We find him reclining in one of those collapsible camping chairs near his tent, reading a large leather-bound book.

"Clara would like to join us," Billy tells him.

For all of two seconds Stephen thinks she just means I want to join them for roasting marshmallows or something, but then he sees the look on my face. "Ah," he says. "I see. I'll call the others."

Within ten minutes I'm standing in the innermost ring of an outward-spreading circle of angel-bloods, the entire congregation assembled again in the middle of the meadow, and every single one of them is looking right at me. I try not to squirm. Stephen asks me a single question: "Do you promise to serve the light, to fight for the side of good, to love and protect the others who serve alongside you?"

I say I do. In that way it's kind of like a wedding ceremony. The congregation unfurls their wings. I've seen them do this before, with my mother, when they were saying good-bye to her the last time I was here. But now it's me in the center of the circle, and it's night, so when they summon glory around me, it kind of feels like the sun rising in my soul. I haven't felt glory since the Garter, and something releases inside when the light floods me. I feel warm, for the first time in more than a week. I feel safe. I feel loved. Their light fills the meadow, and it's different from the glory I call up in myself, fuller, like the beating heart of every person in the circle is my heart, and their breath is my breath, their voices my voice.

God is with us, they say in Latin, for what I assume is the team motto, their words a swelling hum around me. *Clara lux in obscuro.* Bright light in the darkness.

"I'm thinking about Chicago," Christian says, the day after we get back to Lincoln. He's sitting at the dining table in our hotel, surfing the internet on his laptop.

I look up from where I'm preparing Web's morning bottle. "What are you thinking about it?"

"We should move there," he says. "I've found us the perfect little house."

I promptly lose count of how many spoonfuls of powdered formula I've scooped into the bottle. "Oh. A house." He's looking at houses. For us. Even though I feel lighter after the glory in the meadow the other night, the idea of hiding away

311

with Christian and Web, creating a whole new identity for myself, still doesn't sit right.

But Christian's excited about it. He's making plans.

He sees the freaked-out expression on my face, or maybe he feels it. "Clara, don't worry. We can take this whole thing really slow. One step at a time, with everything. Let's stay here for a couple more weeks, if you want. I know it's hard."

Does he? I wonder. Walter is gone, I think. Christian's an only child. He's not leaving anything behind.

"That's not fair," he says quietly. "I had friends at Stanford. I had a life there, too."

"Stop reading my mind!" I exclaim, then say stiffly, "I have to feed Web," and leave the room.

I'm being childish, I think. It's not Christian's fault we're on the run.

After Web is fed and changed, I slink back into the kitchen. Christian's closed his laptop. He's watching TV. He looks up at me warily.

"Sorry," I say. "I didn't mean to yell."

"It's fine," he says. "We've been cooped up."

"Will you take Web for a while? I need to take a walk. Clear my head."

He nods, and I hand Web over to him.

"Hey, want to hang out, little man?" Christian asks him, and Web coos happily in response.

I beeline it for the door.

It's raining outside, but I don't care. The cool air feels good on my face. I stuff my hands in the pockets of my sweatshirt, pull up my hood to cover my head, and walk to a park a few blocks from the hotel. It's deserted. I sit on one of the swings and turn on my phone.

I have to do this one last thing, which I've been avoiding—hoping, maybe, that everything would work itself out. But it's not working itself out.

I have to call Tucker.

"Oh, Clara, thank God," he says when I say hello. He was sleeping, and I woke him, and his voice is rough-edged. "Are you okay?" he rasps.

I am not okay. Just hearing him brings tears to my eyes, knowing what I'm about to do. "I'm fine," I say. "I'm sorry I didn't call sooner."

"I've been going out of my mind, worrying," he says. "You took off like that, half-cocked and frantic and whatnot, and then the Garter was all over the news. I'm so sorry, Clara. I know Angela was one of your best friends." He lets out a breath. "At least you're safe. I thought you were—I thought you might be—"

Dead. He thought I might be dead.

"Where are you?" he asks. "I can come meet you somewhere. I have to see you."

"No. I can't." Just do it, I tell myself. Get it out before you lose your nerve. "Look, Tucker, I'm calling because I have to make you understand something. There's no future for you and me. I don't even know what my future is, at this point. But I can't be with you." A lone tear makes its way down my face, and I wipe at it impatiently. "I have to let you go."

He gives an aggravated sigh. "It doesn't matter, does it?" he says, his voice laced with anger. "All that I said to you before, about us, about what I feel, it doesn't matter. You're making the choice for both of us."

He's right, but that's just how it has to be. I push on. "I wanted to tell you that wherever I am, whatever happens, I'll always think of you, and the time we spent together, as my happiest time. I'd do it all over again, if I had the choice. No regrets."

He's quiet for a minute. "You're really saying good-bye this time," he says, and I can't tell if he's asking me or simply trying to get his head around the idea.

"I'm really saying good-bye."

"No," he says against my ear. "No. I won't accept that. Clara . . ."

"I'm sorry, Tuck. I have to go," I say, and then I hang up. And cry. And cry.

I sit on that swing for a long time, in the rain, thinking, trying to get a grip on myself. I try to picture Chicago, what it will be like, but all I can conjure in my head is a giant silver bean and a bunch of tall buildings. And Oprah. And the Bears.

I gaze up at the gray, shifting clouds.

Is this my destiny? I ask them. *To be with Christian? To go with him? To protect Web because his mother can't be here?*

Is this my purpose?

The clouds don't have a lot of answers.

For the first time in my life, I wish for a vision. I almost miss having them, which is ironic, I know. Every night lately as I lay me down to fragile sleep, I wonder, will it come? Is this the night when the mysterious scene will play like a movie trailer behind my eyelids and the whole process will begin again: sorting through the fragments, the details, the feelings, trying to understand what they add up to? In that moment before I close my eyes and give in to the darkness of night, to sleep, my body tenses under the sheets. My breath quickens. Waiting.

Hoping that a vision will steal over me, and there will be something God wants me to do. Anything.

Hoping for a direction. A path to walk. A sign.

But the vision doesn't come.

From behind me, bells start to toll the hour from a towering redbrick church a couple blocks away. I count the beats—ten of them—and stand up. I should get back to Christian.

But then, as the last notes from the clock fade away, an idea comes to me, a thunderclap of sudden inspiration.

I could make myself have a vision. Or, at the very least, I could try.

315

I glance around. There's no one else in the park, which makes sense. You'd have to be crazy to go out in this down-pour. I'm alone.

I smile and close my eyes. Focus.

And the glory comes, like it never left me. It comes. Thanks largely to the congregation, I think.

I imagine sunshine. A line of palm trees. A row of red flowers along a path of purple-and-tan checkered stones.

I think of Stanford.

I cross.

The quad is largely deserted as I walk to MemChu. The last few steps I practically run into the church. I can't be gone long, I think. Christian will worry.

It's still early here, and there's only one person walking the labyrinth when I get to the front of the nave: a guy in a red sweatshirt, mumbling quietly to himself as he walks the pattern on the floor. I shuck off my damp shoes, pick up at the entrance of the circle and start walking, slowly, following the turns and twists of the pattern, trying to clear my head of all that's clogging it.

Time to meditate. Briefly I worry that I might start to glow in front of red sweatshirt guy, but he seems lost in his own thoughts and I can't wait.

I walk in circles for a while, not thinking but moving my feet automatically, following the path before me, then stop and check my watch.

I've been here for ten minutes, and I haven't even come close to having the vision.

Maybe this is a pipe dream. I couldn't make myself have a vision before. Why would it work for me now?

"You're not going to get the result you want if you keep looking at your watch," says a voice. I turn. Standing on the opposite side of the circle in the red sweatshirt is Thomas.

Good old Doubting Thomas.

"Thanks," I say wryly. "I bet you're not going to get the result you want if you keep stopping to see how everybody else is doing."

"Sorry. I was just trying to help." His eyebrows come together. "How'd you get all wet?"

"Do you come here often?" I ask instead of trying to explain, since this isn't exactly the place I would have expected to find the guy who could never seem to leave well enough alone in happiness class.

He nods. "Since I finished that class. It helps me get my mind off my crazy life."

His crazy life, I think. How crazy could it be?

"I'm not very good at this," I confess, gesturing to the blue vinyl circle. The morning sun is passing through the stained-glass windows, casting a riot of color onto the patterns under our feet. "I don't know what I'm doing. It's just not happening."

317

"Here." He pulls at something around his neck and comes away with the earbuds for an iPod, which he hands me. "Try this."

I tentatively slip the buds into my ears. He presses play, and I'm flooded with a chorus of male voices singing in Latin. Gregorian chant.

Again, Thomas surprises me. I would have pegged him as a rap aficionado.

"Nice," I say to him.

"I don't know what they're saying, but I like it," he says. "It helps."

I listen.

Panis angelicus fit panis hominum . . . Bread of angels becomes the bread of men . . .

Sometimes it doesn't suck to be able to understand any language on earth.

"So now you walk," Thomas says. "Just walk, and listen, and let your mind empty itself out."

I do what he says. I don't think about what I want. I don't think about Angela or Web or Christian. I walk. The monks chant in my ears, and I hear them like I'm standing among them, and I stop for a moment in the center of the circle, and I close my eyes.

Please, I think. *Please. Show me the way.*

That's when the vision hits me like a Mack truck doing seventy. And I am swept away.

17

TWO MINUTES TO MIDNIGHT

In the vision, I'm waiting for someone. I'm standing next to a long metal bench—standing because I'm too nervous to sit down. I take a few steps in one direction. Stop. Walk back the other way. Look around. Check my watch.

Two minutes to midnight.

A cloud drifts in front of the moon, which is full, circled by a hazy grayish ring. I pull my jacket tighter to me even though I'm not cold. My head is full of fear, my chest tight with it, my heart beating fast. This is crazy, I think. Foolhardy, my mother would call it. Insane. But here I am, anyway.

Sanity is overrated.

Behind me something hisses, loud and mechanical, and I turn to look. There's a train, a sleek, silver line of cars stretched along the tracks. It rolls slowly toward me.

Maybe I'm supposed to go somewhere.

The train passes, clacking in a heavy rhythm like my heart. The brakes squeal as it glides to a stop, and the passenger doors slide open. I take a step forward and then look down the empty platform. After a moment the doors close, the engine rumbles, and the train continues on, shaking the earth with its weight, screeching and clacking until the last car passes. It rolls away into the darkness without me.

I check my watch. One minute to midnight.

When I look up again, I see a bird swoop down from the roof of the train depot, dark as a shadow. It lands on a lamppost across the tracks, swivels its head toward me, caws. It's a crow. My heart starts to beat even faster.

"Caw," says the crow, testing me, taunting me, calling me to join him across the tracks.

I start walking to him, and I don't look back.

Because I know this bird.

He's going to be my guide.

I spiral back to myself at the church. I'm stopped in the center of the circle, my face uplifted, the monks singing, singing, singing, their voices gone dark.

"Looks like it worked," Thomas says, smiling, as I hand him back his iPod with shaky hands.

"Are you okay?"

I nod. "I have to go now."

Boy, do I ever have to go now.

I walk to the Oval and sit down under the tree where I always study. I think Samjeeza's name, over and over again, summoning him the only way I know how, hoping that he hasn't given up his creepy stalking now when I'm really counting on him. And I wait.

I feel his presence before I see him. He steps out of the trees at the edge of campus, his amber eyes bewildered but curious.

"You called me," he says.

"Yes, I did." Although I'm as surprised as he is that it worked.

"I didn't expect to see you here again," he says. "You're in some trouble with Big Brother."

So he already knows. Of course he does. I'm sure gossip really gets around in hell. "You could say that. Anyway. I'm ready to tell you a story," I say. "But I want something in return."

He smiles, surprised and pleased and even more curious now. He opens his arms, palms up, and steps back in the semblance of a formal bow.

This guy is cheese to the core.

"What can I do for you, little bird?" he says.

This is it. Don't chicken out now, I tell myself. I meet his eyes.

"The Black Wings took my friend Angela. Do you know where she is?"

"Yes. Asael has her."

"In hell?"

"Naturally."

I swallow. "Have you seen her?"

He nods.

"Is she all right?"

There's a cruel twist to his mouth. "No one is all right in that place."

"Is she . . . alive?"

"Physically speaking, yes, her heart was beating the last I saw her."

"And when was that?" I ask.

He finds the question funny. "Some time ago," he answers with a laugh.

I bite my lip. This is the insane part: Telling him my impromptu plan. Putting it all out there. Letting the chips fall where they may. The wind picks up and sends the trees into a furtive whispering, like a warning. *Don't trust him,* they say.

But I trust the vision, and the vision tells me that I trust him.

Samjeeza's getting impatient. "I told you what I know about your friend. Now tell me the story."

"Not yet. I need something else." I take a deep breath.

Be brave, my darling, my mother told me once. *You're stronger than you think.* I can be brave, I tell myself.

"I need you to take me to Angela," I say then. "In hell."

He lets out a disbelieving laugh. "Whatever for?"

"So I can get her out."

His eyes widen. "You're serious."

"Serious as a heart attack," I say, which is appropriate, because I feel like I'm about to have one.

"Impossible," he says, although his eyes take on an excited gleam.

"Why is it impossible?" I ask, crossing my arms over my chest. "Don't you have the power to do it? You took me there before."

I'm provoking him, and he knows it. Still, he smiles. "I could take you there easily enough. Getting you out would be infinitely more difficult. Chances are you'd lose yourself within a few moments and become as trapped as your friend."

"I'm strong," I tell him. "You've said so yourself."

"Yes, and why is that?" he asks. "Why are you so strong, little Quartarius?"

I smile vaguely.

"You'd be waltzing in right under Asael's nose and taking something that belongs to him," he says, like the idea is not altogether an unpleasant one. He's none too fond of Asael. Which works for me.

"Yes. Will you help me?"

"All that for a mere story? Do you take me for a fool?"

"Then I guess this is a pointless conversation." I shrug and stand up, brush grass off my jeans. "Oh well, it was worth a shot."

"Wait," he says, all the humor gone from his voice now. "I haven't said no, exactly."

Hope and terror bloom simultaneously in my chest. "Then you'll take me?"

He hesitates. "It's very dangerous, for both of us, but especially for you. The likelihood that you will be caught—"

"Please," I say. "I have to try."

He shakes his head. "You don't understand the nature of hell. It will swallow you up. Unless . . ." He starts to pace. He has an idea, something good—I can tell by the way he stands up straighter, by the diabolical bounce in his step. I wait for him to tell me.

"All right," he says at last. "If you cannot be talked out of it, I will take you."

"How soon can we go?" I ask.

"Tonight. That will give you enough time to reconsider." He leans toward me. "This is a futile endeavor, little bird, no matter how strong you think you are."

"When should I meet you? Where?" I ask.

"Where's the nearest train station?"

"A few blocks from here. Palo Alto."

"Meet me at the train station in Palo Alto, then," he says. "Midnight."

I'm light-headed. I already knew the time and place, from the vision, but hearing him say it, knowing for sure that's what the vision is about, shocks me. That and that he's ready to take me so soon. Like, tonight. Tonight I am going to hell.

"Having second thoughts already?" he asks with the hint of a smile.

"No. I'll be there."

"Wear black or gray, nothing conspicuous or flashy, and cover your hair," he says. "Also, you must bring a friend, another of the Nephilim, or I can't take you."

He turns like he's going to walk away.

"A friend? You can't be serious," I gasp.

"If you're going to succeed on this little excursion, you'll need someone to ground you. Someone to help you keep back the sorrows of the damned. Otherwise your gift of feeling what others feel will drown you. You won't last two minutes."

"All right," I say hoarsely.

He turns into a bird. My eye's not quick enough to see the transition, but one second he's a man, the next a crow. He squawks at me.

Midnight, he says in my mind, his voice like a splash of cold water. *And don't forget, you owe me a story.*

I won't forget.

Christian's more than a little surprised when I cross straight into our hotel room and tell him we need to take Web to Billy after all. I'll fill him in later. "Trust me," I say, and his jaw tightens, but he doesn't argue when I go around gathering up Web's supplies and take us to Billy's house in the mountains, where she is obviously expecting us.

He thinks I'm freaking out over the whole motherhood thing. That I don't want to be responsible for Web. He's disappointed, because he thought we could handle it, but he understands.

Or at least he thinks he does.

It kills me to hand Web over to Billy, but I try to smile when I do it. He'll be safer with Billy, I remind myself. But he's uncertain in her arms, whimpering, and my heart squeezes painfully at the way he keeps looking at me.

"It's okay, little dude. Auntie Billy's going to take good care of you," I say, and go over all his stuff one last time, what kind of formula he takes and which one makes him puke like *The Exorcist*, which blanket to swaddle him in at night, which pacifier is his favorite, the vital importance of his stuffed monkey.

"I got it, kid," Billy says, patting my arm. She's feeling emotional, too. Deep down she's always wanted a child. She would have had one with Walter, if she could have. But she herself only has seven more years to live.

"I'll call tonight and sing him a song," I promise, and only barely get out of there without bursting into tears.

And that entire time, Christian stands beside me, waiting for me to tell him what's up.

He's crazy surprised when I cross us to the study room in the Roble basement and not back to Lincoln.

"All right, Clara," he says, trying to hide his alarm. "Where are we? What's going on?"

I tell him.

He has the following reaction:

"You did *what?*"

Yeah, he's a little upset. Understandably.

"I agreed to meet Samjeeza at the Palo Alto train station, at midnight," I say again.

"How could you do that?" He tugs his hands through his hair. "Do you have a death wish?"

"No," I reply coolly. "I have a vision, and it's telling me that I'm going to go meet him."

"You're talking about taking a train ride into hell."

"I know."

He starts shaking his head. "No. No way. No."

"I'll show you," I say, refusing to take no for an answer. "Come on."

Without another word I head off, up the stairs, out of Roble, walking fast across campus, and he doesn't have much of a choice but to follow. He hasn't learned to cross yet—for as amazing as he is with flying and glory swords, I am still light years ahead of him when it comes to calling and using glory. He can't get back without me.

When he sees the church, he suddenly gets where I'm

going, and he doesn't want to come. I take his hand and start pulling him across the quad. We reach the doors of MemChu. I turn to him. "Just go inside with me. Walk the labyrinth. See if you don't have a vision there, too. I'll bet you ten bucks you see a train station."

Uncertainty flashes in his eyes. He's tempted.

"Last time I went in there, I came out thinking you were going to die," he says hoarsely.

"But I didn't. And you did what you were supposed to do. You saved me. You saved Web."

"I killed a person," he whispers.

"I know. But this is what we're supposed to do now. Don't you see? It's our purpose. Maybe all of it, all along, has been about this. Rescuing Angela. Getting her out of hell." I feel like somebody's lit a fire under me. I can hardly stand still, I'm so full of anticipation.

Christian's brow rumples. "All along?" he asks. "What do you mean?"

"What if Angela was always supposed to have Web? I mean, Asael sent Phen to find her, and maybe they were meant to fall for each other, and she was meant to get pregnant. With the seventh—God's perfect number."

"What does that have to do with us?"

"So I had my first vision, which told me that I had to move to Wyoming. So I did. And met you, and Angela. And then I had my second vision—and this one's a stumper, because I never could understand why I kept seeing the cemetery, why God wanted me to know about that moment in advance, but now I think I was being shown two things that I would need to know. I was being shown that Samjeeza was there, so I knew he would be there that day when I went to give him my mother's bracelet. I chose to be kind to him, which changed the way he felt about me. Which is why he's been watching me, talking to me, and why I could go to him and ask for this."

"What's the second thing?" Christian asks.

"You. My cemetery vision showed me that you make me stronger. You and me together, we can get through anything. We can be each other's anchor. We can be each other's strength."

"You sound exactly like Angela right now, you realize?" he says.

I laugh and keep on talking. "And the third vision showed me what happened to her. If I hadn't had that vision, I would never have known that we had to go out to the Pink Garter that night. Angela would have just disappeared, and the twins would have burned down the theater, and Web probably would have died, or they'd have taken him, too. I was meant to be there, Christian. And now I'm meant to go get her."

"Clara, I don't know," he says doubtfully.

"It's not all about me," I say. "It's about Angela. This entire time, it's been about her. Come on." I start tugging him into the welcoming coolness of the church. "Walk the labyrinth one more time, with me."

Ten minutes later we're both sitting in the front pew of the church, catching our breath. There's no one else in the church, but when we talk, I get a sense that all the mosaic angels are listening.

"I saw it again," I say to Christian, quietly, triumphantly. "Two minutes to midnight. The train even has the Caltrain logo on it. One comes in, headed north, and then a few minutes later another, headed south. That's the one we're going to take."

"I didn't see it," he says, his face whiter than normal.

Some of my excitement fades. "You didn't see the train?"

He shakes his head. "I saw Asael," he murmurs.

My breath freezes in my lungs. "You saw him."

"I saw his face. He was talking to me. I don't know what he was saying, but he was less than ten feet away from me."

That's not good news. I mull this over for a minute. "But I see the train so clearly. And I'm waiting for you. I keep looking at my watch. I'm waiting for you to show up."

"What if I don't show up?" he says. "You can't go, then. Samjeeza won't take you without me, right?"

"But Christian, we have to go. It might be Angela's only chance."

"Angela's gone," he says. "She might not be dead, but she's gone where the dead go."

I stand up. "When did you turn into such a coward?"

He gets up, too. There's a vein standing out on his neck that I've never seen before. "It's not cowardly to not want to do something crazy."

"Yes, this is crazy," I admit. "I know that. Even in the vision pretty much all I'm thinking is, This is crazy. This is crazy. But I still do it."

"We don't have to do this, just because you see it," he counters. "You and I both know that the visions never turn out quite how we expect them to."

"I can't leave Angela in hell," I say, gazing up at him. "I won't."

"We'll figure out another way."

"What other way?"

"Maybe the congregation—"

"The congregation already said that they can't help us."

"We could ask your dad."

I shake my head. "You remember what he said, don't you? He said I had to be ready to face—whatever—without him. Helping me is not part of the plan."

He stares up at the angels angrily. "Then what is he good for? What was all of that, the training, the talks, all of it, what good did it do us?" He sighs. "I thought we were partners," he says softly. "I thought we'd decide things together. And here you go making deals with fallen angels without even telling me."

I kneel down beside him. "You're right. I should have

talked to you first. We are partners. I'm counting on it, actually. I need you."

"Because Samjeeza said you needed to bring a friend."

"Because I can't do this without you. I need our strength, Christian."

He looks cornered. This is his worst nightmare come to life, I realize. "And what do you think will happen if we make it, if we get Angela out of there? You think they'll stand idly by? They'll come after us with a vengeance after that."

I hadn't given much thought to what would happen after we got out. I was too busy imagining Angela's grateful tears, the joyous hugs, the "woo-hoo, we're out of hell" feeling.

But he's right. They will come after us. We won't be able to go back to a normal life then, either. It won't change our fate, not that way. It can only make things worse.

Christian sees the realization on my face. "We're here, Clara. We're safe, at least for the moment."

I bite my lip. "But Angela's in hell."

His eyes are sad, resigned. "You can't save everybody, Clara. Some things are beyond our ability to change."

Like Jeffrey. Or my mom dying. Or being with Tucker.

"No," I whisper. "What about the vision?"

He gives a bitter little laugh. "When did you become so faithful all of a sudden?"

It hurts, him saying that, but I'll take it. And what I realize in this moment is that it's his fate, too. It's his choice. I can't make it for him.

"I understand if you don't want to do it," I say then. On impulse I reach up and hook my hand behind his neck, draw myself into his arms for a hug. I let his warmth infuse me, and mine pour back into him.

When I pull away, his eyes are shining.

"If I don't go, you can't either," he says. "He won't take you."

Oh, Christian, I think. Always trying to keep me out of trouble.

"I'll see you at midnight at the train station," I say. "Or I won't. But I really hope I will."

I kiss his cheek, and then leave him alone with the stained-glass angels.

Later I review my mental before-you-go-to-hell checklist: Make sure Web is somewhere safe—check. Tell Christian your plan, hope he doesn't freak out too much—sort of check. And now I have to try to find my brother. The idea that Lucy knows about him, and has sworn to take revenge on me, has me near panic every time I think about it.

As usual, I start at the pizza place. Since the night at the Garter I've been calling like crazy, trying to reach him, but he's never been there.

"He quit," the manager informs me now, clearly ticked off. "He didn't give notice or anything. He just stopped show-ing up about a week ago."

"Do you know where he lives?" I ask.

The manager shrugs. "He always biked to work, even in bad weather. If you see him, tell him we need our uniform back."

"I'll tell him," I say, but there's a sick feeling in my stomach that I'm not going to get that chance anytime soon.

I wander around my old neighborhood, trying to think of where to look for him next. It feels like déjà vu, looking for my brother, the way we did last summer in the first weeks when he was gone. My inclination is to start at my old house, work my way out from there. I call Billy.

"How's Web?" I ask, unable to help myself.

"He's good. He smiled at me. I'll text you the picture."

My heart squeezes. Angela's missing it.

"Hey, you asked the people who moved into our old house if they'd seen Jeffrey around, didn't you? Last June?" I ask.

"First place I checked," she answers. "A real pretty girl lived there, too. Long, black hair. She said she knew Jeffrey, from back when they were in school together, but she hadn't seen him."

"Did she give you her name?" I ask, my heart starting to beat fast. A pretty girl. Long black hair. Who'd gone to school with Jeffrey.

"L something," Billy says. "Let me think."

"Lucy?" I manage to get out.

"That's it," Billy says. "Oh dear," she says, as she realizes what I'm getting at.

The answer that's been staring me in the face all this

334

time now basically head-butts me. Lucy's been involved with Jeffrey for a long time, and we didn't know it. Who knows all the ways she could have been messing with his head?

"He's been staying at our house. Mom never sold it," I murmur to myself.

Mom knew that I was going to run away, he told me. *She even kind of prepared me for it.*

The windows are dark when I get there, no cars in the drive, no bicycle leaning against the garage. We used to keep a spare key under a flagstone on the back patio. I vault completely over the fence and into our old backyard. The swings on my old swing set sway gently as I pass.

Oh, clever, sneaky Mom.

It's not that she didn't care about Jeffrey's vision or that she wasn't interested in his the way she was so involved in mine. It's that she already knew how it would play out. She knew what he would need. I can't help but be annoyed by this. It's like she was enabling him to run away.

The spare key is right where I thought it would be. My hands tremble as I unlock the door and slip into the house.

"Jeffrey?" I call.

Silence.

I send up a little prayer that I don't run into Lucy instead. Because that would be awkward.

I poke around the kitchen. There's a stack of dirty dishes in the sink. I open the fridge and find it mostly empty save for a gallon of chocolate milk that's a week expired and what I think is a foil-wrapped slice of old pizza. It's hard to tell what with the mold.

I call his name again, jog upstairs to his room. He's not here, but his sheets are on the bed, rumpled at the bottom corner. The drawers of his old dresser, the one Mom said she was getting rid of before we moved to Wyoming—in fact, I complained because she bought Jeffrey a whole new set of bedroom furniture for the move, oh clever, sneaky Mom—are full of his clothes. It smells like him in here.

I search the drawers, looking for clues, but I get nothing.

He lives here, clearly. Or he did. It doesn't seem like he's been back here for a while. Add that to what the pizza place manager said about him not showing up to work for a week, and color me officially worried.

Lucy could have him, right now. Asael could have him. Or he could be—

I won't let myself think the word *dead*, won't allow myself to picture Jeffrey with a sorrow blade through his heart. I have to believe that he's out there, somewhere.

I sit down on his bed and dig for a scrap of paper in my purse, a pen. On the back of a Nebraska grocery store receipt I write the following note:

Jeffrey,
I know you're mad at me. But I really need to talk to you.
Call me. Please remember that I'm always in your corner.
Clara

I hope he gets the message.

Outside again, I hide the key back under the flagstone and take a long, last look at the house where I grew up, and I wonder if I'll ever lay eyes on it again after tonight, or if I'll ever get to talk to my baby brother.

Very soon now, I'll have to catch a train.

18

YOU'LL SEE ME AGAIN

At some point in the afternoon it seems like I have nothing to do but wait for night to fall. I glance at my watch. I've got hours to go before I have to make the journey to the train station.

Before I go to hell.

I should do something frivolous, I think. Fun. Ride a roller coaster. Eat a ton of rocky road ice cream. Buy something ludicrous on credit. These very well could be my last hours on this earth.

What should I do? What is the thing that, if everything changed, I'd miss the most?

The answer comes to me like a song on the wind.

I've got to fly.

***

It's stormy at Big Basin. I climb quickly, easily, my nerves giving me even more speed than usual, and take my place on the rock at the top of Buzzards Roost, legs dangling over the edge, staring out across the blue-black tangle of clouds that lies heavy over the valley.

Not good flying conditions. I briefly consider going somewhere else—the Tetons, maybe, crossing there—but I don't. This is our thinking spot, Mom's and mine, and so I'll sit here and think. I'll try to be at peace with whatever's going to happen.

I cast back to the day Mom first brought me here, when she broke the news to me that I was an angel-blood. *You're special,* she kept saying, and when I laughed at her and called her crazy, denied that I was faster or stronger or smarter than any other perfectly normal teenage girl I knew, she said, *So often we only do what we think is expected of us, when we are capable of so much more.*

Would she approve of what I'm about to do, the leap I'm about to make? Would she tell me I'm insane to think that I can do this impossible thing? Or, if she were here, would she tell me to be brave? *Be brave, my darling. You're stronger than you think.*

I'm going to need to come up with a story to tell Samjeeza, I remind myself. That's my payment. A story, about Mom.

But what story?

Something that shows my mother at her very best, I think:

339

lively and beautiful and fun, the things Samjeeza most loves about her. It has to be good.

I close my eyes. I think about the home movies we watched in the days before she died, all those moments strung together like a patchwork of memories: Mom wearing a Santa hat on Christmas morning, Mom whooping in the stands at Jeffrey's first football game, Mom bending to find a round, perfect sand dollar on the beach at Santa Cruz, or that time we went to the Winchester Mystery House on Halloween night and she ended up more creeped out than we were, and we teased her—oh, man, did we tease her—and she laughed and clutched at our arms, Jeffrey on one side and me on the other, and she said, *Let's go home. I want to get in bed and pull the covers up over my head and pretend like there's nothing scary in the world.*

A million memories. Countless smiles and laughs and kisses, the way she told me she loved me all the time, every night before she tucked me into bed. The way she always believed in me, be it for a math test or a ballet recital or figuring out my purpose on this earth.

But that's not the kind of story Samjeeza will want, is it? Maybe what I give him won't be good enough. Maybe I'll tell him, and he'll laugh the way he does, all mocking, and then he won't take me to hell after all.

I could fail at this before I even start.

I feel dizzy and open my eyes, wobble unsteadily at the edge of the rock. For the first time in my life, I feel like I'm too high up. I could fall.

I scramble back away from the edge, my heart hammering in my chest.

Whoa. This is too much pressure, I think. I rub my eyes. It's too much.

A gust of wind hits me, warm and insistent against my face, and my hair picks this moment to slide out of my ponytail and swirl around me, into my eyes. I cough and swipe at it. For all of two seconds I wish I had a pair of scissors. I would hack it all off. Maybe I will, if and when I get back from hell. The new me will need a radical makeover.

I gaze wistfully out at the sky, then catch my breath as I truly look at it. The clouds are all but gone, only a few wisps of white hanging in the distance. The sky is clear. The sun is dropping slowly toward the ocean, glancing off the treetops in a golden blaze.

What happened? I think dazedly. Did I do that? Did I dissipate the storm, somehow? I know that Billy can control the weather, and sometimes things get wonky when she's feeling emotional, but I never thought that I might be able to do it myself.

I stand up. Whatever the reason, it's good. I can fly now, even if it's only for a few minutes. It feels like a gift. I take off my hoodie, stretch my arms up over my head, and prepare to summon my wings.

Just then I hear a rustling below me, then the unmistakable sound of sneakers on rock, the small grunts of exertion as somebody climbs the rock wall. Somebody is coming up.

Bummer. I've never seen anyone else here before. It's a public trail, and anyone can hike it, I suppose, but it's typically deserted. It's a difficult climb. I've always counted on it being a place I could go to be alone.

Well, I guess flying is out.

Stupid somebody, I think. Find your own thinking spot.

But then the stupid somebody's hands appear at the edge of the rock, followed by her arms, her face, and it's not a stupid somebody after all.

It's my mother.

"Oh, hi," she says. "I didn't know there was anybody here."

She doesn't know me. Her blue eyes widen when she sees me, but it's not in recognition. It's in surprise. She's never come across anybody else up here, either.

She is beautiful, is my first thought, and younger than I've ever seen her. Her hair is curled in a fluffy way that I would have teased her about if I'd seen it in a photograph. She's wearing light-colored jeans and a blue sweatshirt that slouches off the shoulder in a way that reminds me of this one time when she made me watch *Flashdance* on cable. She's a poster girl for the eighties, and she looks so healthy, so flushed with life. It makes an achy lump rise in my throat. I want to throw my arms around her and never let her go.

She glances away uncomfortably. I'm staring.

I close my mouth. "Hi," I choke out. "How are you? It's a lovely day, isn't it?"

She's looking at my clothes now, my skinny jeans and black tank top, my loose, blowing hair. Her eyes are wary but curious, and she turns and gazes out at the valley with me. "Yes. Beautiful weather."

I hold out my hand.

"I'm Clara," I say, the picture of friendliness.

"Maggie," she replies, taking my hand, shaking without squeezing, and I get a glimpse of what's going on inside her. She's irritated. This is her spot. She wanted to be alone.

I smile. "Do you come up here often?"

"This is my thinking spot," she says, in a tone that subtly informs me that it's her turn now, and I should be on my way.

I'm not going anywhere.

"Mine, too." I sit back down on my boulder, which is so not what she wants to happen that I almost laugh aloud.

She decides to wait me out. She takes a seat on the other side of the outcropping and stretches her legs in front of her, reaches into her bag for a pair of police-officer-style mirrored sunglasses and puts them on, leans her head back like she's taking in the sun. She stays that way for several moments, her eyes closed, until I can't stand it anymore. I have to talk to her.

"So do you live around here?" I ask.

She frowns. Her eyes open, and I can feel her irritation giving way to a more general wariness. She doesn't like people who ask too many questions, who show up out of the blue in unexpected places, who are too friendly. She's had experiences with that kind of thing before, and none of them ended well.

"I'm just finishing my freshman year at Stanford," I ramble on. "I'm still kind of new to the area, so I'm always hounding the locals with questions about the best places to eat and go out and that kind of stuff."

Her expression lightens. "I graduated from Stanford," she says. "What's your major?"

"Biology," I say, nervous to see what she'll think of that. "Premed."

"I have a degree in nursing," she says. "It's a hard path, sometimes, making people better, fixing them up, but rewarding, too."

I had almost forgotten that about her. A nurse.

We talk for a while, about the Stanford-Berkeley rivalry, about California and which beaches are best for surfing, about the premed program. Before five minutes are up she's acting a whole lot friendlier, still kind of wanting me to leave so she can buckle down and make whatever decision it is that she came up here to make, but also amused by my jokes, curious about me, charmed. She likes me, I can tell. My mom likes me, even if she doesn't know that she's supposed to love me. I'm relieved.

"Have you ever been inside Memorial Church?" I ask her when there's a lull in the conversation.

She shakes her head. "I don't go to church, as a rule."

Interesting. Not that Mom was ever fanatical about church or anything, but I always got the impression growing up that she liked church. We only stopped going when I got to be a teenager, maybe because she thought that I'd do something in church that would give away that there was more to our family than met the eye. "Why not?" I ask. "What's wrong with church?"

"They're always telling you what to do," she says. "And I don't like to take orders."

"Even from God?"

She glances at me, one corner of her mouth hooking up into a quiet smile. "Especially from God."

Very interesting. Maybe I'm having a little too much fun with this conversation. Maybe I should tell her who I am, point-blank, stop messing around, but how do you break it to someone that you're actually their as-yet-not-even-conceived child, come to visit them from the future? I don't want to freak her out.

"So," she says after a minute. "What did you come up here to think about?"

How to put this? "I'm supposed to go on a . . . trip, to help a friend who's in a bad place."

She nods. "And you don't want to go."

"I want to. She needs me. But I have a feeling that if I go, I won't ever be able to really come back. Everything will change. You know?"

"Ah." She's looking at my face intensely, seeing something there. "And there's a guy you're leaving behind."

Trust her to miss nothing, even now. "Something like that."

"Love is a many-splendored thing," she says. "But it is also a pain in the ass."

I give a surprised laugh. She swore. I've never heard her truly swear before. Young ladies, she used to tell me all the time, do not swear. It's undignified.

"Sounds like the voice of experience," I say teasingly. "Is that what you came up here to think about? A man?"

I watch her carefully frame the words before she says them. "A marriage proposal."

"Whoa!" I exclaim, and she chuckles. "That's serious."

"Yes," she murmurs. "It is."

"So he asked you?" Holy crap. This must be Dad she's talking about. She's up here trying to decide whether or not to marry Dad.

She nods, her eyes distant like she's remembering something bittersweet. "Last night."

"And you said . . ."

"I said I needed to think about it. And he said that if I wanted to marry him, to meet him today. At sunset."

I give a low whistle, and she smiles in a pained way. I can't help myself. "So are you leaning toward yes, or toward no?"

"Toward no, I think."

"You don't . . . love the guy?" I ask, suddenly out of breath. This is my future we're talking about here, my entire existence on the line, and she's leaning toward no?

She gazes down at her hands, at her ring finger, where there is very conspicuously no gorgeous engagement ring. "It's not that I don't love him. But I don't think he's asking me for the right reasons."

"Let me guess. You're loaded, and he wants to marry you for the money."

She gives a little snort. "No. He wants to marry me because he wants me to have his child."

Child, singular. Because she doesn't know that there's a Jeffrey in the plan.

"You don't want kids?" I ask, my voice a tad higher than usual.

She shakes her head. "I like children, but I don't think I want to have my own. I'd worry too much. I don't want to love something that much and then have it taken away." She looks off across the valley, embarrassed by how much she's given away about herself. "I don't know if I can be happy in that life. Housewife. Mother. It's not for me."

It's quiet for a minute while I try to think of something smart to say, and miraculously, I hit on it. "Maybe you shouldn't look at it in terms of whether or not you'll be happy as this guy's wife, but if being his wife is true to the kind of person you want to be. We think of happiness as something we can take. But usually it comes from being content with what we have, and accepting ourselves."

Happiness class is coming in handy, at last.

She looks over at me sharply. "How old are you, again?"

"Eighteen. Sort of. How old are you?" I ask with a grin, because I already know the answer. I've done the math. When Dad asked her to marry him, she was ninety-nine.

She reddens. "Older than that." She sighs. "I don't want to become someone else simply because it's what's expected of me."

"So don't. Be more," I say.

"What did you say?" she asks.

"Be more than what's expected of you. Look beyond that. Choose your own purpose."

At the word *purpose*, her eyes narrow on my face. "Who are you?"

"Clara," I answer. "I told you."

"No." She gets up, walks to the edge of the rock. "Who are you, really?"

I stand and stare at her, meeting her eyes. Time to show my hand, I think. I swallow.

"I'm your daughter," I say. "Yeah, it's kind of weird to see you, too," I continue, as her face goes sheet white. "What's today's date, anyway? I've been dying to know ever since I saw your outfit."

"It's July tenth," she says dazedly. "1989. What are you playing at? Who sent you?"

"Nobody. I guess I was missing you, and then I crossed through time by accident. Dad said I would see you again, when I needed it most. I guess this is what he meant." I take a step forward. "I really am your daughter."

She shakes her head. "Stop saying that. It's not possible."

I hold up my arms, shrug. "And yet here I am."

"No," she says, but I can see her scrutinizing my face in an entirely different way, seeing my nose as her nose, the shape of my face, my eyebrows, my ears. Uncertainty flickers in her eyes. Then panic. I start to get worried that she might jump off this rock and fly to get away from me.

"This is a trick," she says.

"Oh yeah? And what I am trying to trick you into?"

"You want me to . . ."

"Marry Dad?" I fill in. "You think he—Michael, my father, an angel of the Lord and all that—wants to trap you into a marriage that you don't want to be in?" I sigh. "Look, I know this is surreal. It feels strange to me too, like any minute I might disappear like I was never born, which would be a total bummer, if you know what I mean. But I don't care, really. I'm so glad to see you. I've missed you. So much. Can't we just . . . talk about it? I'm going to be born on June 20, 1994." I take a slow step toward her.

"Don't," she says sharply.

"I don't know how to convince you." I stop and think about it. Then I hold up my hands. "We have the same hands," I say. "Look. The exact same. See how your ring finger is slightly longer than your index finger? Mine too. You always joked that it was a sign of great intelligence. And I have this big vein that goes horizontally across the right one, which I think looks kind of weird, but you have that too. So I guess we're weird together."

She stares at her hands.

"I think I should sit down," she says, and drops heavily to sit on the rock.

I crouch next to her.

"Clara," she whispers. "What's your last name?"

"Gardner. I think it's what Dad chooses as his mortal sur-name, but I'm not sure, actually. Clara, by the way, was like the most popular girl's name in something like 1910, but not so much since then. Thanks for that."

She stifles a smile. "I like the name Clara."

"Do you want me to tell you my middle name, or can you come up with it on your own?"

She puts her fingers to her lips and shakes her head incredulously.

"So," I say, because the sun is definitely on its way toward the horizon now, and she's going to have to go soon, "I don't want to pressure you or anything, but I think you should marry him."

She laughs weakly.

"He loves you. Not because of me. Or because God told him to. Because of you."

"But I don't know how to be a mother," she murmurs. "I was raised in an orphanage, you know. I never had a mother. Am I any good at it?"

"You're the best. Seriously, and I'm not just trying to make my case here, but you are the best mother. All my friends are superjealous of how amazing you are. You put all the other moms to shame."

Her expression's still cloudy. "But I'll die before you grow up."

"Yes. And that sucks. But I wouldn't trade you for somebody who'd live to be a thousand."

"I won't be there for you."

I put my hand over hers. "You're here now."

She nods her head slightly, swallows. She turns my hand over in hers and examines it.

"Amazing," she breathes.

"I know, right?"

We sit for a little while. Then she says, "So tell me about your life. Tell me about this journey you're going on."

I bite my lip. I worry that if I tell her too much about the future, it will disrupt the space-time continuum or something and destroy the universe. When I tell her this, she laughs.

"I've seen the future all my life," she says. "It tends to work as a paradox, in my experience. You find out something is going to happen, and then you do it because you know that's

351

what happens. It's a chicken-or-the-egg scenario."

Good enough for me. I tell her everything I think I have time for. I tell her about my visions, about Christian and the fire, the cemetery, and the kiss. I tell her about Jeffrey, which shocks her, because she never considered that she might have more than one child.

"A son," she breathes. "What's he like?"

"A lot like Dad. Tall and strong and obsessed with sports. And a lot like you. Stubborn. And stubborn."

She smiles, and I feel a glimmer of happiness in her at the idea of Jeffrey, a son who looks like Dad. I blab on about how Jeffrey's vision got him all messed up and how he ran away and has been living at our old house, how he's dating a bad Triplare, how I can't find him now, and she sobers right up.

And finally, I tell her about Angela and Phen and Web, and what happened in the Garter, and how I'm starting to believe that Angela's what my purpose is really about.

"So what do you have to do," she asks, "to save her?"

"I made a deal with the devil, so to speak."

"What devil?"

"Samjeeza."

She flinches like I've slapped her. "You know Samjeeza?"

"He considers himself a friend of the family."

"What does he want?" she asks grimly.

"A story. About you. I don't know why, really. He's obsessed with you."

She bites the end of her thumb gently, contemplating. "What kind of story?"

"A memory. Something where he can imagine you alive, like a new charm on your bracelet." She looks surprised. "Which you gave me, and I gave back to him, the day of your funeral. It's complicated. I need a story. But I can't think of anything good enough."

Her eyes are thoughtful. "I'll give you a story," she says. "Something that he'll want to hear."

She takes a deep breath and gazes down at the trees below us. "As I said before, I was a nurse once, during the Great War, working at a hospital in France, and one day I met a journalist."

"At a pond," I supply. "In your underwear."

She looks up, startled.

"He's told me some stories, too."

She's mortified at the idea, but pushes on. "We became friends, of a fashion. We became more than friends. At first I think it was only a game for him, to see if he could win me, but as time went on it became . . . more. For both of us."

She pauses, her eyes scanning the horizon like she's searching for something, but she doesn't find it.

"Then one night the hospital was bombed by the Huns." Her lips tighten. "Everything was on fire. Everyone was . . ." She closes her eyes briefly, then opens them again. "Dead. I clawed my way out of there, and it was just fire, fire everywhere, and then Sam rode in on a horse and said my name, and reached out his hand for me, and I took it, and he pulled me up behind him. He took me away from there. We spent the night in an old stone barn near Saint-Céré. He pumped some water and made me sit down, and he washed the soot and blood off my face. And he kissed me."

Kissed in a barn. Must be a genetic thing.

But this story isn't going to cut it, I realize. Samjeeza already knows it. It's the horse charm.

"He'd kissed me before," Mom continues. "But after that night it was different, somehow. Things had changed. We talked until the sun came up. He finally admitted to me what he was. I had already guessed that he was an angel. I felt it when we first met. At the time I wanted nothing to do with angels, so I tried to ignore him."

"Right." I smile. "Angels can be a pain in the ass."

Her mouth twists, her eyes twinkling for a moment before she gets serious again. "But he wasn't merely an angel. He told me how he had fallen, and why. He showed me his black wings. And he confessed that he'd been trying to seduce me because the Watchers wanted angel-blood offspring."

"Whoa. He just admitted it?"

"I was furious," she says. "It was all that I'd been running away from my entire life. I slapped him. He caught my wrist and asked me to forgive him. He said he loved me. He asked me if I could ever love him back."

She stops again. I am transfixed by her story. I can see it, the images pouring out with her feelings into my brain. His eyes, earnest, full of sorrow and love, pleading. His voice, soft as he told her, *I know that I'm a wretch. But is it possible that you would ever love me?*

I gasp. "You lied."

"I lied. I said I could never care for him. I told him I never wanted to see him again. And he looked at me for a long moment, and then he was gone. Just like that. I never told anyone about that night. Michael knows, I think, in the way he seems to know everything. But I haven't ever talked about it until now." She exhales through her lips like she's just set down something heavy. "So there's your story. I lied."

"You did care for him," I say carefully.

"I loved him," she whispers. "He was my sun and moon for a time. I was crazy about him."

And now he's crazy about you, I think. Emphasis on *crazy*.

She clears her throat. "It was a long time ago."

And yet we both know that time can be a tricky thing.

"That must be uncomfortable for you to hear," she says, seeing my frown. "Me saying I loved a man who's not your father."

"But I know you love Dad." I remember Mom and Dad together in her last days, how obvious the love was between them, how pure. I smile at her, bump my shoulder into hers. "You loooove him. You do."

She laughs, pushes back against me. "All right, all right, I'll marry him. I couldn't very well refuse him now, could I?" She suddenly gasps. "I have to go," she says, jumping up like Cinderella late to the ball. "I'm supposed to meet him."

"On the beach at Santa Cruz," I say.

"I told you about it?" she asks. "What do I say to him?"

"You just kiss him," I tell her. "Now go on before you're late and I cease to exist."

She moves to the edge of the rock and summons her wings. I'm startled by how gray they are, when normally, when I knew her best, they were so piercingly white. They're still beautiful now, but gray. Undecided. Uncertain.

She hesitates.

"Go," I say.

There are tears in her eyes. *I don't want to leave you,* she says in my mind.

Don't worry, Mom, I answer, calling her Mom for the first time since I came here. *You'll see me again.*

She smiles and caresses my cheek, then turns and takes off, the wind from her wings blowing back my hair, and glides toward the ocean. Toward the beach, where my father is waiting.

I wipe my eyes. And when I look up again, I'm back in the present, like this entire afternoon has been some kind of beautiful dream.

19

SOUTHBOUND TRAIN

Two minutes to midnight.

For real, this time.

The vision hasn't prepared me for the sheer enormity of
this moment. I feel like I'm going to jump out of my skin.
I feel each tick of my watch's second hand like an electric
charge pulsing through me again and again.

I can do this, I tell myself, fiddling with the zipper of my
black hoodie.

Tick, tick.

Tick, tick.

The northbound train comes and goes. Samjeeza arrives,
claims the lamppost, squawks at me.

But Christian's not here.

I turn a slow circle, looking for him, my eyes lingering on every empty space, every shadow, hoping to find him, but he's not here.

He's not coming.

For a minute I think my fear is going to eat me up.

"Caw," says the crow impatiently.

It's midnight.

I have to go. With or without him.

I face the stretch of pavement that will take me across the tracks. One step at a time, my heart going like a rabbit's, my breath coming in shallow gasps, I cross the tracks.

On the other side Samjeeza unfolds himself into a man. He looks pleased with himself, excited, the fox-in-the-henhouse kind of excited, a wicked gleam in his eye. My skin prickles at the sight of him.

"A fine night for a journey." He glances around. "I told you to bring a friend."

"Do you have any friends who'd go to hell for you?" I ask, trying to keep my bottom lip from trembling.

His gaze is piercing. "No."

He has no friends. He has no anyone.

He *tsks* his tongue like he's disappointed in me. "This will not work without someone to ground you."

"You could ground me," I say, lifting my chin.

The corner of his mouth turns up. He leans forward, not

touching me but close enough to envelop me in the cocoon of sorrow that's always enclosing him. It is a deep, gut-wrenching agony, like everything beautiful and light in this world has slowly withered and died, crumbled to ash in my hands. I can't breathe, can't think.

How did Mom ever manage to get close to this creature? But then, she didn't have the way with feelings I have. She couldn't know how black and bone-chillingly cold he truly is inside, how shattered.

"Is this what you want to be bound to?" he asks in a rumbling voice.

I step back and gasp when I'm able to get my breath again, like he's been choking me.

"No." I shudder.

"I didn't think so," he says. "Ah, well." He looks down the tracks, where in the distance I can hear the very faint whistle of an approaching train. "It's probably for the best," he says.

I'm going to miss my chance.

"Wait!"

I turn to see Christian hurrying across the tracks, wearing his black fleece jacket and gray jeans, his eyes wide, his voice ragged as he calls, "I'm here!"

My breath leaves me in a rush. I can't help but smile. He reaches me and we hug, clutching at each other's arms for a minute, murmuring "I'm sorry" and "I'm so glad you're here" and "I couldn't miss it" and "You don't have to do this" back

359

and forth between us, sometimes out loud, sometimes in our heads.

Samjeeza clears his throat, and we step back from each other and turn to him. He cocks his head at Christian.

"Who is this?" he asks. "I've seen him hanging around you like some lovesick puppy. Is he one of the Nephilim?"

Christian inhales sharply. He's never seen Samjeeza before, never been this close to a Black Wing. I wonder for a moment if he wasn't wrong about seeing Asael. Asael and Samjeeza look enough alike that maybe he confused the two. It's possible. This could still be his vision, I think.

"He's a friend," I manage, grabbing Christian's hand. Immediately I feel stronger, more balanced, more focused. We can do this. "You said I needed a friend, and here he is. So now you can take us to Angela."

"Forgetting something, are we?" Samjeeza says. "Your payment?"

What payment? Christian demands in my head. *Clara, what payment? What did you promise him?*

"I didn't forget."

The train is approaching, a dull red light at its head, advancing down the tracks. I'll have to make this fast.

"I have a story," I tell him. "But I'll show you."

With my free hand I reach up and touch Samjeeza's cheek, which is smooth and cool, inhuman. His sorrow floods me, making Christian gasp as it reverberates through me and into him, but I surge against it, squeeze Christian's hand tighter, and focus on today, the hour with my mother on the top of Buzzards Roost. I pour it all into Sam's shocked and open mind: her voice telling the story, the wind blowing her long auburn hair, the way she felt as she told it, the warm soft clasp of her hand holding mine, and finally, the words.

I lied.

I loved him.

Samjeeza flinches. It is more than he expected. I feel him start to tremble under my hand. I step back and let him go.

We wait to see what he will do. The train's approaching the station. It's different from the northbound one; this one is smudged with dirt or soot or something black and nasty so that I can't read the words on the sides. The windows are crowded with black shapes. Gray people, I realize. On their way to the underworld.

Sam's eyes are closed, his body absolutely still, like I've turned him into stone.

"Sam . . . ," I prompt. "We should go."

His eyes open. His eyebrows push together, the space between them wrinkling like he's in pain. He regards Christian and me like he doesn't know what to do with us anymore. Like he's having second thoughts.

"Are you absolutely certain that you want to do this?" he asks, his voice hoarse. "Once you board this particular locomotive, there's no turning back."

"Why do we have to take a train?" Christian asks impulsively. "Can't you take us there, the way you did with Clara and her mother before?"

Samjeeza seems to gain back a bit of his equilibrium. "For me to expend energy in that way would call attention to what I'm doing, and the trail could be followed. No, you must go like all the common damned of this world, into the depths by ferry, or carriage, or train."

"All right," Christian says tightly. "Train it is, then."

Are you sure? I ask him silently, looking into his eyes.

I'll go where you go, he answers.

I turn back to Sam. "We're ready."

He nods.

"Listen to me carefully. I will take you to your friend, where I have arranged for her to be at the given time, and you must convince her to go with you."

"Convince her?" Christian interjects again. "Won't she be eager to get out of there?"

Samjeeza ignores him, focuses on me. "Speak to no one else but the girl."

What, does he think I'll stop to chat with the first person I stumble across? "No problem."

"No one else," he repeats sharply, talking loudly to make himself heard over the engine of the train as it slows to a halt in front of us. "Keep your heads down. Do not look anyone in the eyes." He glances at Christian. "Try to maintain physical contact with your friend, but any outward sign of affection or connection between you will be noticed, and you do not want to be noticed. Stay close to me, but do not touch me. Do not look directly at me. Do not speak to me in public. If I am to stay with you, you must do exactly as I tell you, when I tell you, without question. Do you understand?"

I nod mutely.

The train shudders to a complete stop. Samjeeza takes two golden coins from his pocket and drops them into my hand. "For passage." I pass one to Christian.

"Your hair," he says, and I pull my hood up over my head.

The doors hiss open.

I step closer to Christian so that our shoulders touch, take a deep breath of what is all at once oily, stale air, and let go of his hand. Together we follow Samjeeza into the waiting car. The doors close behind us. There's no going back.

This is it.

We're going to hell.

It's dark inside the car. I'm immediately overpowered by a claustrophobic feeling, like the grimy walls are shrinking, enclosing us, trapping us. It's not helped by the fact that there are people crowded around us like shadows, insubstantial and ghostlike, sometimes immaterial enough that I can see right through them or they seem to overlap one another, occupying the same space. There's an occasional moan from one of them, the sound of a man who's coughing wretchedly, a woman weeping. The lights over our heads are red and flickering, buzzing like angry insects. Outside the window is nothing but black, like we are passing through an endless tunnel.

I'm scared. I want to clutch at Christian's hand, but I can't. People would notice. We don't want to be noticed. We can't be noticed. So I sit, head down, eyes on the floor, my heart going *pump pump pump*, and every now and then my leg brushes his, and his anxiety in this situation, his own fear, pulses through me and mixes with my own until I can't tell who's feeling what exactly. The train shudders and rocks, the air inside heavy and stifling and cold, like we're underwater and slowly freezing into a solid block of nothingness. I have to fight not to shiver.

I'm scared, yes, but I'm also determined. We're going to do this, this impossible task that lies before us now. We're going to rescue Angela.

And I'm thankful, in that moment, full to the brim with gratitude that Christian is with me. He's here. My partner. My best friend.

I don't have to do this alone.

If I had my gratitude journal on me now, that's what I would write.

We stop, and more people get on. A man in a black uniform passes through the car and takes the gold coins. I wonder where the gray people get them, if there's some sort of coin dispenser for the dead somewhere out there in the world, or if someone gives it to them, like the coin is a metaphor for what people want to take with them from one life to the next, only now they must give it to the man in the black uniform. Some of them seem reluctant to hand it over. One guy claims he doesn't have a coin, and at the next stop the man in the black uniform takes this guy by the shoulders and hurls him off the train. Where will he go, I wonder? Is there a place that's worse to go than hell?

The man in the black uniform gives a wide berth to Samjeeza and asks him no questions, I notice.

At the third stop, Samjeeza moves toward the door. He glances at me, a signal, and steps out. Christian and I stand up and push through the gray people, and each time I brush hard enough against one of them I receive a jolt of some raw and ugly feeling: hate, lost love, resentment, infidelity, murder. Then we're standing on the platform, and I can breathe again. I try to look discreetly for Samjeeza, and I find him a few feet away. Already he looks different here; his humanness is fading. He's larger and more menacing by the moment, the blackness of his coat a stark contrast to the gray of those around him.

Where are we? Christian asks in my mind. *This looks familiar.*

I turn around.

It's Mountain View, I recognize immediately. The

structure of the buildings is largely the same, only there's a cold, thick mist passing between the buildings, and no color to be seen, like we've stepped onto the set of a horror movie inside a black-and-white television.

Look at them, Christian says with an inner shudder of revulsion.

The gray people are walking all around us, heads down, some with black tears flowing down their faces, some scratching at themselves violently, their arms and necks raw with the marks of their fingernails, some muttering as if they're talking to someone, but no one speaks to anyone else. They are adrift in their own oceans of solitude, all the while pressed in from every side by others just like them, but they never look up.

He's on the move, I say to Christian as Samjeeza starts to walk, down what would be Castro Street on earth. We wait for a few seconds before we follow. I slip my hand in Christian's under the edge of his jacket, thankful for the warmth of his fingers, the smell of his cologne that I can only faintly detect in this congested mixture of what I identify as car exhaust and burned-out fire and the reek of mildew.

Hell stinks.

The street is empty of cars, no one driving, but the mass of people on the sidewalk never ventures onto the road. They part around Samjeeza as he walks among them, sometimes moaning as he passes by. A black sedan is idling at the corner.

As we approach, the driver gets out and crosses to open the door for Samjeeza. He is something other than the gray people, something like the man in the black uniform was, and indeed he wears a kind of uniform himself, a fitted black suit and a chauffeur hat with a curved, shiny brim.

Don't stare, Christian warns me. *Keep your head down.*

I bite my lip when I see that the driver does not have any eyes or mouth, just a smooth expanse of skin from nose to chin, a pair of slight indentations in his face where his eye sockets should be. Even so, he appears to look at us when we stop behind Samjeeza, and without words he seems to ask a question:

Where?

"I am taking these two to be marked for Asael," Samjeeza says. He puts a finger to his lips, and the message to us is clear: *This man can't speak, but he can hear. Be quiet.*

The driver nods once.

I feel Christian's wave of anxiety at Asael's name like a new surge of adrenaline hitting my system. This could be a trap. We are walking right into it.

Technically we're being driven right into it, I say to try to lighten the moment, but he doesn't have time to respond before Samjeeza puts a hand in the middle of Christian's back and shoves him into the backseat, and I follow. Samjeeza slides in beside me, his shoulder touching mine now, and he likes it, this light, tantalizing contact, my human smell, the way my lips are slightly parted in terror. He likes how a strand of my hair has come undone from my ponytail, slipping out of my hoodie, how in this colorless world it shines pure white.

I press closer to Christian, who waits until Samjeeza closes the door of the car before putting his arm around me, drawing my head into his shoulder, away from Sam.

Ah, so protective, Sam says into our minds. *Who are you, again? I thought she was in love with someone else.*

Christian clenches his teeth but doesn't respond.

We pass through the hell version of downtown Mountain View quickly, past Church and Mercy Streets, city hall, where there is a line of the gray people waiting outside; past the shops and restaurants, some boarded up but others open, people slouched one to a table over bowls of indistinguishable food. We reach what would be El Camino Real, the main street that connects all these little cities between San Francisco and San Jose, and turn south. Still there are no other cars on the road.

Does hell surprise you? Samjeeza asks silently. His inner voice has a bite to it, a burn, like the aftertaste of something bitter.

I guess I didn't think there would be restaurants and stores.

It is a reflection of earth, he says. *What's true on earth is more or less true in this place.*

So all these people are trapped here? I gesture out the window at the throngs of gray people pushing along the streets, always on their way somewhere, it seems, but at the same time aimless, without any true direction.

Not trapped, but kept. Most of them do not realize they're in hell. They have died, and gravitated to this place because that is where they have willed themselves. They could leave at any time they choose, but they will never choose to.

Why not?

Because they will not let go of what it is that brought them here to begin with.

We pull into a parking lot, and the car squeaks to a stop.

Remember what I told you, Samjeeza says. *Don't speak to anyone but your friend, and only when I tell you to do so.*

The driver opens the doors, and we climb out. I suck in a breath when I see where we are.

A tattoo parlor.

Samjeeza pushes us toward the building, then opens and holds the door as we step inside. It's all in black and white, the leather couches a deep charcoal gray, the large neon word TATTOO glowing a stark, eye-piercing white, the designs on the walls flapping like startled birds with the sudden gust of wind we let in. The floor is dirty; there's a stickiness and grit under our feet. We stand for a moment in the reception room, waiting. A bubble rises up in the water cooler: gray water in a gray container.

Then: a muffled scream from somewhere in the building.

A man comes out from the back, a small, thin, black man with a shaved head. An angel, I think, although not like any

I have seen before. His nonexistent eyebrows lift in surprise when he sees us.

"Samyaza," he says, inclining his shining head in a kind of bow.

"Kokabel." Samjeeza greets him the way a king might acknowledge the court jester.

"To what do I owe the honor?"

"I have brought these two for my brother. They are of the fallen."

It's taking every ounce of Christian's self-control not to bolt for the door and drag me with him. I shift closer and try to steady him. *Stay calm,* I want to whisper in his mind, but I don't know if this new angel will be able to hear our connection.

"Live Dimidius?" Kokabel asks, again surprised.

Samjeeza's eyes glint as he looks at me. "Quartarius. But a matched pair, and I think he'll find them amusing."

"Why stop here? Why not bring them directly to the master?"

"I thought it would please him to have them marked first," Samjeeza says. "Can you fit them in today? I had hoped to present them to Asael shortly, if possible."

"What is today?" Kokabel answers, grinning. He jerks his head toward the hallway. "Bring them back. Will we need to restrain them?" He looks like he might relish the task.

"No," Samjeeza answers smoothly. "I have broken them

thoroughly. They shouldn't offer any resistance."

We follow Kokabel down a narrow corridor into a small room, like an exam room at a doctor's office. There is a person reclined on a large leather chair, with a man—Desmond, I recognize—leaning over her, a buzzing tattoo gun in his hand. From this angle I can't see her face, only her hands as they clutch the arms of the chair.

She's wearing dark gray nail polish, but I'm guessing that on earth it would be purple.

Christian and I each suck in a breath at the same time. Kokabel pushes us farther into the room like we are livestock, and I wish I could hold Christian's hand as Angela's despair crashes over me. Desmond is tattooing something on her neck on one side. She's wearing a hueless camisole almost the same color as her pale skin, and dirty, torn jeans, no shoes. The soles of her feet are black. Her hair is pulled back in a ratty knot at the base of her skull, her bangs overgrown so that they almost obscure her eyes, a few lanky strands sticking out like straw on a scarecrow. Her entire right arm is covered in words, some easily readable, some overlapping and indecipherable.

Jealous, I make out along her forearm. *Insufferable know-it-all. Bad friend. Careless.*

Selfish, it reads in the curve of her elbow.

Slut, in the tender space where her arm meets her shoulder.

And other things, more specific sins, like *I lied to my*

mother, I lied to my friends, I started a rumor, I hid the truth, in tiny scribbled print all along her bicep, the word *LIAR* spelled broadly across it.

"Sit," Samjeeza commands us, and we sink obediently into a pair of folding chairs against the far wall. I try to keep my eyes down, but some part of me can't look away from Angela.

"Desmond, we've brought you some new customers," Kokabel says.

"I'm just finishing up here." Desmond sniffles like he has a cold, wiping his nose on the back of his hand. His eyes flit to Samjeeza, then quickly away.

I lift my gaze to Angela's neck, the spot where Desmond is currently leaving a line of characters. He spreads his fingers to stretch the skin there, touching the gun into the tender space under her ear, wiping away a smear of black ink with a dirty cloth. The letters are dark and startling against the fragile whiteness of her flesh.

Bad mother.

"A bad mother," Samjeeza remarks. "Who's her unlucky offspring?"

Kokabel shakes his head. "Penamue's, I believe. I thought he didn't have it in him to sire children, but they say he's the father. She's a troublesome one. Asael sends her back to us every time she displeases him, which is often."

Angela takes a sudden breath, a strangled whimper escaping her, the cords on her neck standing out and halting Desmond's progress. Without blinking an eye he rears back and slaps her, hard, across the face. I have to bite my lip to keep from crying out. She slides down on the chair, closes her eyes. Gray tears slip down her cheeks as he finishes the words.

Samjeeza turns to Kokabel. "I'd like to choose the design for the female," he says. "Will you show me your book?"

"Yes. This way," Kokabel says. "I'll be back for the girl," he directs at Desmond, and then he steps into the hall. Samjeeza holds back a moment longer, reaches to slip something into Desmond's hand, a plastic bag, then follows Kokabel to deliberate on my ink.

I'm thinking it's not going to be a pretty butterfly on my hip.

Desmond puts the bag in his pocket and pats it, like it's a pet or something. He scoots his stool up to my chair. I force my eyes down as he takes my chin and turns my head from side to side.

"Lovely skin," he says, his breath like sour cigarettes and gin. "I can't wait to work on you."

Christian's body tightens like a bowstring.

Don't, I tell him with a look, not daring to speak even with my mind in here.

Desmond gets up and peels off his gloves, throws them onto a counter in the corner, stretches, wipes at his nose again.

"I need a refreshment," he says, clicking his fingers together in a kind of nervous rhythm. Then he goes out, sniffling and rummaging for the bag Samjeeza gave him, and closes the door behind him.

You have perhaps five minutes to make your escape, comes Samjeeza's disembodied voice in my head, the second we're alone with Angela. *Go back to the train station and take a north-bound train, which will come shortly. Hurry. In a few minutes the whole of hell will be after you, including me. And remember what I told you. Don't speak to anyone. Just go. Now.*

Christian and I rush to Angela's side.

"Ange, Ange, get up!"

She opens her eyes, the dark traces of tears still on her cheeks. She frowns as she looks at me, like my name isn't quite coming to her.

"Clara," I supply. "I'm Clara. You're Angela. This is Christian. We have to go."

"Oh, Clara," she says wearily. "You were always so pretty." Absently she rubs at her arm where it says *jealous*. "I'm being punished, you know."

"Not anymore. Let's go."

I pull at her arm, but she resists. She whispers, "I've lost them."

"Ange, please . . ."

"Phen doesn't love me. My mother did, but now she's lost, too."

"Web loves you," Christian says from beside me.

She stares up at him with anguish in her eyes. "I left him

374

for you to find. Did you find him?"

"Yes," he says. "We found him. He's safe."

"He's better off," she says. Her fingers drift up to scratch at the fresh words on her neck. *Bad mother.*

I grab her hand. Her self-loathing churns through me. I get the sharp taste of bile in the back of my throat. No one loves her. She can never go back.

Yes, you can, I whisper in her mind. *Come with us.* But I don't know if she can hear me. She never learned how to receive.

"What's the point? It's over. Ruined," she says. "Lost."

In that instant I know that her soul is wounded. She'll never wake up from this trance she's in, not like this. She'll never agree to come with us.

We came here for nothing.

No one loves me, she thinks.

No. I will not let this happen, not again. I grab her shoulders, force her to look at me. "Angela. *I* love you, for heaven's sake. You think I would have come all this way, to freaking hell, to rescue you if I didn't love you? I love you. Web loves you, and what's more, he needs you, Ange, he needs his mother, and we don't have any more time to waste with you feeling sorry for yourself. Now *get up!*" I command her, and at that precise instant I send the smallest blast of glory straight into her body.

Angela jerks, then blinks, shocked, like I threw a glass of water in her face. She looks from Christian to me and back again, her eyes going wide.

"Angela," I whisper. "Are you okay? Say something."

Her lips slowly curve up into a smile.

"Geez," she says. "Who died and made you boss?"

We stare at her. She jumps to her feet. "Let's go."

No time to celebrate. We slip into the hallway, back to the deserted waiting room. It takes all of two seconds flat for us to be out the door and down the street, staying close together, Christian leading us north, toward the train station, followed by me close behind him, trying to walk in step to keep some kind of subtle physical contact between us, trailed by Angela. In this chain we make our way past a row of dingy, falling-down apartments and onto Palo Alto Street, which on earth has a charming, hometown-America feel but in hell is like something out of a Hitchcock film, lined with twisted, leaf-less black trees that seem to claw at us as we pass, the houses decaying, the windows broken or boarded over, the paint peeling in gray flakes. We pass a woman standing in the mid-dle of a yard, holding a hose, watering a patch of grassless, muddy ground, mumbling something about her flowers. We see a man beating a dog. But we don't stop. We can't stop.

The rundown neighborhood gives way to more open city, commercial buildings, restaurants, and offices. Angela's look-ing around like she's never seen this place before, which I find odd, considering she's the one who's been here for almost two weeks. We pop out on Mercy Street near the library, and city hall looms over us, a huge granite building with lots of blackened windows, and suddenly the street is flooded with the gray people again, groaning and crying and tearing at their skin. It's hard going, since the lost souls on the sidewalk are mostly moving south, the wrong direction. We're like fish pushing our way upstream against the current, but at least we're getting there, step by slow step. It feels like we've been walking for hours, but we can't have been gone longer than five or ten minutes.

Very, very soon, they're going to notice we're gone.

We're just going to walk out of here? Angela thinks incredulously.

That's the plan. I give her a tiny nod, not sure that she can hear me. *There are no locks in this place. It's not a prison. They could all leave,* I tell her, glancing at the people walking by, *if they chose to.* I'm suddenly overcome by the urge to grab one of these gray people by the shoulders and say, *Come with us,* and lead them out of here single file.

But I can't. It would break the rule Samjeeza laid out for us very plainly. *Don't speak to anyone.*

At last we turn onto Castro, the main drag. We're in the heart of downtown Mountain View, the street lined with restaurants and coffee shops and sushi bars. My eyes go straight to a building that on earth was my favorite bookstore: Books Inc., a place Mom and I used to go to simply hang out and drink coffee and sit in the comfy chairs. But here something has scratched away the word *Books* from above the door, leaving deep gouges in the stone like the building was set upon by an enormous beast. The black awnings are tattered and hanging in shreds, and smoke pours out from the shattered windows from a fire burning somewhere in the back.

We trudge on about another two blocks, keeping our heads down as much as we can, like we are walking into the wind, until the black wrought-iron archway that marks the entrance to the train station comes into view. My heart lifts at the sight of it.

Almost there, Christian says. *I hope we don't need a coin or something to get out of here, because Sam didn't give us anything for a return trip.*

We start moving faster. One block to go. One block and we're home free. Of course, I know it's not over. Getting out is only the first step, and then we'll have to run, hide, and stay hidden, leave everything behind for good. But at least we're all alive. I don't know if, deep down, I really expected to survive this journey in one piece. It turned out to be so simple. Almost—dare I say it?—easy.

But then I see the pizza place.

I stop so suddenly that Angela bumps into me from behind. Christian yelps as I jerk on his arm. The gray souls jostle into us, moaning, shouting, but I stay for a minute with my feet planted and stare across the street at the small, boxlike build-ing where my brother used to work.

Don't tell me you want pizza at a time like this, Angela says.

Christian mentally shushes her. *Clara?*

He stopped showing up, I think.

I step off the curb and into the empty street.

Clara, Jeffrey's not in there, Christian says urgently. *Come back on the sidewalk.*

How do you know? I have a horrible, aching feeling in the pit of my stomach.

Because he's not dead. He doesn't belong here.

We're not dead. Angela wasn't dead, I say, and take another step, pulling them into the street with me.

We have to go, Christian says, glancing wildly toward the black arch. *We can't get off course now.*

I have to check, I say at the same time, and then I let go and pull away from their hands.

Clara, no!

But I'm going. The emotions of the souls wash over me all at once, now that I don't have Christian's added strength to help me block them out, but I grit my teeth and move quickly across the street, onto the opposite sidewalk. Toward the pizza place. Each step draws me closer to the front window, which has a long, horizontal crack in the glass, like it might collapse into a thousand shards at any moment, but through the hazy pane I see Jeffrey, his head down, a filthy dish towel in his hand, swiping at a table in absent circles.

It's worse than I thought.

My brother's in hell.

20

ZOMBIELAND

I don't take time to think. I burst through the door and go to him, knowing that any second now Kokabel and Samjeeza and who knows who else could be after us, painfully aware that I promised Samjeeza I wouldn't talk to anybody but Angela, but I don't care. He's my brother. In that moment it occurs to me that maybe my purpose in coming to hell wasn't all about Angela, after all. Maybe I was meant to save Jeffrey.

He does a double take when I approach him, then scowls. "Clara, what are you doing here?"

I guess I shouldn't expect him to be happy to see me.

There's no time for small talk, no time for explanations. I spot Angela and Christian on the sidewalk right outside the window, their mouths open in horror that I was right. "I need you to do what I tell you, just this once," I say quietly, glancing around at the gray people in the restaurant, one person to a table, but none of them look up. Yet. I grab his hand and tug him toward the door. "Come with me, Jeffrey. Now."

He jerks away from me. "You can't show up here and order me around. This is my job, Clara. My meal ticket. It sucks, but one of the things about having a job is that I can't exactly come and go whenever I please. Bosses tend to frown on that."

He doesn't know where he is. He thinks this is his normal life. I don't have time to ruminate about how depressing it is that my brother can't tell the difference between normalcy and eternal damnation.

"This is not your job," I say, trying to keep calm. "Come on. Please."

"No," he says. "Why should I listen to you? Last time you were really freaking rude to me, and you yelled at me, and then you didn't come back for all this time, and now you expect me to—"

"I didn't know you were here," I interrupt. "I would have come sooner if I'd known."

"What are you talking about?" He tosses his dishcloth down on a nearby table and glares at me. "Have you gone mental or something?"

Oh, I'm on my way. Already the barrier I've erected

between me and the emotions of all these people around me is corroding, and little whispers are getting through.

None of her business.

I hate him. I deserve better.

Cheated. They cheated me.

I blink furiously and try to clear my head, concentrate on Jeffrey, but then—

What is she doing here?

Oh, crap. I stare over Jeffrey's shoulder, and there's Lucy, framed in the doorway, her expression totally shocked to see me.

"You . . . What are you doing here?" she marches up and demands, her eyes full of fury, but her voice controlled. She slips her arm into Jeffrey's. Just seeing her again brings the memory of that night at the Pink Garter rushing back, the fireball she hurled at us, her shriek as Christian cut Olivia down, what she vowed afterward. *I swear I will kill you, Clara Gardner. And I'll make sure you suffer first.*

"Let go of him," I say in a low voice.

Christian is suddenly by my side, staring at Lucy with fierce eyes that dare her to attack us here, like he's reminding her that he killed her sister and he might have a glory sword with her name on it. Which makes me wonder if glory swords work in hell.

I really, *really* hope they do.

Lucy stares at me wordlessly, her hold on my brother's arm

tightening. I feel her hatred of me but also her fear. She wants to hurt me, to sever me in two with her blade, to avenge her sister, to earn the respect of her father, but she's scared of me. She's scared of Christian. Deep down, she's a coward.

"We're going," Christian says. "Now."

"I'm not going with you," Jeffrey says.

"Shut up," I snap. "I'm taking you out of here."

"No," Lucy says, her voice much calmer than what I can feel churning inside of her. "You aren't." She smiles at Jeffrey sweetly. "I can explain all of this, baby, I promise, but first, I have to handle something. You stay right here, okay? I have to go for a minute, but I'll be right back. Okay?"

"Okay . . . ," Jeffrey agrees, frowning. He's confused, but he trusts her.

She leans up to kiss him softly on the mouth, and he relaxes. Then she lets go of him, which kind of shocks me, that she's releasing him without a fight. I brace myself for a sudden sorrow blade to the chest, but she brushes past me without a second look in my direction.

Then I feel what she intends to do. She's going to the club, three blocks away. To find her father. To bring a whole world of hurt down on our heads.

She hopes that Asael will turn us all, me and Christian and Angela, to tiny piles of ash.

When she's out of sight I turn to Jeffrey, who goes back to wiping down the table. "Jeffrey. Jeffrey! Look at me. Listen.

We're in hell. We have to go, like now, so we can catch a train out of here."

He shakes his head. "I told you, I have to work. I can't leave." He moves to another empty table and starts stacking dishes.

"This isn't the place where you work," I say, careful to keep my voice even. "This is hell. Hades. The underworld. It looks like the pizza joint, but it's not. It's only a reflection of earth. This isn't real pizza, see?" I cross to a table and grab a slice of fake pizza from the plate, hold it up next to Jeffrey's face. It's like a hunk of soggy cardboard, gray and texture-less, dissolving in my hand. "It isn't real. Nothing's real here. Nothing's solid. This is *hell*."

"There's no such thing as hell," he murmurs, his gaze on the pizza, vaguely concerned. "It's something church people made up to scare us."

"Did Lucy tell you that?"

He doesn't answer, but I see it in his eyes, the beginnings of doubt. "I can't remember."

"Come with me, and we'll take a train, and everything will get clear again. I promise."

He resists as I pull at his arm. "Lucy said that she'd be right back. She said she'd explain."

"There's nothing to explain," I say to Jeffrey. "It's simple. We're in hell. We need to get out. Lucy's a Black Wing, Jeffrey. She brought you here."

He shakes his head, jaw tightening. "No. Not possible."

Christian is pacing at the door, unwilling to wait any longer. *You have to come now.*

I turn to Jeffrey. "Come on, Jeffrey. Trust me. I'm your sister. I'm the only family you've got. We have to stick together. That's what Mom told us, remember? Do this for me now."

His silver eyes get mournful, and I feel behind my ever-crumbling wall how hurt he is by all that's happened: the inexplicable vision and his failure to enact it, the way everything was always about me and never him, Dad abandoning us, Mom dying and leaving him with so many unanswered questions, everything turning to ashes right before his eyes. Everyone's gone, and there's nobody left for him but Lucy, and there's something that he knows is missing in her, something important, and he doesn't know if it's all his fault, if it's because he's not the person he's supposed to be, but he doesn't want to lose her, too. *Who am I?* he thinks. *Why am I here? Why do I have to hurt so much all the time? Why does it never, never get any easier?*

And he wishes it would just stop.

He wishes he were dead.

"Oh, Jeffrey," I gasp. "Don't think that." I throw my arms around him, my heart in my throat. "I love you, I love you," I'm saying over and over. "And Mom loves you, and Dad loves you, he does; we all love you, silly. Don't think that."

"Mom's dead. Dad's gone. You're busy," he says without inflection.

"No." I pull back and look into his eyes, tears streaming down my face. I put a hand on his cheek the way I did with Samjeeza earlier and flood him with the memory of Mom on Buzzards Roost this afternoon, hoping he can receive it, focusing on the moment when I first told her about Jeffrey, how happy she was at the very idea of him. Then I show him heaven. Mom walking into the distant light. The warmth of it. The peace. The lingering traces of love all over her.

"Don't you see? It's real," I whisper.

He stares at me, a sheen of tears in his eyes.

"Let's go home," I say.

"Okay." He nods. "Okay."

All my breath leaves me in a relieved rush. We move to the door. Christian's practically bouncing on the balls of his feet, looking all around like the very shadows are going to jump us. *Over there,* he says, looking to the west, to the waning light. *Something's coming.*

I grab Christian's hand, still gripping Jeffrey's. "Come on."

There's the clear sound of a train whistle, high and sweet. I've never heard a more welcome sound in my life.

The people on the street turn toward the noise.

It's coming. It's almost here.

But now we've caught the attention of the damned. I was concentrating on Jeffrey before, not looking at the other lost souls in the pizza parlor, but they are all looking at me. Even the gray people out on the street are turning slowly toward us, their faces raised instead of bent to the ground. They look directly at us, and where their eyes should be are black, empty holes. They open their mouths, and the insides are black—their teeth are black, their tongues—and I become aware of another noise, like the buzzing of flies. Death.

Christian swears under his breath. Angela grabs Jeffrey's hand.

One of the gray people lifts a bony finger to point at us. Then another, and another. Then they start to move in our direction.

"Run!" Angela yells, and we take off toward the train station down the middle of the street, our arms bumping and jarring as we struggle to keep holding on to one another. We can do it. We've only got like half a block to go, if that. We're so close. Minutes away from safety. We can do this. We can get there.

But we don't make it ten feet before the gray people start to pour onto the asphalt to block our way. They are lighter than real people, easier to shove back, to push past, but soon there are so many of them, too many of them now, an army of the damned between us and the station. Their fingers are cold and damp, zombielike, their hands tearing at my hoodie and then at my hair, Angela kicking and screaming and crying, Jeffrey being jerked out of my grasp. They're all around us, on every side, moaning, yelling things in a language I don't understand, a litany of low, guttural noises, shrieks.

We're going to be torn to pieces, I think. We're going to die right here.

But then they stop, as suddenly as they turned on us. They back away, then cast their faces down again, leaving the four of us gasping and panting in a small empty circle in the middle of the road. We're trapped.

I warned you not to speak to anyone, comes Samjeeza's voice ringing in my head, and I feel a kind of eagerness from him. Fear. Excitement. He expected this. He knew that Jeffrey was in hell, and he knew that I'd talk to him. He knew that I'd give us all away.

I'm beginning to think he tricked us.

Please, I say desperately. *Help us.*

I can't help you now. Asael has you, and then Samjeeza's presence vanishes as quickly as it came. He's deserted us.

The crowd of gray people is parting to let someone come through. I can't see him yet, but I feel him. I know him. My blood turns to ice at the wave of malevolent delight that radiates out of this man, this angel, which overcomes his sense of sorrow to the point that it chills my bones to think all that he could be capable of. He is powerful. He is hate. And he carries the image of a drowned woman like a tattoo on his heart.

"Asael," I whisper.

I turn to Christian. He smiles at me sadly, lifts my hand to his lips and kisses my knuckles. Angela puts her tattooed hand on my shoulder and squeezes.

"Thanks for trying," she says. "It means a lot that you tried."

"What's happening?" Jeffrey asks.

"We're done," I answer. "There's no way out."

"You could cross us." Christian's eyes meet mine, flaring with hope. "Call the glory, Clara. This is it. You were right. This is your purpose, this right now. Call the glory. Get us out of here."

I reach for the glory, but the sorrow presses in.

"I can't," I say helplessly. "There's too many of them, too much sorrow; I can feel them——"

"Forget them." He takes my face in his hands. "Forget Asael. Just be with me."

I stare up into his warm green eyes, so close that I can see the flecks of gold.

"I love you," he murmurs. "Can you feel that? You. Not some destiny I think I'm called to. You. I'm with you. My strength. My soul. My heart. Feel it."

I feel it. I feel his strength, and more importantly, I feel mine. He's right. I can do this.

I have to do this.

My light explodes around us. And I send us away.

The light takes a while to fade. I step back from Christian, my breath coming in ragged gasps. He gently brushes a strand of hair away from my face, the back of his hand lingering against my cheek. He wants to kiss me.

"Get a room, you two," Angela says, taking her hand off my shoulder. With the other hand she's holding on to Jeffrey's ear. He pushes her hand away almost absentmindedly.

We made it out.

Christian glances around. "Where are we?"

A cow lows nervously from the darkness, and everybody but me turns to look. I hold up my hand and call glory into it so they can all see what I already know is there: a set of stalls against one side, saddles and tack, farm equipment, an old rusted tractor in the far back, a hayloft over us.

"Pretty," says Angela, staring into my glory lantern. "I want one."

I stumble over to the wall to turn on the light. My knees feel funny as I let the glory blink out. I've expended a lot of energy in the past few minutes. I'm tired.

"What is this?" Christian asks, still sounding dazed. "A barn?"

"The Lazy Dog," I say, staring into the dirt to avoid the sudden comprehension in his eyes. "The Averys' barn."

Angela bursts out laughing. "You brought us to Tucker's barn," she says, her eyes bright.

"Sorry," I whisper up to Christian.

"Sorry?" Angela repeats. "You're sorry? You brought us out of hell. You brought us home." She lifts her tattooed arm over her head and breathes in deep like this manure-scented place where we've landed is the freshest, freest air she's ever smelled.

Jeffrey sits on a bale of hay, his face pale, clutching at his stomach like he's been punched. "You brought us out of hell."

"You brought us out of hell," Christian repeats with such proud conviction in his voice that tears spring to my eyes.

"I was in hell," Jeffrey whispers, like he only now gets it. "Did you see those people's eyes? I was in freaking *hell*. How did I end up in hell?"

"Where's Web?" Angela asks suddenly. "Where is he?"

"He's with Billy. He's safe."

"I want to see him. Can we go see him? I bet he won't even recognize me. He's probably taller than me by now. Where is he, did you say? Where's Web?"

Christian and I exchange worried glances. "He's with Billy," I say again, slowly. "He's still a baby, Ange. He's not even three weeks old."

She stares at me, then at Christian. "Three weeks?"

"We've been taking good care of him. He's great, Ange. I mean, he cries. A lot. But outside of that he's the best baby."

"But——" She closes her eyes, brings a trembling hand to her mouth. She laughs again, wildly. "So I didn't miss it. Every day I thought, I'm missing it. I'm missing his life. All those years I wondered." Her eyes lift to mine. "But you brought me back."

I knew time worked differently in hell, but I didn't expect

this. Angela had been gone for ten days when we decided to go find her, but it sounds like, on her end, she's been gone for longer.

Much longer.

She stumbles, and Christian and I catch her between us, guide her to a hay bale, and sit her down. She grabs my wrist suddenly, and I'm flooded with the tangle of her emotions, amazement and relief and rage, a deep desire to see Web, to hold him and smell that place behind his ears, a fear that it won't smell the same, that place, or that she won't be the same. She's fractured now, she thinks, a broken doll with glassy eyes.

"Ange, it's okay," I say.

"Thank you for coming," she murmurs, then shakes her head, brushes her bangs out of her eyes, and looks up at me earnestly. "Thank you," she tries again. "For coming for me. How did you find me?"

"Yes, how *did* you find her?" booms a voice from behind us. "That's the part I couldn't figure out."

Angela looks up. Then she bends her head to her knees and groans, a dying, hopeless noise.

I spin around. There, standing in the shadows at the back of the barn, is Asael.

He looks like Samjeeza, I think. They're both tall, but that's kind of a given for angels, with coal-black, glossy hair. This man's is cut so that it ends just past his ears, a bit wavy whereas Samjeeza's is straight, but they have the same deep-set amber eyes. I see Angela in his face, too, something about the Roman nose with the slight hook at the bridge, her full bottom lip. And there's something else about him that strikes me as familiar, but I can't put my finger on it.

Lucy is standing beside him, arms crossed, looking pouty. Jeffrey stands up. "Luce? Mr. Wick?"

Mr. Wick. Lucy's dad. The man who owns the club and the tattoo parlor.

"Hello, Jeffrey," Asael says. He takes a step forward. I counter by summoning a circle of glory around us. I'm so tired. It starts to waver immediately, but before it goes out, Christian replaces it with his own glory. I sigh with relief. At least for the moment we're safe.

Asael stops short, annoyance on his face, like we've done something incredibly rude. He looks first at Jeffrey, who's staring at him all freaked out, the way you naturally would if you ever encountered your girlfriend's dad in a random barn in another state, then at Angela, who doesn't move or raise her head, then at Christian. Then me.

"I don't believe we've met," he says, lingering on me. "I'm Mr. Wick."

"You're Asael," I say. "You're the leader of the Watchers," I say, for Jeffrey's sake. "A Black Wing."

Asael turns his hands up imploringly. "Why must you insist on such labels? Black, white, gray, what does it matter?

393

Jeffrey, you know me. Have I ever been unkind to you?"

"No," says Jeffrey, but he's starting to look queasy, confused.

"It does matter," I say to my brother. "Good and evil exist, Jeffrey. They're real. This guy is about as evil as they come. Can't you feel it?"

Asael laughs like the idea is preposterous, and Lucy joins in.

"Come on, Jeffrey," she says. "Come back with us. You don't belong with these people. You belong with me."

"In hell?" he asks.

Her eyes flash. "That wasn't hell. It's an alternate world to our own, yes, but it's not hell. Did you see any boiling pit of lava or a guy in a red suit with a tail and a pitchfork? That's a myth, baby. What's important is that we can be together. We're meant to be together, right?"

For an awful second I think he's going to say, *Right*, and walk across to them, and I'll lose him again, this time forever, but then his jaw tightens.

"No," he says quietly. "I don't belong with you."

"What?" She sounds truly shocked. "What are you saying?"

"He's saying that he thinks the two of you should see other people," I quip.

Enough with the small talk, I say to Christian, mind-to-mind. *Let's get out of here. I'd feel a lot better if we were on hallowed ground.*

Can you do it? Christian asks. *You're not too tired?*

394

I'm tired. But I'm pretty motivated to give the getting-the-heck-out-of-here plan a try. *I'm fine.*

Christian takes my hand, and instantly I feel stronger. I can do this, I think. Christian bends and whispers something to Angela. She stands, studiously not looking at Asael or Lucy, and tucks her arm in his.

I hold my hand out to Jeffrey. *Let's go home,* I say.

"Jeffrey, listen to me——" Lucy says.

I start to imagine our place in Jackson, only a few miles from here, the aspen tree in the front yard, the wind in the pines, the sense of well-being and warmth that I always associate with our house, the squirrels staking out their territory in the trees, chattering, the birds flitting from branch to branch. That's where I'll take us. We'll be safe there. We can figure things out.

Jeffrey takes my hand, which makes me feel stronger still. "Let's go," he says.

Asael makes an angry noise in the back of his throat, but he can't stop me, he can't touch me, and I close my eyes.

I'm two seconds from willing us out of there. Two seconds.

But then the barn door opens and Tucker walks in.

I know the minute I see him that we're screwed.

21

SAFE AND SOUND

Tucker doesn't see Asael or the others immediately. He only has eyes for me. "You came back," he says, such relief in his voice that I want to cry, and then before I can warn him Asael is by his side, moving faster than the human eye can perceive, blocking the way out.

"And who is this, come to join the party?" Asael asks.

For a moment nobody speaks. Tucker stands up straighter, and I know he's wishing that he'd brought the shotgun this time. Not that the shotgun would do any good.

Lucy approaches from the back, giving us and the glory a wide berth. "This must be Tucker," she says, coming to stand on the other side of him. "Jeffrey's told me all about him. He's Clara's boyfriend."

"Ah. And a fragile human one at that," Asael says. "Interesting."

I find my voice. "He's not my boyfriend."

"Oh, no?" Asael turns to me with an amused expression, like he can't wait to hear what I'm about to say. He's enjoying this, the way he's got us all standing so completely still, afraid. He thrives on this.

"We broke up. It's like you said, he's a human. He didn't understand me. It didn't work." Christian's hand tightens in mine as he registers how, even though what I'm saying is technically the truth, it's also a lie, and he can feel how desperately I want to be convincing in this lie. Because if Tucker's not worth anything to me, he can't be used as leverage.

But then, if Tucker's not worth anything to me, he can also be discarded like an empty paper cup, used and thrown away. I have to be careful.

"She's with me now," Christian says. He's so much better at lying than I am. There's no telltale catch in his voice.

"It's true that you two seem awfully fond of each other," Asael says thoughtfully. "But then it begs the question: Why did you come here? Why, out of all the places on earth you could have gone, did you send yourself here, to this boy?"

I meet Tucker's eyes and swallow. This is the lie I'm not going to get away with.

Because he's my home.

"Lucy, be a dear and hold the human, will you?" Asael says, and now there's a black blade at Tucker's throat. Lucy takes his arm and pulls him a few steps away from Asael, her own eyes glinting with the excitement of it all. I hear the sorrow that makes up the blade sizzle slightly as it touches Tucker's neck, and he flinches.

Asael appears happy, like his day is looking up.

"Now," he says, suddenly all business. "Let's negotiate. I think a trade might be in order. A life for a life."

"I'll go," Angela volunteers immediately. She clears her throat and says it again louder. "I'll come back with you, Father." Her voice wavers on the word.

Asael scoffs. "I don't want you. You've been nothing but a disappointment since I found you. Look at you." His eyes sweep up and down her body, lingering at the markings on her arm. *Bad daughter.*

She doesn't answer, but part of her seems to shrink inside herself. *No one loves me* passes through her mind.

"I want Jeffrey," Lucy says, like a child demanding her favorite toy. She looks at him, smiles. "Come on, baby. Come with me."

Jeffrey takes a deep brave breath and starts to step forward, and I catch his arm and pull him back.

"Dear, sweet Lucy," Asael says as Jeffrey and I argue without words for a minute. "I know you have a crush on the boy, and I know you've put a lot of work into him, but I think I'd rather have that one."

He points at me.

"No," Christian and Tucker say at the same time.

Asael smiles wickedly. "Ah, you see? She's valuable. And easy on the eyes." His gaze on me is like a touch, and I shiver, draw my arms over my chest. "I'm looking forward to hearing how you managed to cross out of hell. You'll tell me, won't you? Who's been teaching you?"

"Take me," Christian says then.

Asael waves his hand dismissively. "I don't even know who you are. Why would I want you?"

"He's the one who killed Liv," Lucy accuses.

Asael's eyes flash. "Is that true? You killed my daughter?"

I understand Christian's intention about a second too late. "Christian, don't—"

"Yes," Christian says. "But I'm your son."

His son.

Oh, boy. I didn't see that one coming. But Christian, I realize, has been seeing this moment. This is his vision, facing down the man who killed his mother. His father.

Lucy gasps, her face turning up again, eyes wide. If Christian is Asael's son, it means that he's also her brother. Her brother and Angela's brother. It's quite the family reunion we're having in here.

How long has he known that? I wonder. Why didn't he tell me?

Asael's eyes widen. "My son? Why ever would you think that you're my son?"

399

"You're the collector, right?" Christian looks down at his feet. "You collected my mother. Bonnie was her name. A Dimidius. You met her in New York City, 1993."

"Ah, I remember," Asael says. "Green eyes. Long, pale hair."

Christian's jaw clenches.

"A shame what had to happen with her," Asael continues. "I hate to destroy beautiful things. But she simply would not tell me where I could find you. Tell me, do you have black spots on your wings?"

"Shut up," Christian mutters. I've never felt that kind of rage from him before, and it's a frightening thing. He'd kill Asael, if he could.

Asael squints at him thoughtfully, oblivious. "Well now, that does change things. Perhaps I want you, after all. Even though you'll have to be punished, I suppose, for killing Olivia."

"No," I say firmly, shaking my head. "I'll go with you. Tucker is my responsibility, no one else's. I'll go."

Clara, Christian growls in my mind. *Stop talking and let me do this.*

You are not the boss of me, I send back fiercely. *Think about it. What you did just now, telling him that, was unbelievably brave and selfless, and I know you did it for me, but it was . . . stupid. I don't care what the vision told you. We need to be smart about this. Out of all of us, I'm the most likely to be able to get out of hell on my own. I can get out.*

Not without me, he says. *You'll go crazy in there without some-one to ground you.*

He has a point, but I try to ignore it. *Find my dad,* I say. *Maybe he can come for me.*

I remember Dad's exact words last time we talked. *I can't interfere,* he said. He can't save me. Still, it's what I have to do. And I'm actually starting to form the beginnings of a plan.

I'm going. No more arguing, I tell Christian. *Besides, you're the one holding the glory,* I say, and then before he can answer, I step out of it.

Tucker groans when I walk toward them.

"Let him go," I say, my voice traitorously thick. "A life for a life, like you said."

Asael nods at Lucy, whose dagger disappears, but she still has hold of Tucker's coat.

"Let him walk to the glory," I say.

"First, you come to me," Asael insists.

"How about we do it at the same time?"

He smiles. "All right. Come."

I step toward Asael, and Lucy steps toward the circle of glory with Tucker.

Don't let him touch you, Angela whispers fervently in my mind. *He'll poison you.*

That's a problem I don't know how I am going to avoid. Asael holds out his arms like he's welcoming me home. I can't help but let him touch me, and within seconds his hands are on my shoulders, then his arms are around me like he's embracing me, and Angela's right—my mind fills with regret. All the failures, every wrong move I've ever made, every doubt I've ever had about myself, they all rise up inside me at once.

I was a selfish girl, selfish at the core, spoiled, flippant with the people around me. I was an ungrateful, disobedient daughter. A bad sister. A terrible friend.

Weak. Coward. Failure.

Asael murmurs something under his breath, and his wings appear, an ebony cloak that he draws around me. The world is fading into blackness and cold, and I know that in one more moment we'll be in hell again, and this time there will be no way to fight the sorrow. It will swallow me whole.

I turn my head to get a final glimpse of Tucker through Asael's oily black feathers.

I lied to him. I broke his heart. I treated him like a child. I wasn't faithful. I hurt him.

"Yes," Asael says, a snake's hiss in my ear. He strokes my hair. "Yes."

But that's not all, a small, bright voice in my head chimes in. My own voice.

You sought to protect him. You've sacrificed yourself, your very soul, so that he may live. You've put his welfare ahead of your own.

You love him.

I love him. I will pack that thought away inside of me where nothing can touch it. I will preserve it, somehow. I will shape it into something I can use, to protect me when I'm taken to hell.

Asael makes a choking noise. I push back against him, the weight of his wings heavy around me, and struggle to see anything but black. His mouth is open, gasping like he's out of air, and still he makes the thick, wet noise in the back of his throat.

"Father?" Lucy asks uncertainly.

He staggers, taking me with him. His wings drop from around me, and that's when we all see my glory sword buried in his chest.

I have struck his heart.

The blade brightens as I readjust my grip on the handle. All around the wound his flesh sizzles, it heats and burns, the way it did that day in the woods with Samjeeza so long ago, when I destroyed his ear with glory, but this wound is on a much greater scale. Asael's mouth opens and closes, but no words come. The light of my sword is pouring into him. He looks at me like he doesn't recognize me, his hands grasp at my shoulders, but he is suddenly weak, and I am strong, so very, very strong.

I push the sword in deeper.

He screams, then, a boom of agony that rattles the walls of the barn and makes everyone but me cover their ears. The lightbulb over our heads shatters and rains down on us. Smoke pours off Asael as he leans against me, and I want to get away from him. My teeth come together as I put my hand against his collarbone and draw the bright sword out of his body. I step back. He falls to his knees, and my arm moves almost with a mind of its own, a mighty sweep that severs one enormous black wing from his shoulder. It bursts into bits of feathers and smoke.

Asael doesn't even seem to feel it. His hand is still at his heart, and suddenly he lifts his arms toward the sky in some sort of silent plea.

"Forgive me," he croaks, and then he falls onto his face on the dirt floor of the barn, and disappears.

No one speaks. I bow my head for a minute, my hair falling wild around my face, the heat of the glory sword still moving through me, up my arm, curling around my elbow in bright tendrils. Then I look up at Lucy. She's still clutching Tucker by the arm, her face slack with horror and dismay.

"Let go of him," I say.

She pulls him closer. The sorrow blade appears in her hand again, wavering but there, substantial enough to do damage, and she holds it out, gestures at all of us.

"Get back," she says, her dark eyes wild with panic. She's outnumbered now, outmatched without her big bad father to get her what she wants, but she's still dangerous. She could kill Tucker, easily.

She wants to.

"Let go of him," I say again more firmly.

"Luce," Jeffrey says gently, stepping forward. Christian has dropped his circle of glory, and the barn feels plunged in darkness. I don't even know what time it is, day or night, the pale light outside the barn window sunrise or sunset. Since time is wonky there, I don't know how long we were in hell.

"No," Lucy says. She glares at me, dashes tears from her eyes with the back of her sleeve. "You. You have taken everything from me."

"Luce," Jeffrey cajoles her. "Put down the knife."

"No!" she screams. "Get back!"

I raise the sword, threatening, and she shrieks. Her wings are out in a flurry of black feathers, like Christian's but the opposite, obsidian with spatters of pure white across them, and she lifts Tucker effortlessly, caught by one arm and the front of his coat, her wings beating furiously, carrying them upward, crashing through the high window in the hayloft. For the second time that night glass showers down on us, and I cover my face with my arm to keep it out of my eyes, and when I look again she's gone.

My glory fizzles out.

She's taken Tucker.

Without a word I'm after them. I'm flying before my wings are all the way unfurled. I pause in the air above the ranch, turning, searching for where she's gone, and to the east I see a small black smudge against the light of the sun rising in the east. It's morning, then. I hear Christian's voice somewhere

405

behind me, his cry of "Wait! We'll go at her together!" but I can't wait. I streak off after her, flying harder, faster than I've ever flown before. I fly and fly, following her, over the mountains, high, where the air grows thin and cold. I follow her as she veers north and then east again, and it becomes clear to me that she doesn't know where she's going. She has no destination. She's simply flying to get away. She's running scared.

Anywhere you go, I will follow, I promise her silently. She's strong, what with the sorrow blade and the speckled wings and all, the child of Asael and some unfortunate angel-blood like Christian's mother. She's fast, and powerful.

But she can't fly forever.

Within minutes we're deep in Grand Teton National Park, Jackson Lake appearing below like a long gleaming mirror against the land. Lucy pushes higher, moving more upward than out now, and I wonder what she's planning. The air is very thin, and my throat feels dry with each labored breath I take; my lungs complain for oxygen.

Stop! I scream at her.

She slows and hovers, her wings threshing the air almost gently. She's tired.

"Enough," she pants when I'm about twenty-five feet away, her voice ragged. She turns to me in the air. Tucker is limp against her, his arms and legs dangling, his head thrown back. We're so high up, seemingly level with the tops of the Grand Teton. I worry that he can't breathe at this altitude. I worry that she's stabbed him with the black dagger. I worry about that half-crazy look in her eye.

"Give him to me," I say.

She smiles slightly, ironically, and I can see Angela's "oh yes, I'm scheming" expression on her face. I wonder if I'll ever be able to see Angela the same way again, as only herself and not related to these people.

"Then come and take him," she spits out.

The sorrow blade singing through the air catches me off guard.

It's a bad throw, but it clips my shoulder and part of my left wing. The pain is intense, piercing, the kind of pain that slows the mind, and so it takes me a few beats longer than normal to understand what she's done.

She's flying off again.

And Tucker is falling. Down, down, he's falling.

Toward the lake, so very far below us.

I forget about Lucy. There's only Tucker, and I know the moment I start for him that I'm not going to be able to catch him.

I try. I narrow my body, I push toward him through the air, but he's still too far away to stop him.

It's terrible, those few seconds, but a peaceful kind of terrible, the way he turns over and over in the air as he falls, gently, gracefully, almost like a dance, his eyes closed, his lips parted, his hair, which has grown longer over the months

I haven't seen him, caressing his face. The world opens up below us in a rush of blue and green.

And then he strikes the water.

I'll hear that sound in my nightmares for the rest of my life. He comes down on his back, hits the surface so fast, with so much force, that he might as well have hit concrete. The splash is enormous, obscuring everything. I hit the water a few moments later, only thinking to retract my wings at the last second. The water closes around me, over me, cold as a knife stabbing me, knocking the air out of my lungs. I push upward, break the surface, gasping for air. There's no sign of Tucker. I turn in the water frantically, searching, praying for a sign, some bubbles, something to give me an idea of where to look, but there's nothing.

I dive. The water is dark and deep. I kick downward, my eyes open wide, my fingers out and groping.

I have to find him.

Feel for him, comes that voice in my head. *Feel for him with more than just your hands.*

I push deeper, turn in a different direction. My chest asks for more air and I deny it. I dive deeper, reaching for him with my mind, a tiny flicker of something that might be him, and when I'm about to give up hope and go for more air, my fingers catch his boot.

It takes an agonizingly long time for me to get him to the surface, then to the shore, then out of the water. I drag him up on the rocky bank, screaming for help at the top of my lungs, then fall to my knees beside him and put my ear near his chest.

His heart's not beating. He's not breathing.

I've never learned CPR, but I've seen it on television. I'm crying raggedly, stifling my sobs so I can breathe into his mouth. I press on his chest and hear a bone crack, which makes me cry harder, but I keep doing the compressions, willing his heart to pump. I can feel when I touch him that he's already hurt so badly, so many bones broken, organs inside of him injured, maybe beyond repair. Bleeding inside.

"Help!" I scream again, and then stupidly remember that I'm more than a human girl in this situation, that I have the power to heal, but I'm so shaken that it takes me a few tries to summon glory. I lean over him, the glory shining through me like a beacon on the shore of Jackson Lake, where anybody out on an early morning hike could see me now, but that doesn't matter. I only care about Tucker. I put my glowing hands on his body and will his flesh to mend. I stretch my body along his, my cheek to his cheek, my arms around him, covering him with my warmth, my energy, my light.

But he doesn't take a breath. My glory fades with my hope.

I hear wings behind me. A voice.

"Now you know how it feels," she says, and I raise my arm to block her dagger, but I'm not quick enough. She's going to kill me too, I think dazedly.

But then she doesn't. There's a strange noise, something whistling by my head.

And then there's a glory arrow sticking out of Lucy's chest.

Jeffrey's standing behind her, his face resolute but also shocked, like he didn't even know what he was doing up until now. He drops his arms.

Lucy's dagger is gone. She crumbles to the ground, gasping like a beached fish.

"Jeffrey," she says, reaching for him. "Baby."

He shakes his head.

She turns onto her stomach like she's going to drag herself away from us. Then without warning she rolls into the lake, and she's gone.

I turn back to Tucker and bring the glory again.

Christian comes down on the shore next to Jeffrey.

"What happened?" he asks.

I look up at him.

"Can you help me?" I whisper. "Please. I can't make him breathe."

Jeffrey and Christian exchange glances. Christian goes to his knees beside us and puts his hand on Tucker's forehead, like he's feeling for a fever, I think numbly, although that's not what he's feeling for. He sighs. Puts his hand gently on my arm.

"Clara . . ."

"No." I pull away, grasping on to Tucker more tightly. "He's not dead."

Christian's eyes are dark with sorrow.

"No," I say, scrambling to my knees. I pull up Tucker's T-shirt, lay my hands on the strong, brown expanse of his chest, over the heart I've heard beating under my ear so many times, and pour my glory into him like water, using all of it, every bit of life and light there is inside me, every spark or flicker of light that I can find. "I won't let him die."

"Clara, don't," Christian pleads. "You'll hurt yourself. You've already given too much."

"I don't care!" I sob, swiping at my eyes and pushing at Christian's hands as he tries to pull me away.

"He's already gone," Christian says. "You've healed his body, but his soul's gone. It's slipped away."

"No." I lean down and put my hand to Tucker's pale cheek. I bite my lip against the wail that wants to tear out of me, and taste blood. The ground shifts under me. I feel dizzy, faint. I gather Tucker's body into mine, hold him against me, my hands curling and uncurling in his coat, spilling out jelly beans on the wet rock beneath us. I stay that way for a long time, letting my tears run against his shoulder. The sun gets warmer and warmer, drying my hair, my clothes, drying his.

Finally I raise my head.

Christian and Jeffrey are gone. The lake's so clear that it makes a perfect reflection of the Tetons on the water, the pink-tinged sky behind them, the lodgepole pines along the opposing shore. It's so incredibly still in this place. No sound but my breath. No animals. No people. Just me.

411

It's like I've stopped time.

And Tucker is standing behind me, his hands shoved in the pockets of his jeans, looking down at me. His body has mysteriously vanished from my lap.

"Huh," he says bemusedly. "I had a feeling you might be in my heaven."

"Tucker," I gasp.

"Carrots."

"This is heaven," I say breathlessly, looking around, noticing at once how the colors are brighter, the air warmer, the ground under me more solid, somehow, than it is on earth.

"It would appear so." He helps me up, keeps my hand in his as he leads me along the shore. I stumble, the rocks on the bank too hard for my feet. Tucker has less trouble, but it's difficult for him, too. Finally we make our way up to a sandier spot and sit, shoulder to shoulder, looking out at the water, looking at each other. I'm drinking in the sight of him unbroken and healthy, perfect in his beauty, warm and smiling and alive, his blue eyes even bluer here, sparkling.

"I don't think this dying thing is half so bad as it's cracked up to be," he says.

I try to smile, but my heart's breaking all over again. Because I know that I can't stay here.

"What do you think I'm supposed to do now?" he asks.

I peer over my shoulder at the mountains. On earth the sun would be on the other side of them as it rises, to the east, but here the light is behind them. Always growing. It's always sunrise in heaven, the way that hell is in perpetual sunset, never breaking into the full light of day, but there's the promise of it, soon, maybe.

"Go into the light," I say, and scoff at how cliché it sounds.

He snorts. "Get out of town."

"No, seriously. You're supposed to go that way."

"And you know this because . . . ?"

"I've been here before," I say.

"Oh." He didn't know that. "So you can come and go? You could come back?"

"No, Tucker. I don't think so. Not where you're going. I don't belong here."

"Hmm." He stares off at the lake again. "Well, I'm glad you found a way this time."

"Yeah. Me too."

He reaches for my hand, takes it in both of his, strokes my palm. "I love you, you know."

"I love you, too," I say. I would cry, but I don't think I have a tear left in me. "I'm so sorry this happened. You had this beautiful life in front of you, and now it's gone." It's good to be here with him, to see him safe and sound, but my heart hurts when I think of Wendy and his parents, the way his death is going to open a big black gaping hole in their lives, a wound that won't ever fully heal.

I hurt when I think of spending my whole long life on

earth without seeing him again.

He tilts my chin up. "Hey, it's okay."

"If I'd just left you alone . . ."

"Don't do that," he says. "Don't regret us. I don't. I won't, ever."

We sit there together like that for I don't know how long, our hands tangled, my head against his shoulder. He tells me about all the things I missed this year, how he took up bull riding at the rodeo, for the adrenaline of it, he says, because he wanted something to make him feel alive when he was otherwise feeling pretty low.

"You're lucky you didn't break your neck," I say.

He grins. Shrugs.

"Okay, not so lucky."

"I missed you every minute. I wanted to drive out to California and grab you by that pesky hair of yours and drag you back to Wyoming and make you see sense. Then I thought, well, if I can't bring her to me, I'll go to her."

"So you applied to UC Santa Clara."

"Wendy told you about that?" he asks, surprised. I nod. "What a tattletale." He sighs, thinking of her. Sobers. "You sure we can't stay here forever?" he asks wistfully.

"No. You're supposed to move on."

"You too, I guess. Can't hang out with a dead guy all your life."

"I wish I could."

"Prescott's a good egg," he says, his voice strained. "He'll take care of you."

I don't know what to say. He stands up, brushes the non-existent heavenly dirt off his pants out of sheer force of habit. "Well, I should let you go, I think. I've got a hike ahead of me."

He pulls me into his arms. We've had some good-byes, Tucker and me, off and on again, but nothing like this. I cling to him, breathing in his smell, his cologne and horse sweat and hay, a hint of Oreo cookies, feeling the solidness of his arms, knowing this is the last time I'll feel that, and I look up at him all desperate and heartbroken, and then we're kissing. I hang on to him for dear life, kissing him like the world's about to end, and I guess in a way it is. I kiss him like I probably should be embarrassed to do in a place like heaven, which feels like church, a place where God is looking right at you, but I don't stop. I give him my whole heart through my lips. I love him. I open up my mind and show him how much I love him. He gives a startled, agonized laugh, and breaks away, breathing hard.

"I can't leave you," he says hoarsely.

"I can't leave you either," I say, shaking my head. "I can't."

"Then don't," he says, and grabs me behind the neck and kisses me again, and the world is tilting, tilting, and everything goes black.

22

THE PROPHET

I wake up in my room in Jackson. For a minute I consider whether or not it was all a bad dream. It feels like one. But then reality settles over me. I groan and turn onto my side, curling into the fetal position, pressing my hands to my forehead until it hurts, rocking, rocking, because I know that Tucker is gone.

"Ah, now," says a voice. "Don't cry."

There's an angel sitting on the edge of my bed. I can feel that he loves me. He's thankful that I'm all right. Home. I can feel his relief that I'm safe.

I turn over to look at him. "Dad?"

It isn't Dad. It's a man with clean-cut auburn hair, eyes the color of the sky after the sun's gone down, when the light has almost left it. He smiles.

"Michael couldn't come this time, I'm afraid, but he sends his love," he says. "I am Uriel."

Uriel. I've seen him before. Somewhere in my brain I'm storing an image of him standing next to Dad, looking all fierce and regal, but I don't know where that comes from. I sit up and am instantly flooded with weakness, a hollowness in my stomach, like I haven't slept in days. Uriel nods sympathetically as I sink back onto the pillows.

"You've had quite the adventure, haven't you?" he says. "You did well. You did what you were meant to do. And perhaps more than you were meant to do."

But not well enough, I think, because Tucker's dead. I'll never see him again.

Uriel shakes his head. "The boy is fine. He's more than fine, as a matter of fact. That's why I've come to talk to you."

It's like my whole body goes limp with relief. "He's alive?"

"He's alive."

"So I'm in trouble?" I ask. "Was I not supposed to save him?"

Uriel gives a little laugh. "You're not in trouble. But what you did for him, the way you poured yourself into him, it saved him, yes, but it will also have changed him. You need to understand."

"It changed him?" I repeat, dread uncurling in my gut. "How?"

He sighs. "In the old days we called a person with so much glory, so much of the power of the divine inside them, a prophet."

"What does that mean, a prophet?"

"He will be slightly more than human. The prophets of the past have sometimes been able to heal the sick, or conjure fire or storms, or see visions of the future. It affects the little things: their sensitivity to the part of the world humans don't usually see, their awareness of good and evil, their strength in both body and spirit. Sometimes it also affects their longevity."

I take a minute to digest this information. And wonder what the word *longevity* actually means in this case.

Uriel's expression is almost mischievous. "You should keep an eye on him. Make sure he doesn't get into trouble."

I stare at him. Try to swallow. "What about Asael? Is he going to come after us?"

"You've dealt with Asael quite efficiently," he says, a touch of pride in his voice.

"Did I . . . kill him?"

"No," he answers. "Asael's returned to heaven. His wings are white once more."

"I don't understand."

"A glory sword is not just a weapon. It is the power of God, and you thrust it right into the center of Asael's being. You filled him with light, vanquished him with truth."

Like maybe I am that Buffy-type chick.

"All I did was use a sword one time," I say, embarrassed at the thought.

"Oh, is that all?" he asks lightly, like he's teasing me, but I can't be sure.

"What about the other Watchers? Will they come?"

"When Asael fell, leadership of the Watchers reverted back to Samjeeza. And for some mysterious reason, I don't believe he's going to attack you."

That worked out well, I think. It all seems too good to be true, if I'm being honest. I'm supposed to keep my eye on Tucker. I'm safe from the Black Wings. I'm not, for once, in trouble. I'm waiting for the other shoe to drop any time now.

"You're not safe from the Black Wings," Uriel says a bit sadly. "The Watchers are only a small faction of the fallen, who will still be seeking out the Nephilim and pursuing their agenda all over the world."

"And what is their agenda, exactly?"

"To win the war, my dear. We will need to be vigilant in our work against them, all of us, from the mightiest of the angels to the smallest of the angel-bloods. There is much work to be done. Many battles."

"Is that what my purpose is? To fight?" I ask. I'm the daughter of the Smiter, after all.

Uriel sits back. "Is that what you think it is?"

That's my mom's best trick: answer a question with a question. Which, frankly, I'm getting sick of. I think about the sizzling noise the glory sword made when I pushed it into

419

Asael's chest, his scream of anguish, his gray face. Revulsion ripples through me. "No. I don't think I'm a fighter. But what am I, then? What is my purpose?" I lift my eyes to Uriel's, and he gives me a sympathetic, close-lipped smile. I sigh. "Oh, that's right. You're not going to tell me."

"I can't tell you," he says, which startles me. "You are the only one who can decide what your purpose is, Clara."

I decide? Now he says I decide? Hello, news flash. "But the visions—"

"The visions show you forks in the path along becoming who you are meant to be."

I shake my head. "Wait. So which turn in the road am I supposed to go down? I mean, which is it: I decide or it's meant to be?"

"Both," he says.

Okay, so that's an infuriating answer.

"What is your purpose, Clara?" Uriel asks me gently.

Christian, I think immediately. In every vision, there's Christian. He's present, anyway, at every fork in my path. But does that mean he is my purpose? Can a person be a purpose?

My purpose is you, my mother told me once. But what did she mean by that? Was she being literal? Or was she, too, talking about some kind of decision?

Every answer leads me to five more questions. It's not fair.

"I don't know," I admit. "I want to be good. I want to do good things. I want to help."

He nods. "Then you must decide what will allow you to do that."

"Will there be more visions?" Somehow, even before he answers, I think the answer is yes.

"Do you think there will be more forks in your path?" Uriel asks, another question for a question. He has familiar eyes, knowing, blue with tiny lights in them.

I know those eyes.

"Are you . . . ?" I start to sit up again, to get a better look at his face.

His hands gently push my shoulders back down. He draws the covers up over me.

"No," he says. "Sleep, my dear. That's enough for now. You need to rest."

And before I can argue, before I can ask him who he really is, he puts his hand at my temple, and I fade back into a deep and dreamless sleep.

I open my eyes to Christian's face hovering over mine.

"Hi," he whispers. "How are you feeling?"

"Fine." I look around for Uriel, but there's no sign of him. Christian gives me room to sit up. I put my hand to my forehead. I feel better now, more like myself. Or maybe it's only because Christian's here. "How long have I been out?"

"Oh, you know. A few days," he answers cheerfully. "Like, three."

Whoa, three days? "Well, a girl has to get her beauty sleep," I say.

He laughs. "I'm kidding. Maybe like eight hours. Not that long."

"Where's Tucker?" I ask immediately. "Is he okay?"

There's a shade of loss in his smile, a resignation that makes something twist inside me.

"He's fine. He's downstairs in your mom's room. He's been asking about you, too."

"What happened? At the lake, I mean."

"You healed him," he says. "You healed him until you passed out, until you stopped breathing yourself for a few seconds, and then Jeffrey thumped him on the chest a few times, gave him a couple of puffs that I'm sure neither of them will ever want to talk about again, and he came back. He coughed out about a gallon of lake water, but he came back." Christian looks me in the eyes. "You saved him."

"Oh."

"Yeah," he says with a smirk. "You're a little bit of a show-off. First you get us out of hell. And then you defeat like the biggest, baddest Watcher on the books, and then you go on a high-speed, very high-altitude chase, and then you resuscitate the dead. Are you done? Because seriously, I don't know if I can take any more excitement."

I look away, pressing my lips together to keep from smiling. "I think so." Then I tell him about Uriel's visit.

"Why Uriel?" Christian asks when I'm done. "Why send him?"

"I think he's my grandfather," I say slowly. "He didn't tell me that, but I kind of got the impression that he thought of me as family."

"Your mom's father?"

"Yeah." I relate what Uriel said about Asael and Samjeeza, and Christian looks even more relieved, and oddly troubled, like this is not all good news to him. "So maybe we can go back to Stanford?" I say. "We're free to live a normal life for a while. No angel-blood protection program. Good, right?"

He bites his lip. "I'm going to take some time off from school, I think."

"Why?" I ask.

He brushes his hair out of his eyes and looks a bit sheepish. "I don't think that I went to Stanford for the right reasons. I don't know if I belong there."

He doesn't want to be around me is what I get from that answer.

"So you're taking off."

"I might travel around with Angela and Web, find a place to lie low for a while. Angela needs some rest."

"How come you never told me that she's your sister?" I ask.

He shrugs. "I was still getting used to the idea. I read in her journal about her father being a collector, she called him,

423

and I connected the dots. But it didn't feel real until——"

Until he saw Asael face-to-face.

"So Web's your nephew," I say.

He nods, happy at the thought. "Yeah. He is."

They're a family. I feel a flash of something like envy mixed with loss. There won't be any more days with Christian and Web and me. But it's for the best. I imagine them walking along the sand on some deserted beach, like in that place Dad liked to train us, Web squishing the sand between his chubby fingers, laughing at the surf.

"I've always liked the beach," he says.

"When?" I ask.

"Nowish. I only wanted to say good-bye." He sees my stricken expression. "Don't worry. I'll keep in touch."

He gets up. He smiles like everything's peachy, but I can feel that this is killing him. Leaving me goes against all his instincts, all that his heart is telling him.

"I meant it, what I said in hell," he says. "You're my glory sword, you know that? My truth."

"Christian——"

He holds his hand up like, *Let me finish.* "I saw the look on your face when he died. I saw what was in your heart, and it's real. All this time I kept telling myself that it was a crush, and you'd get over it, and then you'd be free to be with me. But it's not a passing phase, or this stubborn refusal to accept what you think is your destiny. You're not going to get over it. I know that. You belong with him now." He swallows. "I was wrong to kiss you that day in the cemetery."

There are tears in my eyes. I wipe at them. "You're my best friend," I whisper.

He looks down. "You know I'm always going to want to be more than that."

"I know."

An awkward silence stretches between us. Then he shrugs and gives me his devil-may-care smile, rakes his hand through his wavy brown hair. "Well, you know, that Tucker guy's not going to be around forever. Maybe I'll catch up with you in a hundred years or so."

My breath hitches. Does he mean it, or is he being flippant to save face? I swing my legs over the side of the bed and stand up, carefully, in case I'm still weak. But I feel surprisingly fine—refreshed, even. I look at him solemnly. I think about the word *longevity*. "Don't wait around for me, Christian. That's not what I want. I can't promise you—"

He smirks. "I won't call it waiting," he says. "I have to go."

"Wait. Don't go yet."

He stops, something in his expression that doesn't quite dare to be hope. I cross the room to him and pull up his shirt. For a second he looks totally confused, but then I put my hand on the long gash in his side, which still hasn't healed. I clear my head as much as I can, then call the glory to my fingers. And it comes.

He gives a pained gasp as his flesh knits itself back together. When I take my hand away, the cut is completely healed, but there's a long silver scar stretching down his ribs.

"Sorry about the scar," I say.

"Wow," he laughs. "That was just like *E.T.* Thank you."

"It's the least I could do."

He moves to my window and pulls it open, bends to step out onto the eaves. Then he turns to me, the wind ruffling his hair, his green eyes full of sorrow and light, and he lifts his hand in a wave. I lift mine.

See you later, he says in my mind, and summons his wings, and flies.

I take a bath. I scrub every part of my body, shave my legs, work the dirt from under my fingernails, until finally, at long last, I feel clean. Then I sit at my desk in my bathrobe and tackle the arduous task of combing the tangles out of my hair. I smooth moisturizer over my face, put on some lip balm on a hopeful whim. In my closet I stand for a while staring at a yellow sundress my mom once gave me for my birthday, which I wore the night Tucker first took me to Bubba's, which was, in a backward way, our first date. I put it on, along with some strappy white sandals, and go downstairs.

My black hoodie, the one I was wearing all through this whole ordeal, is laid carefully across the back of the couch. I pick it up. It smells like lake water and blood. I walk to the laundry room to toss it in there, but first I check the pockets.

Inside the left pocket is a silver charm bracelet. I hold it in my palm, examining each charm. A horse, for when they took off across the countryside. A fish, for when they met. A heart. And now a new charm.

A tiny silver sparrow.

I put it on. It tinkles against the bones of my wrist as I walk down the hallway to Mom's old room. My heart starts to beat fast, my breath quickens, but I don't hesitate. I want to see him. I open the door.

The bed's empty, the sheets pulled up in a messy way, like someone tried to straighten the covers in a hurry. No one's here. I frown.

Maybe I took too long to come find him. Maybe he left.

I smell something burning.

I find Tucker in the kitchen, attempting and spectacularly failing to make scrambled eggs. He pushes at the blackened mess with a spatula, tries to flip it, burns himself, fights back a cuss word, and starts shaking his hand like he can get the pain off it. I laugh, and he whirls around, startled. His blue eyes widen.

"Clara!" he says.

My heart lifts looking at him. I walk up to him and take the spatula out of his hand.

"I thought you'd be hungry," he says.

"Not for that." I smile and grab a dish towel, pick up the frying pan, march it over to the trash can, and scrape the eggs into it. Then I go to the sink and rinse it out. "Let me," I say.

He nods and pulls himself up onto one of the kitchen stools. He's not wearing a shirt, just a pair of my brother's old pajama pants. Even so he looks like Sunday morning, I think the expression goes. I try not to flat-out stare as I go to the refrigerator and get out a carton of eggs, crack them into a bowl, add milk, whisk it all together.

"How are you?" he asks. "Jeffrey told me you were sleeping."

"You saw Jeffrey?"

"Yeah, he was here for a while. He seemed kind of distracted. He tried to give me an envelope full of money."

"Uh, sorry?" I offer.

"You California yuppies think you can buy anything," Tucker jokes.

And he is joking. He's getting pretty fond of California yuppies.

"I'm good," I say with a cough, to answer his initial question. "How are you?"

"Never felt better," he says.

I stop whisking and look him over. He doesn't seem changed, I think. He doesn't look like any prophet I've ever heard of.

"What?" he asks. "Do I have egg on my face?"

"I'm not really hungry," I say, pushing aside the eggs. "I need to talk to you."

He swallows. "Please don't let this be the part where you tell me what's best for me again."

I shake my head, laugh. "Why don't you put on some clothes?"

"That's a great idea," he says. "But they seem to be missing. I guess they got thrashed beyond repair earlier. Maybe you could take me home real quick."

"Sure." I walk over to him and take his hand, draw him off the stool. He looks at me uncertainly.

"What are you doing?" he asks.

"Do you trust me?"

"Of course."

I delight in his quick intake of breath as I reach up and cover his eyes with both of my hands. I call the glory, a warm, pulsing circle of light around us. I close my eyes, smiling, and send us both to the Lazy Dog. To the barn. On purpose.

"Okay, you can look," I say, and take my hands away, and the light slowly fades around us, and he gasps.

"How did you do that?"

I shrug. "I click my heels three times and say, 'There's no place like home.'"

"Uh-huh. So . . . you think this is your home? My barn?"

His tone is playful, but the look he's giving me is dead serious. A question.

"Haven't you guessed by now?" I say, my heart hammering. "My home is you."

He's got a kind of laughing disbelief all over his face. He clears his throat. "And I don't feel sick with the glory this time. Why is that?"

"I'll tell you all about it," I promise. "Later."

"So," he says. "Does poking that guy through the heart

with a sword mean you don't have to run away now?"

"I'm not running away."

He grins. "That's the best news I've ever heard. Ever." He puts his hand on my waist, pulls me closer. He's going to kiss me. "So did you really mean all that stuff you said when I was a dead man?"

"Every word."

"Could you say it again?" he asks. "My memory's a little fuzzy."

"Which part? The part where I said I wanted to stay with you forever?"

"Yeah," he murmurs, his face close to mine, his breath hot on my cheek.

"When I said that I love you?"

He pulls back a little, searches my eyes with his. "Yes. Say it."

"I love you."

He takes a deep, happy breath. "I love you," he says back. "I love you, Clara."

Then his gaze drops to my lips again, and he leans in, and the rest of the world simply goes away.

EPILOGUE

"Look at me, look at me," Web shouts from Midas's back, as Tucker leads him around the pasture.

From the porch, where I'm sitting with Angela drinking lemonade, I raise my hand and wave. Every time I see him he's like a foot taller, that kid, although he's small for a nine-year-old, always talking your ear off (he takes after his mother that way), always grinning up at you with mischievous golden eyes from underneath his mop of unruly blue-black hair. As we watch, he gives Midas a little kick to get him to go faster, and Tucker has to jog along beside them to keep up.

"You be careful out there!" Angela calls, more to Tucker than to her son.

Tucker nods, rolls his eyes, pats Midas on the neck, and slows him down. As if falling off a horse would do anything besides startle that indestructible little boy.

"You're kind of a helicopter parent, you know that?" I tease.

She scoffs and lifts her arms above her head in a stretch. If I look hard I can see the faint markings on her right arm, only a few left now. The tattoos started to fade the moment she held Web in her arms again—like his love is washing her clean, she always says.

Still, I wonder if the words will ever completely go away.

"I think I'm more an attachment-style parent," she argues.

"Of course you are."

In a few hours the whole loud bunch of us will be gathered around the Averys' big table in the farmhouse for supper: Tucker's parents, Wendy and Dan and little Gracie, Angela and Web up from the Windy City, and, if I play my cards right, Jeffrey. We'll all eat and laugh and talk about the news and everybody's jobs, and I'll almost certainly take some flack, mostly from Angela, for going to Stanford to get my fancy medical degree fully intending to wind back up here as a plain old family doctor. I'll joke about the fine weather in Wyoming and how I couldn't bear to leave. Tucker will squeeze my knee under the table. And I will get a brief sense of togetherness, of everything being how it should be, but I'll also feel an absence, like there's an empty chair at the table.

At that point the topic of conversation will inevitably turn to Christian, as if me thinking about him makes everyone think about him, and Angela will tell us about the buildings he's working on and Web will gush about the last adventure the two of them went on together: to the Lincoln Park Zoo or the Chicago Children's Museum or the observatory on the ninety-fourth floor of the John Hancock Center. And then the conversation will move on to other things, and I'll feel normal again. I'll feel right.

Angela's still talking about parenting styles, something called Love and Logic. She offers to loan me her books about it, and I smile and say I'll take a look at them. I set my lemonade down and stand up, step off the porch to walk toward the pasture, passing through the shadow of the big red barn, the sky overhead empty and blue.

"Look at me, look at me, Clara," Web says again when he spots me. After dinner I'll take him flying, I think, if Angela will let me. The sound of him giggling as Tucker guides the horse along the fence makes me smile. I take a moment to admire the view of Tucker from the back, the way he walks with a kind of funny cowboy grace, the fit of his jeans.

"I see you! Hi there, handsome," I say to Tucker.

He leans over the fence to kiss me, taking my face between his hands, the plain gold band on his finger cool against my cheek. Then he steps back and drops his head for a minute, his eyes closed in a way I've come to be familiar with over the years. I put my hand on his shoulder.

"You okay? Another vision?" I ask.

He glances up at me, grins. "Yes, I'm having a vision," he says with a laugh in his voice. "I'm having a vision that I just know is going to come true."

"And what's that?" I ask him.

"We're going to be happy, Carrots," he says, tucking a strand of my flyaway hair behind my ear. "That's all."

ACKNOWLEDGMENTS

And now I've come to the end of a long road, and there are so many people to thank.

My first big thanks goes to Katherine Fausset. Best. Agent. Ever. You were my pillar of sanity this time around. Thank you for brainstorming sessions, for chocolate chip cookies, for standing by me through the laugh-filled ups and the tear-filled downs, and for always fighting for me. I am so very glad to have you in my corner.

Thank you to my trio of amazing editors, starting with Farrin Jacobs, for believing in Clara and her story from the rough little first draft of *Unearthly*. I will miss the blue pencil. Thanks to Catherine Wallace, who was with me every step of the way on this journey, quietly asking all the tough questions that would make my book so much better. And a huge thanks to Erica Sussman, my last-minute hero. I can't express what your enthusiasm, your smart ideas, and your quirky sense of humor meant to me at this stage in the game. I can't wait to work together again!

Thanks to the rest of the team at HarperTeen: Mary Ann Zissimos, my publicist, who I'm just going to go ahead and thank in advance this time around, Sasha Illingworth, who created such a gorgeous set of covers that people could not help but pick them up, and all of those awesome people who've been so supportive from the beginning, including Kate Jackson, Susan

Katz, Christina Colangelo, Melinda Weigel, Cara Petrus, and Sarah Kaufman.

I also would like to thank the people who helped me explore and research my northern California setting, starting with my dear friend Wendy Johnston, who chauffeured me to signings and tried out strange pizza and wrangled my kids so I could sneak pictures of a tattoo parlor. Not to mention all the other ways that you are the epitome of a good friend, better than any character I could make up. And I'm sorry all the Wendy scenes keep getting cut. . . .

I owe a big thanks to Keith Ekiss, for helping me find resources at Stanford, and an even bigger thanks to Estela Go, the awesome student who walked me all around campus, didn't so much as raise an eyebrow when I wanted to excessively photograph the laundry room, and answered my hours (oh yes, hours!) of questions. Clara got to experience Band Run and eat Tater Tots and run up to the Dish because of you! Also, thank you to Dayo Mitchell, the dorm advisor at Roble, for helping me understand how one might approach Clara's undecided-ness and Angela's delicate situation. Clara's life at the Farm blossomed after I spent some time with all of you.

While I'm on the subject of Stanford, I'd like to thank Dr. Quynh Le, my boss while I worked at Stanford so many years ago. Thank you for taking a chance on me and for encouraging me to write after my day's work was finished. You always said I'd be published someday, and that meant so much to me.

And now thanks to my friends: To Lindsey Terrell, my

bestest bestie, for being unapologetically Team Christian when everyone else was pulling for Tuck. To Melissa Stockham, who made me feel like my book was "shiny," even those times when I kind of hated it. To Joan Kremer, for always being so willing to read for me and to write with me. I am so happy we stumbled into each other as newbies. To Sarah Hall, who has cheered from the sidelines and put my book into so many hands at your library. And last, but certainly not least, to Amy Yowell, who impresses and inspires me daily with your own drive and determination as a writer. I have no doubt that you'll be putting me into *your* acknowledgments someday soon.

I also want to thank my writer buddies, starting with the amazing and hilarious Brodi Ashton, a kindred spirit if there ever was one. Fate is a funny thing, but I am so glad it drew us together. To Anna Carey, Tahereh Mafi, and Veronica Rossi, for being the best tour mates and confidantes ever. To Jodi Meadows, for her quiet support and knitted fingerless gloves, and the lovely Courtney Allison Moulton, for giving me permission to have Midas chow down on jelly beans the way Pia does. You're still on to name the horses in my next book. Finally, a huge thank-you to Kiersten White, for waxing poetic on how much you love Erica—I will always be grateful that you put her on my radar. You rock.

And now thanks to my family:

My mother, Carol Ware, for the hours that you hovered in the corners at bookstores and middle schools with my baby strapped to your chest. Thanks for your wholehearted love for Clara and her story, from the first time I read you the prologue over the phone. And to Jack Ware, thank you for your warmth, your kindness, your humor, and for all the innumerable ways that you offer your support. I'm so glad to be part of your family.

My dad, Rod Hand, for listening whenever I called to rant or worry and always making me feel, by the end of those conversations, like I was capable of doing whatever I set my mind to. And to Julie Hand, for always being eager to read my drafts and giving me your honest opinion.

To my beautiful and hilarious children, Will and Maddie, thank you for keeping me grounded and teaching me to see life from fresh eyes. Squeeze, I love you.

And finally, to my husband, John. This year was a long haul for you, too, and there's so much to thank you for: for being such a smart, insightful first editor, who helped me unravel so many problems and story lines, for all those brainstorming sessions over dinner, all those late-night last-minute read-throughs, for taking care of the kids without complaint when I had to travel or spend a day working, for your insistence that the book was good and I was good and I could do it, and for sometimes just offering me the hug I needed at the end of the day. I would never have come so far without you by my side.

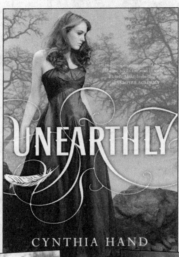
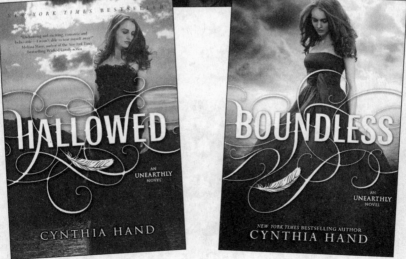